ARDEN HIGH

Twelfth GRADE Night

Written by Molly Horton Booth
and Stephanie Kate Strohm

Illustrated by Jamie Green

Lettering by Chris Dickey

HYPERION

Los Angeles   New York

For Jenny and for Ali
—MHB & SKS

For my college roommates at Bayou #2006
—JG

First Edition, October 2022

10 9 8 7 6 5 4 3 2 1

FAC-034274-22238

Printed in the United States of America

This book is set in CCScoundrel/Fontspring; with hand-lettering by Jamie Green

Illustrated by Jamie Green
Lettered by Chris Dickey
Designed by Tyler Nevins

Library of Congress Cataloging-in-Publication Data
Names: Booth, Molly, author. • Strohm, Stephanie Kate, author. •
    Green, Jamie (Illustrator), illustrator. • Shakespeare, William, 1564-1616.
    Twelfth night.
Title: Twelfth grade night / by Molly Booth and Stephanie Kate Strohm ;
    illustrated by Jamie Green.
Description: New York : Disney-Hyperion, 2022. • Series: Arden High;
    book 1 • Audience: Ages 12–18. • Audience: Grades 10–12. •
    Summary: New student Vi finds herself falling for Orsino, even though he
    wants Vi's help asking Olivia to the school dance.
Identifiers: LCCN 2021042567 • ISBN 9781368062398 (hardcover) •
    ISBN 9781368064651 (paperback) • ISBN 9781368063838 (ebook)
Subjects: CYAC: Graphic novels. • Love—Fiction. • Twins—Fiction. •
    Brothers and sisters—Fiction. • High schools—Fiction. •
    Schools—Fiction. • LCGFT: Graphic novels.
Classification: LCC PZ7.7.B664 Tw 2022 • DDC 741.5/973—dc23
LC record available at https://lccn.loc.gov/2021042567
Reinforced binding

Visit www.HyperionTeens.com

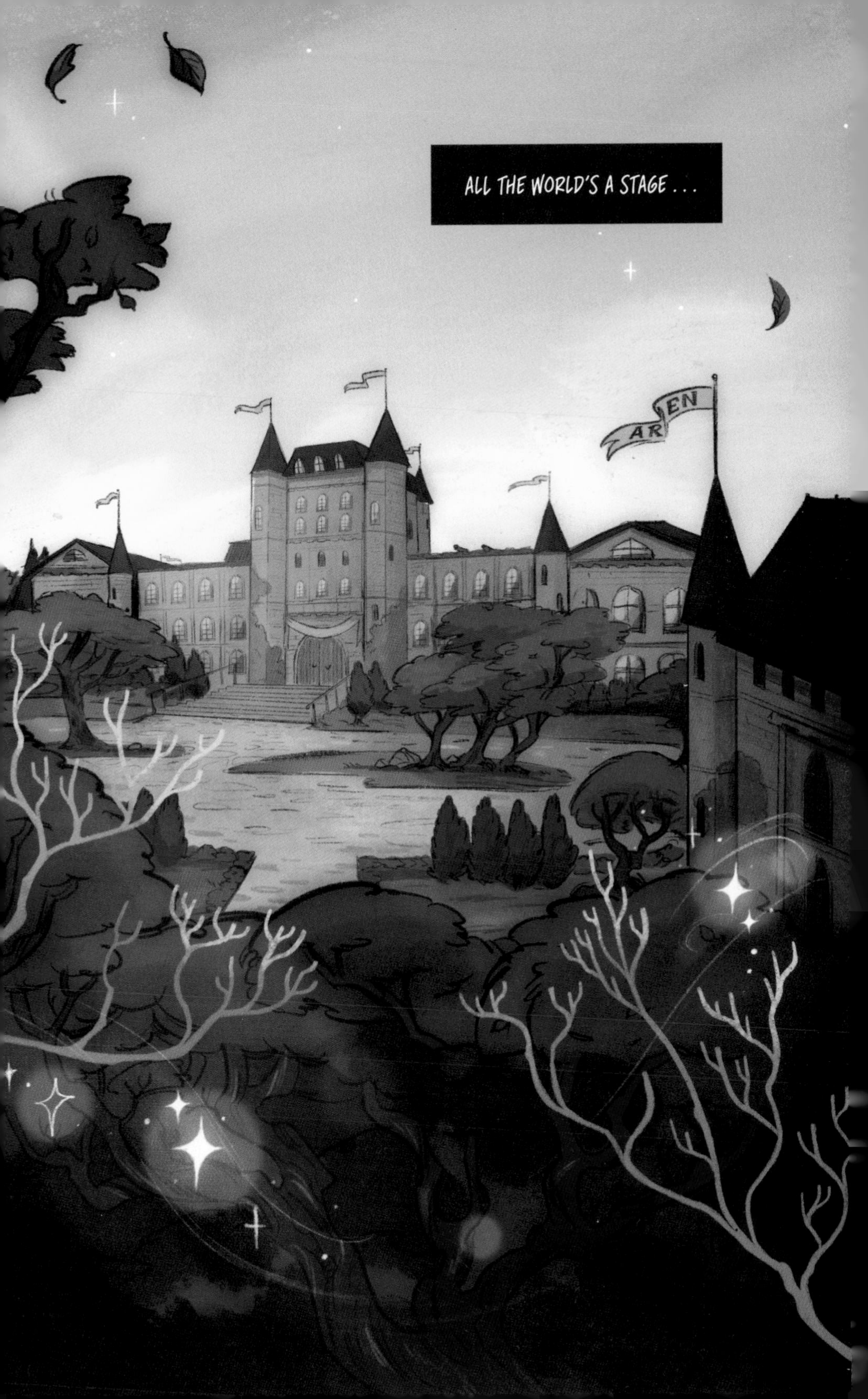
ALL THE WORLD'S A STAGE . . .
AR EN

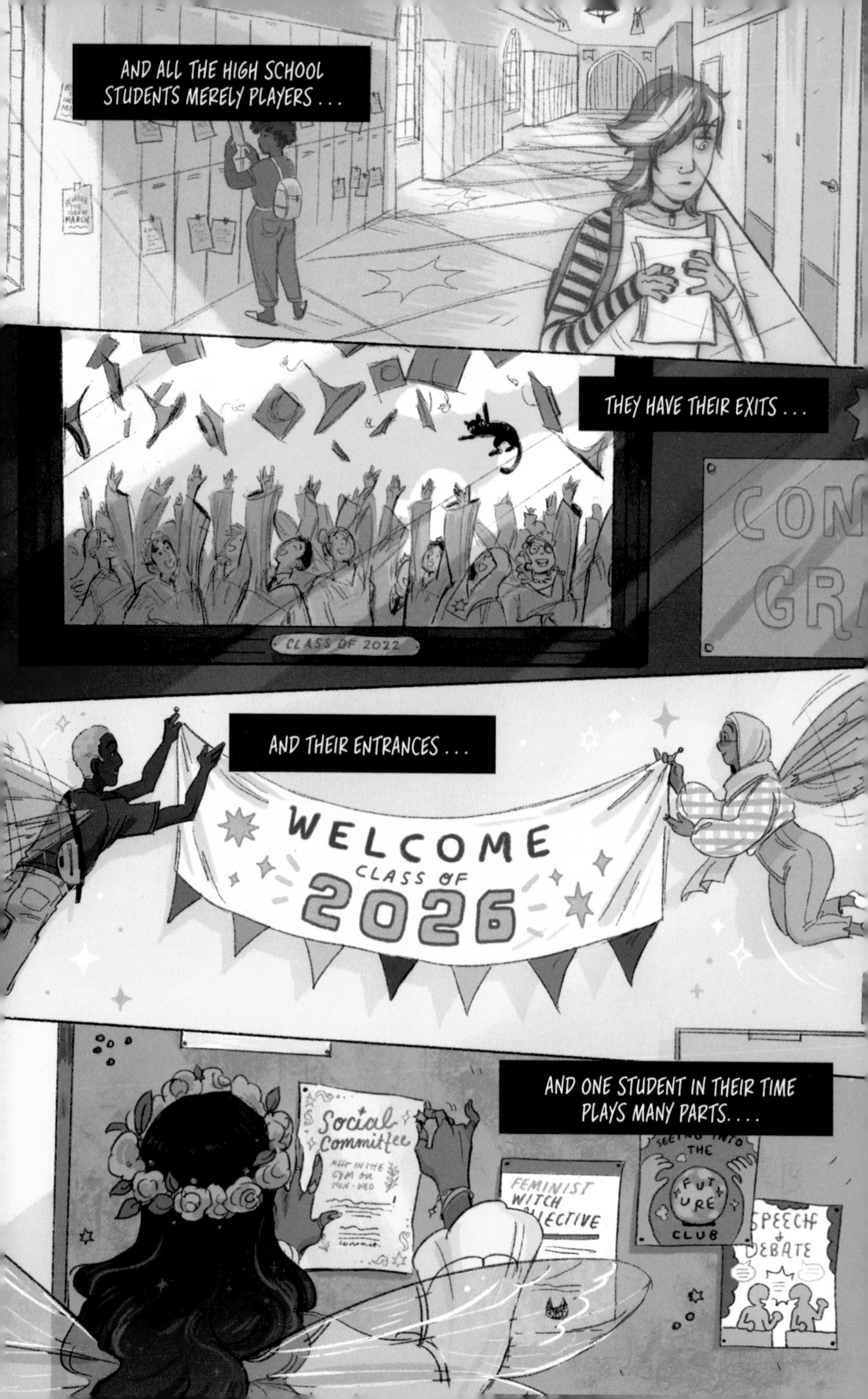
AND ALL THE HIGH SCHOOL STUDENTS MERELY PLAYERS . . .
THEY HAVE THEIR EXITS . . .
CLASS OF 2022
AND THEIR ENTRANCES . . .
WELCOME CLASS OF 2026
AND ONE STUDENT IN THEIR TIME PLAYS MANY PARTS. . . .
Social Committee
FEMINIST WITCH
THE FUTURE CLUB
SPEECH + DEBATE

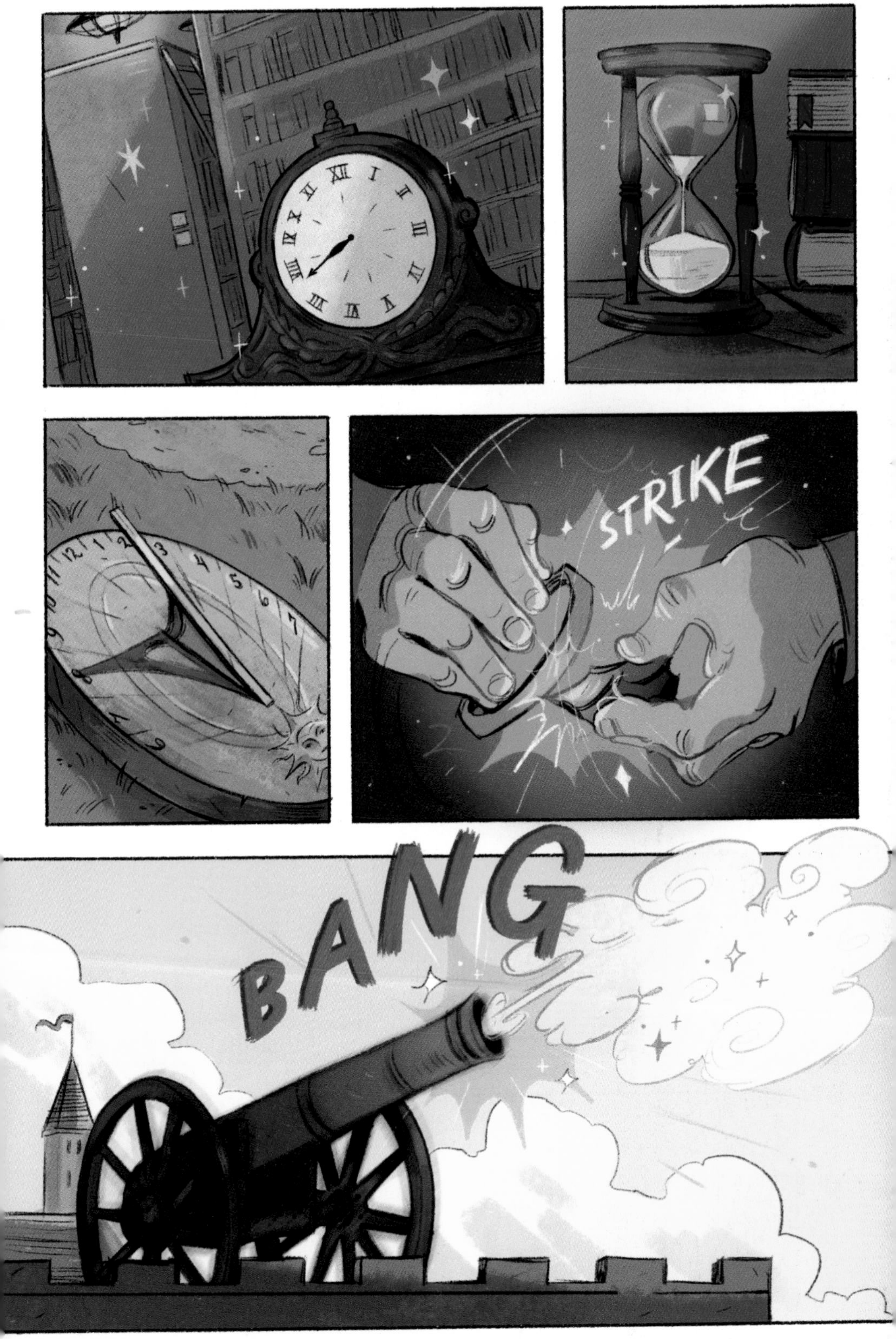
STRIKE
BANG

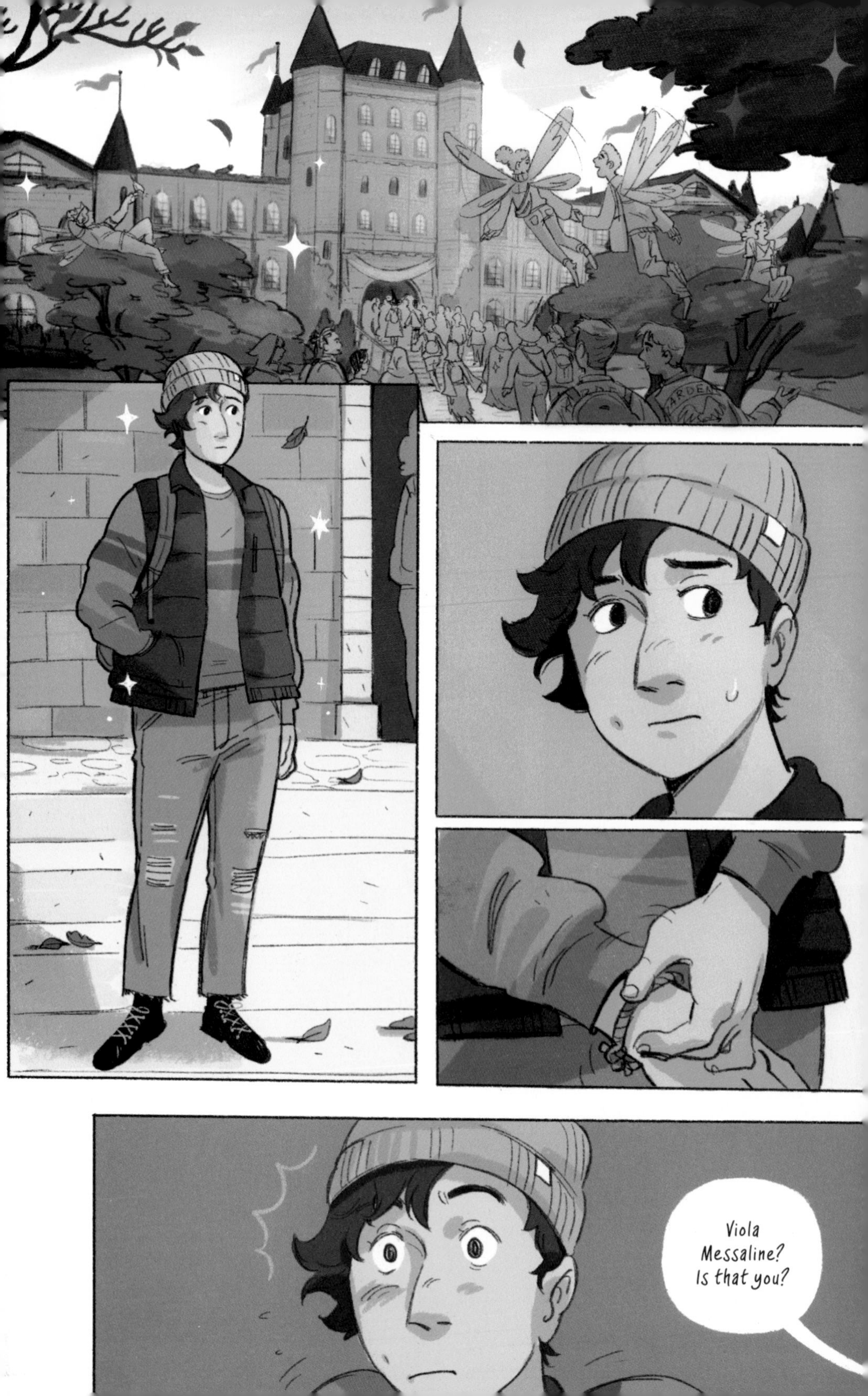
ARDEN
Viola Messaline? Is that you?

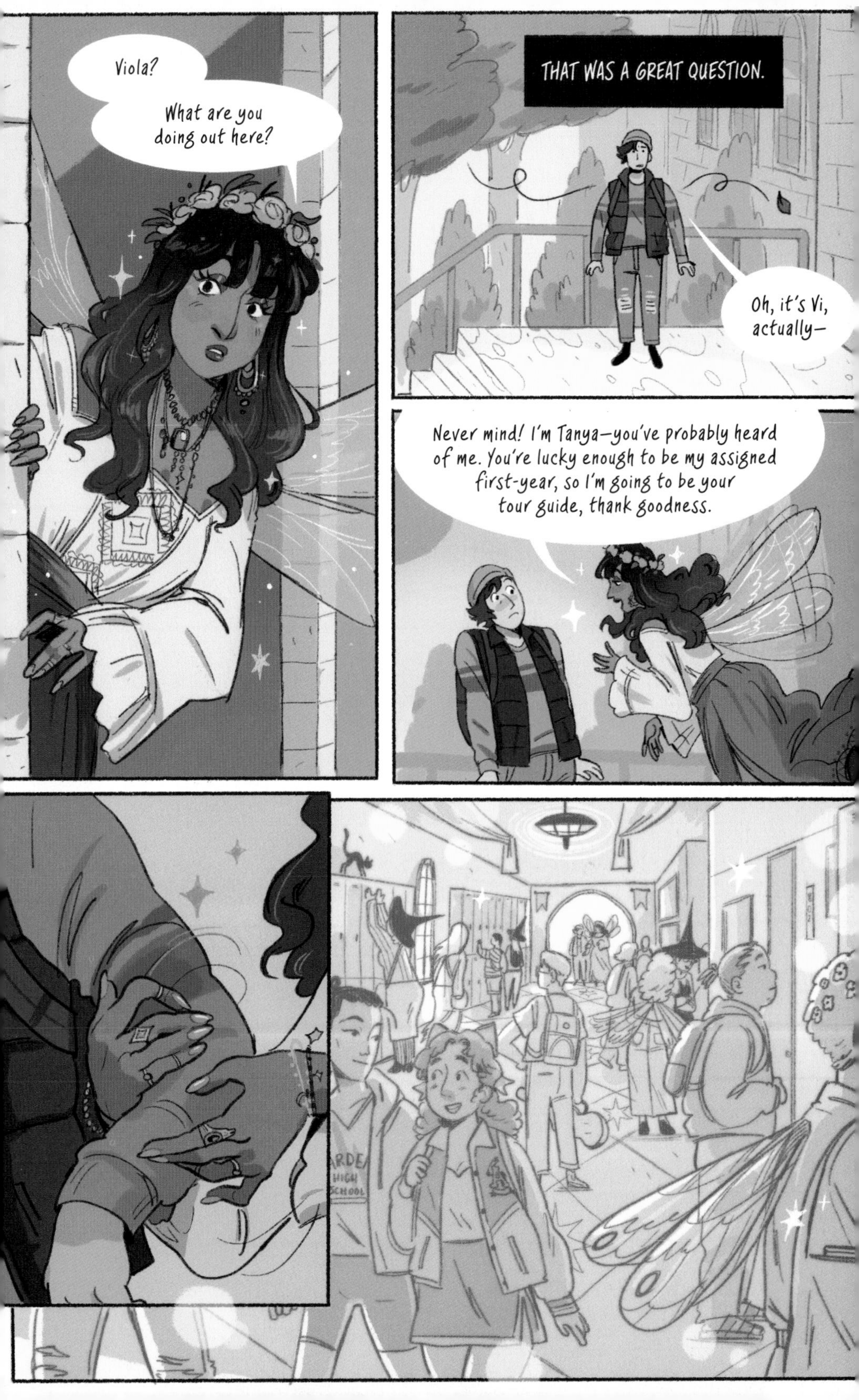
Viola?
What are you doing out here?
THAT WAS A GREAT QUESTION.
Oh, it's Vi, actually—
Never mind! I'm Tanya—you've probably heard of me. You're lucky enough to be my assigned first-year, so I'm going to be your tour guide, thank goodness.

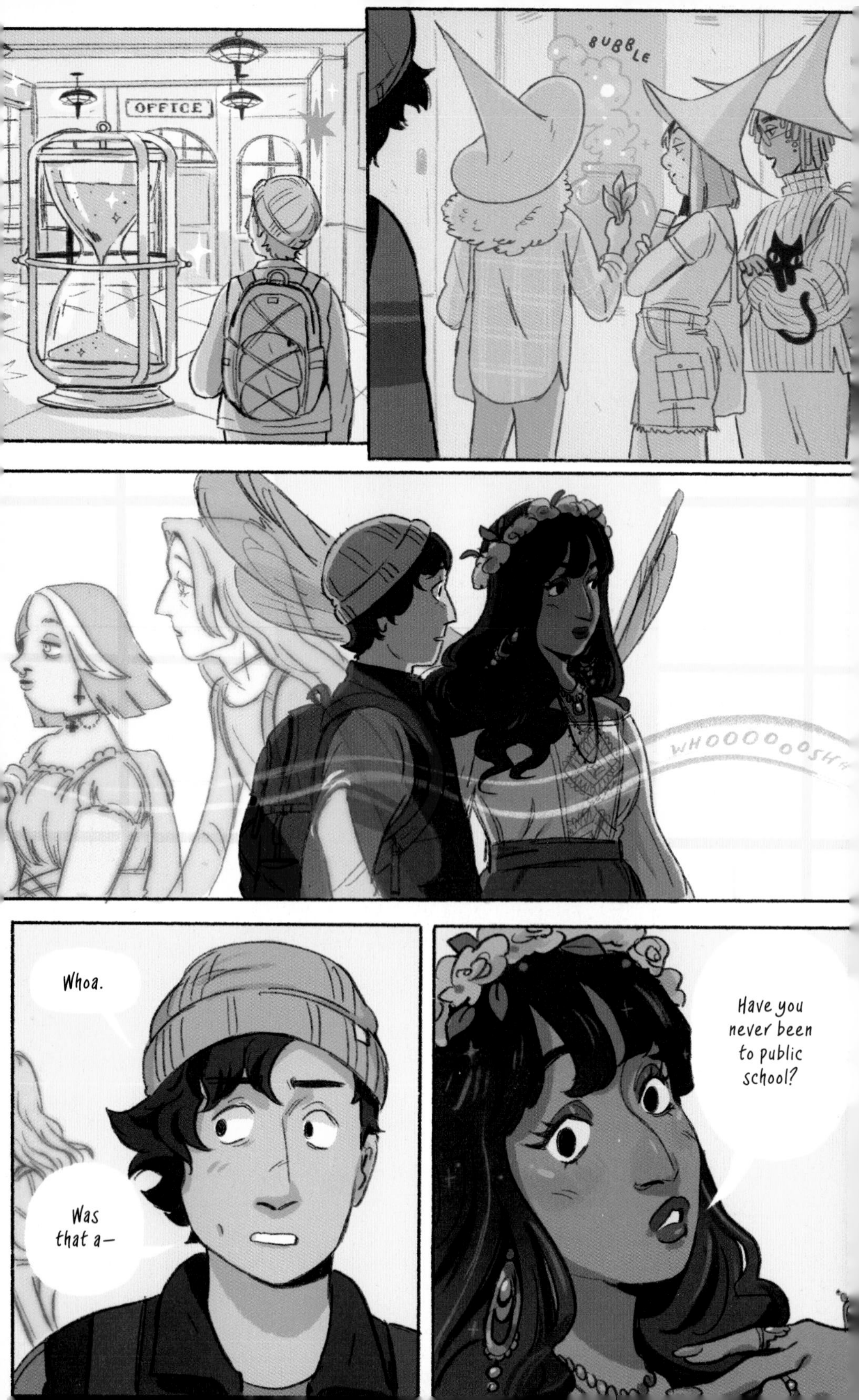
OFFICE
BUBBLE
WHOOOOOOSHH
Whoa.
Was that a—
Have you never been to public school?

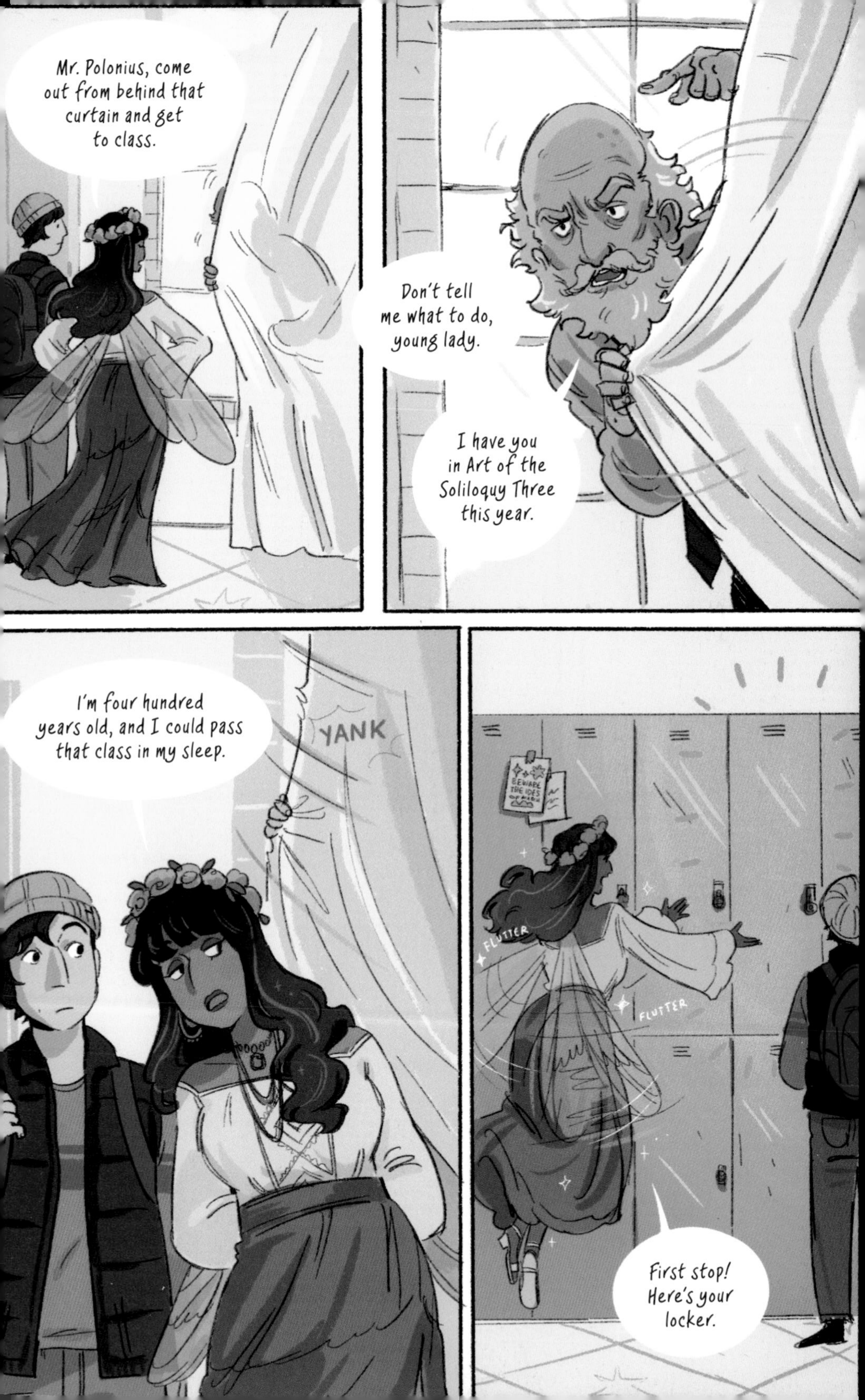
Mr. Polonius, come out from behind that curtain and get to class.
Don't tell me what to do, young lady.
I have you in Art of the Soliloquy Three this year.
I'm four hundred years old, and I could pass that class in my sleep.
YANK
FLUTTER
FLUTTER
First stop! Here's your locker.

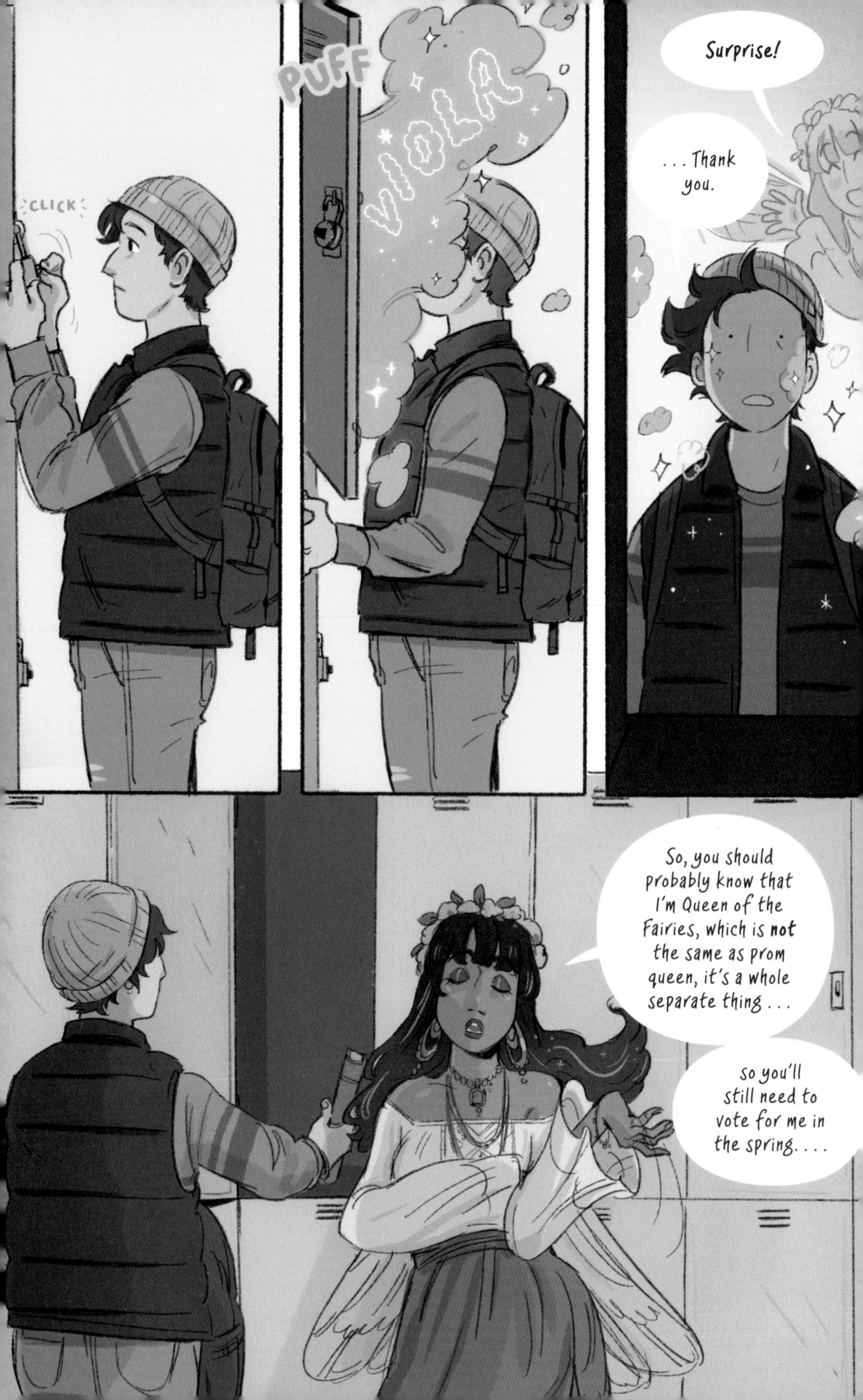
CLICK
PUFF
VIOLA
Surprise!
. . . Thank you.
So, you should probably know that I'm Queen of the Fairies, which is **not** the same as prom queen, it's a whole separate thing . . .
so you'll still need to vote for me in the spring. . . .

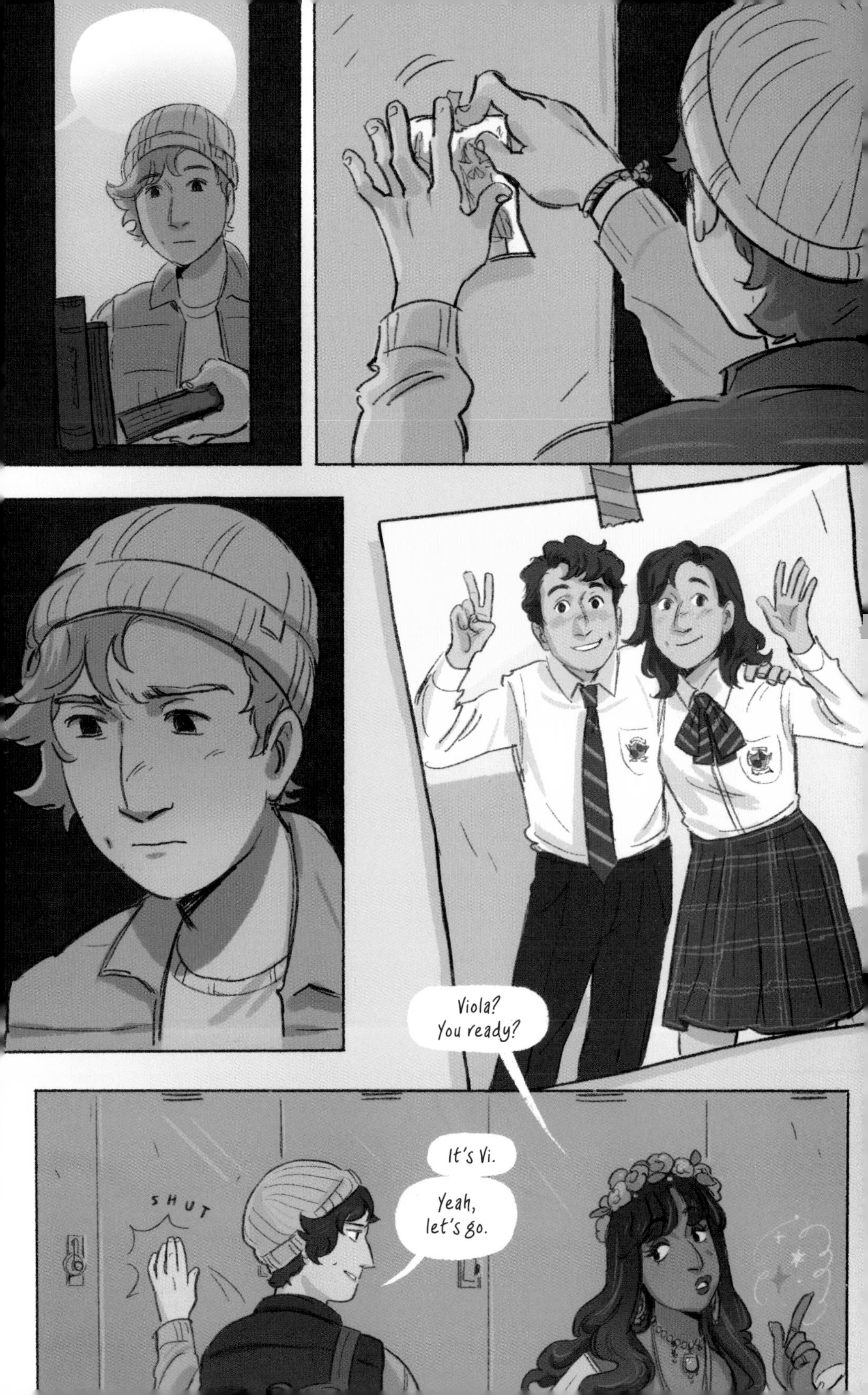
Viola?
You ready?
It's Vi.
Yeah,
let's go.
SHUT

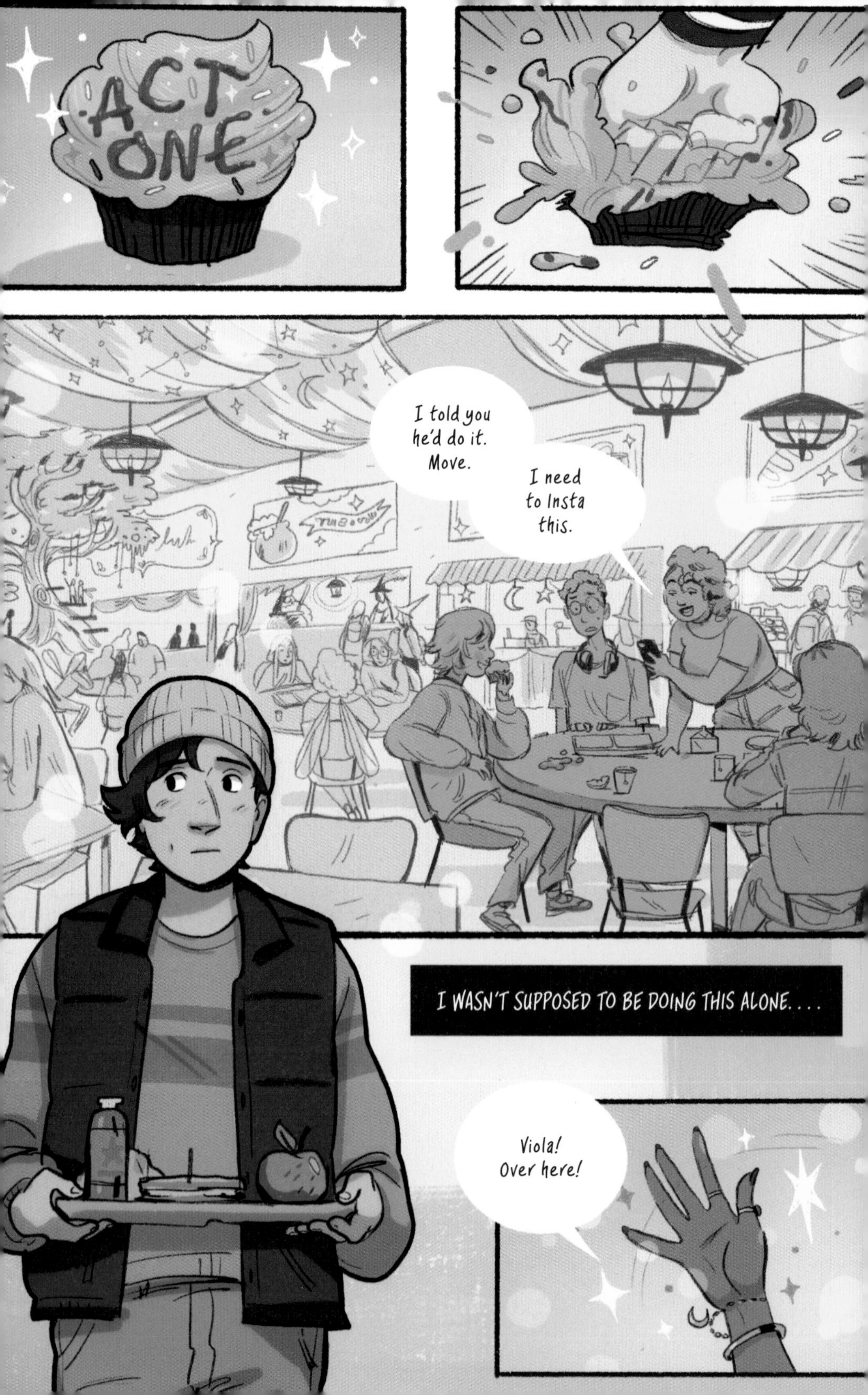
ACT ONE
I told you he'd do it. Move.
I need to Insta this.
I WASN'T SUPPOSED TO BE DOING THIS ALONE. . . .
Viola! Over here!

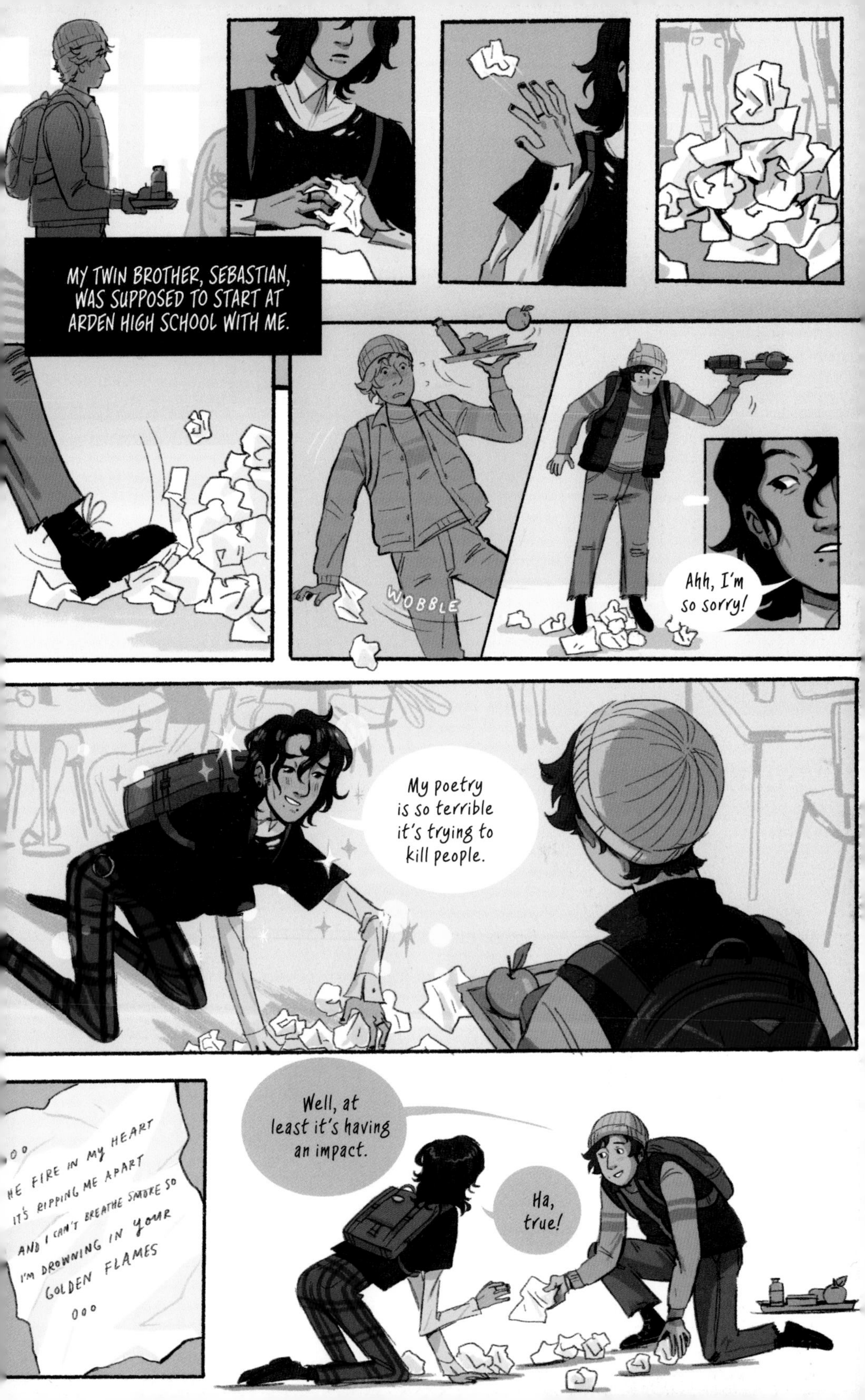
MY TWIN BROTHER, SEBASTIAN, WAS SUPPOSED TO START AT ARDEN HIGH SCHOOL WITH ME.
WOBBLE
Ahh, I'm so sorry!
My poetry is so terrible it's trying to kill people.
OO
HE FIRE IN MY HEART
IT'S RIPPING ME APART
AND I CAN'T BREATHE SMOKE SO
I'M DROWNING IN YOUR
GOLDEN FLAMES
OOO
Well, at least it's having an impact.
Ha, true!

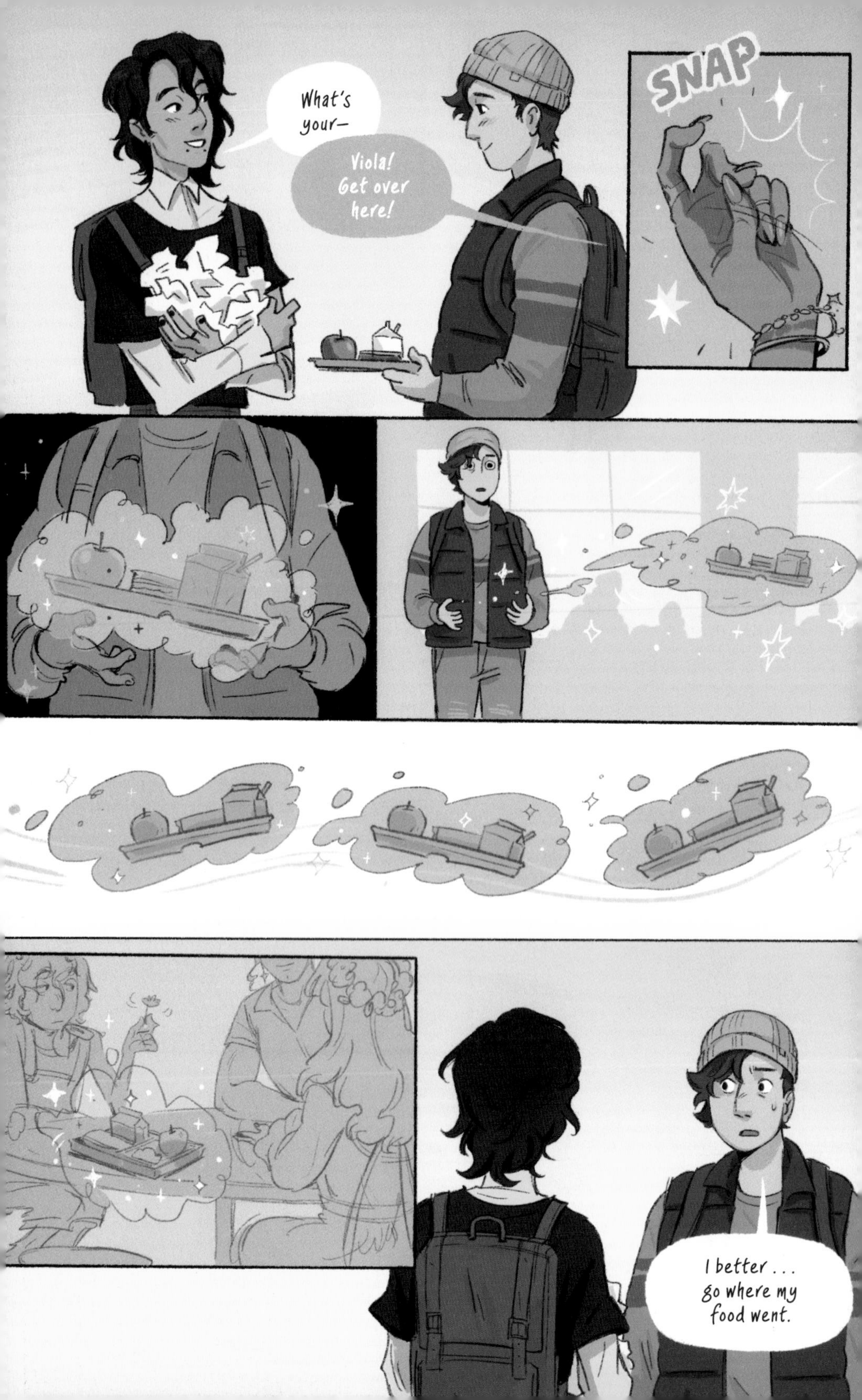
What's your—
Viola! Get over here!
SNAP
I better . . . go where my food went.

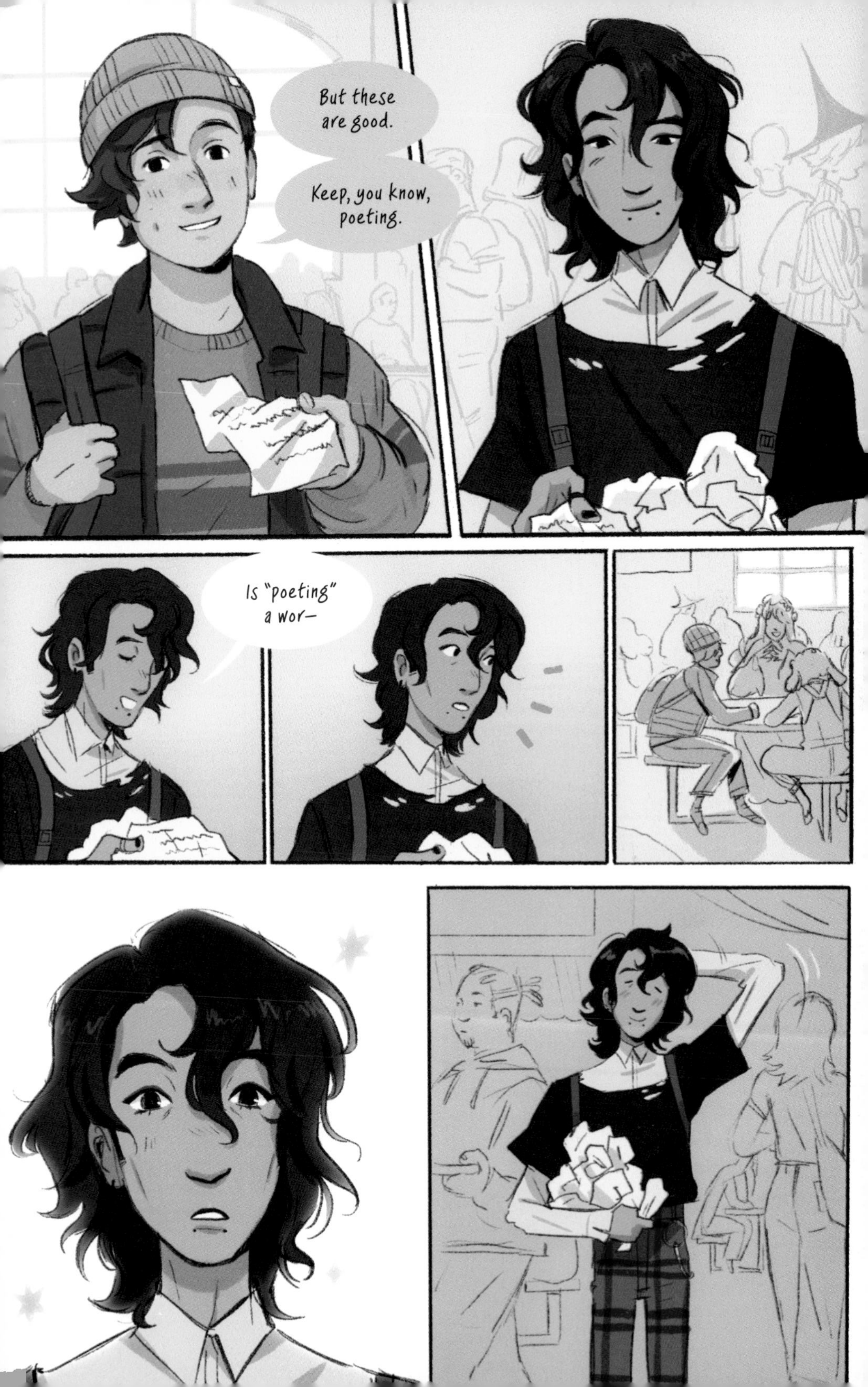
But these are good.
Keep, you know, poeting.
Is "poeting" a wor—

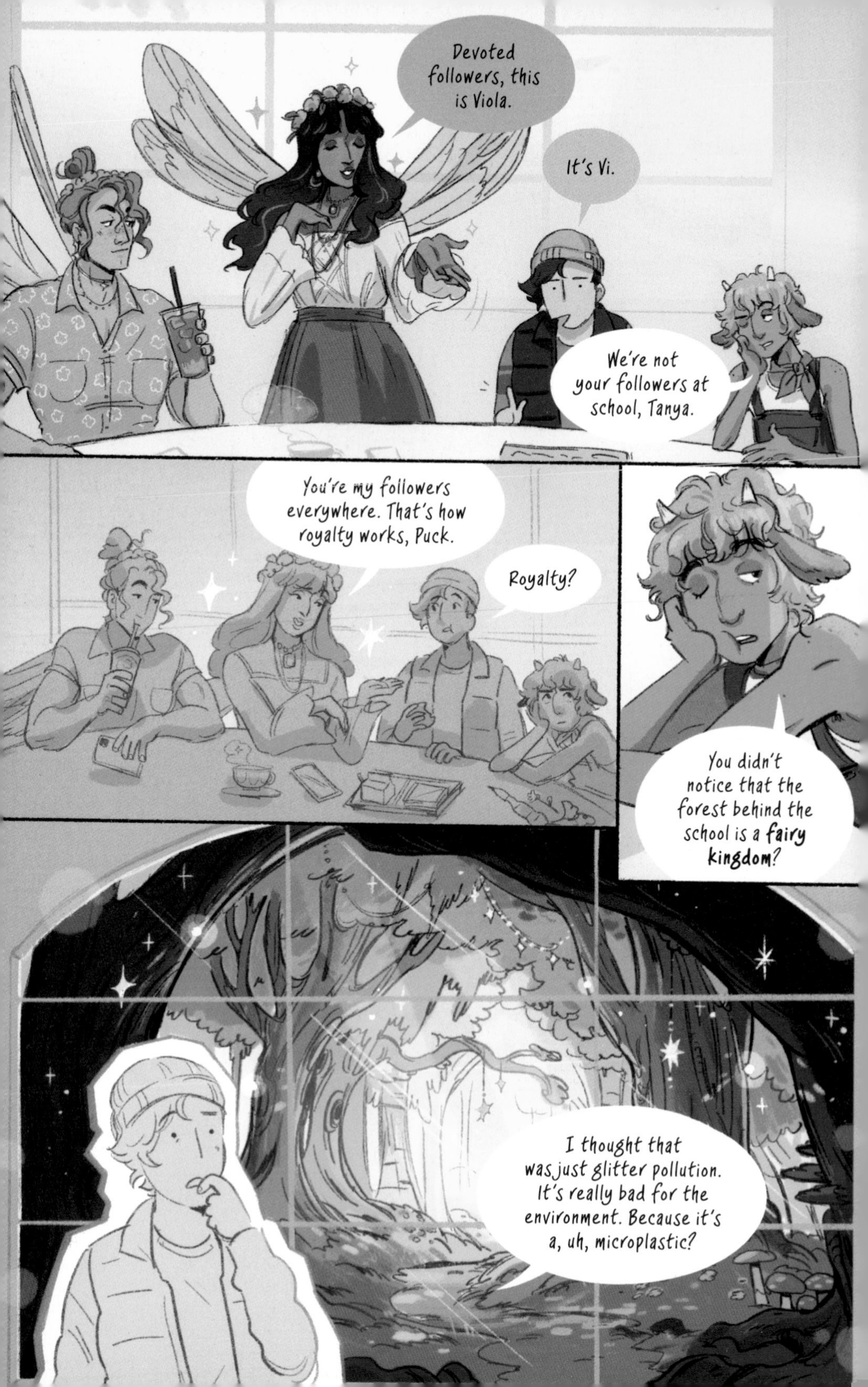
Devoted followers, this is Viola.
It's Vi.
We're not your followers at school, Tanya.
You're my followers everywhere. That's how royalty works, Puck.
Royalty?
You didn't notice that the forest behind the school is a **fairy kingdom**?
I thought that was just glitter pollution. It's really bad for the environment. Because it's a, uh, microplastic?

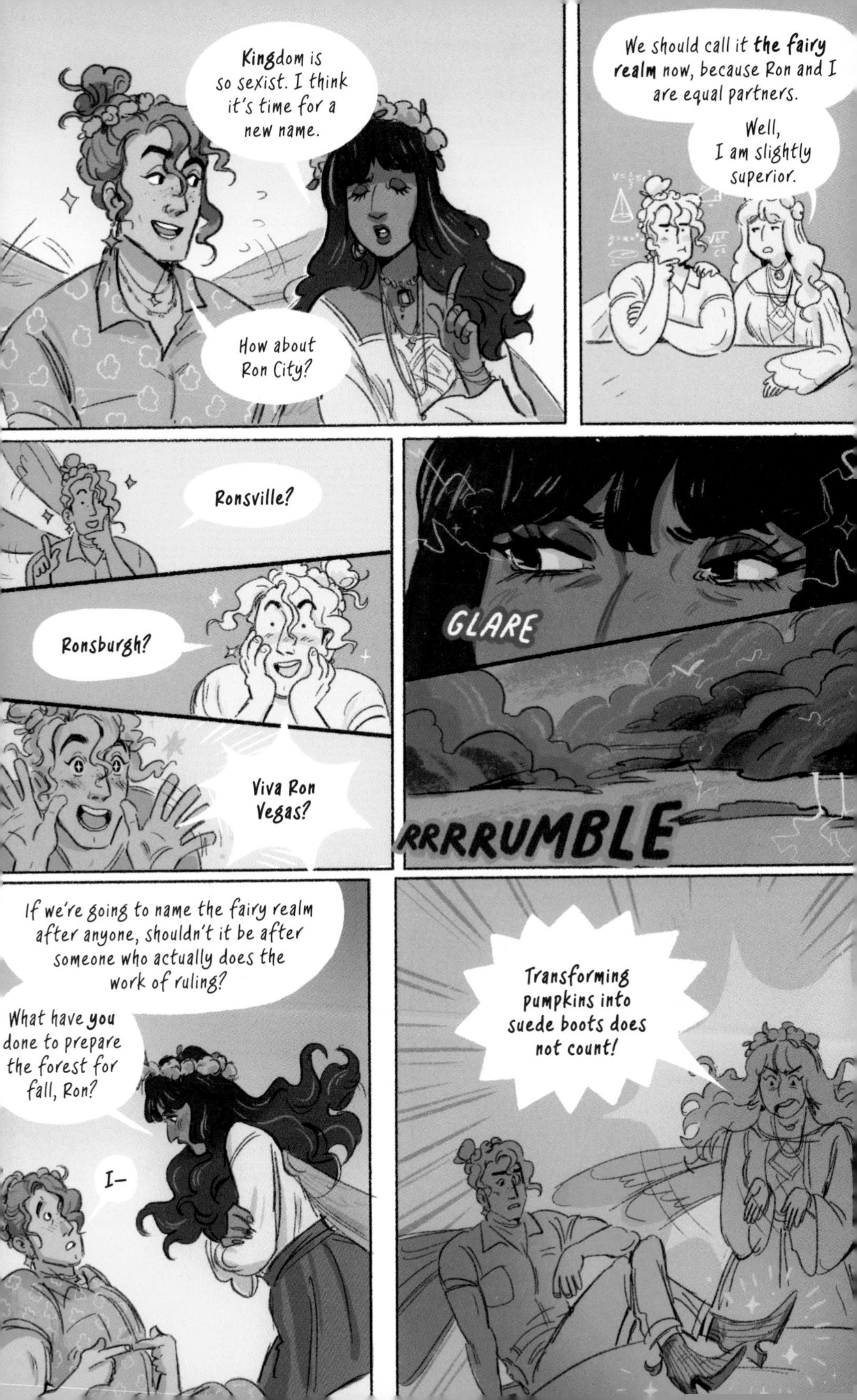
Kingdom is so sexist. I think it's time for a new name.
How about Ron City?
We should call it **the fairy realm** now, because Ron and I are equal partners.
Well, I am slightly superior.
Ronsville?
Ronsburgh?
Viva Ron Vegas?
GLARE
RRRRUMBLE
If we're going to name the fairy realm after anyone, shouldn't it be after someone who actually does the work of ruling?
What have **you** done to prepare the forest for fall, Ron?
I–
Transforming pumpkins into suede boots does not count!

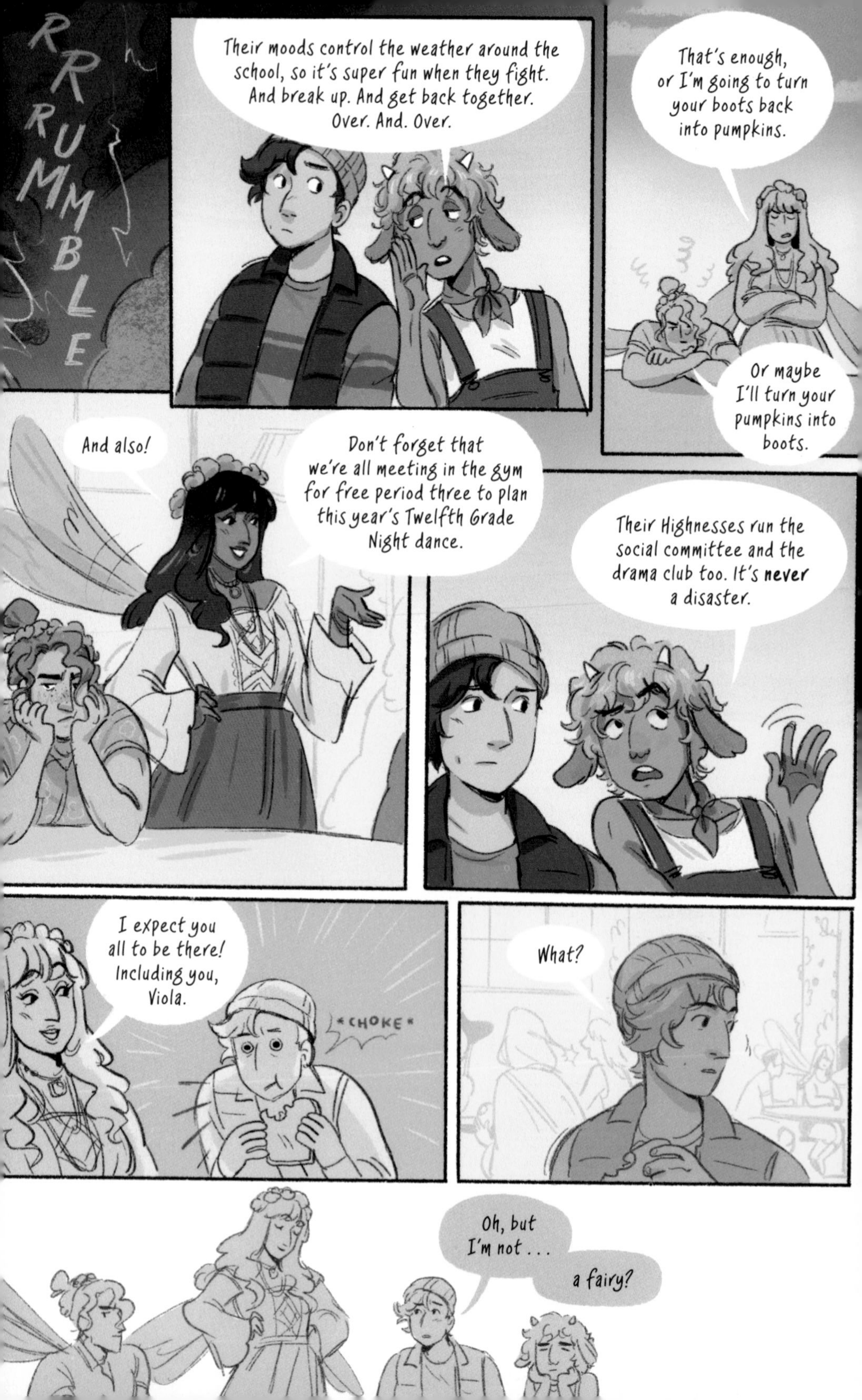
RRRUMMBLE
Their moods control the weather around the school, so it's super fun when they fight. And break up. And get back together. Over. And. Over.
That's enough, or I'm going to turn your boots back into pumpkins.
Or maybe I'll turn your pumpkins into boots.
And also!
Don't forget that we're all meeting in the gym for free period three to plan this year's Twelfth Grade Night dance.
Their Highnesses run the social committee and the drama club too. It's **never** a disaster.
I expect you all to be there! Including you, Viola.
CHOKE
What?
Oh, but I'm not . . .
a fairy?

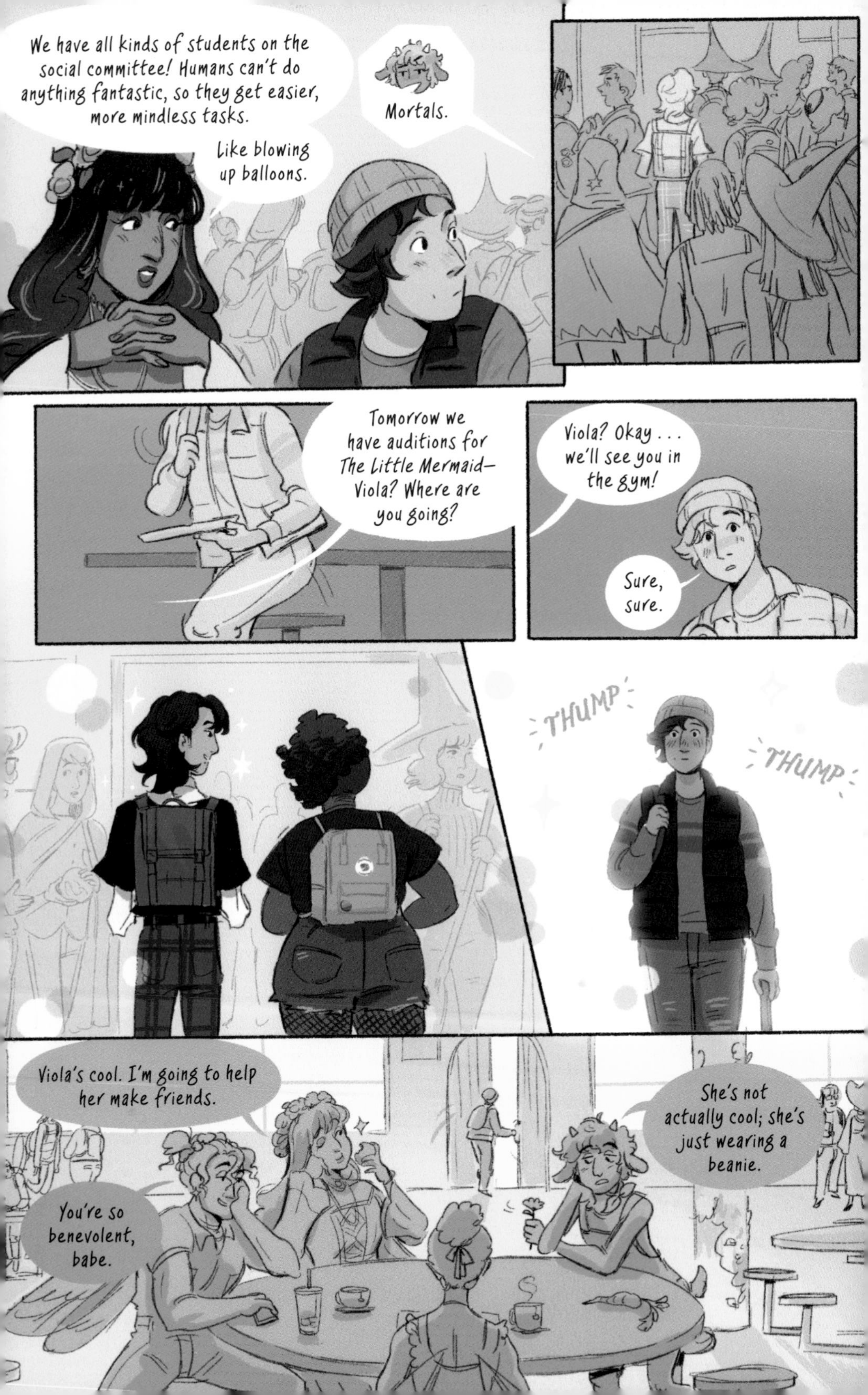
We have all kinds of students on the social committee! Humans can't do anything fantastic, so they get easier, more mindless tasks.
Like blowing up balloons.
Mortals.
Tomorrow we have auditions for The Little Mermaid— Viola? Where are you going?
Viola? Okay . . . we'll see you in the gym!
Sure, sure.
THUMP
THUMP
Viola's cool. I'm going to help her make friends.
You're so benevolent, babe.
She's not actually cool; she's just wearing a beanie.

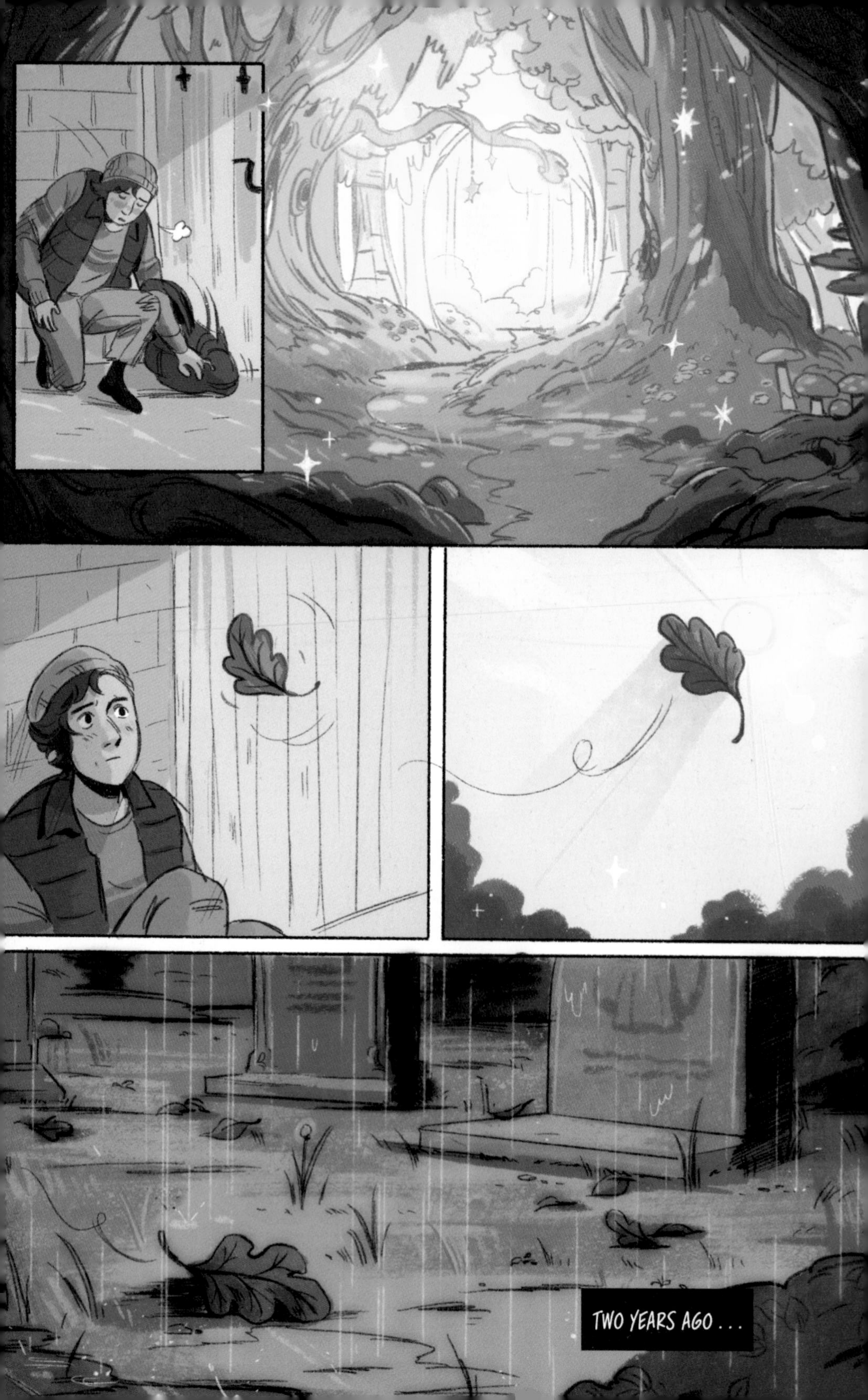
TWO YEARS AGO . . .

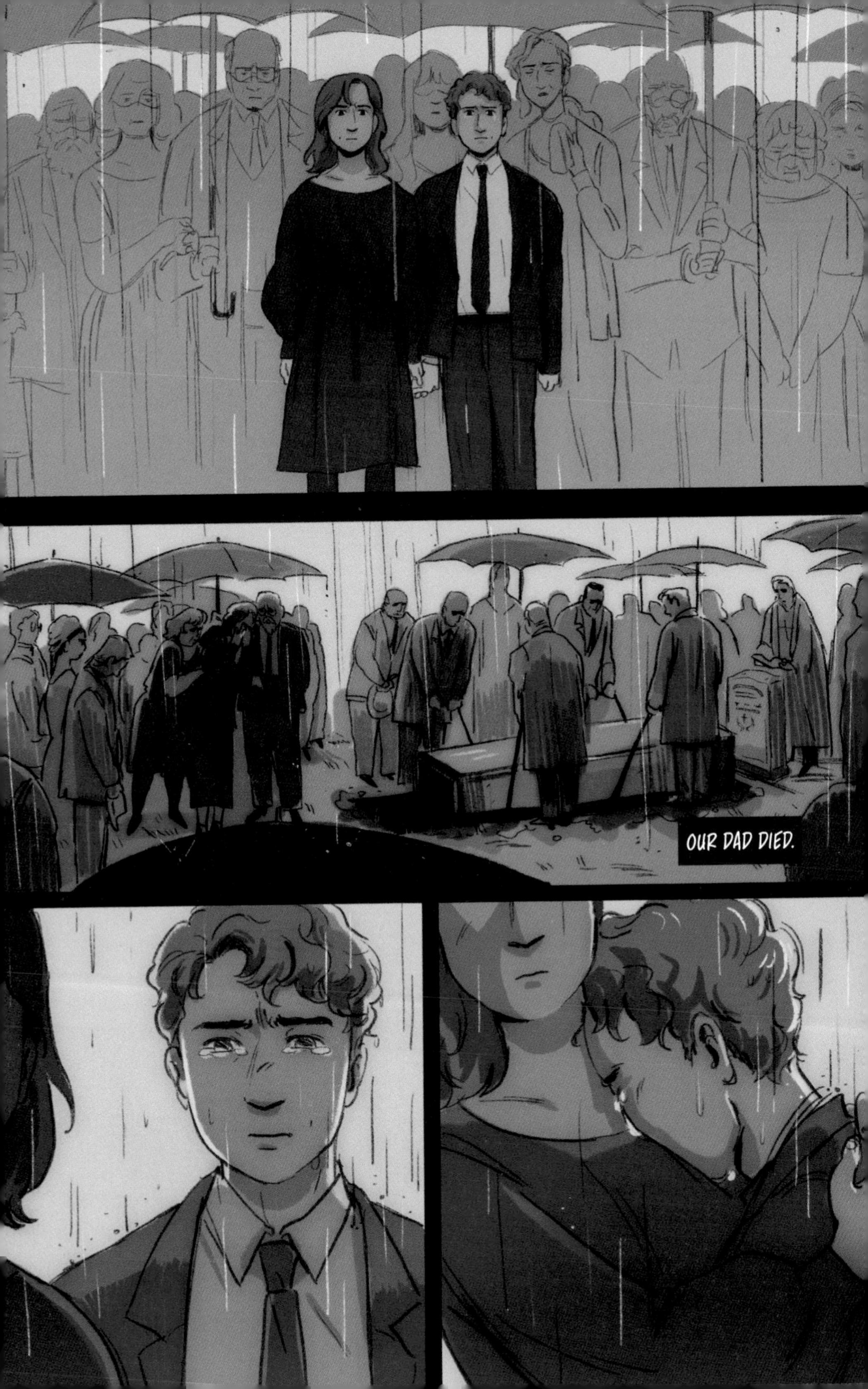
OUR DAD DIED.

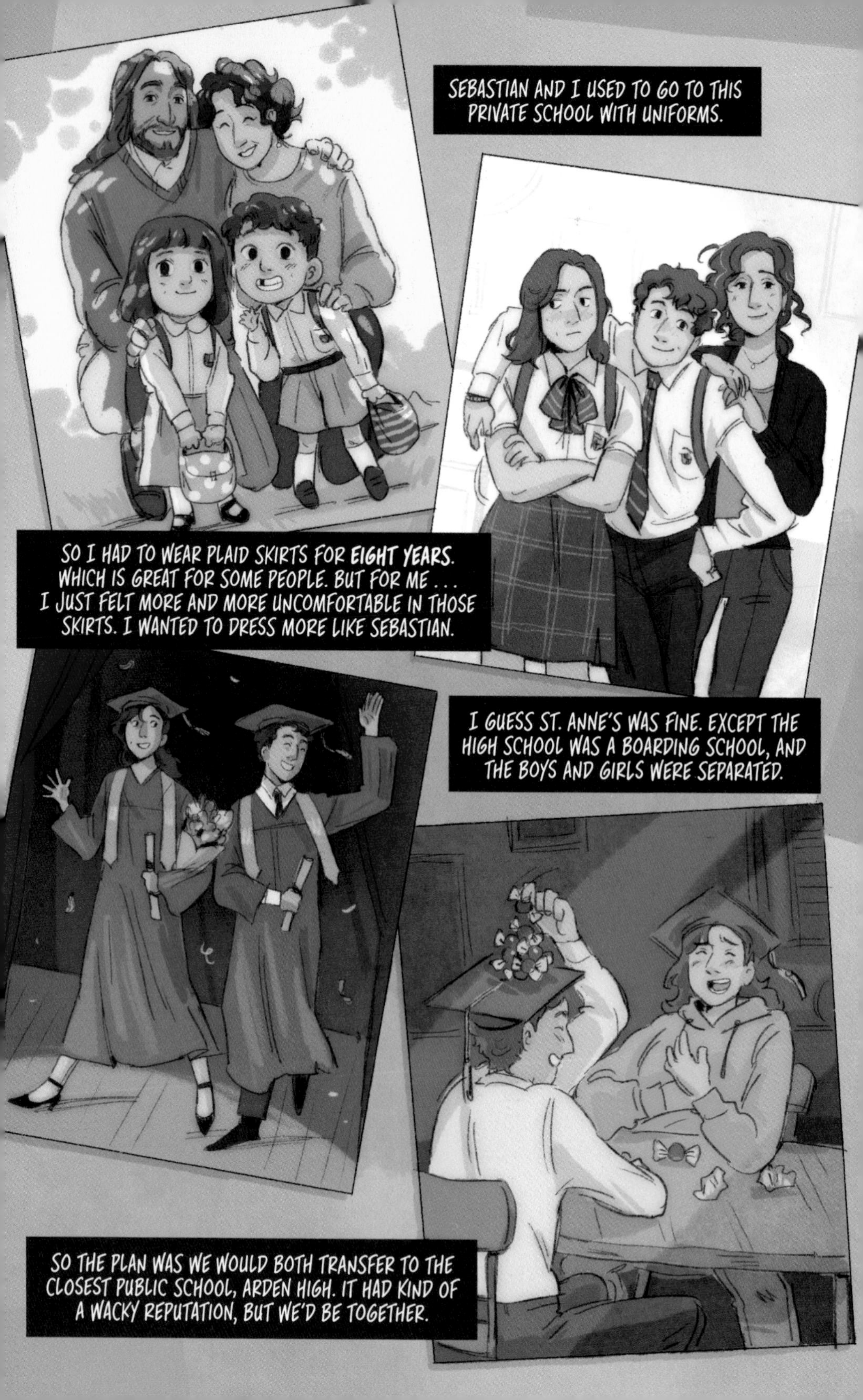

SEBASTIAN AND I USED TO GO TO THIS PRIVATE SCHOOL WITH UNIFORMS.
SO I HAD TO WEAR PLAID SKIRTS FOR **EIGHT YEARS**. WHICH IS GREAT FOR SOME PEOPLE. BUT FOR ME . . . I JUST FELT MORE AND MORE UNCOMFORTABLE IN THOSE SKIRTS. I WANTED TO DRESS MORE LIKE SEBASTIAN.
I GUESS ST. ANNE'S WAS FINE. EXCEPT THE HIGH SCHOOL WAS A BOARDING SCHOOL, AND THE BOYS AND GIRLS WERE SEPARATED.
SO THE PLAN WAS WE WOULD BOTH TRANSFER TO THE CLOSEST PUBLIC SCHOOL, ARDEN HIGH. IT HAD KIND OF A WACKY REPUTATION, BUT WE'D BE TOGETHER.

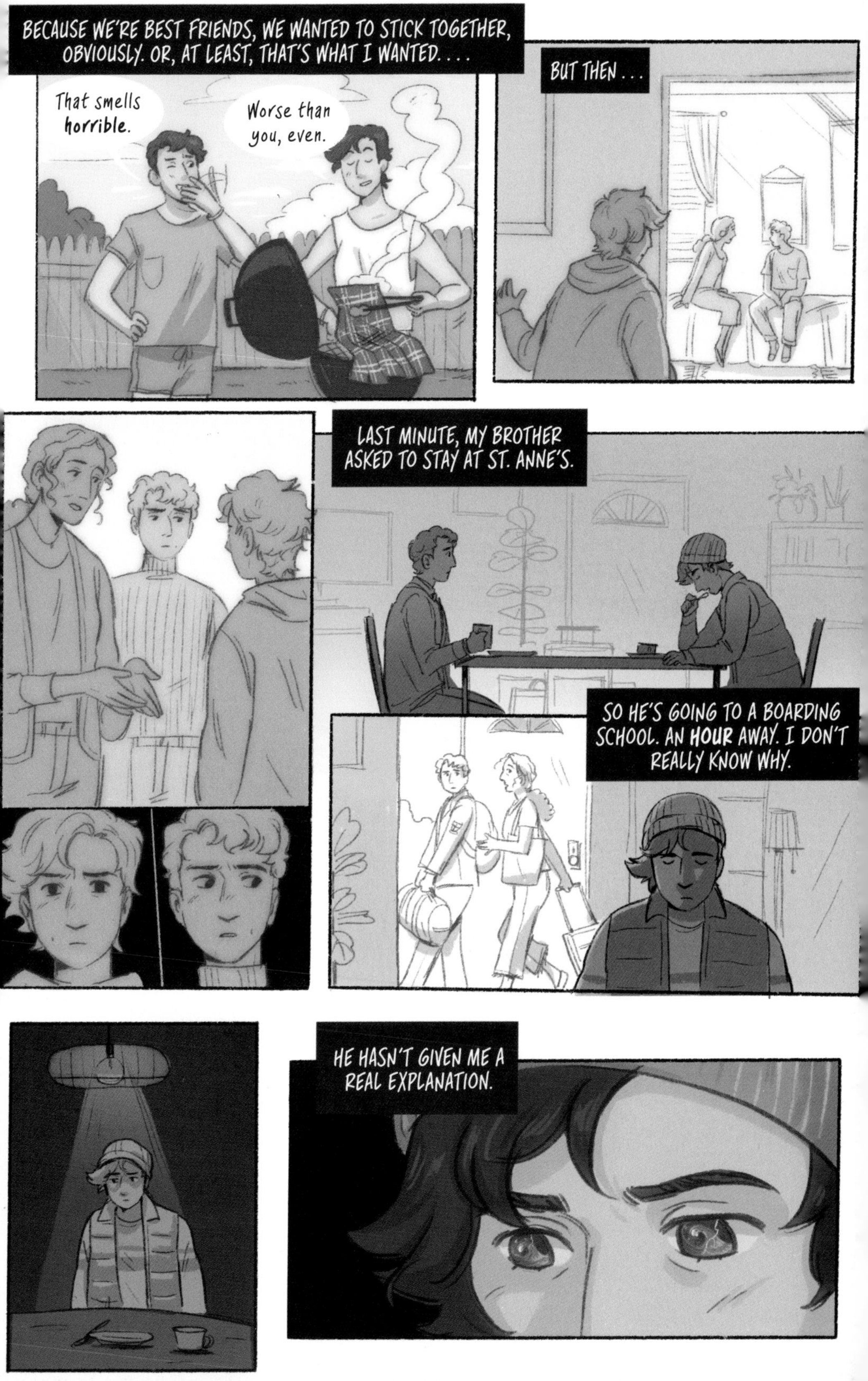
BECAUSE WE'RE BEST FRIENDS, WE WANTED TO STICK TOGETHER, OBVIOUSLY. OR, AT LEAST, THAT'S WHAT I WANTED. . . .
That smells **horrible**.
Worse than you, even.
BUT THEN . . .
LAST MINUTE, MY BROTHER ASKED TO STAY AT ST. ANNE'S.
SO HE'S GOING TO A BOARDING SCHOOL. AN **HOUR** AWAY. I DON'T REALLY KNOW WHY.
HE HASN'T GIVEN ME A REAL EXPLANATION.

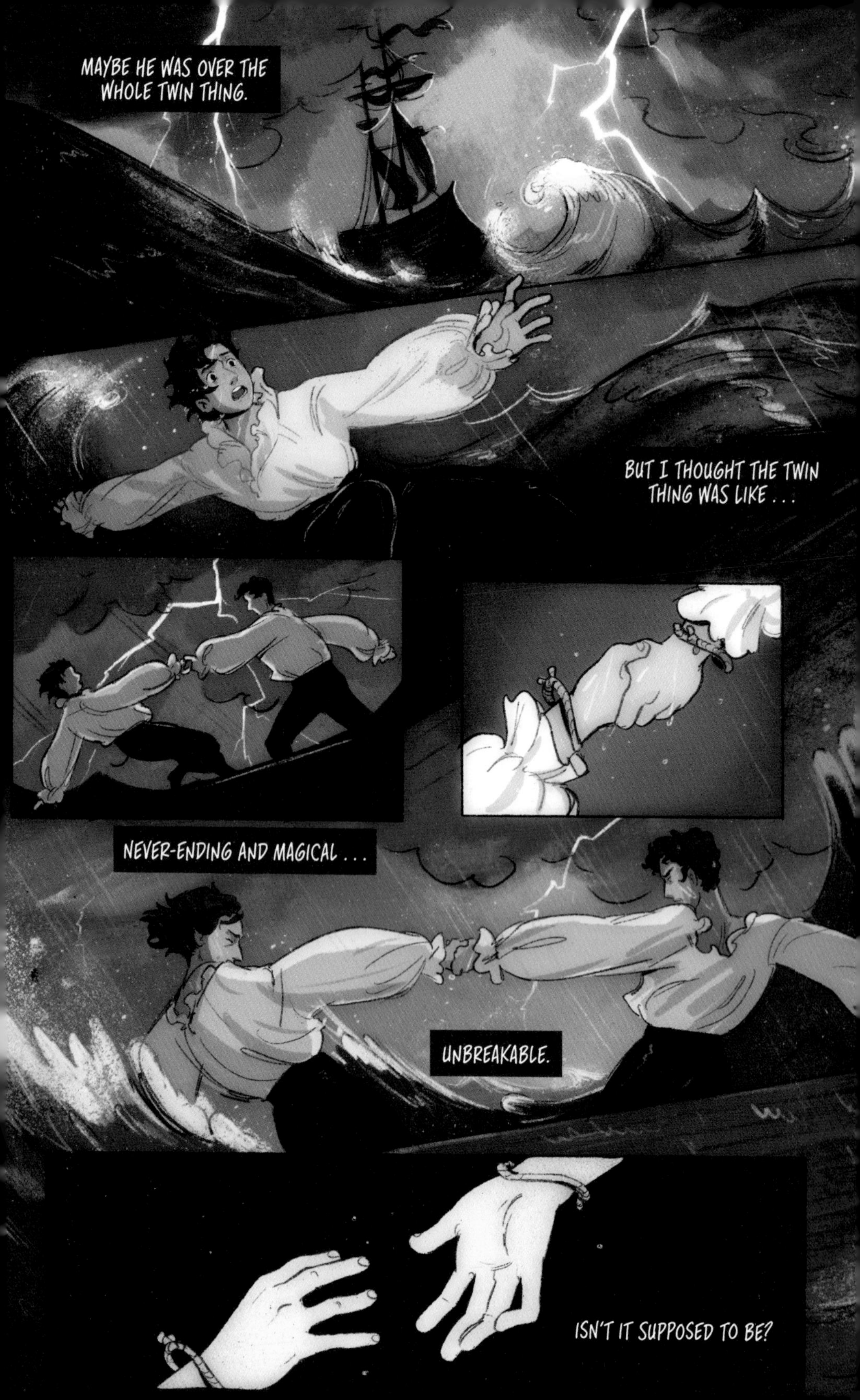
MAYBE HE WAS OVER THE WHOLE TWIN THING.
BUT I THOUGHT THE TWIN THING WAS LIKE . . .
NEVER-ENDING AND MAGICAL . . .
UNBREAKABLE.
ISN'T IT SUPPOSED TO BE?

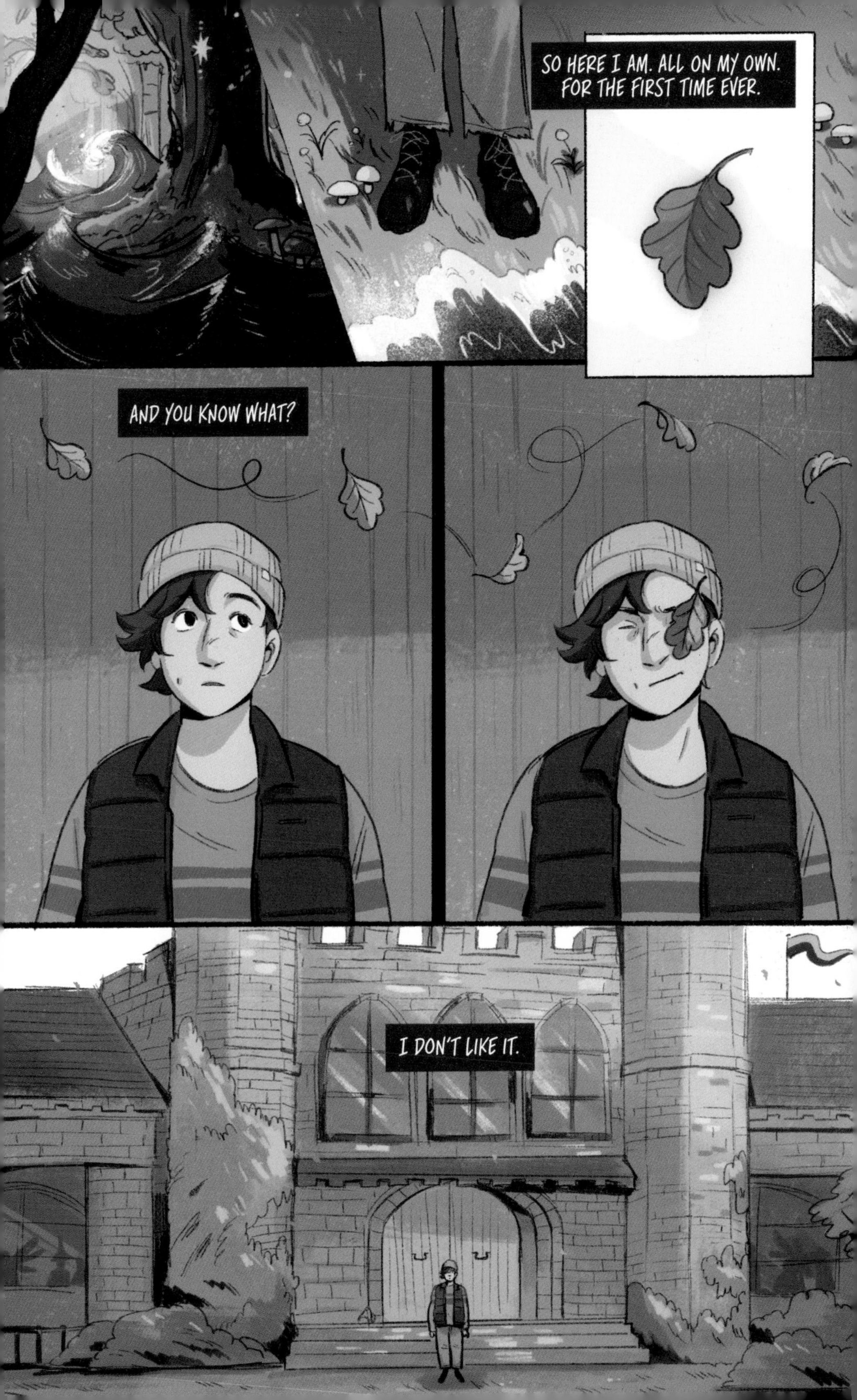
SO HERE I AM. ALL ON MY OWN. FOR THE FIRST TIME EVER.
AND YOU KNOW WHAT?
I DON'T LIKE IT.

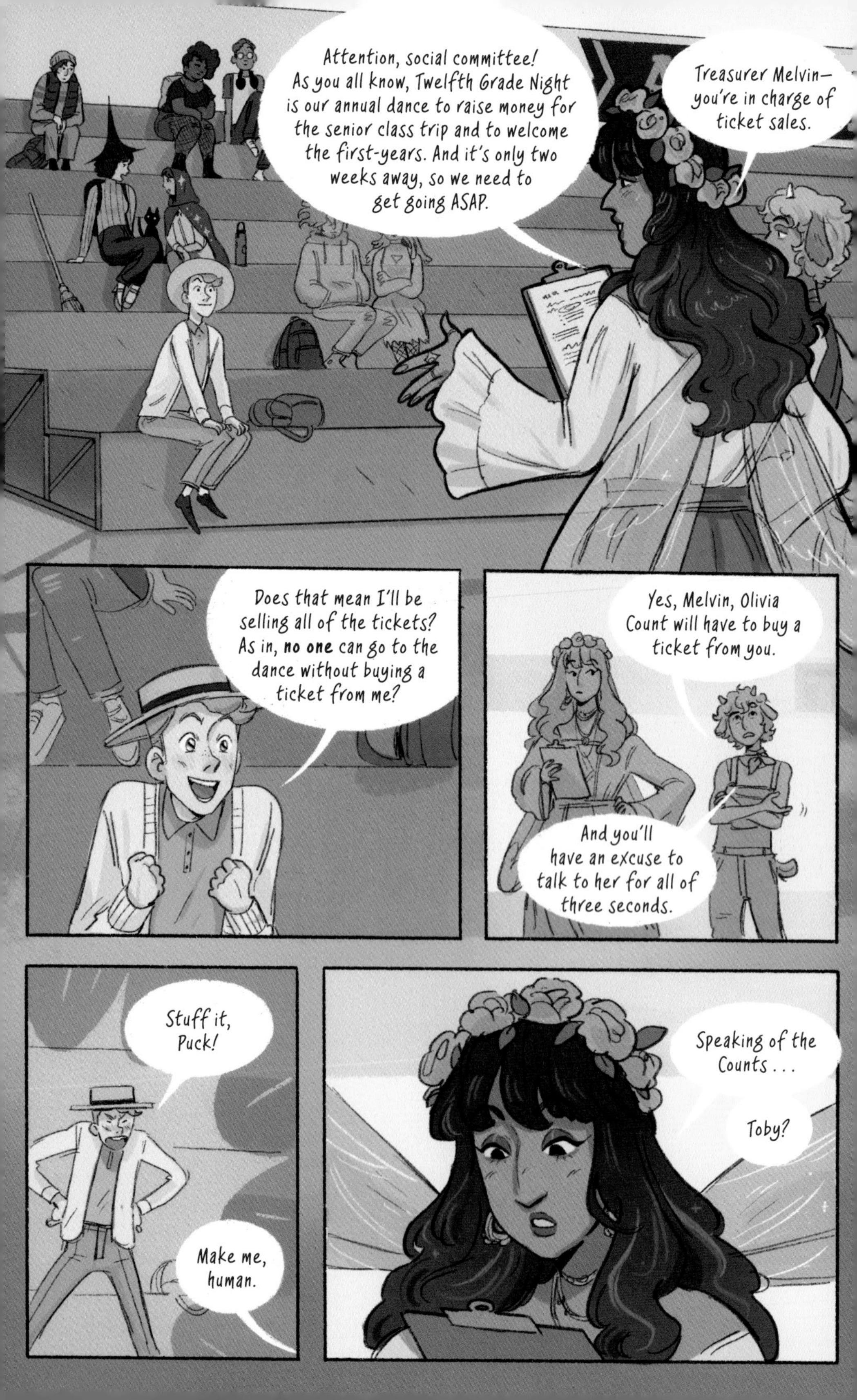

Attention, social committee! As you all know, Twelfth Grade Night is our annual dance to raise money for the senior class trip and to welcome the first-years. And it's only two weeks away, so we need to get going ASAP.
Treasurer Melvin—you're in charge of ticket sales.
Does that mean I'll be selling all of the tickets? As in, **no one** can go to the dance without buying a ticket from me?
Yes, Melvin, Olivia Count will have to buy a ticket from you.
And you'll have an excuse to talk to her for all of three seconds.
Stuff it, Puck!
Make me, human.
Speaking of the Counts . . .
Toby?

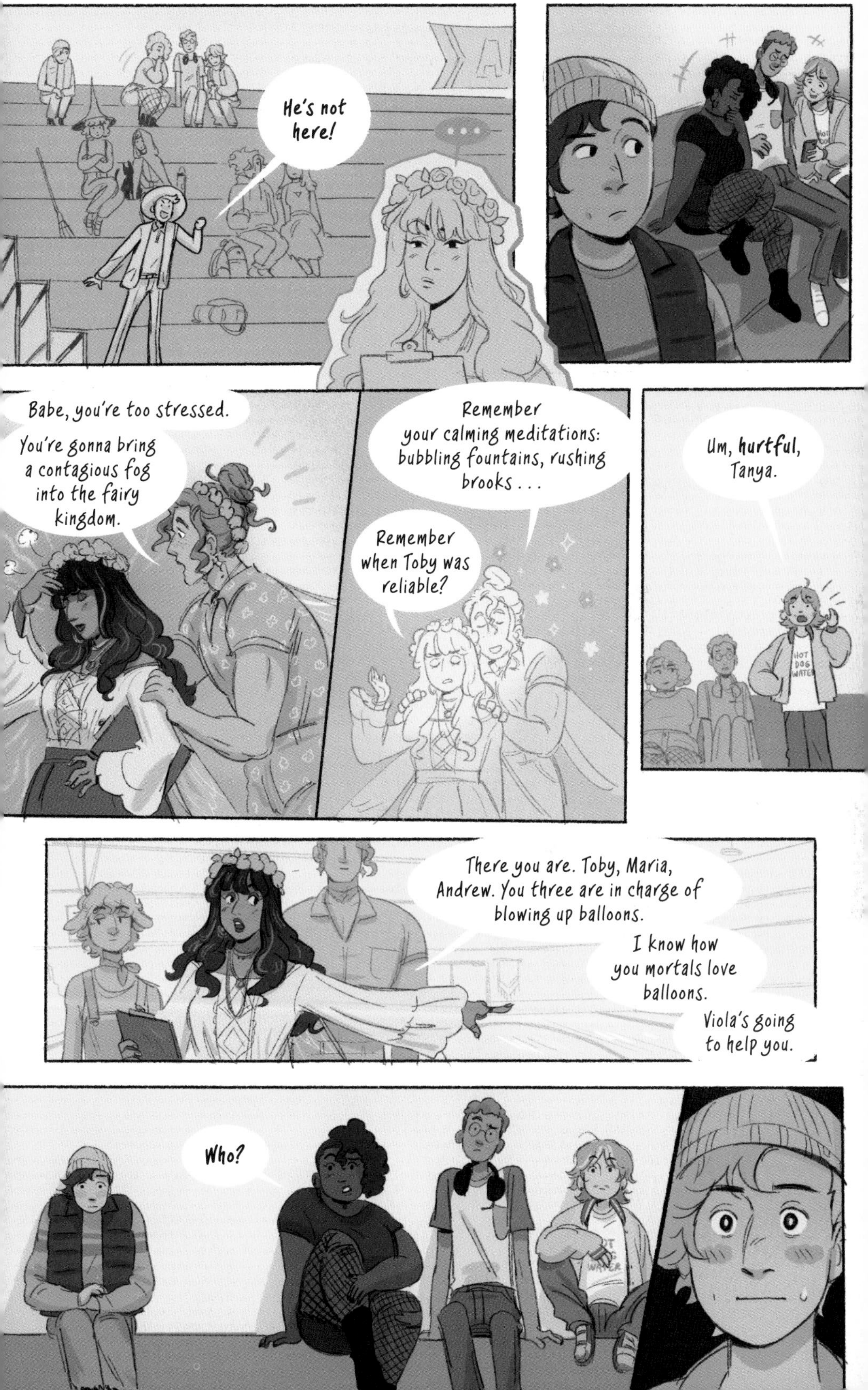
He's not here!
Babe, you're too stressed.
You're gonna bring a contagious fog into the fairy kingdom.
Remember your calming meditations: bubbling fountains, rushing brooks . . .
Remember when Toby was reliable?
Um, **hurtful**, Tanya.
HOT DOG WATER
There you are. Toby, Maria, Andrew. You three are in charge of blowing up balloons.
I know how you mortals love balloons.
Viola's going to help you.
Who?

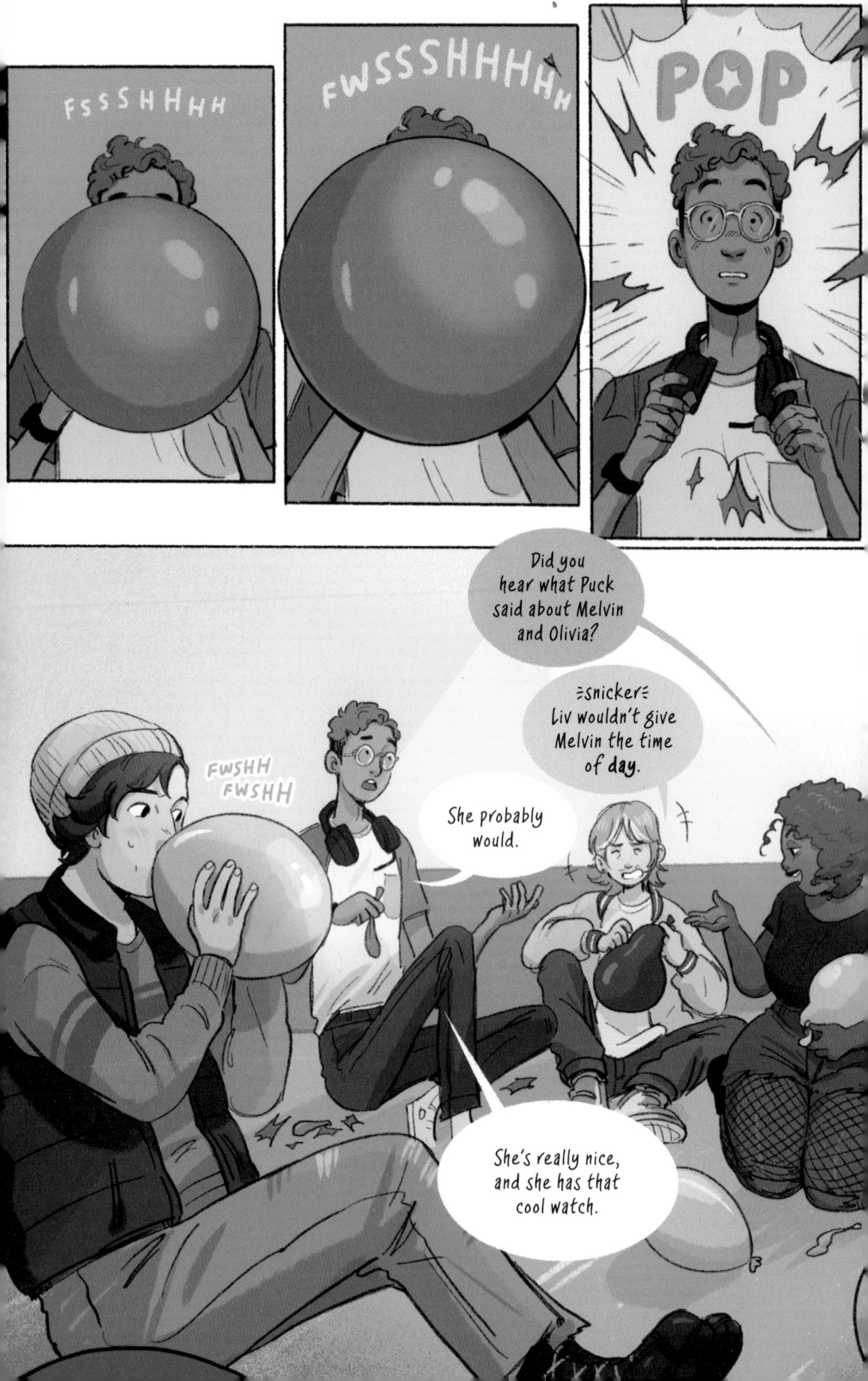
FsSSHHHHH
FWSSSHHHHHH
POP
Did you hear what Puck said about Melvin and Olivia?
≈snicker≈ Liv wouldn't give Melvin the time of day.
FWSHH FWSHH
She probably would.
She's really nice, and she has that cool watch.

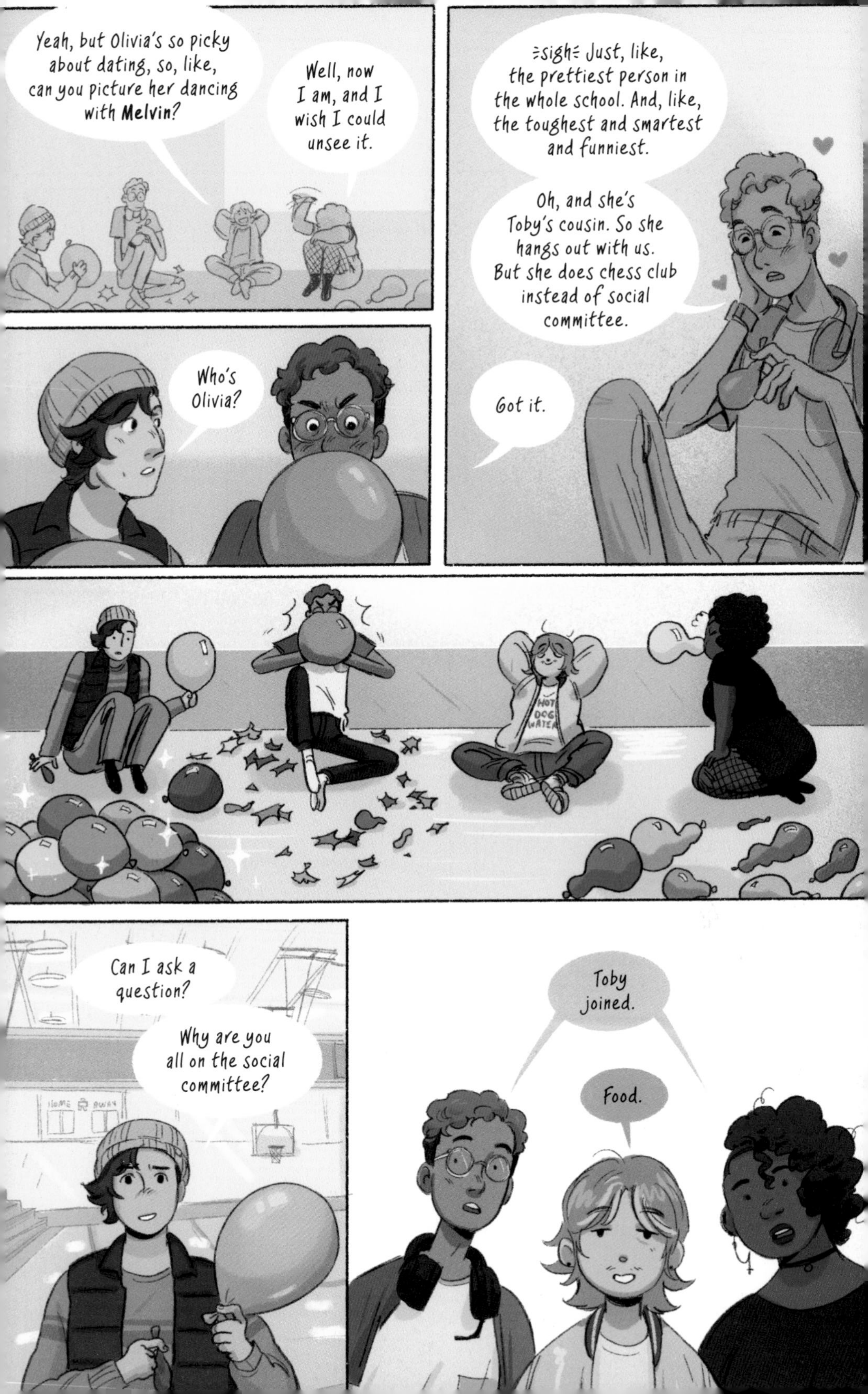
Yeah, but Olivia's so picky about dating, so, like, can you picture her dancing with **Melvin**?
Well, now I am, and I wish I could unsee it.
=sigh= Just, like, the prettiest person in the whole school. And, like, the toughest and smartest and funniest.
Oh, and she's Toby's cousin. So she hangs out with us. But she does chess club instead of social committee.
Who's Olivia?
Got it.
HOT DOG WATER
Can I ask a question?
Why are you all on the social committee?
HOME AWAY
Toby joined.
Food.

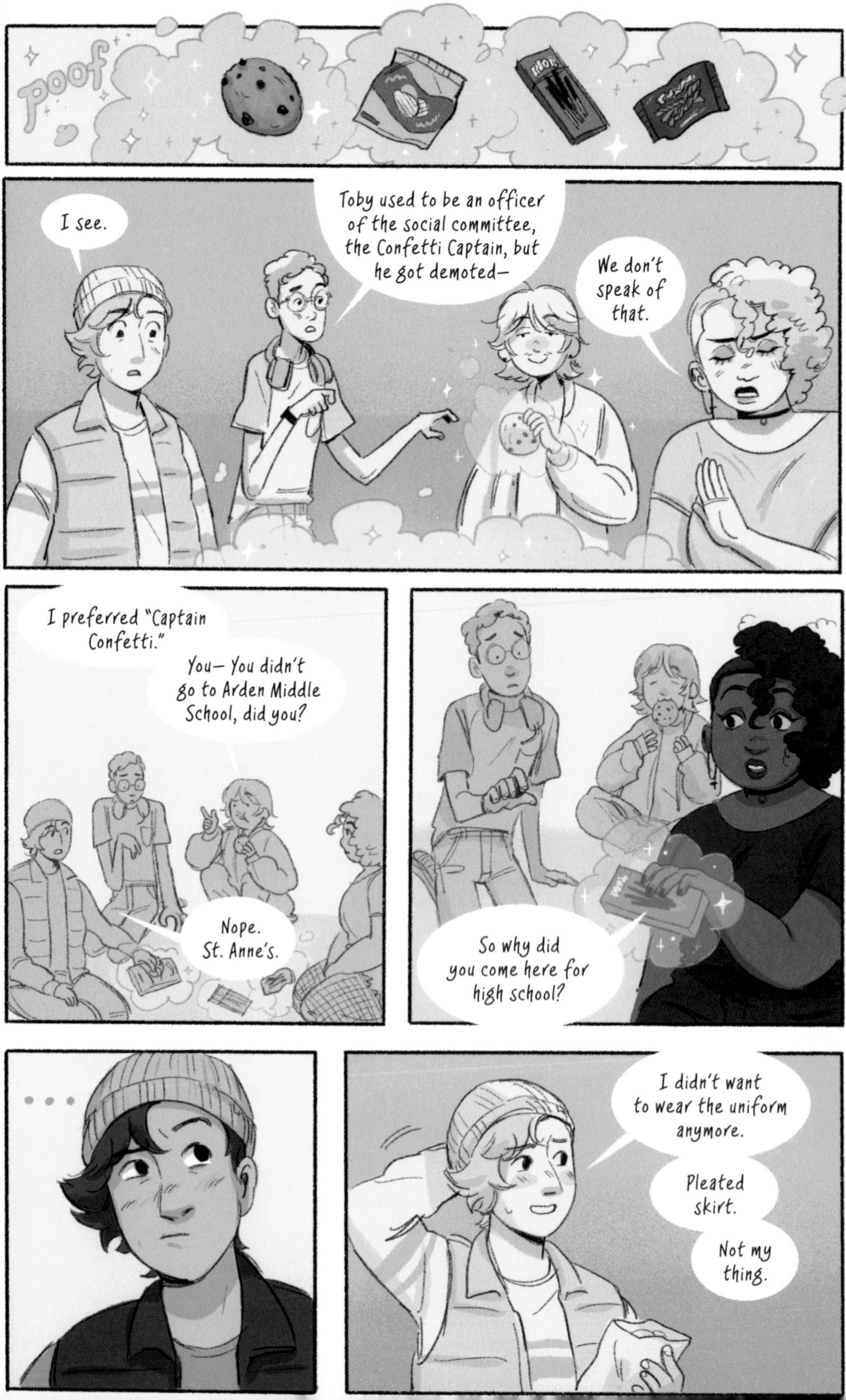
poof
I see.
Toby used to be an officer of the social committee, the Confetti Captain, but he got demoted—
We don't speak of that.
I preferred "Captain Confetti."
You— You didn't go to Arden Middle School, did you?
Nope. St. Anne's.
So why did you come here for high school?
...
I didn't want to wear the uniform anymore.
Pleated skirt.
Not my thing.

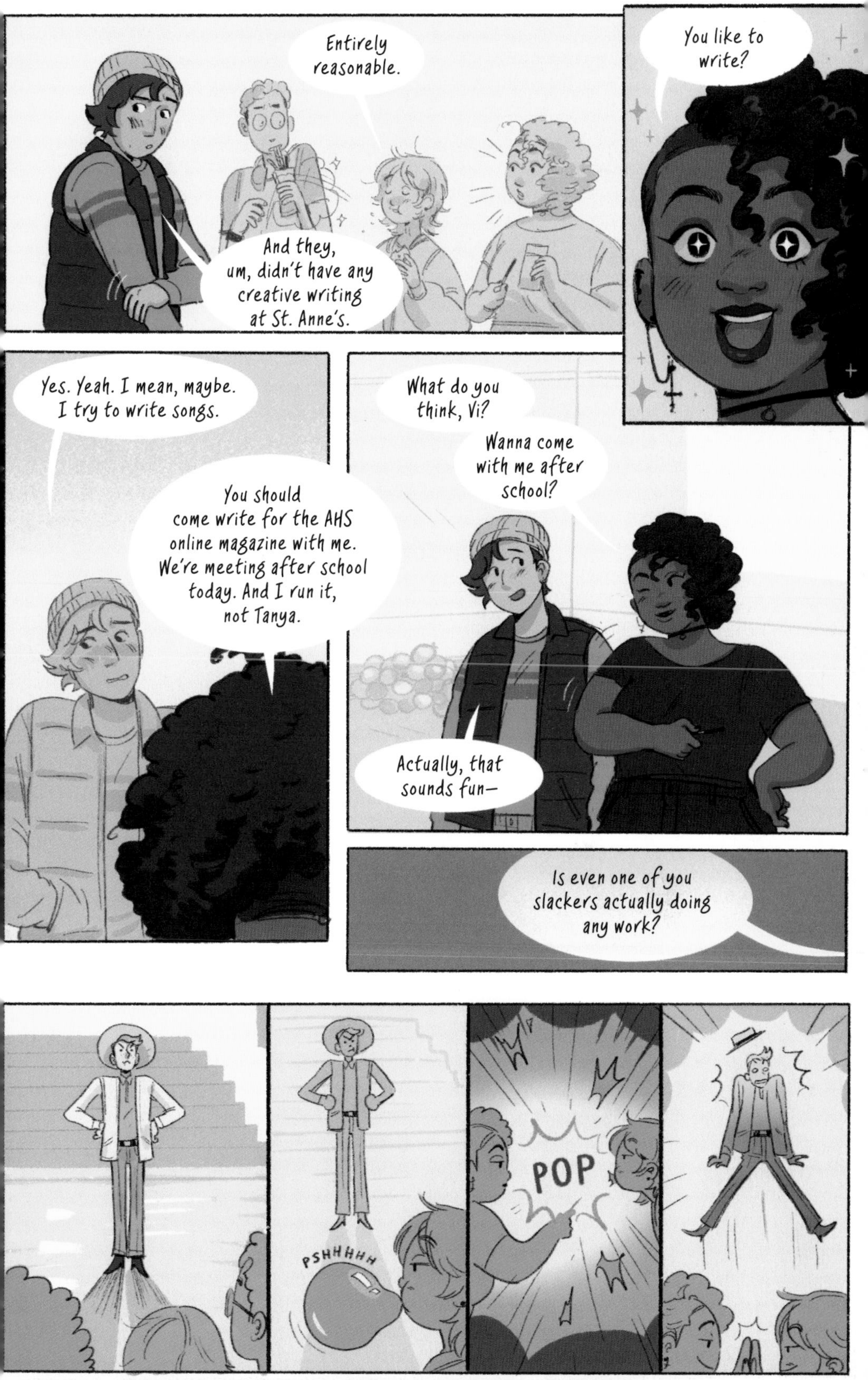
Entirely reasonable.
And they, um, didn't have any creative writing at St. Anne's.
You like to write?
Yes. Yeah. I mean, maybe. I try to write songs.
You should come write for the AHS online magazine with me. We're meeting after school today. And I run it, not Tanya.
What do you think, Vi?
Wanna come with me after school?
Actually, that sounds fun—
Is even one of you slackers actually doing any work?
PSHHHHH
POP

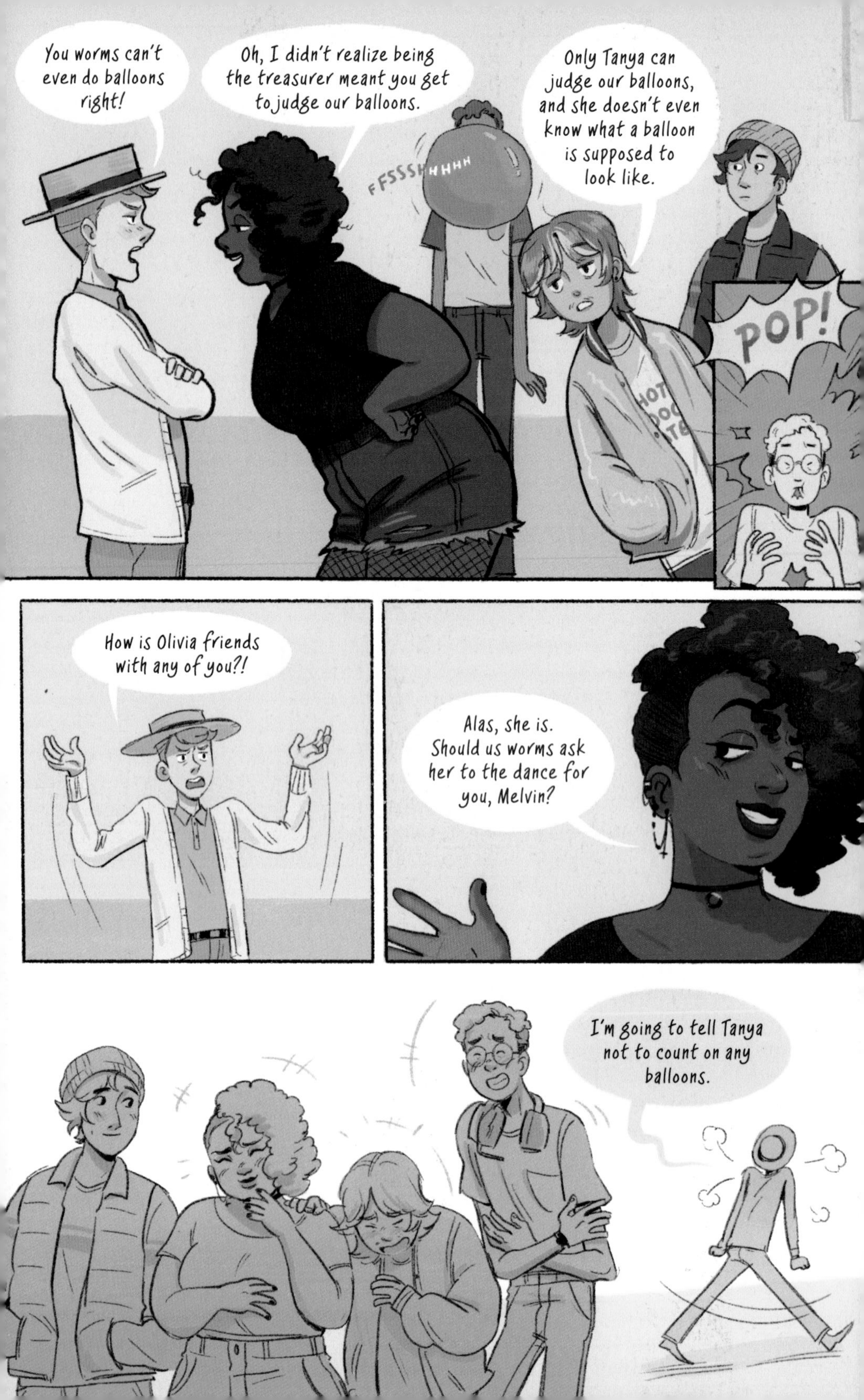
You worms can't even do balloons right!
Oh, I didn't realize being the treasurer meant you get to judge our balloons.
FFSSSHHHHH
Only Tanya can judge our balloons, and she doesn't even know what a balloon is supposed to look like.
POP!
How is Olivia friends with any of you?!
Alas, she is. Should us worms ask her to the dance for you, Melvin?
I'm going to tell Tanya not to count on any balloons.

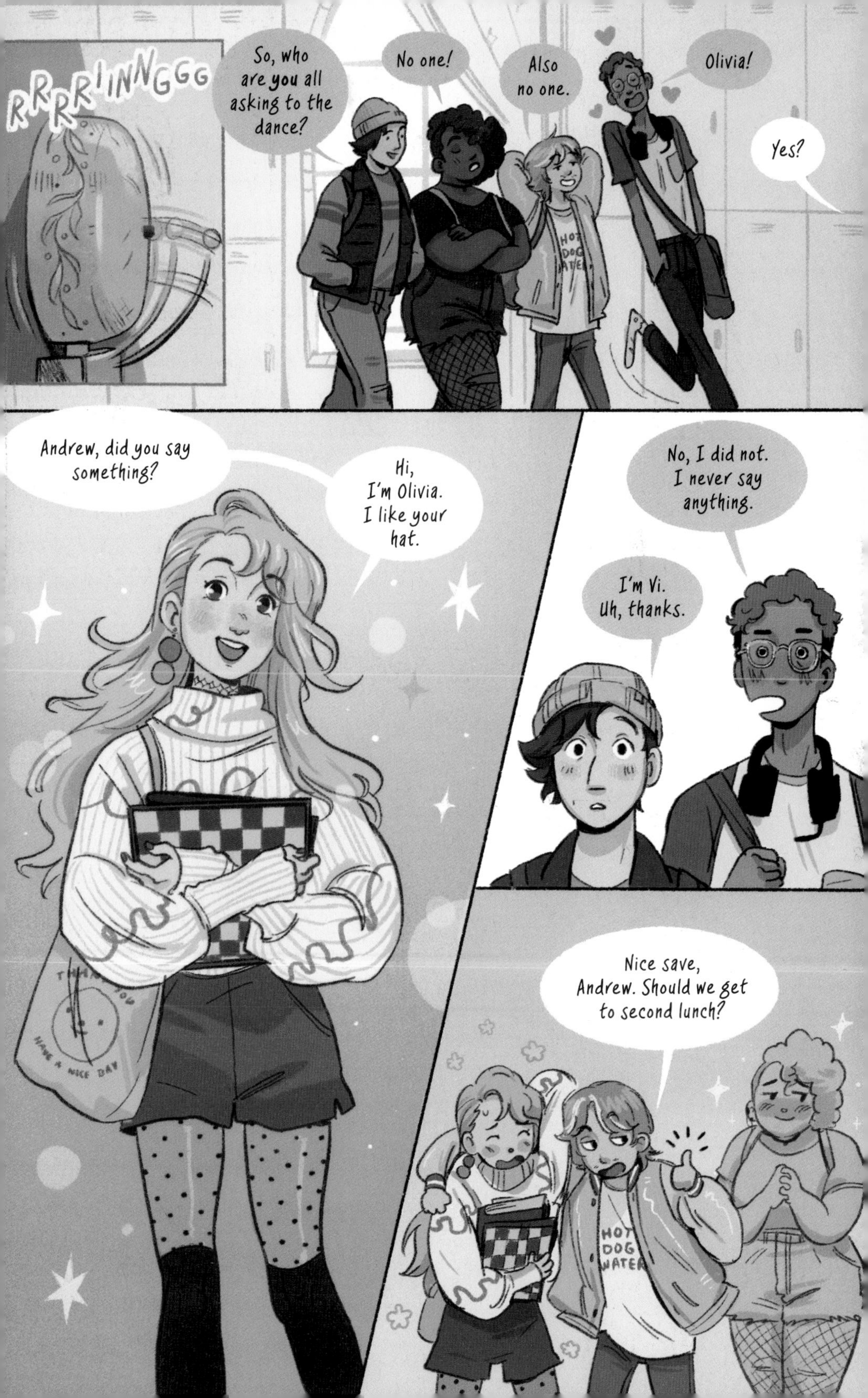
RRRRINNGGG
So, who are you all asking to the dance?
No one!
Also no one.
Olivia!
Yes?
Andrew, did you say something?
Hi, I'm Olivia. I like your hat.
No, I did not. I never say anything.
I'm Vi. Uh, thanks.
Nice save, Andrew. Should we get to second lunch?
HOT DOG WATER
HAVE A NICE DAY

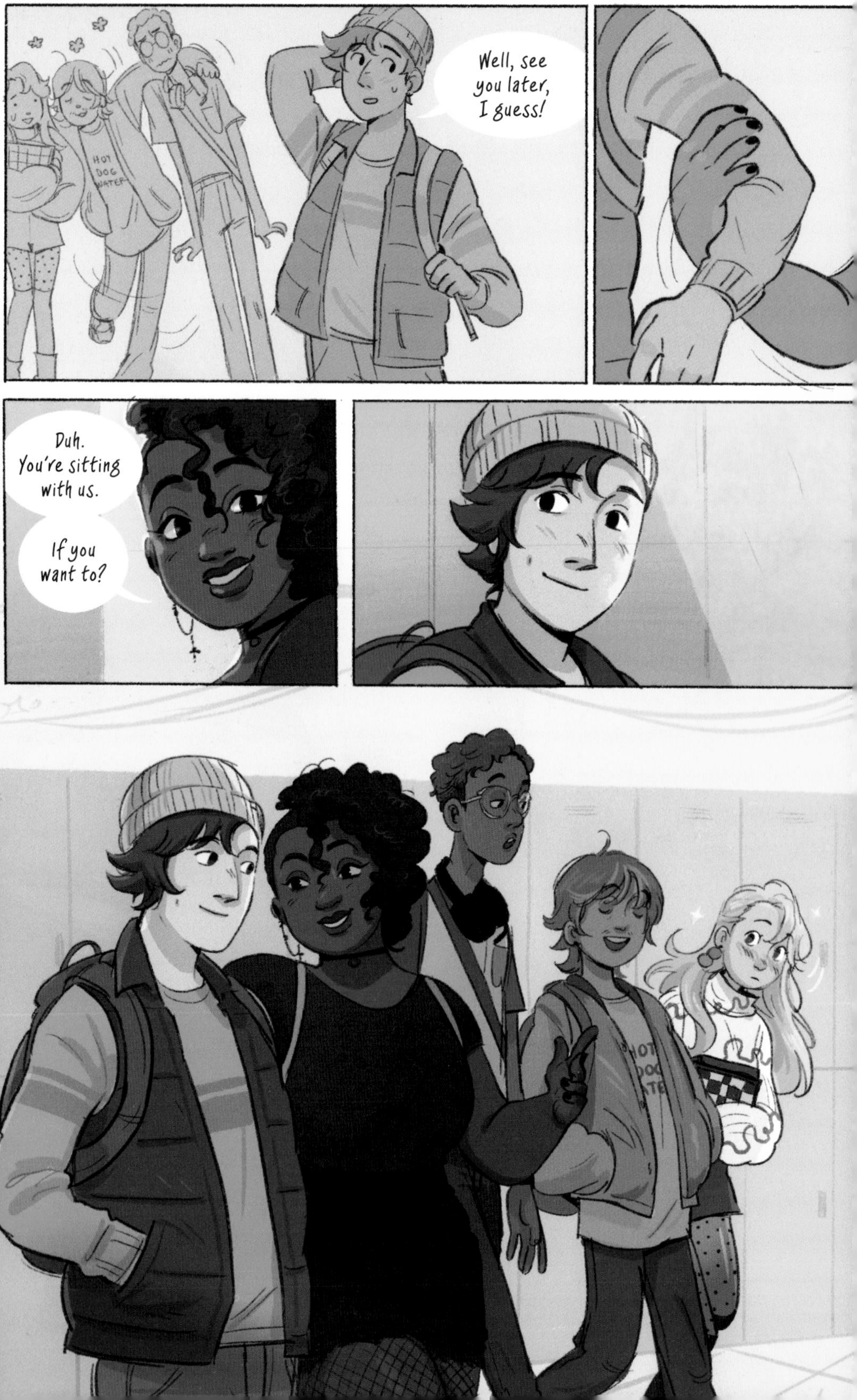

HOT DOG WATER
Well, see you later, I guess!
Duh. You're sitting with us.
If you want to?

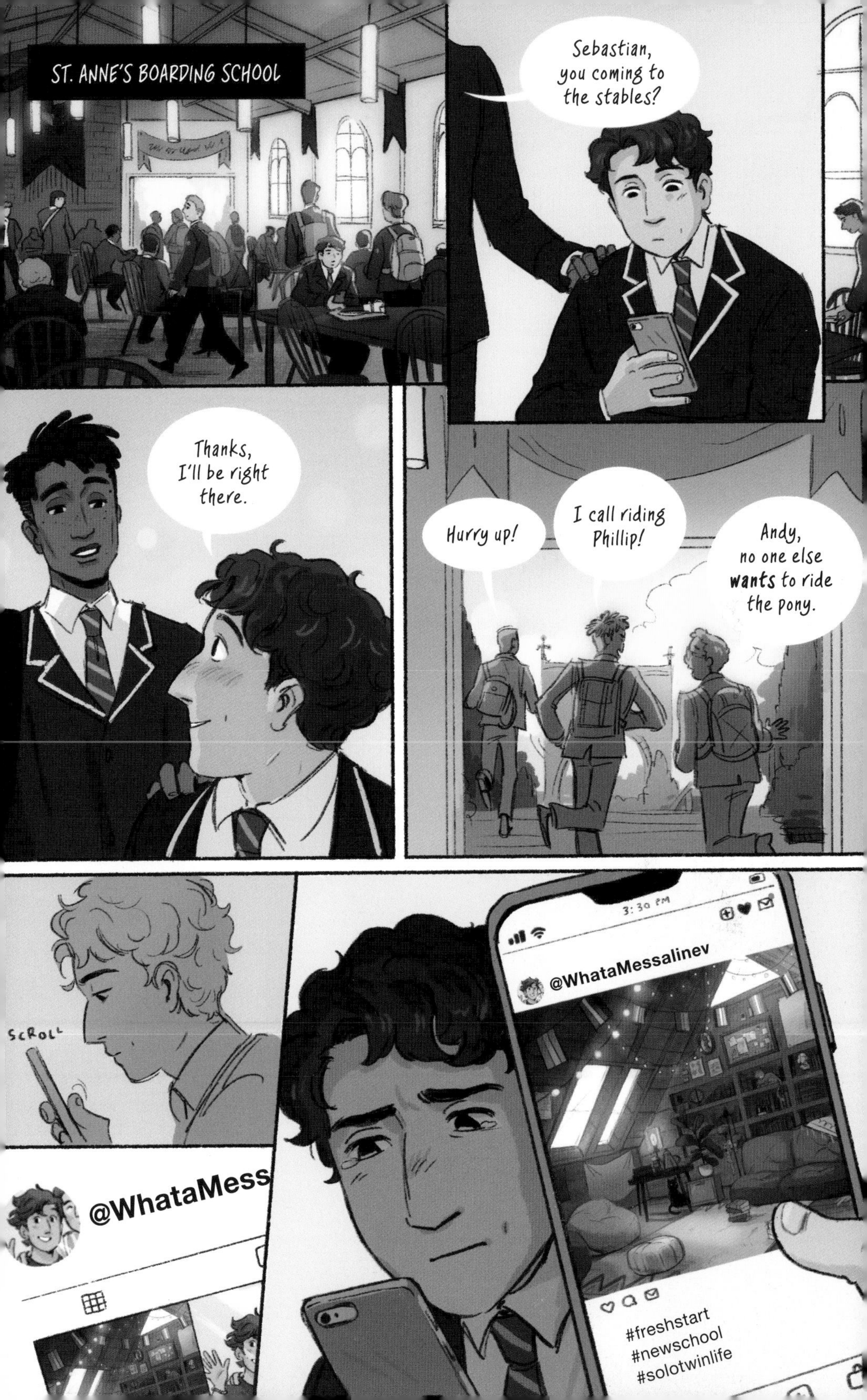
ST. ANNE'S BOARDING SCHOOL
Sebastian, you coming to the stables?
Thanks, I'll be right there.
Hurry up!
I call riding Phillip!
Andy, no one else wants to ride the pony.
SCROLL
3:30 PM
@WhataMessalinev
#freshstart
#newschool
#solotwinlife
@WhataMess

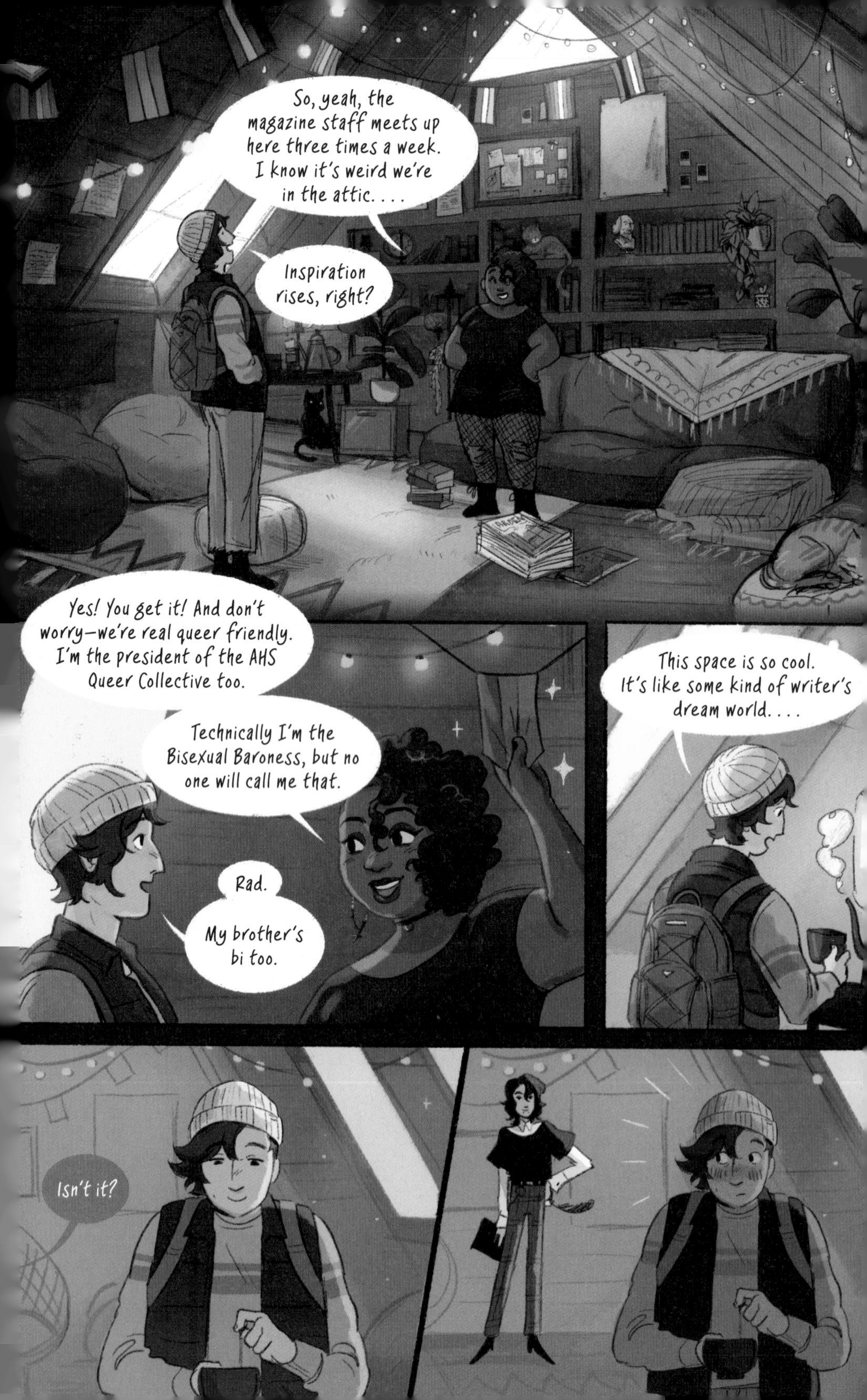
So, yeah, the magazine staff meets up here three times a week. I know it's weird we're in the attic. . . .
Inspiration rises, right?
Yes! You get it! And don't worry—we're real queer friendly. I'm the president of the AHS Queer Collective too.
Technically I'm the Bisexual Baroness, but no one will call me that.
Rad.
My brother's bi too.
This space is so cool. It's like some kind of writer's dream world. . . .
Isn't it?

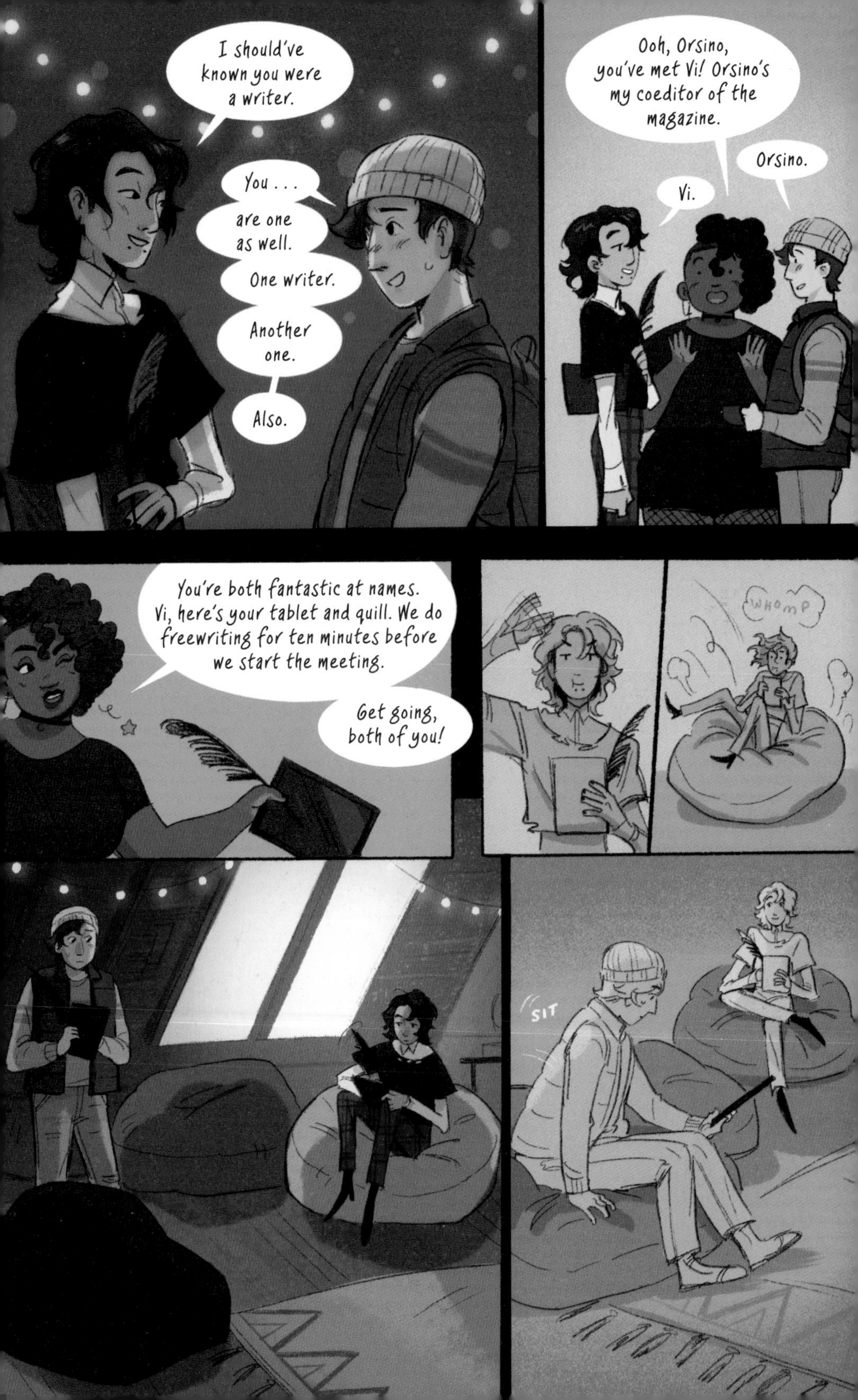
I should've known you were a writer.
You . . .
are one as well.
One writer.
Another one.
Also.
Ooh, Orsino, you've met Vi! Orsino's my coeditor of the magazine.
Vi.
Orsino.
You're both fantastic at names. Vi, here's your tablet and quill. We do freewriting for ten minutes before we start the meeting.
Get going, both of you!
WHOMP
SIT

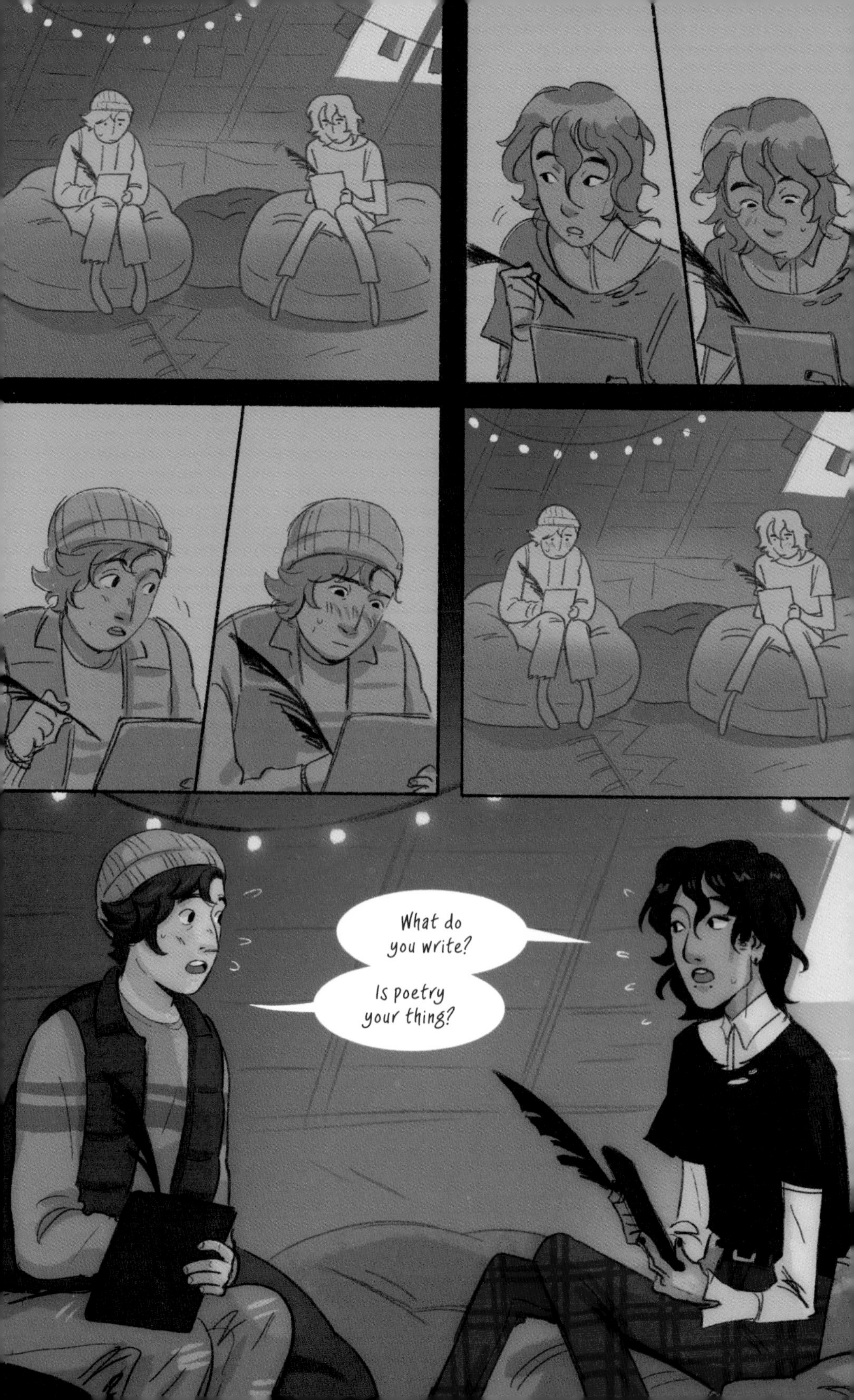
What do you write?
Is poetry your thing?

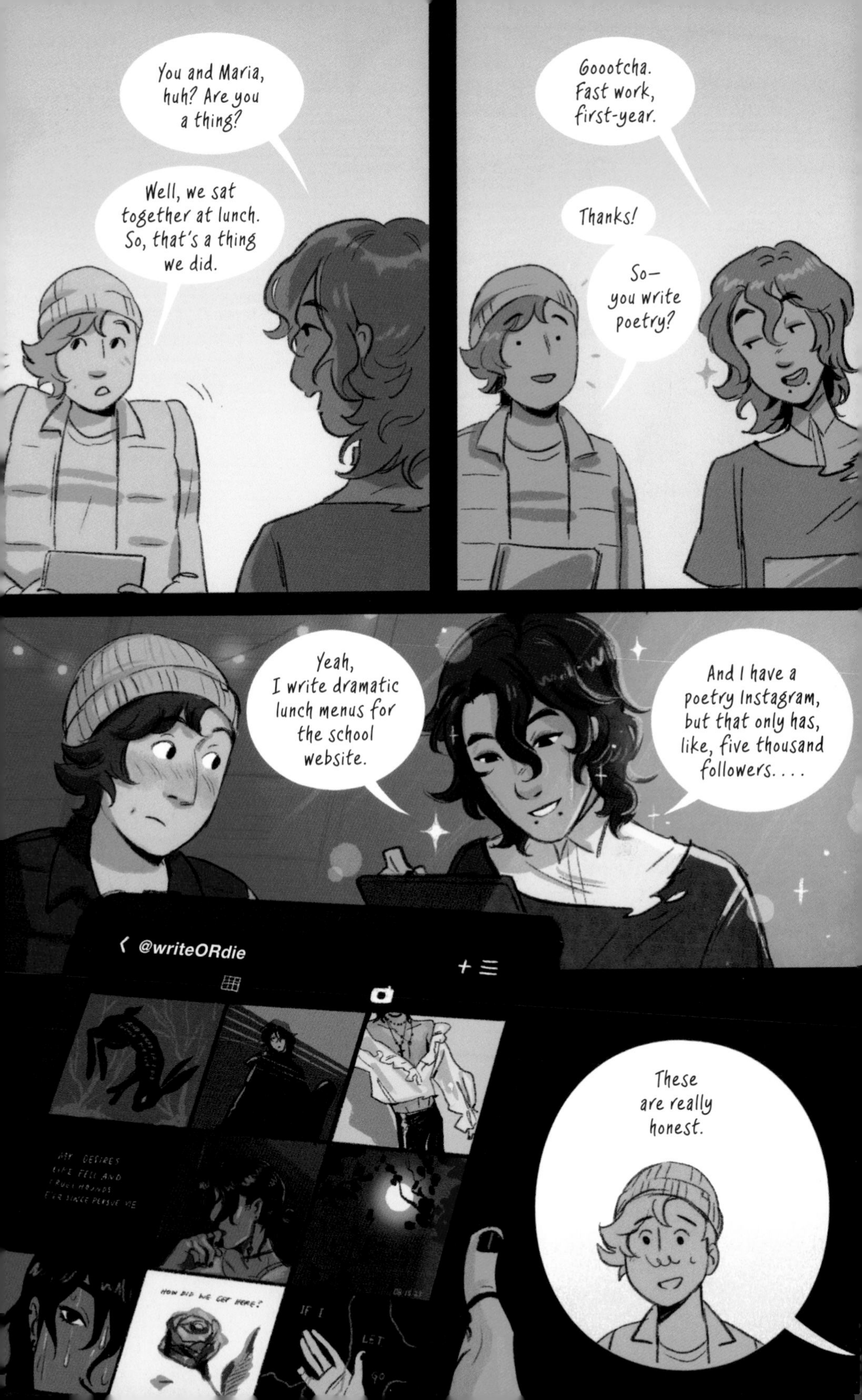

You and Maria, huh? Are you a thing?
Well, we sat together at lunch. So, that's a thing we did.
Gooootcha. Fast work, first-year.
Thanks!
So— you write poetry?
Yeah, I write dramatic lunch menus for the school website.
And I have a poetry Instagram, but that only has, like, five thousand followers. . . .
@writeORdie
HOW DID WE GET HERE?
IF I LET GO
These are really honest.

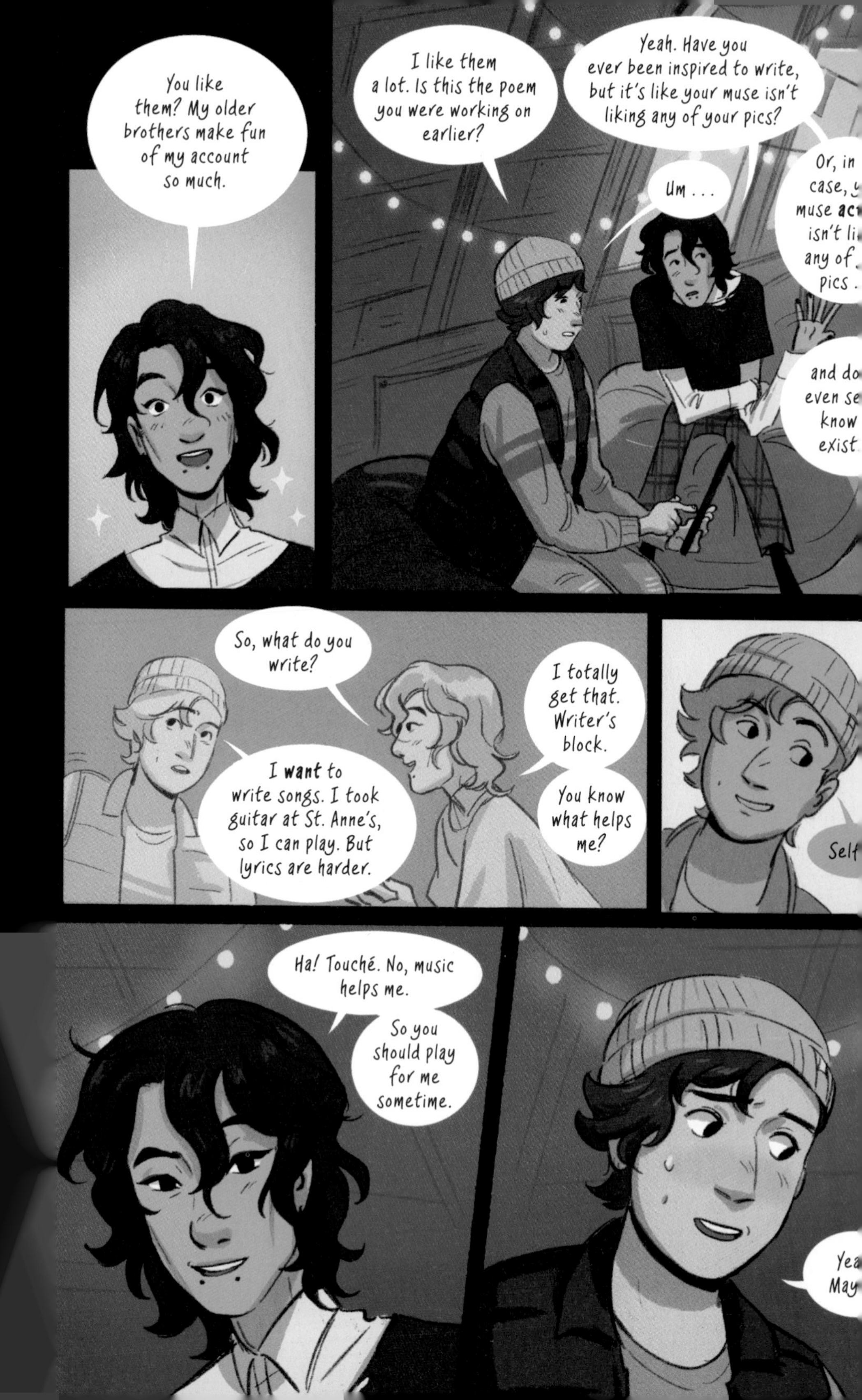
You like them? My older brothers make fun of my account so much.
I like them a lot. Is this the poem you were working on earlier?
Yeah. Have you ever been inspired to write, but it's like your muse isn't liking any of your pics?
Um . . .
So, what do you write?
I **want** to write songs. I took guitar at St. Anne's, so I can play. But lyrics are harder.
I totally get that. Writer's block.
You know what helps me?
Ha! Touché. No, music helps me.
So you should play for me sometime.

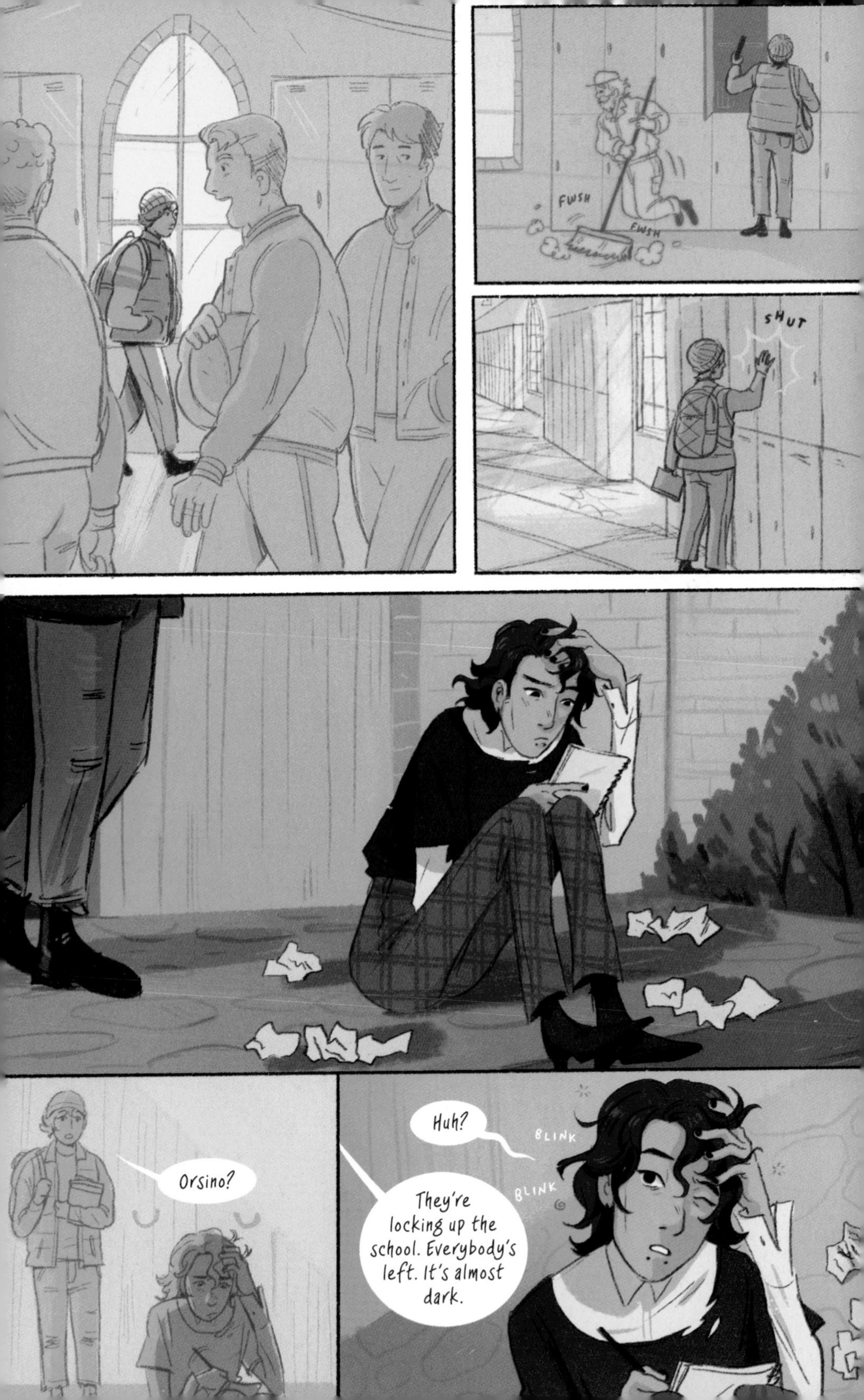
FWSH
FWSH
SHUT
Orsino?
Huh?
BLINK
BLINK
They're locking up the school. Everybody's left. It's almost dark.

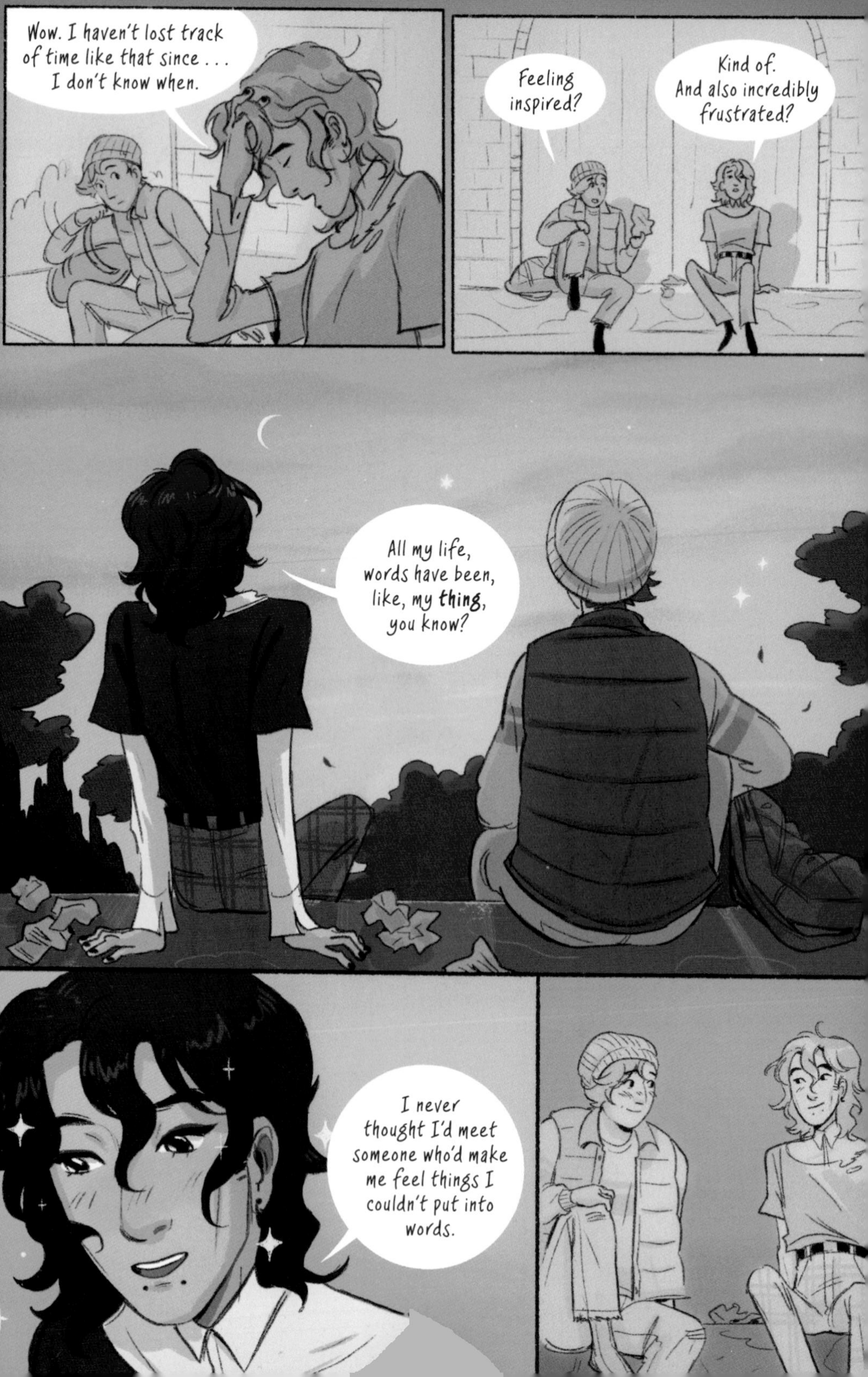
Wow. I haven't lost track of time like that since . . . I don't know when.
Feeling inspired?
Kind of. And also incredibly frustrated?
All my life, words have been, like, my **thing**, you know?
I never thought I'd meet someone who'd make me feel things I couldn't put into words.

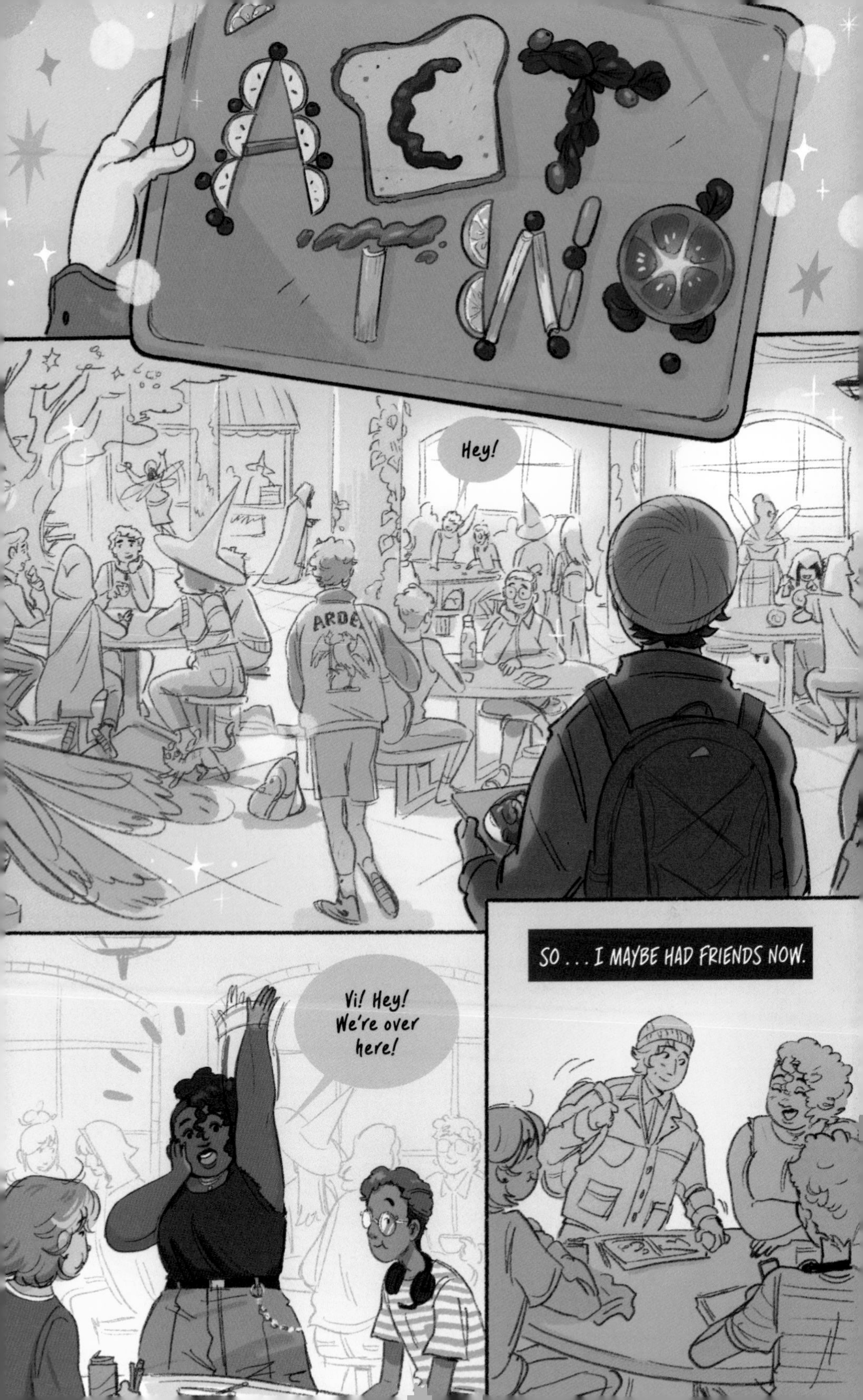
ACT TWO
Hey!
Vi! Hey! We're over here!
SO . . . I MAYBE HAD FRIENDS NOW.

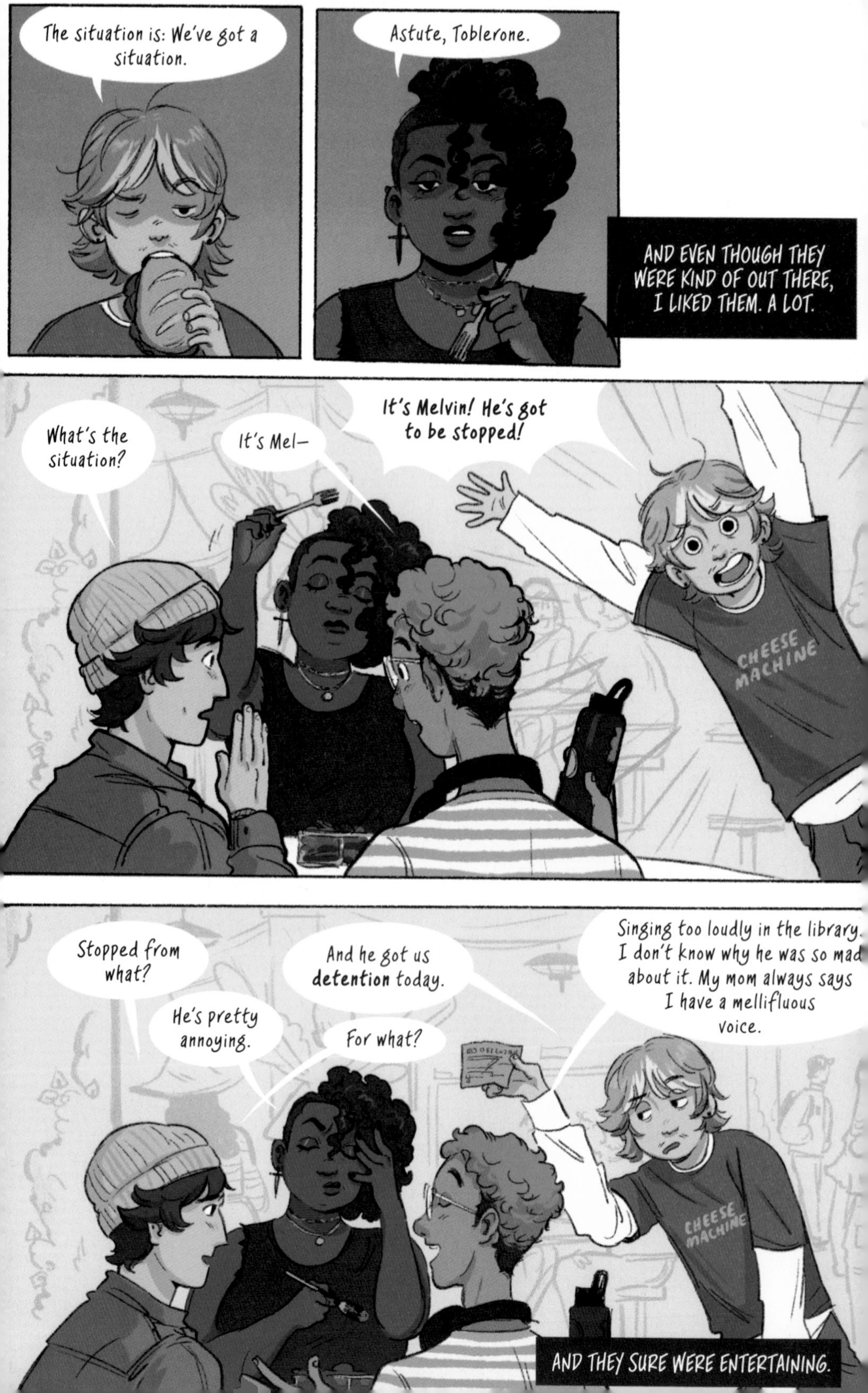
The situation is: We've got a situation.
Astute, Toblerone.
AND EVEN THOUGH THEY WERE KIND OF OUT THERE, I LIKED THEM. A LOT.
What's the situation?
It's Mel—
It's Melvin! He's got to be stopped!
CHEESE MACHINE
Stopped from what?
He's pretty annoying.
And he got us **detention** today.
For what?
Singing too loudly in the library. I don't know why he was so mad about it. My mom always says I have a mellifluous voice.
CHEESE MACHINE
AND THEY SURE WERE ENTERTAINING.

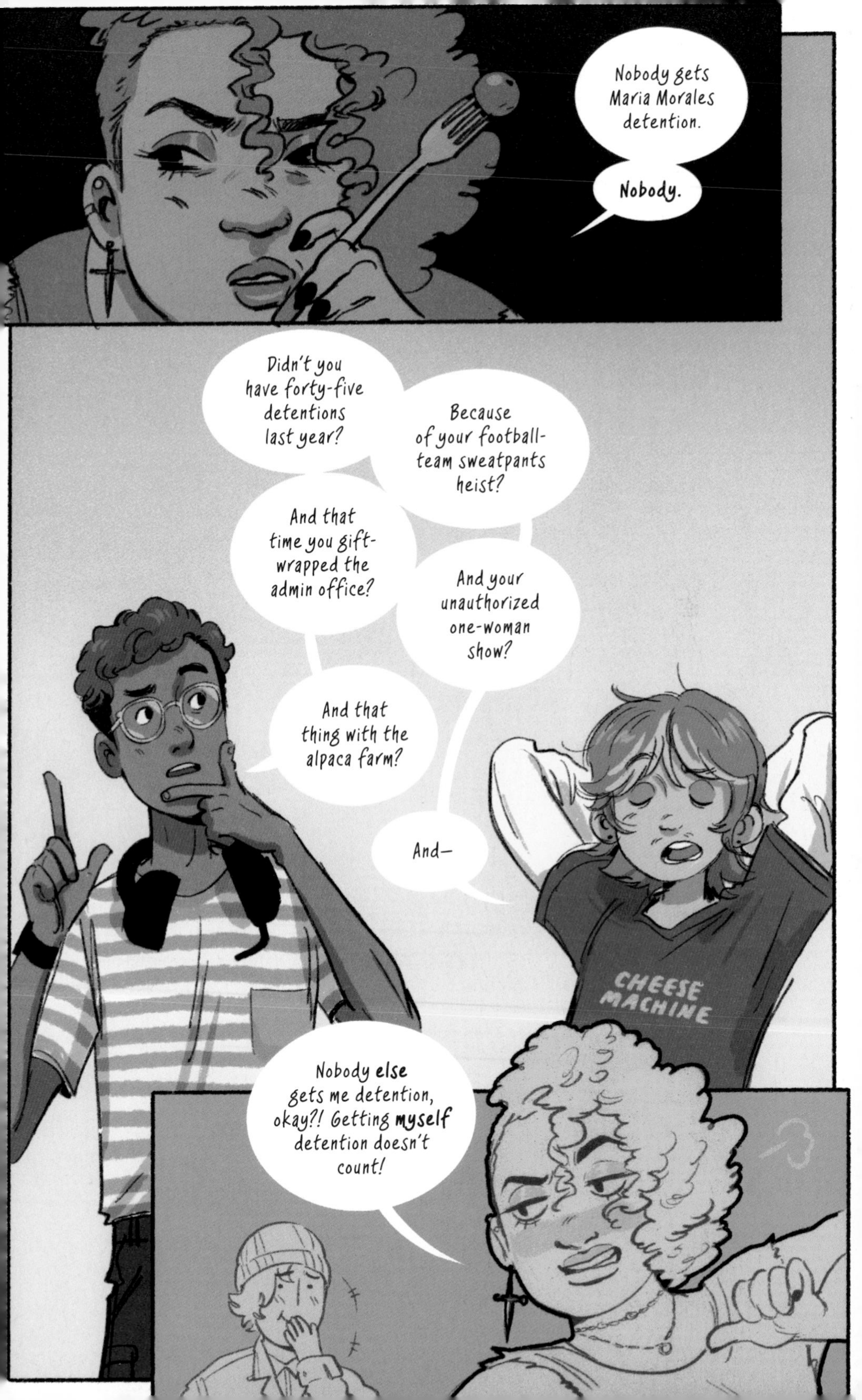
Nobody gets Maria Morales detention.
Nobody.
Didn't you have forty-five detentions last year?
Because of your football-team sweatpants heist?
And that time you gift-wrapped the admin office?
And your unauthorized one-woman show?
And that thing with the alpaca farm?
And—
CHEESE MACHINE
Nobody **else** gets me detention, okay?! Getting **myself** detention doesn't count!

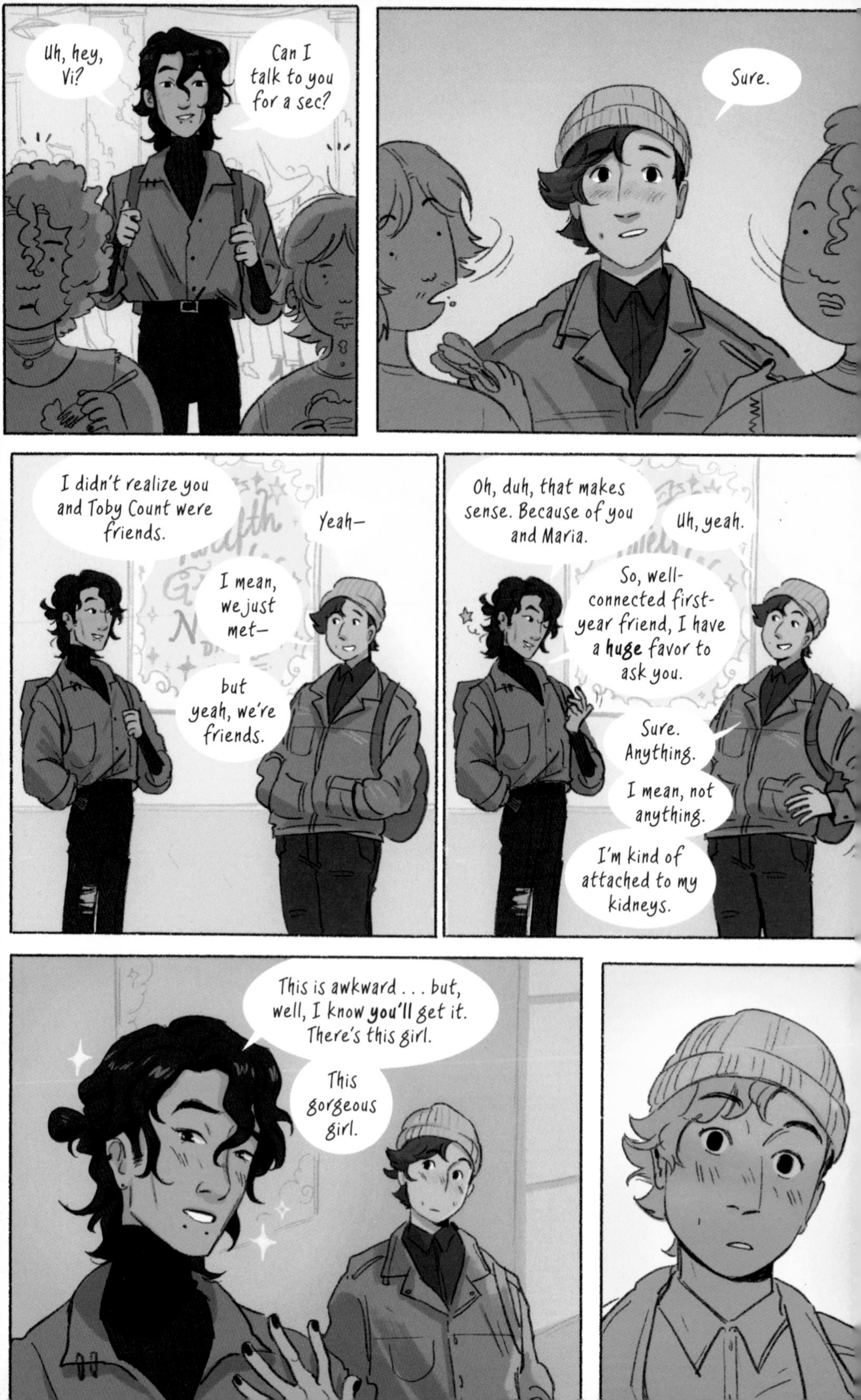
Uh, hey, Vi?
Can I talk to you for a sec?
Sure.
I didn't realize you and Toby Count were friends.
Yeah—
I mean, we just met—
but yeah, we're friends.
Oh, duh, that makes sense. Because of you and Maria.
Uh, yeah.
So, well-connected first-year friend, I have a **huge** favor to ask you.
Sure. Anything.
I mean, not anything.
I'm kind of attached to my kidneys.
This is awkward . . . but, well, I know **you'll** get it. There's this girl.
This gorgeous girl.

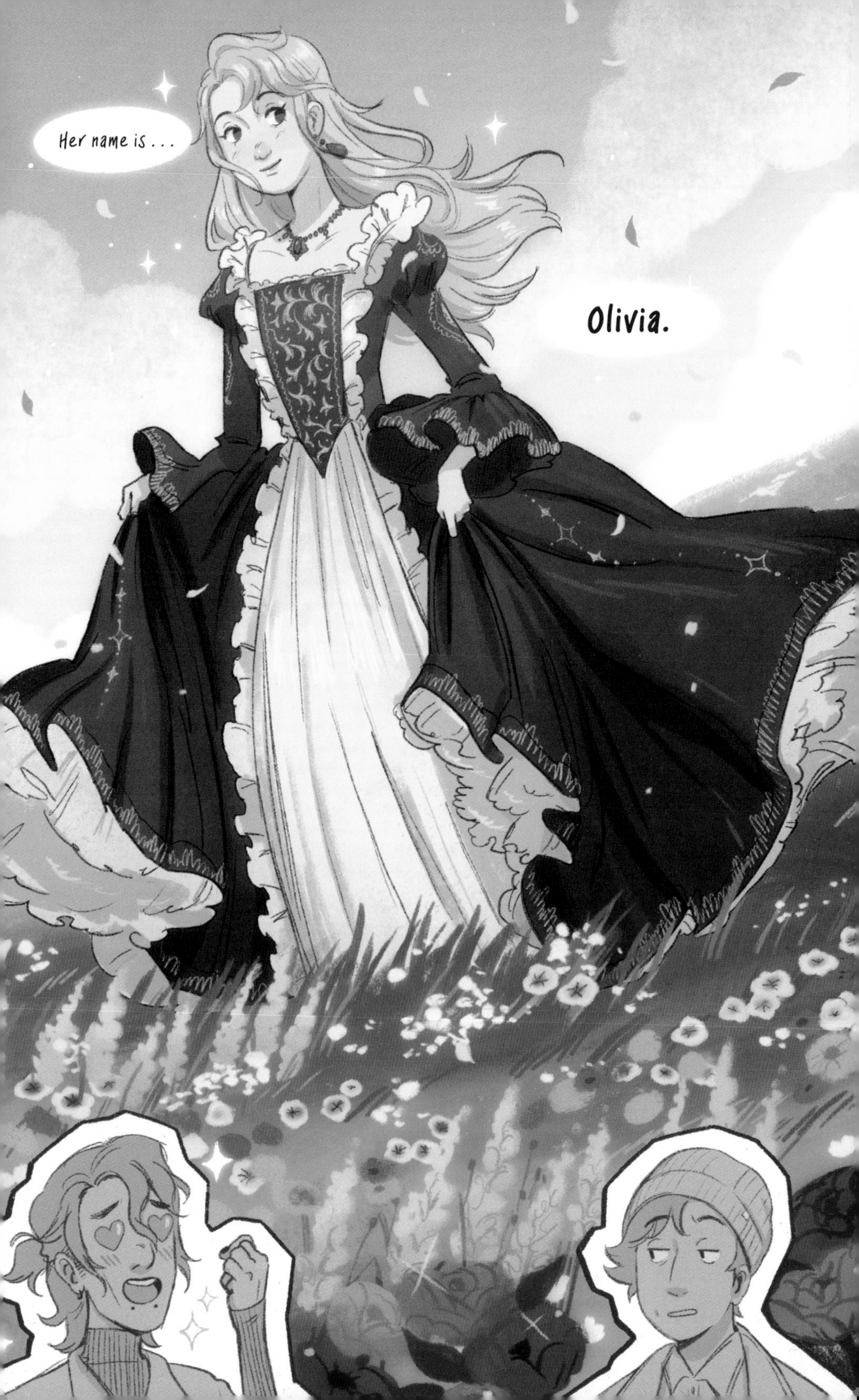
Her name is . . .
Olivia.

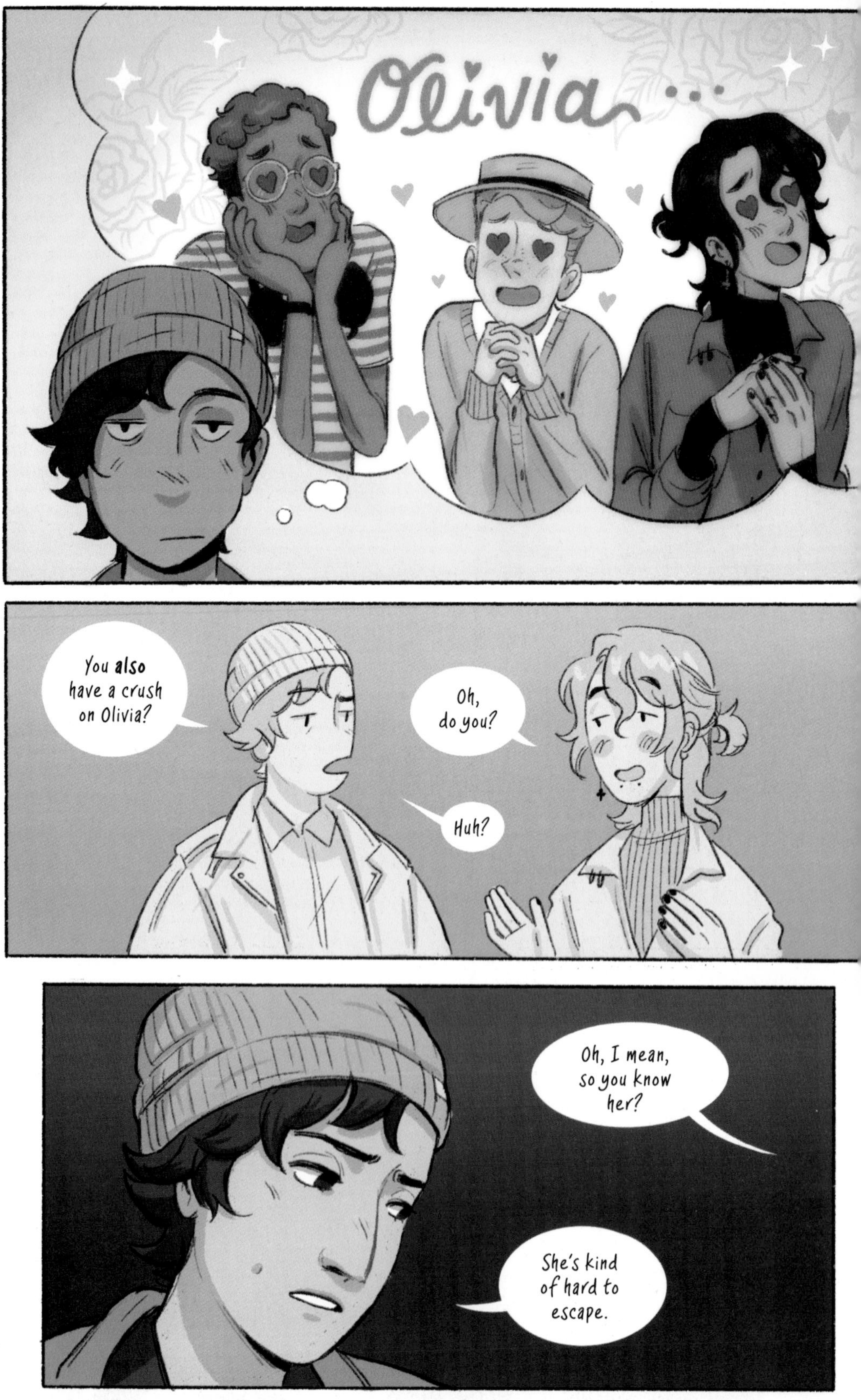
Olivia...
You **also** have a crush on Olivia?
Oh, do you?
Huh?
Oh, I mean, so you know her?
She's kind of hard to escape.

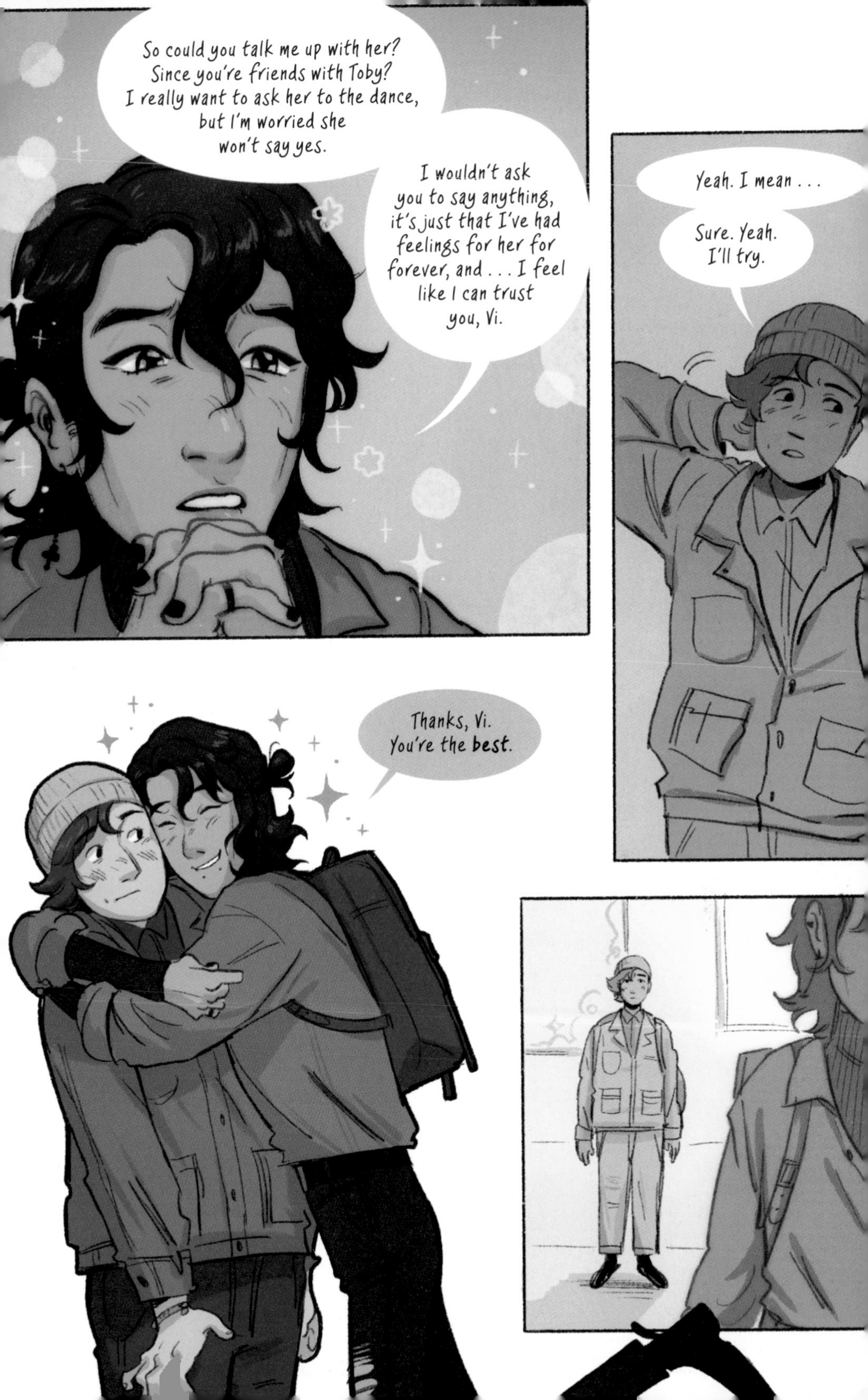
So could you talk me up with her? Since you're friends with Toby? I really want to ask her to the dance, but I'm worried she won't say yes.
I wouldn't ask you to say anything, it's just that I've had feelings for her for forever, and . . . I feel like I can trust you, Vi.
Yeah. I mean . . .
Sure. Yeah. I'll try.
Thanks, Vi. You're the **best**.

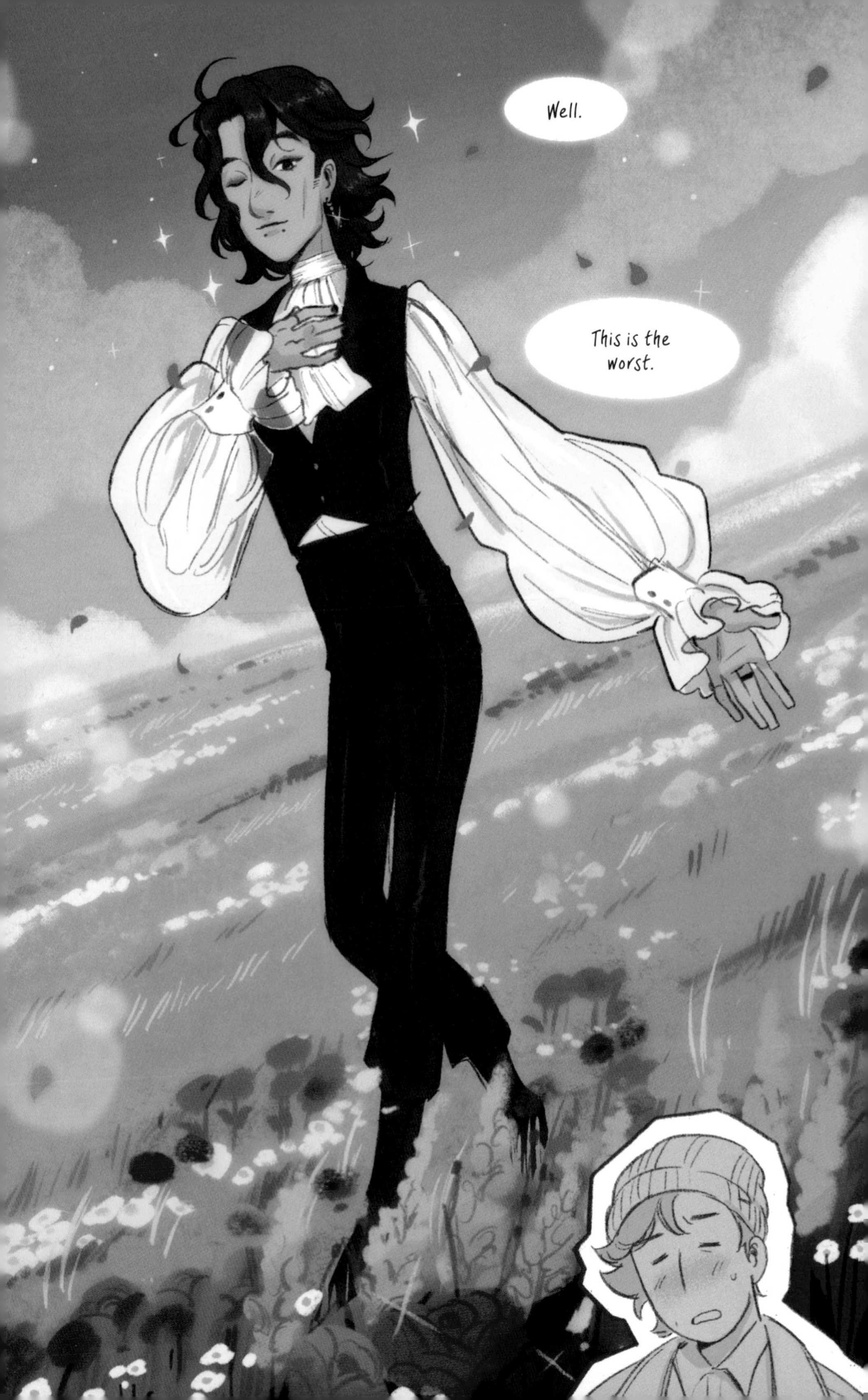
Well.
This is the worst.

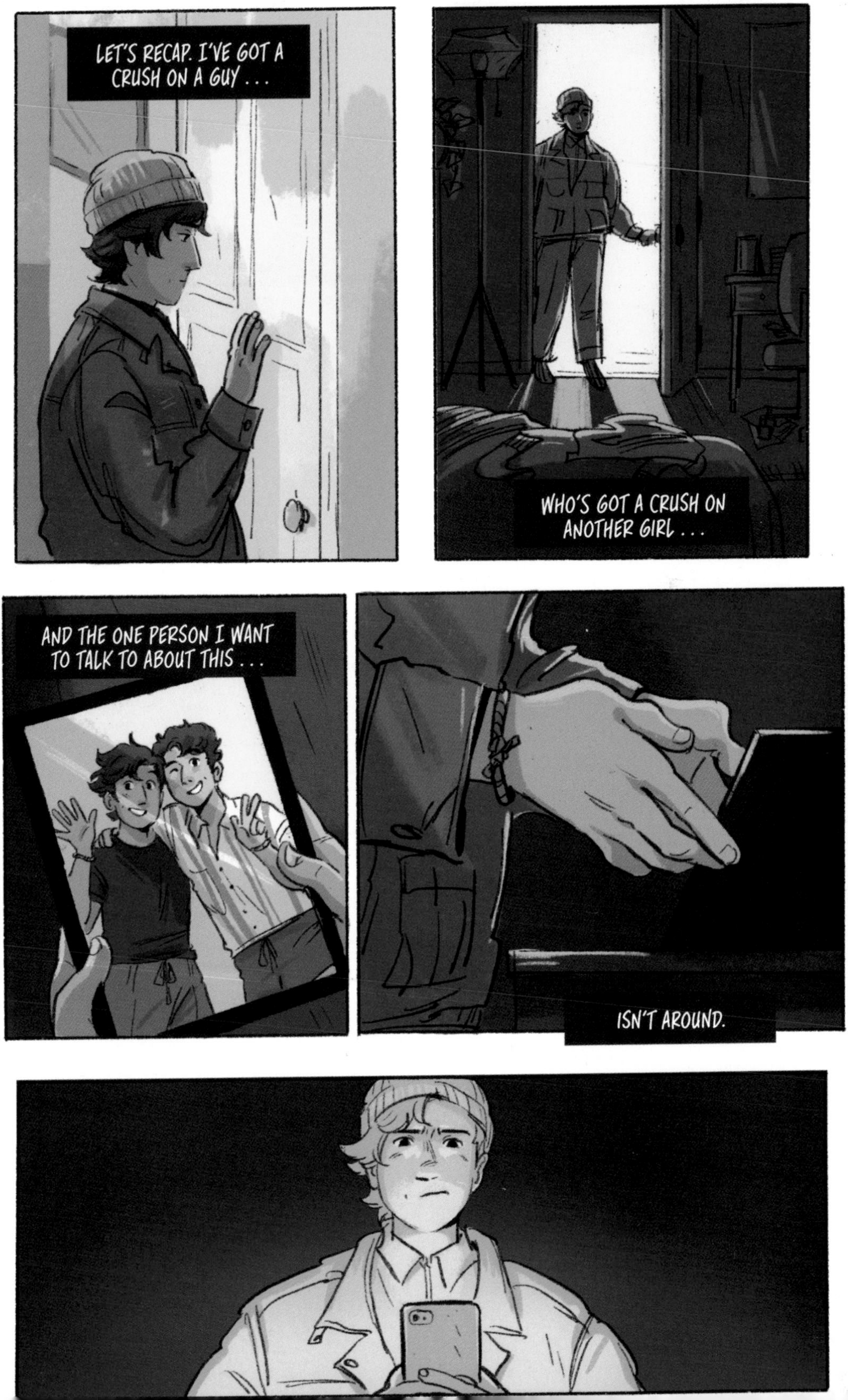
LET'S RECAP. I'VE GOT A CRUSH ON A GUY . . .
WHO'S GOT A CRUSH ON ANOTHER GIRL . . .
AND THE ONE PERSON I WANT TO TALK TO ABOUT THIS . . .
ISN'T AROUND.

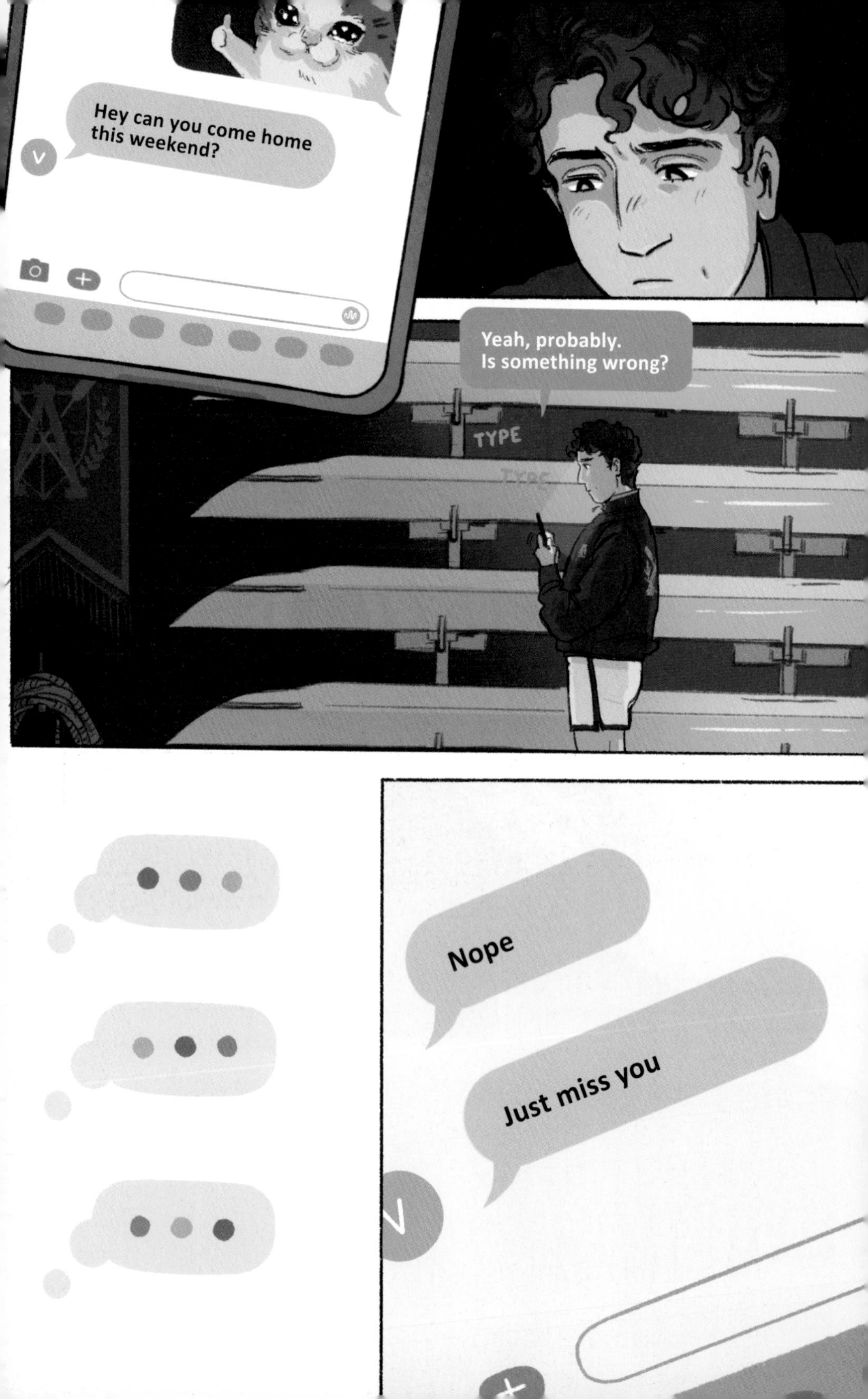
Hey can you come home this weekend?
Yeah, probably.
Is something wrong?
TYPE
Nope
Just miss you

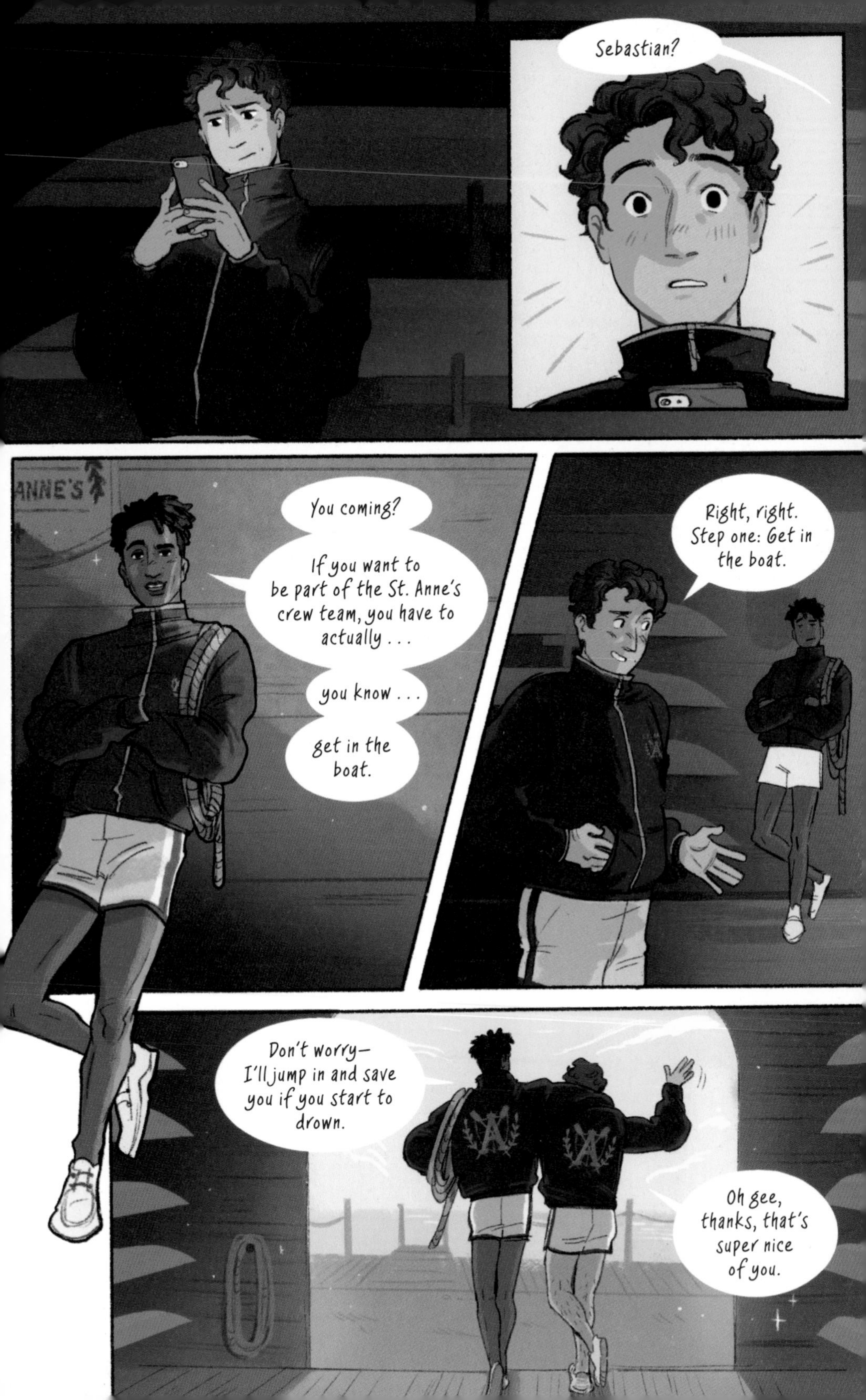
Sebastian?
You coming?
If you want to be part of the St. Anne's crew team, you have to actually . . .
you know . . .
get in the boat.
Right, right. Step one: Get in the boat.
Don't worry—I'll jump in and save you if you start to drown.
Oh gee, thanks, that's super nice of you.

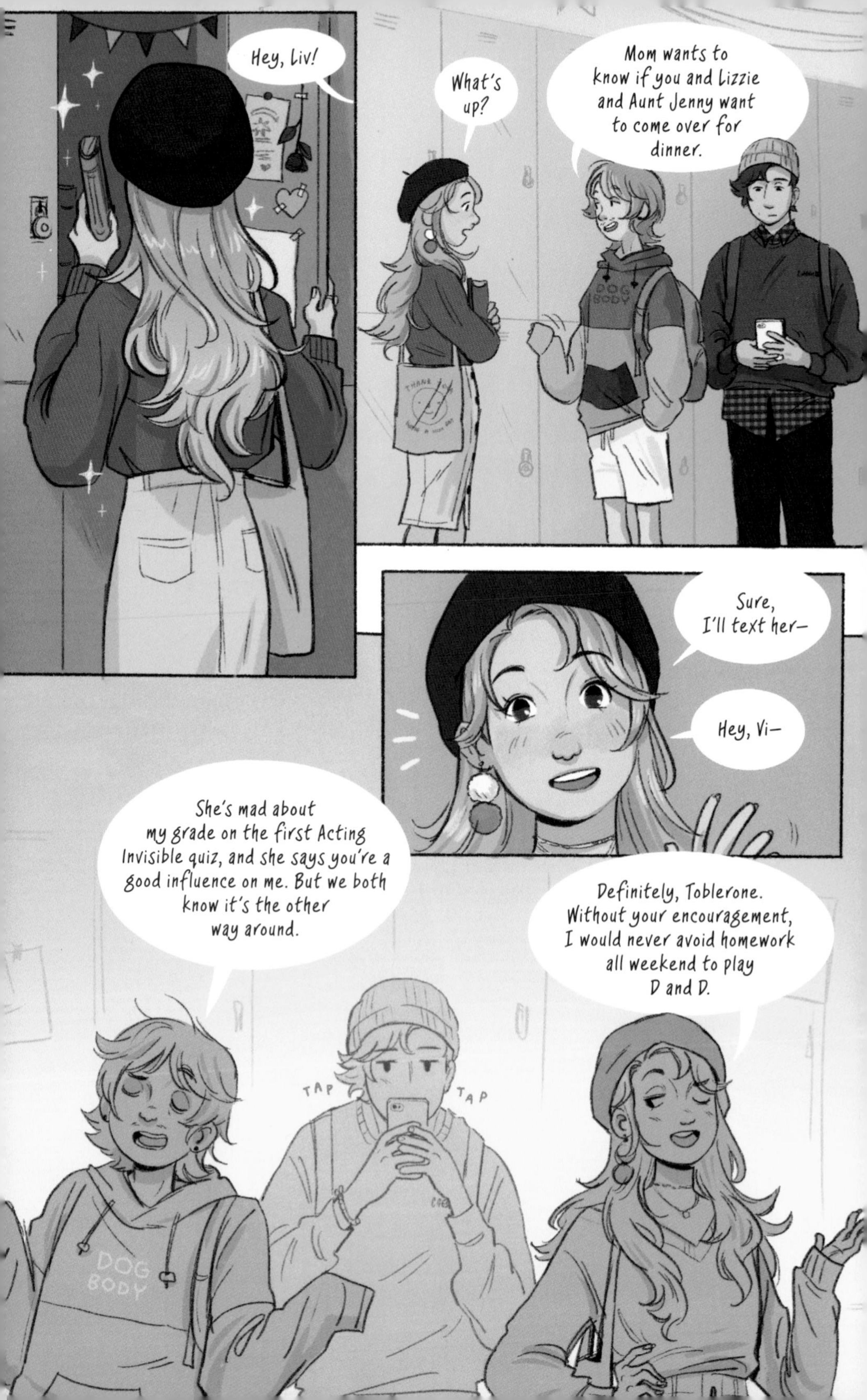
Hey, Liv!
What's up?
Mom wants to know if you and Lizzie and Aunt Jenny want to come over for dinner.
Sure, I'll text her—
Hey, Vi—
She's mad about my grade on the first Acting Invisible quiz, and she says you're a good influence on me. But we both know it's the other way around.
Definitely, Toblerone. Without your encouragement, I would never avoid homework all weekend to play D and D.
TAP
TAP
DOG BODY

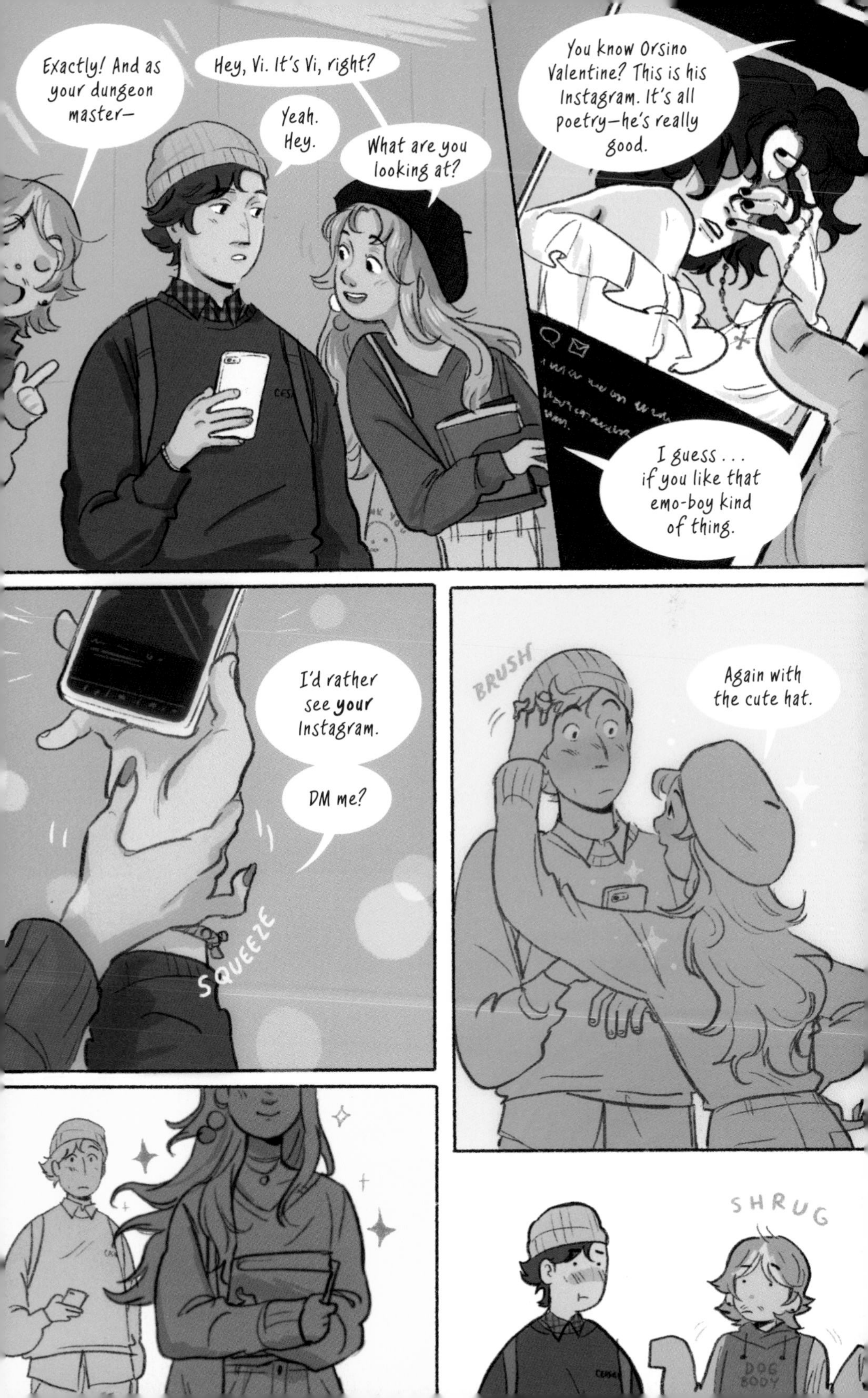

Exactly! And as your dungeon master—
Hey, Vi. It's Vi, right?
Yeah. Hey.
What are you looking at?
You know Orsino Valentine? This is his Instagram. It's all poetry—he's really good.
I guess . . . if you like that emo-boy kind of thing.
I'd rather see **your** Instagram.
DM me?
SQUEEZE
BRUSH
Again with the cute hat.
SHRUG
DOG BODY

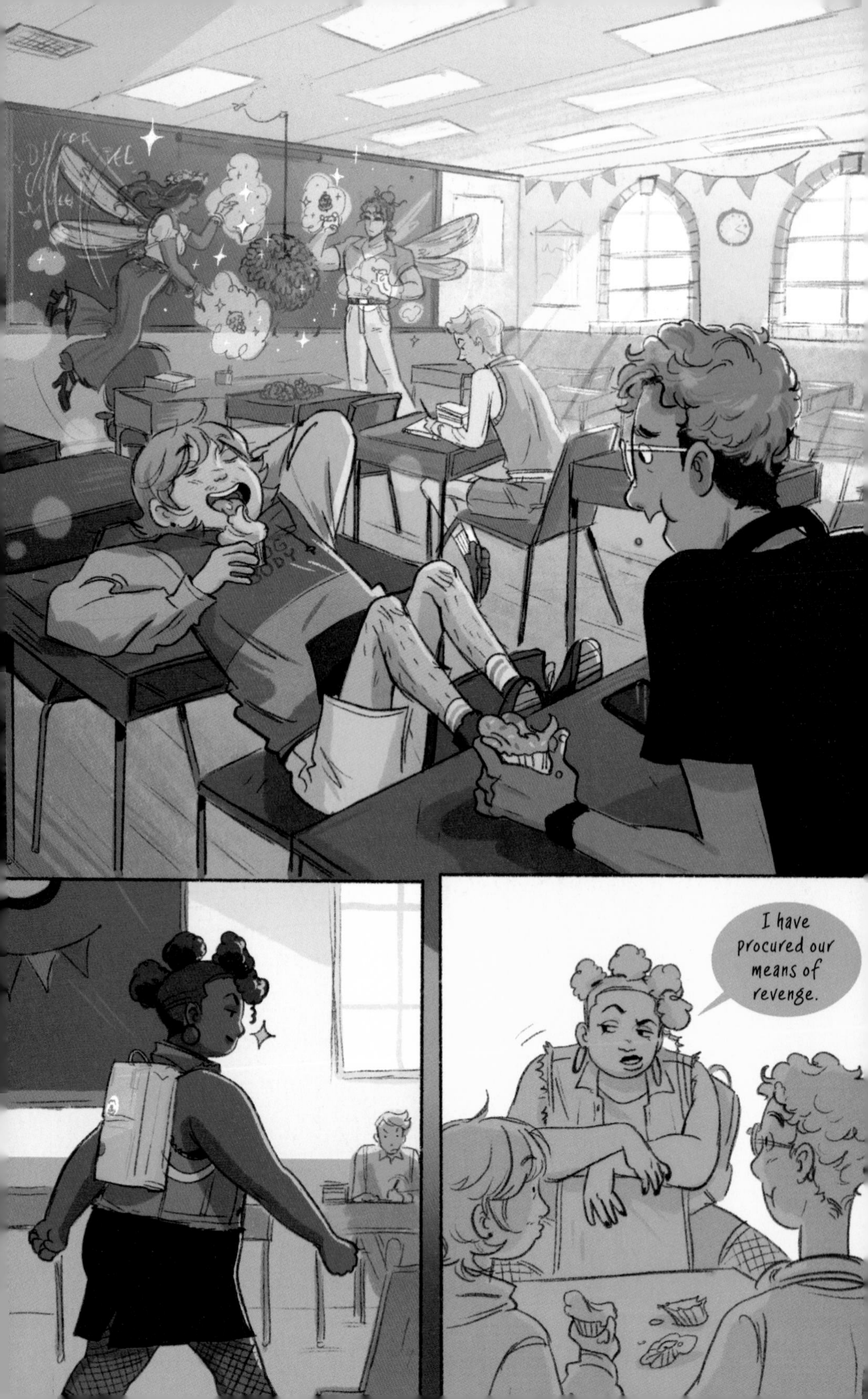
I have procured our means of revenge.

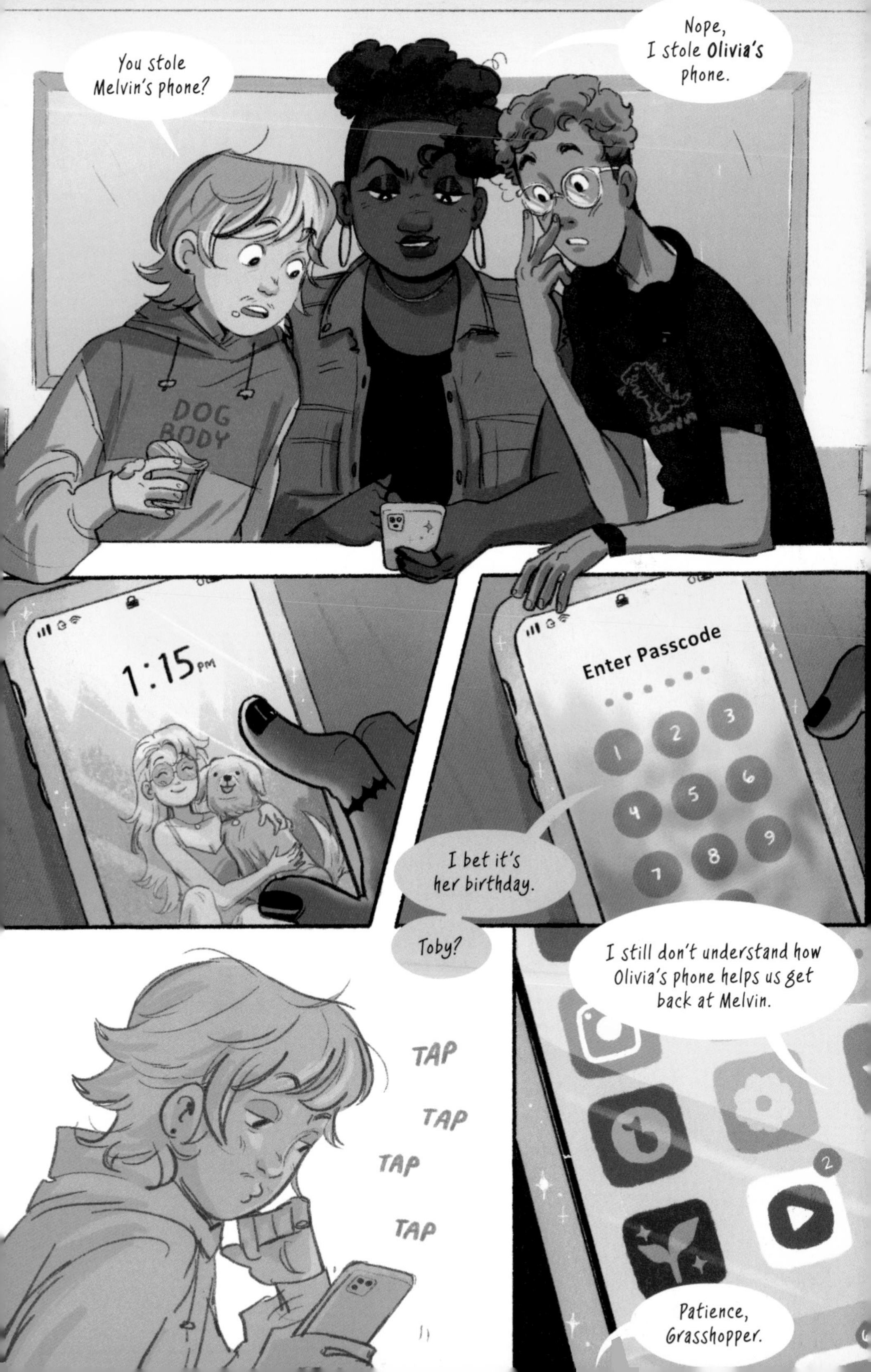
You stole Melvin's phone?
Nope, I stole Olivia's phone.
DOG BODY
1:15 PM
Enter Passcode
1 2 3 4 5 6 7 8 9
I bet it's her birthday.
Toby?
I still don't understand how Olivia's phone helps us get back at Melvin.
TAP
TAP
TAP
TAP
2
Patience, Grasshopper.

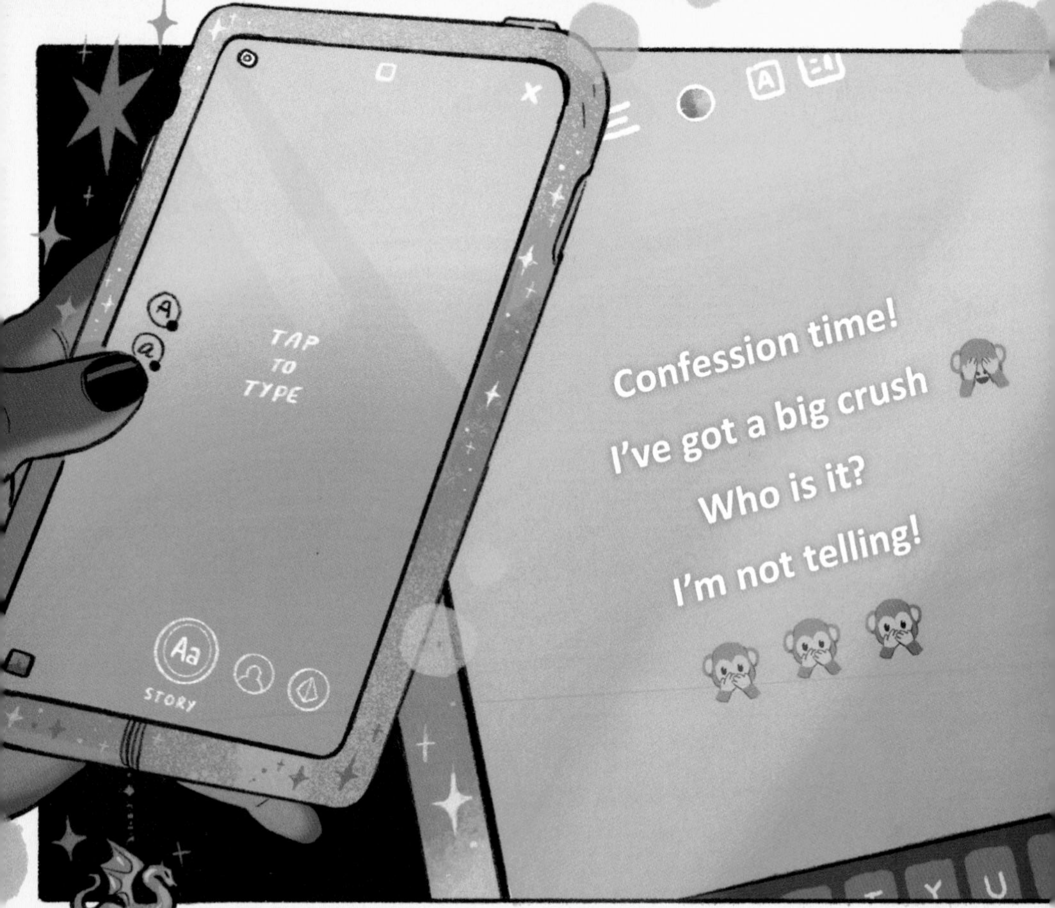
TAP TO TYPE
Aa
STORY
Confession time!
I've got a big crush
Who is it?
I'm not telling!

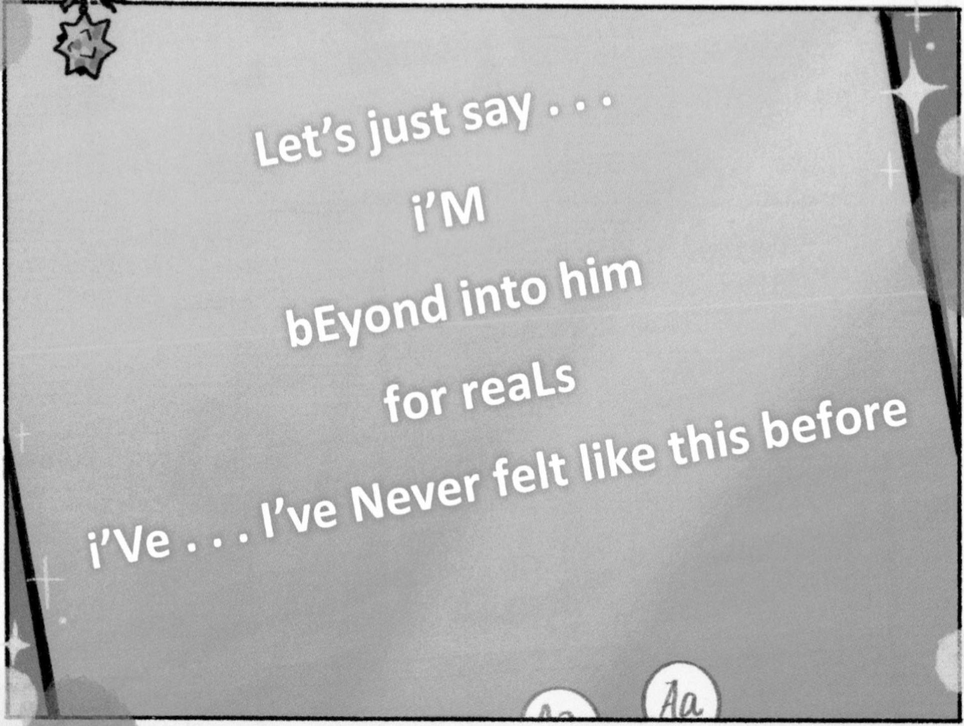
Let's just say . . .
i'M
bEyond into him
for reaLs
i'Ve . . . I've Never felt like this before
Aa

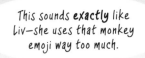

This sounds **exactly** like Liv—she uses that monkey emoji way too much.

Shh, I'm thinking.

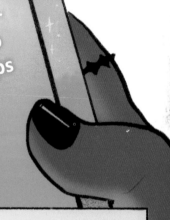

You know who you are ;))) You're my 🖼️ to true love. If you feel the same way, ask me to the Twelfth Grade Night dance—in front of everybody at lunch next week! Prove to me you have what it takes 😍

Also please wear yellow knee-high socks (my fav color!!) so I can see your hotttt kneecaps 🔥🔥🔥

What's up with the socks?

Liv hates yellow.

And she's grossed out by kneecaps.

It's a whole thing.

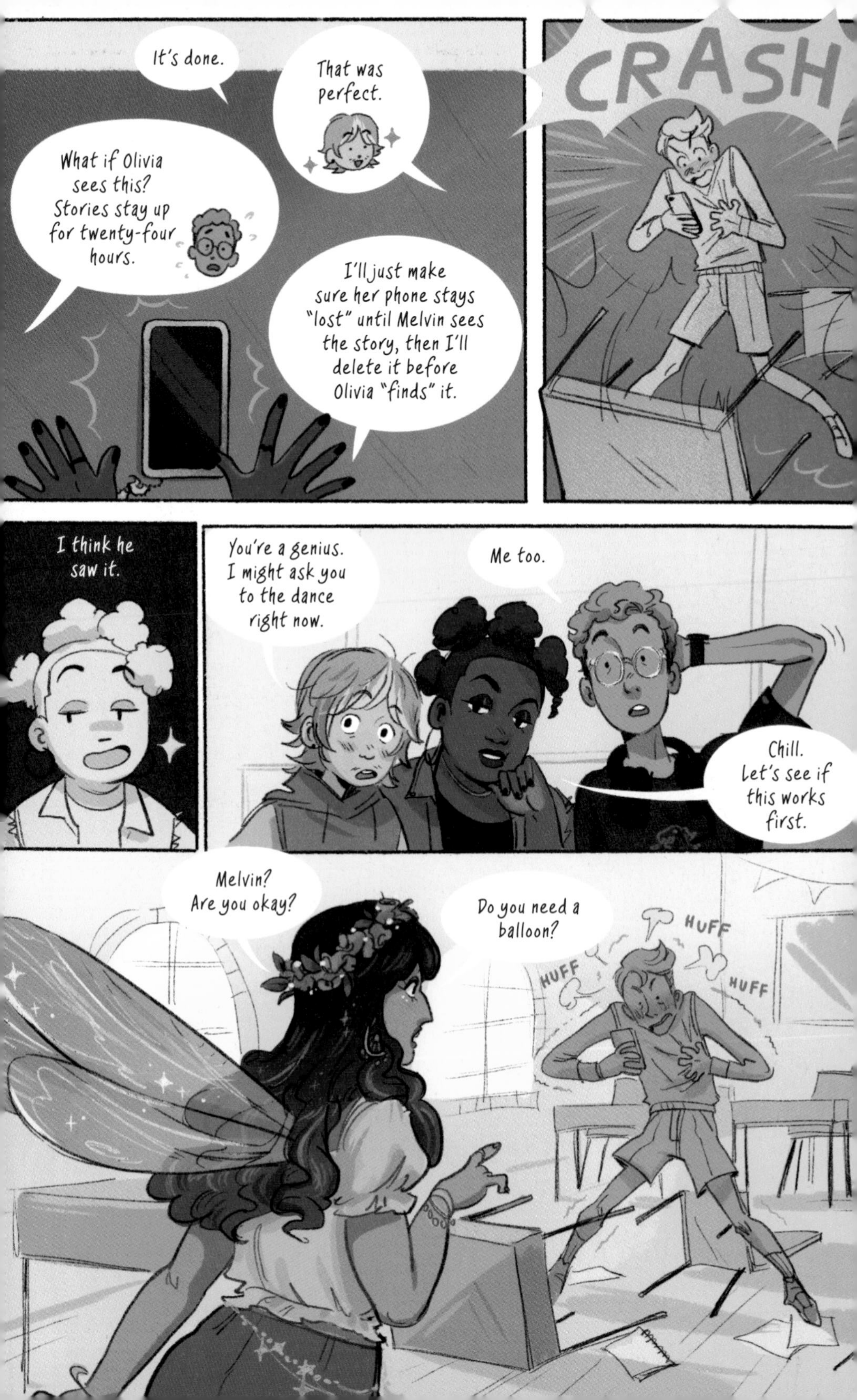
It's done.
That was perfect.
What if Olivia sees this? Stories stay up for twenty-four hours.
I'll just make sure her phone stays "lost" until Melvin sees the story, then I'll delete it before Olivia "finds" it.
CRASH
I think he saw it.
You're a genius. I might ask you to the dance right now.
Me too.
Chill. Let's see if this works first.
Melvin? Are you okay?
Do you need a balloon?
HUFF
HUFF
HUFF

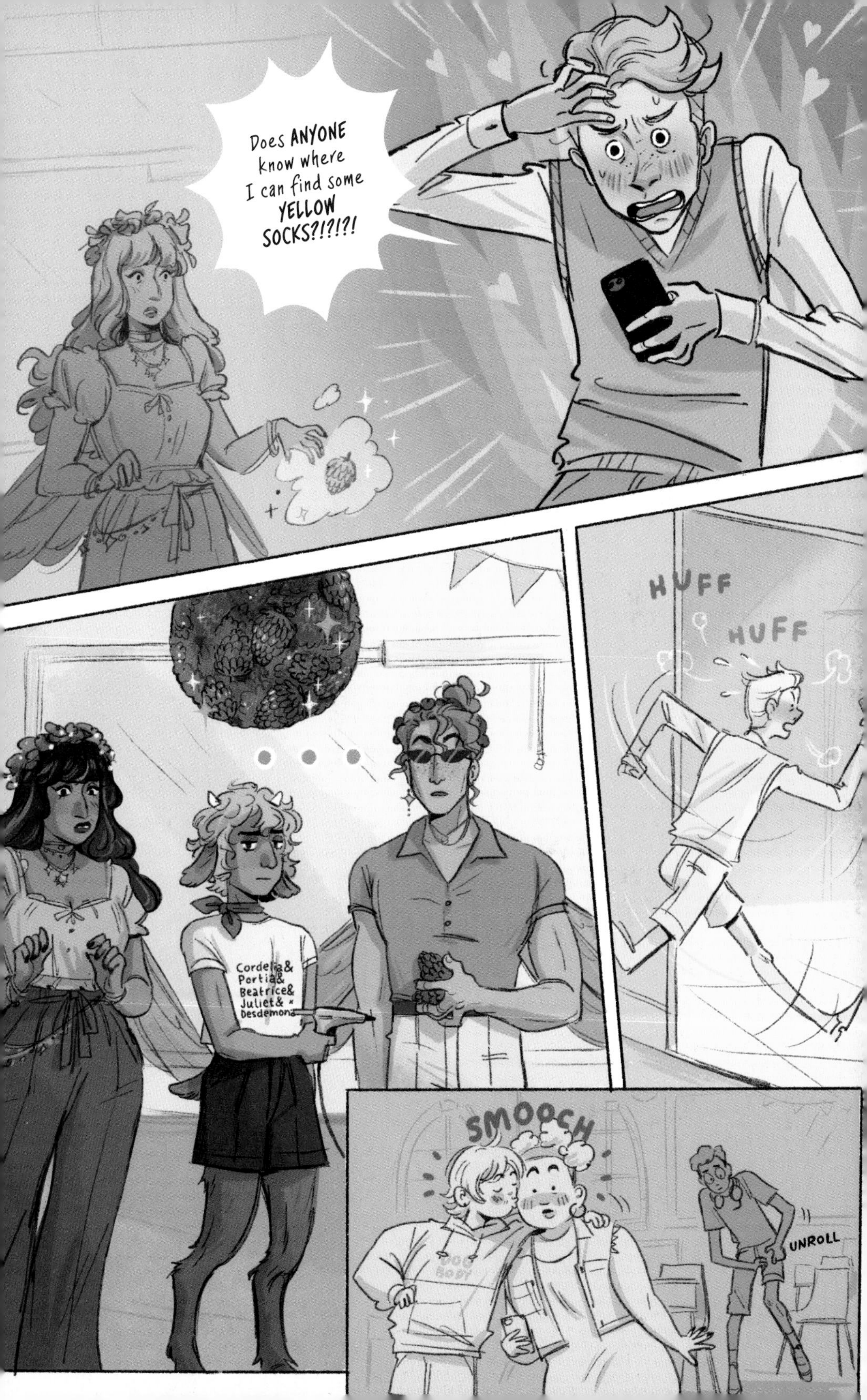
Does ANYONE know where I can find some YELLOW SOCKS?!?!?!
HUFF
HUFF
Cordelia& Portia& Beatrice& Juliet& Desdemona
SMOOCH
UNROLL

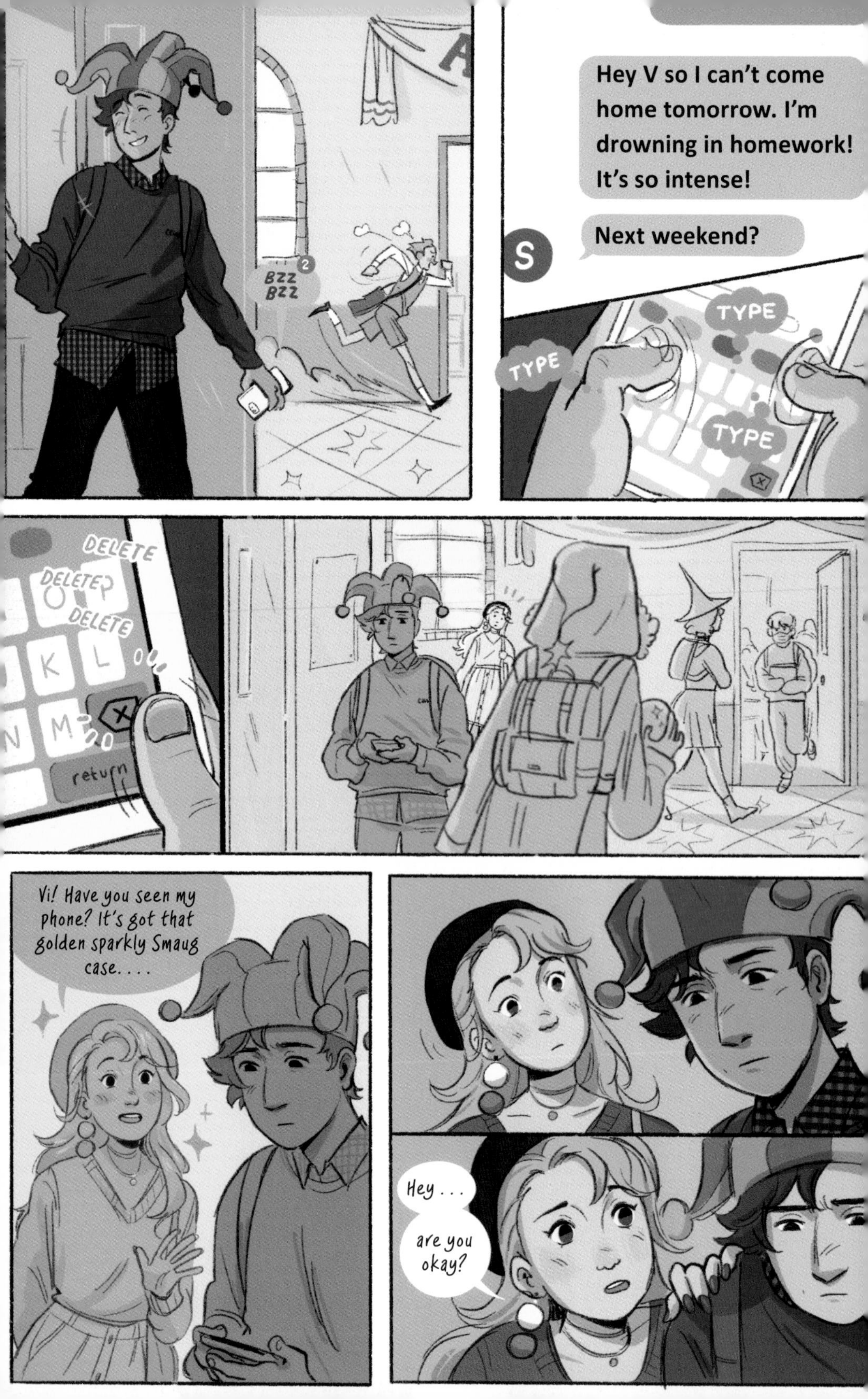
BZZ BZZ
2
Hey V so I can't come home tomorrow. I'm drowning in homework! It's so intense!
S
Next weekend?
TYPE
TYPE
TYPE
DELETE
DELETE?
DELETE
return
Vi! Have you seen my phone? It's got that golden sparkly Smaug case. . . .
Hey . . .
are you okay?

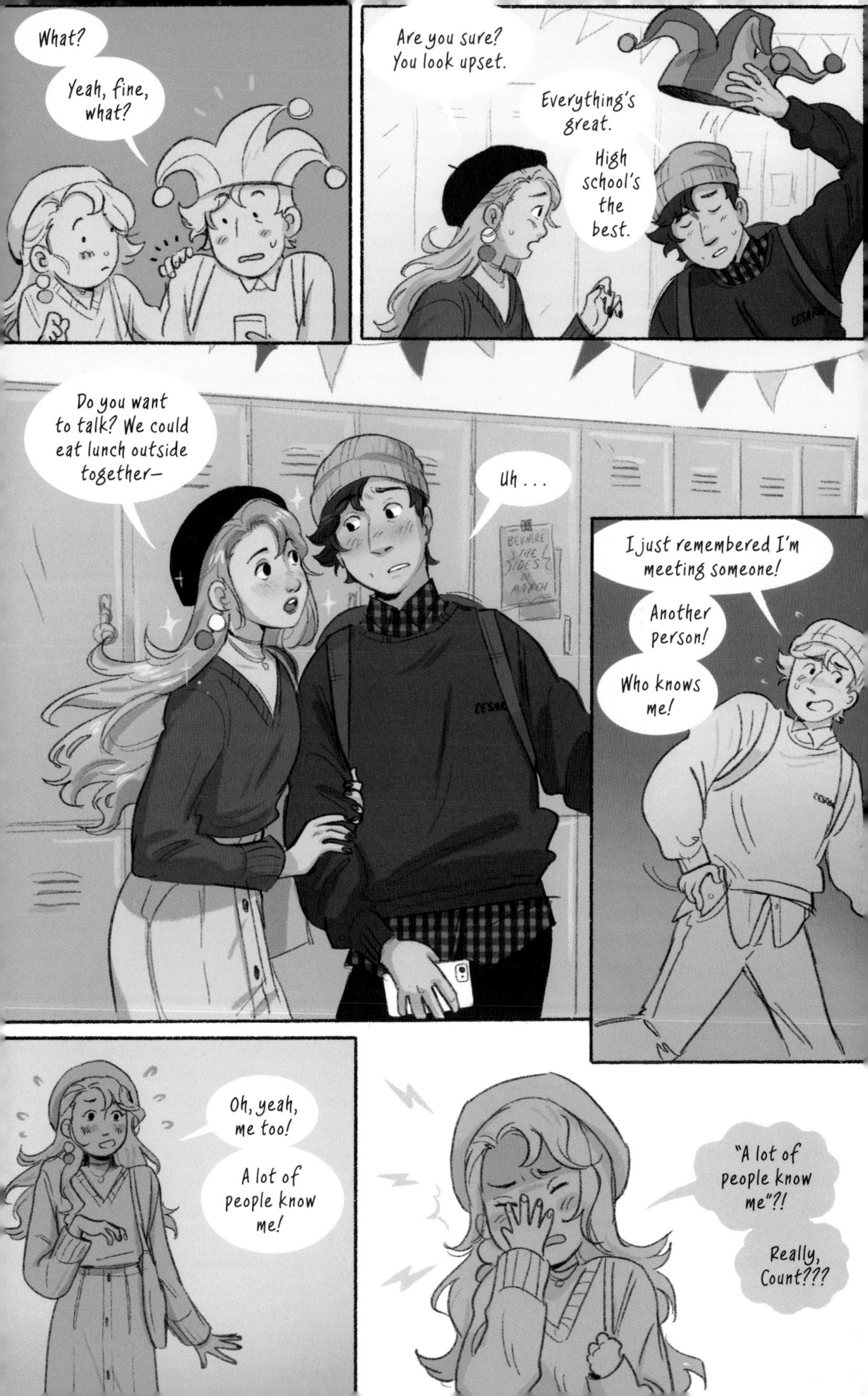
What?
Yeah, fine, what?
Are you sure? You look upset.
Everything's great.
High school's the best.
Do you want to talk? We could eat lunch outside together—
Uh . . .
BEWARE THE IDES OF MARCH
I just remembered I'm meeting someone!
Another person!
Who knows me!
Oh, yeah, me too!
A lot of people know me!
"A lot of people know me"?!
Really, Count???

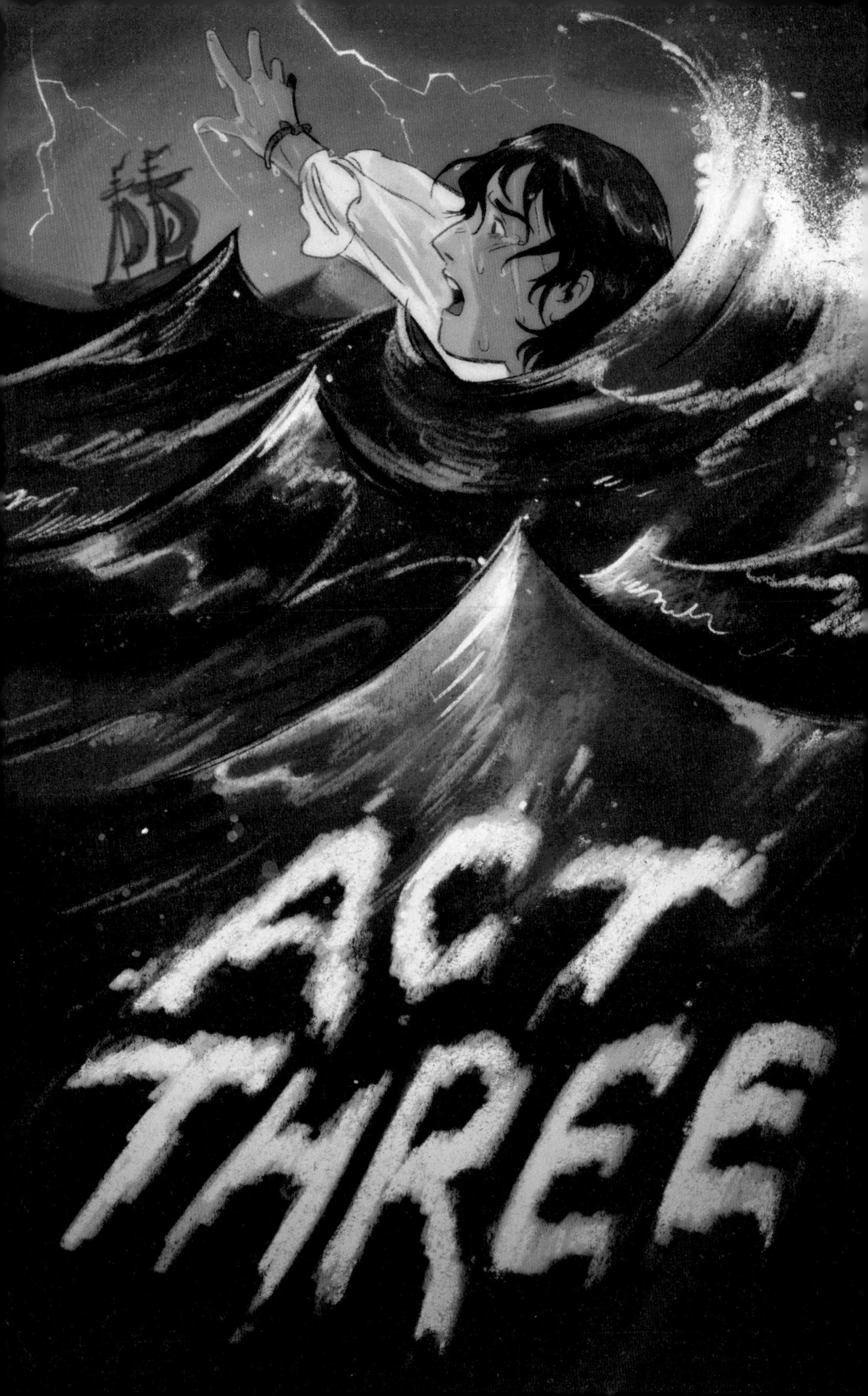
ACT
THREE

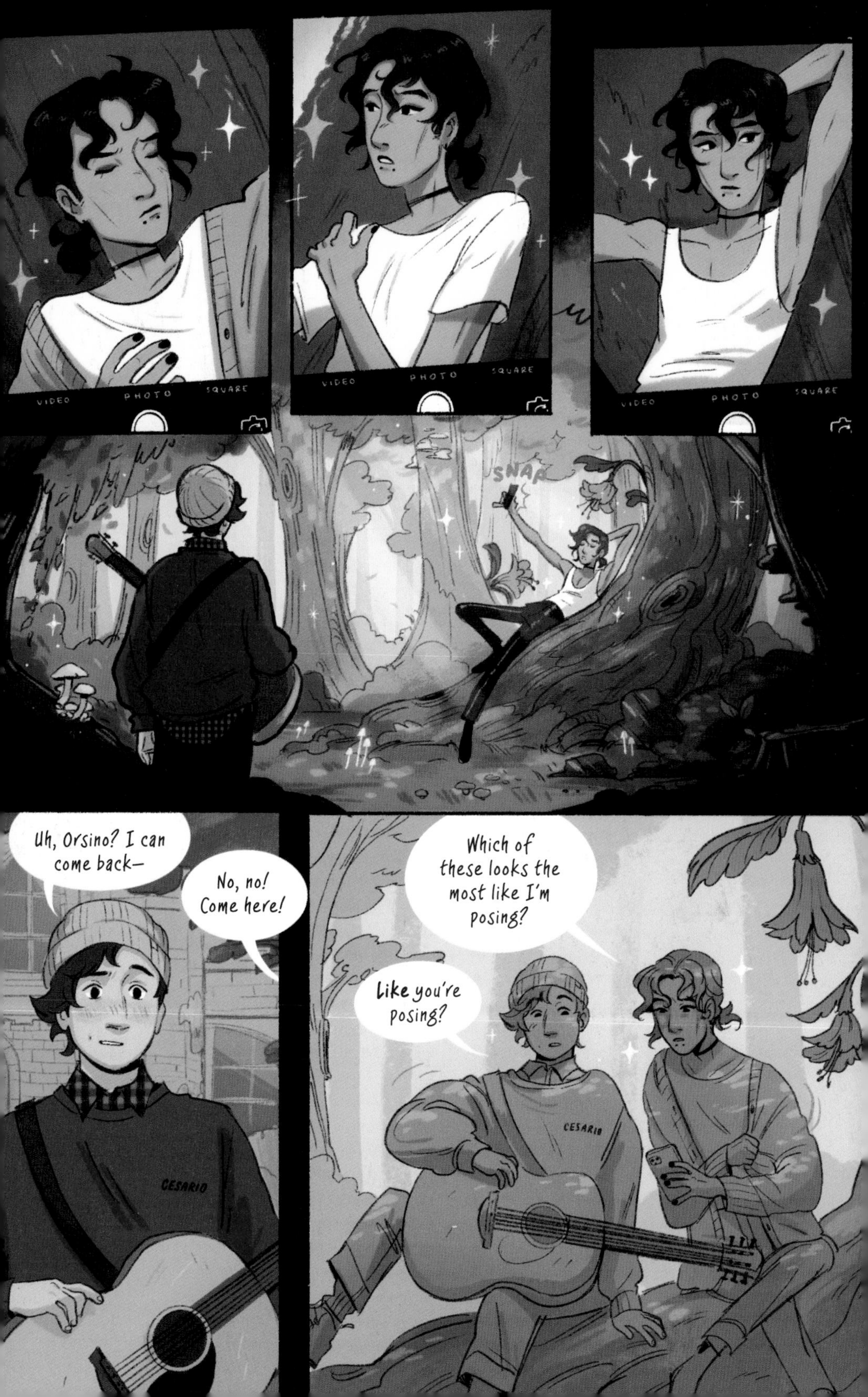
VIDEO PHOTO SQUARE
VIDEO PHOTO SQUARE
VIDEO PHOTO SQUARE
SNAP
Uh, Orsino? I can come back—
No, no! Come here!
CESARIO
Which of these looks the most like I'm posing?
Like you're posing?
CESARIO

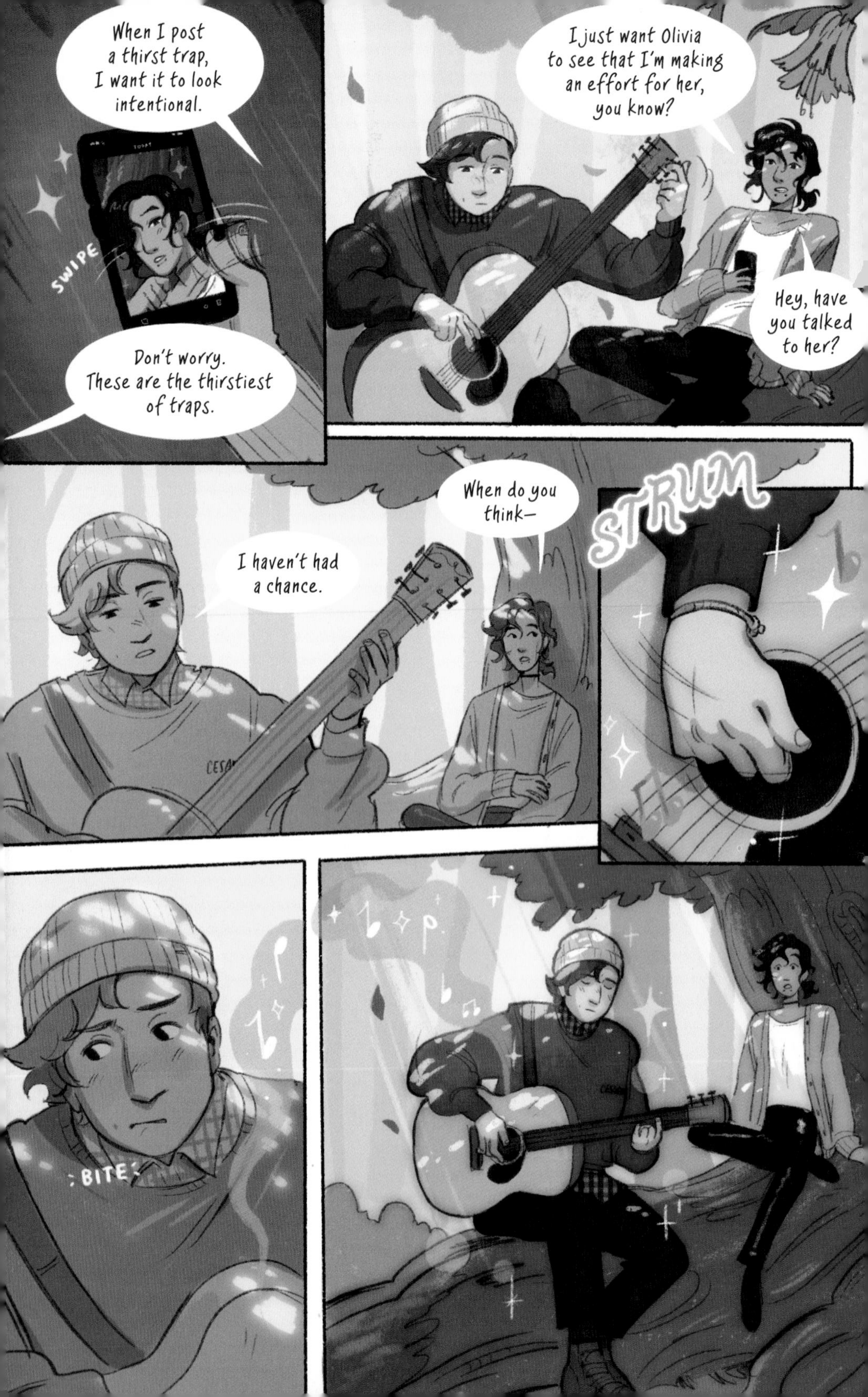
When I post a thirst trap, I want it to look intentional.
SWIPE
Don't worry. These are the thirstiest of traps.
I just want Olivia to see that I'm making an effort for her, you know?
Hey, have you talked to her?
I haven't had a chance.
When do you think—
STRUM
BITE

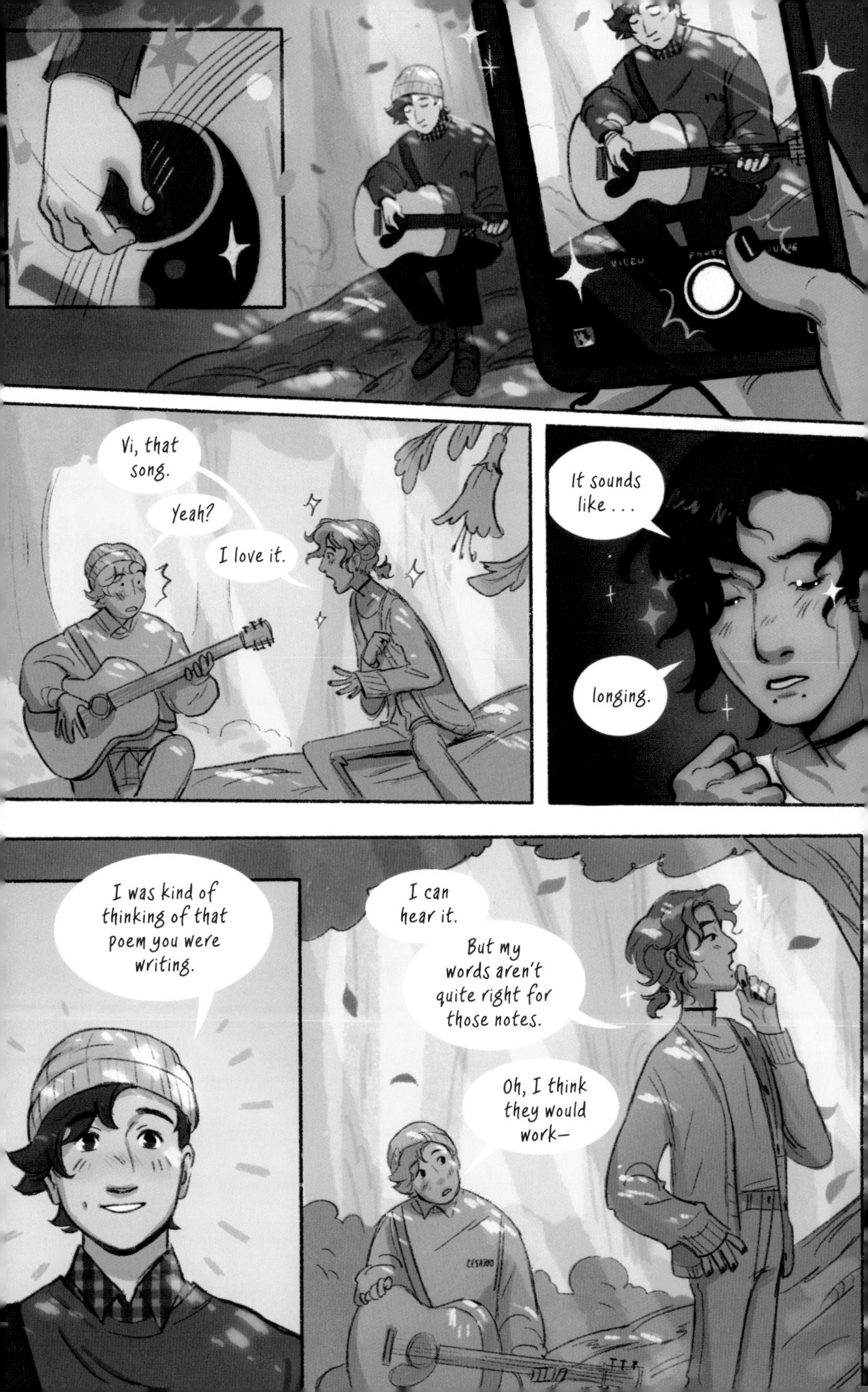

Vi, that song.
Yeah?
I love it.
It sounds like . . .
longing.
I was kind of thinking of that poem you were writing.
I can hear it.
But my words aren't quite right for those notes.
Oh, I think they would work—

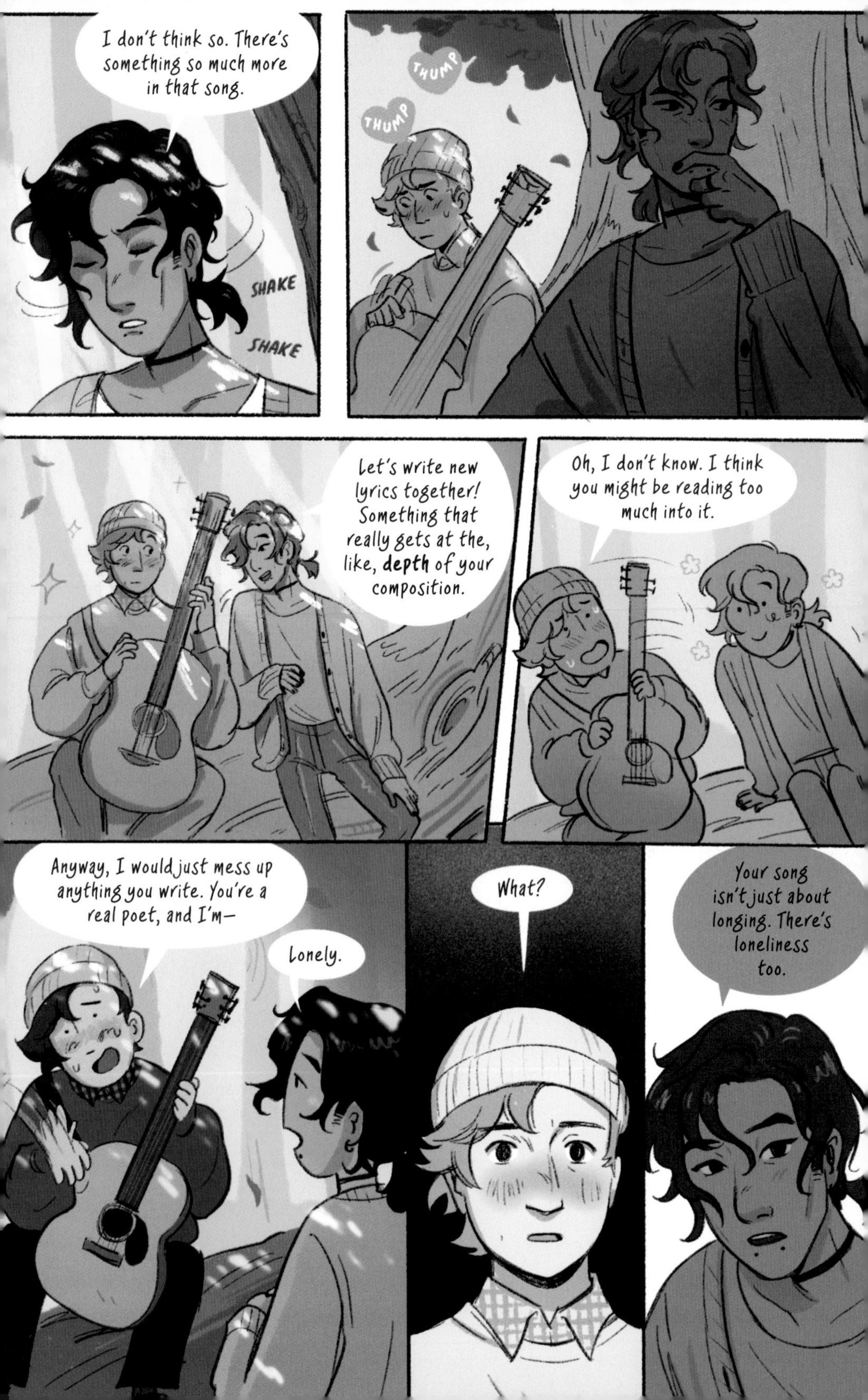
I don't think so. There's something so much more in that song.
SHAKE
SHAKE
THUMP
THUMP
Let's write new lyrics together! Something that really gets at the, like, depth of your composition.
Oh, I don't know. I think you might be reading too much into it.
Anyway, I would just mess up anything you write. You're a real poet, and I'm—
Lonely.
What?
Your song isn't just about longing. There's loneliness too.

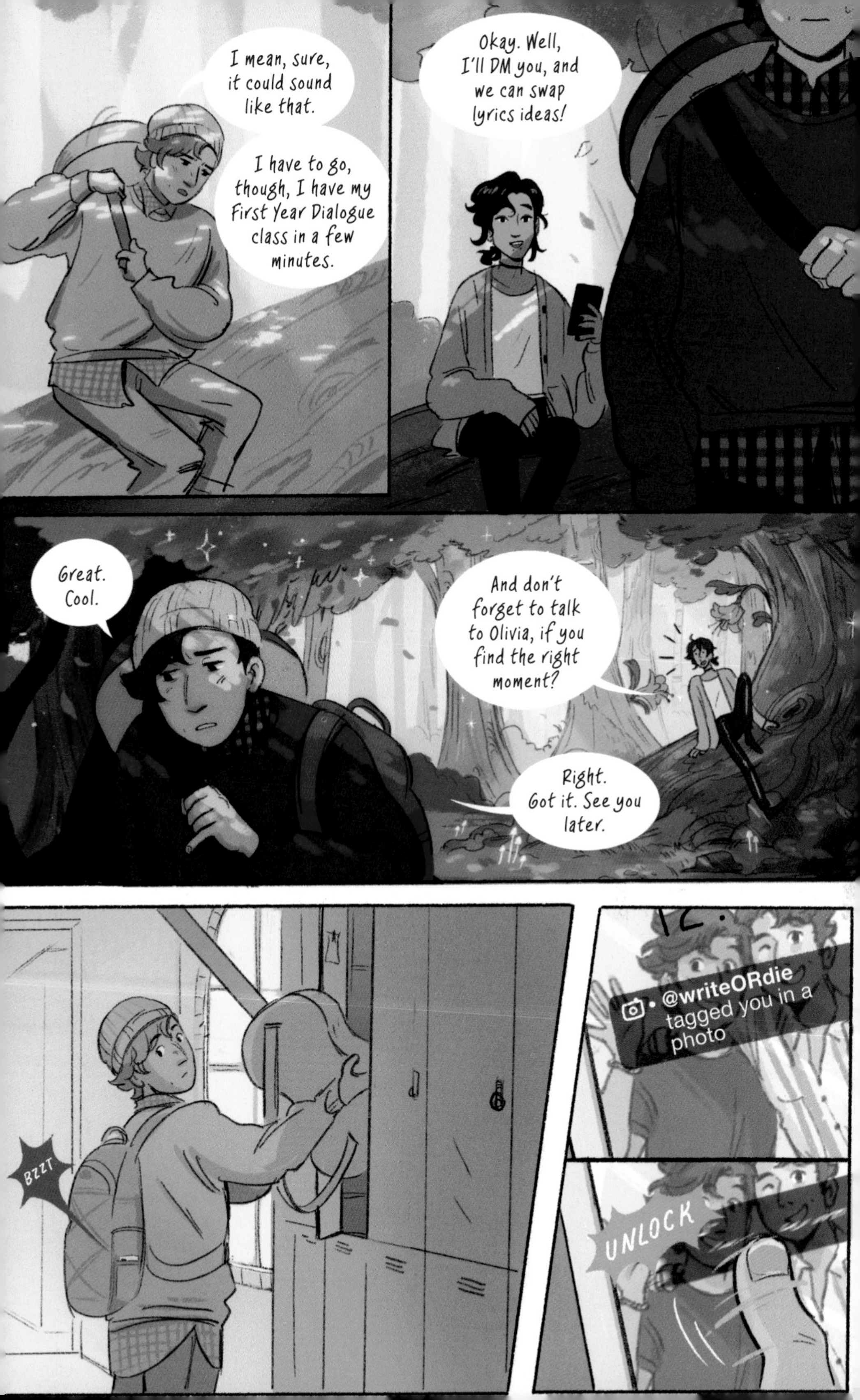
I mean, sure, it could sound like that.
I have to go, though, I have my First Year Dialogue class in a few minutes.
Okay. Well, I'll DM you, and we can swap lyrics ideas!
Great. Cool.
And don't forget to talk to Olivia, if you find the right moment?
Right. Got it. See you later.
BZZT
@writeORdie tagged you in a photo
UNLOCK

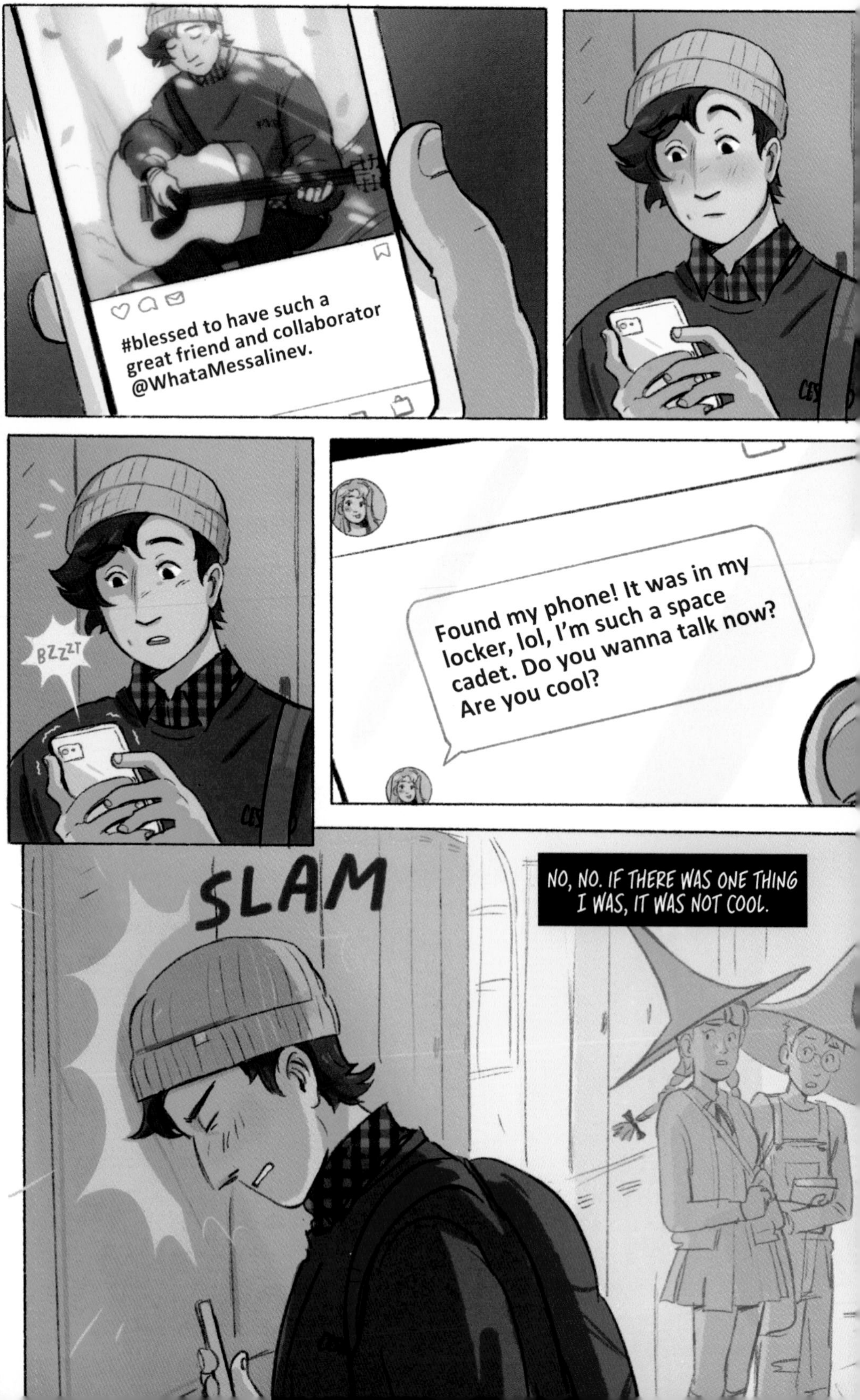

#blessed to have such a great friend and collaborator @WhataMessalinev.
BZZZT
Found my phone! It was in my locker, lol, I'm such a space cadet. Do you wanna talk now? Are you cool?
SLAM
NO, NO. IF THERE WAS ONE THING I WAS, IT WAS NOT COOL.

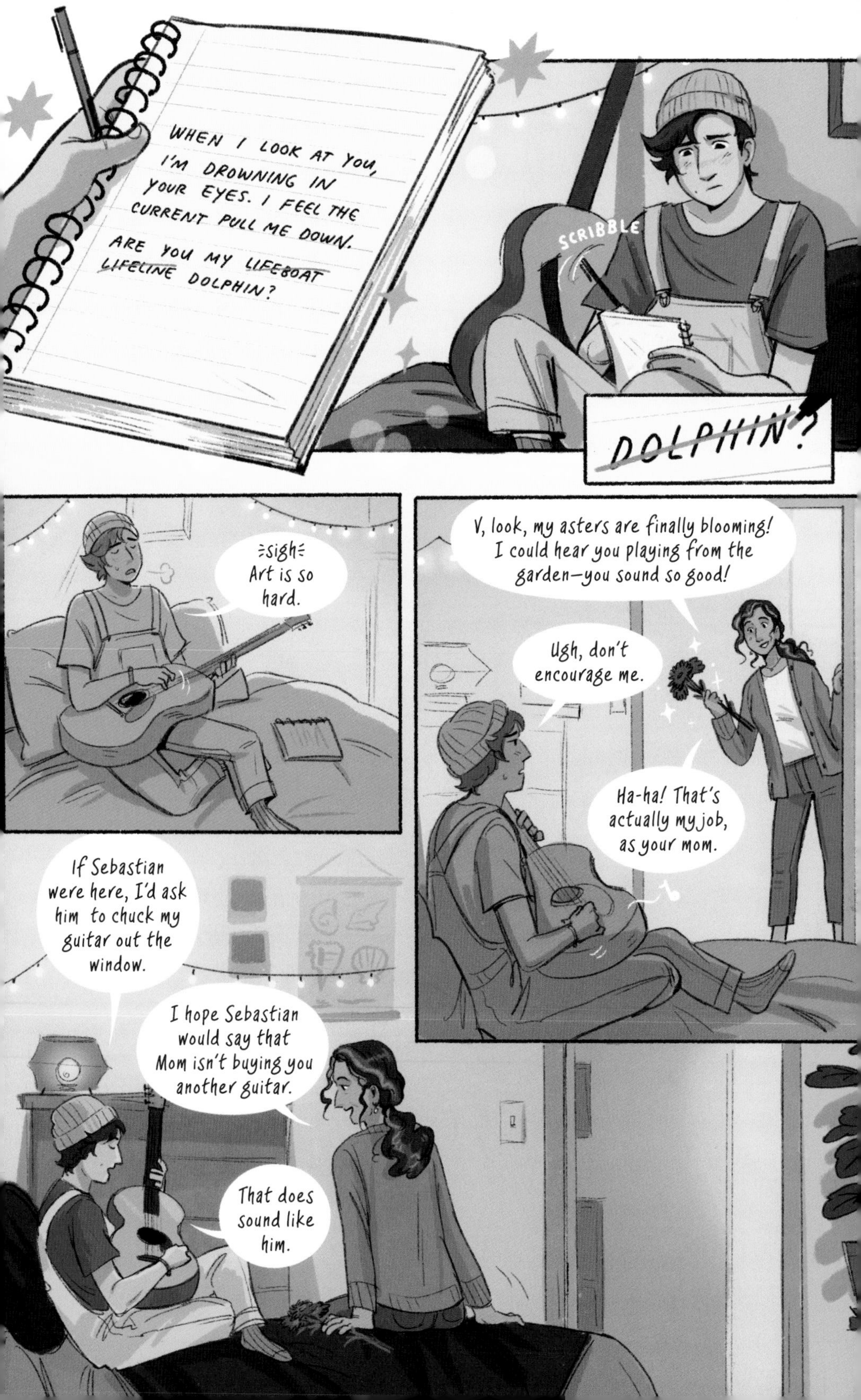

WHEN I LOOK AT YOU, I'M DROWNING IN YOUR EYES. I FEEL THE CURRENT PULL ME DOWN.
ARE YOU MY ~~LIFEBOAT~~ ~~LIFELINE~~ DOLPHIN?
SCRIBBLE
~~DOLPHIN~~?
=sigh= Art is so hard.
V, look, my asters are finally blooming! I could hear you playing from the garden—you sound so good!
Ugh, don't encourage me.
Ha-ha! That's actually my job, as your mom.
If Sebastian were here, I'd ask him to chuck my guitar out the window.
I hope Sebastian would say that Mom isn't buying you another guitar.
That does sound like him.

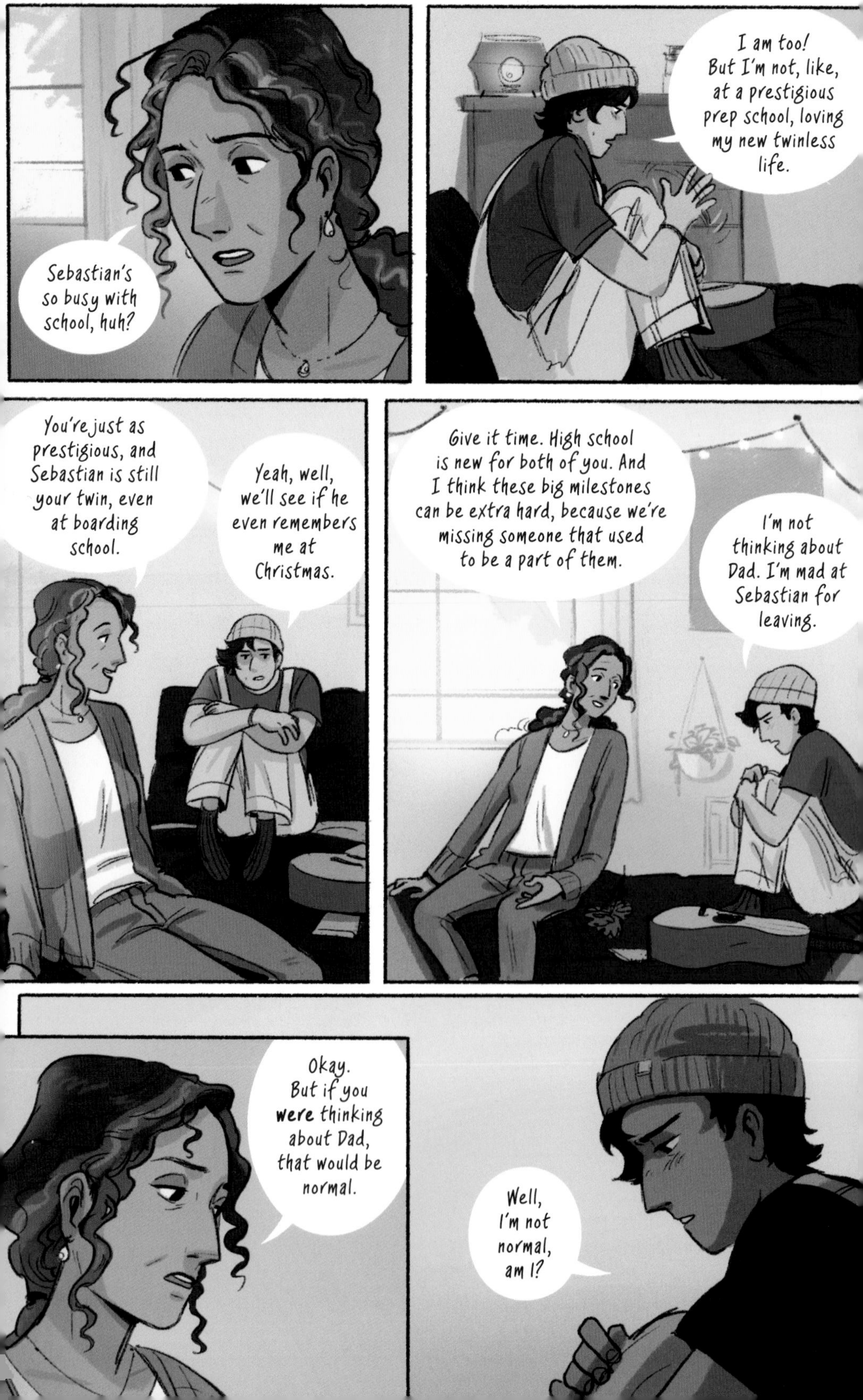
Sebastian's so busy with school, huh?
I am too! But I'm not, like, at a prestigious prep school, loving my new twinless life.
You're just as prestigious, and Sebastian is still your twin, even at boarding school.
Yeah, well, we'll see if he even remembers me at Christmas.
Give it time. High school is new for both of you. And I think these big milestones can be extra hard, because we're missing someone that used to be a part of them.
I'm not thinking about Dad. I'm mad at Sebastian for leaving.
Okay. But if you **were** thinking about Dad, that would be normal.
Well, I'm not normal, am I?

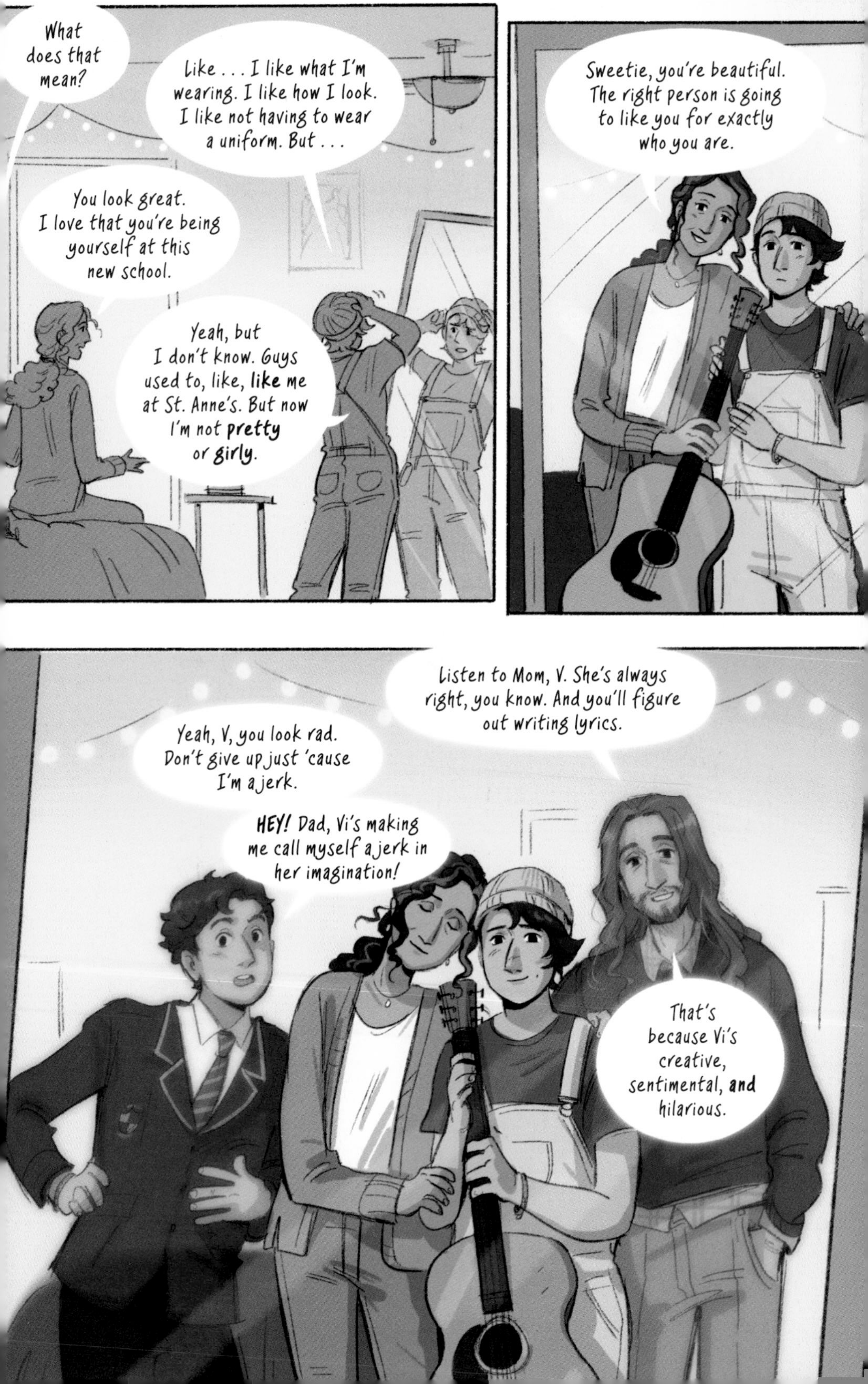
What does that mean?
Like . . . I like what I'm wearing. I like how I look. I like not having to wear a uniform. But . . .
You look great. I love that you're being yourself at this new school.
Yeah, but I don't know. Guys used to, like, **like** me at St. Anne's. But now I'm not **pretty** or **girly**.
Sweetie, you're beautiful. The right person is going to like you for exactly who you are.
Listen to Mom, V. She's always right, you know. And you'll figure out writing lyrics.
Yeah, V, you look rad. Don't give up just 'cause I'm a jerk.
HEY! Dad, Vi's making me call myself a jerk in her imagination!
That's because Vi's creative, sentimental, **and** hilarious.

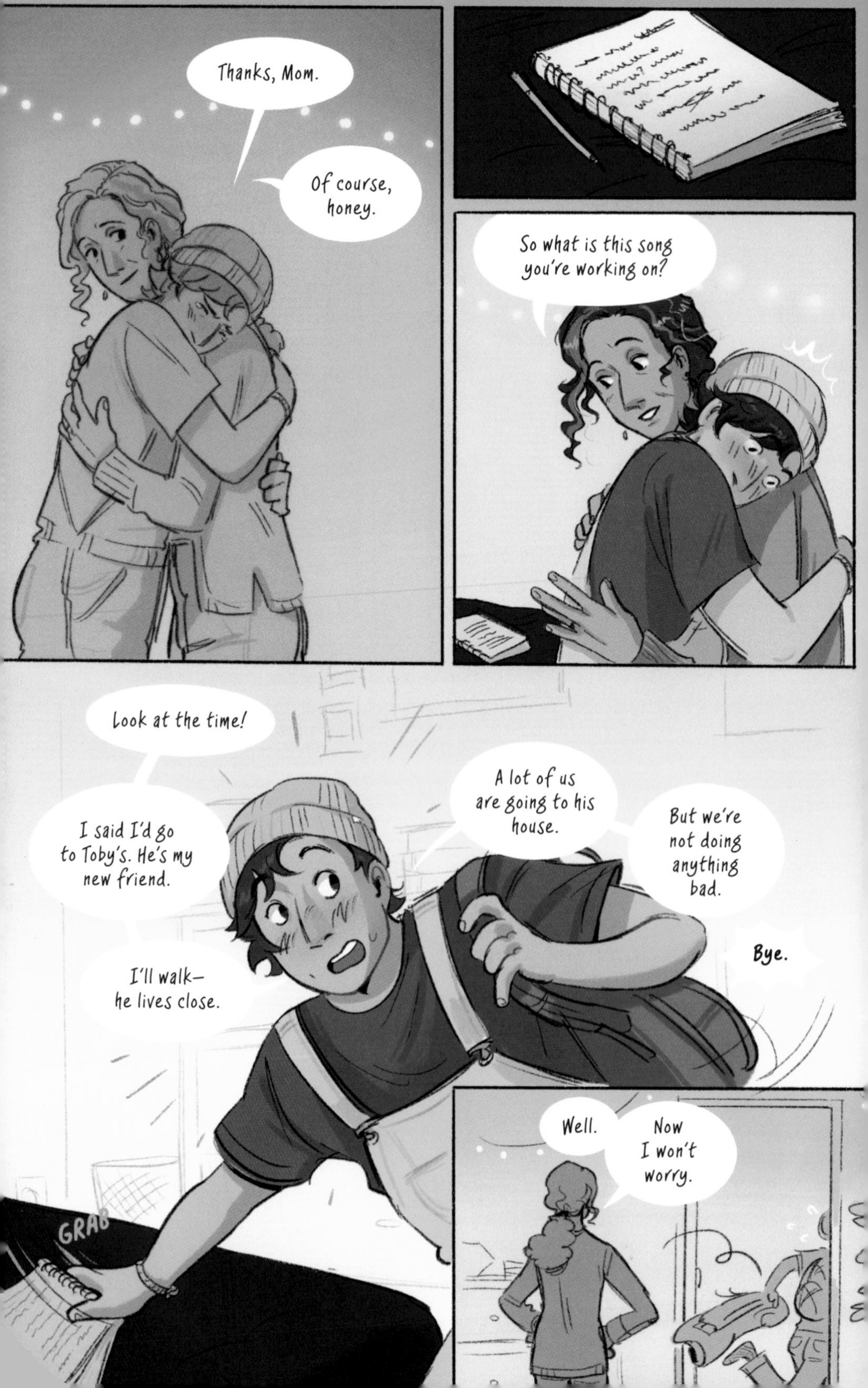
Thanks, Mom.
Of course, honey.
So what is this song you're working on?
Look at the time!
I said I'd go to Toby's. He's my new friend.
I'll walk—he lives close.
A lot of us are going to his house.
But we're not doing anything bad.
Bye.
GRAB
Well.
Now I won't worry.

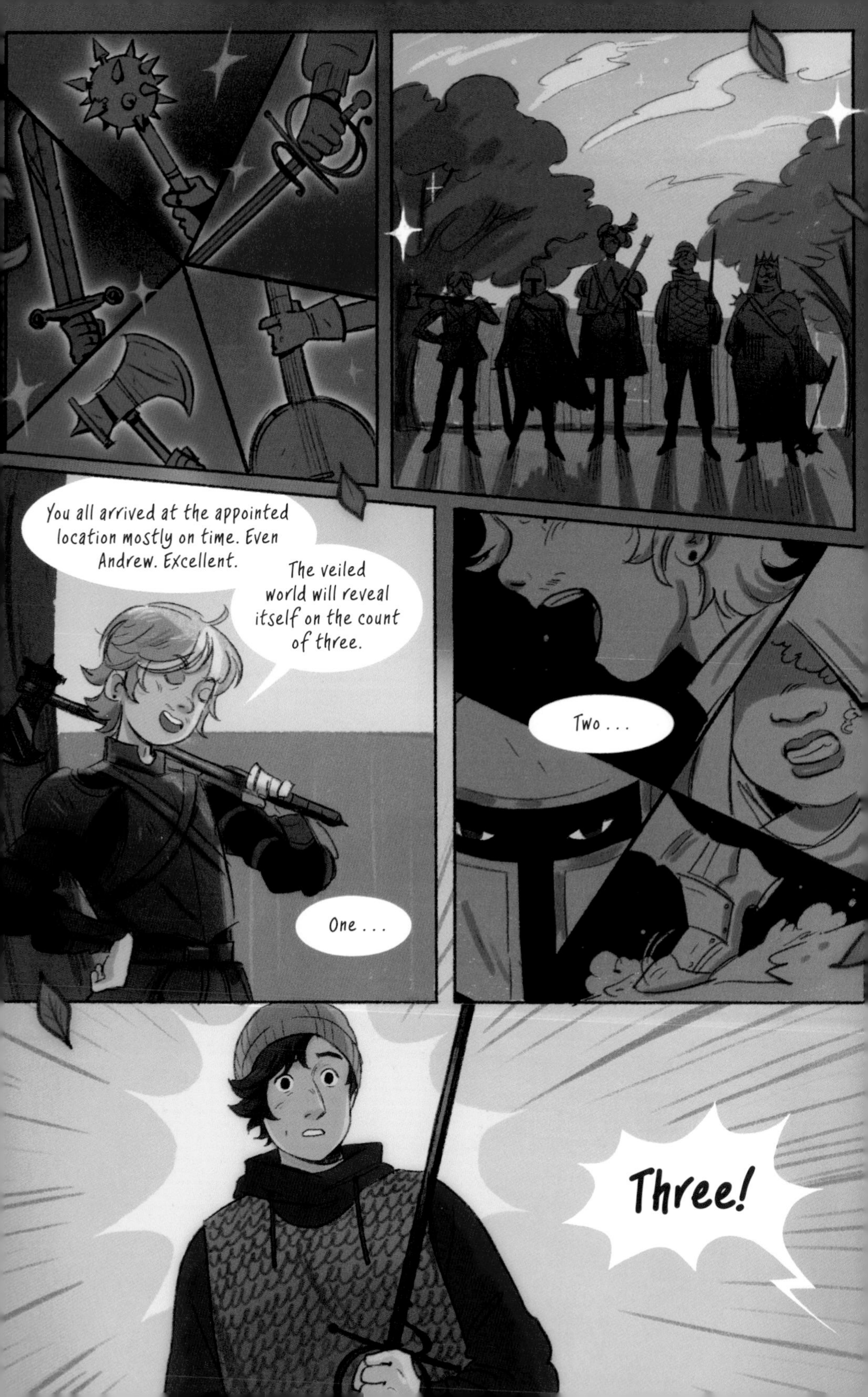
You all arrived at the appointed location mostly on time. Even Andrew. Excellent.
The veiled world will reveal itself on the count of three.
One . . .
Two . . .
Three!

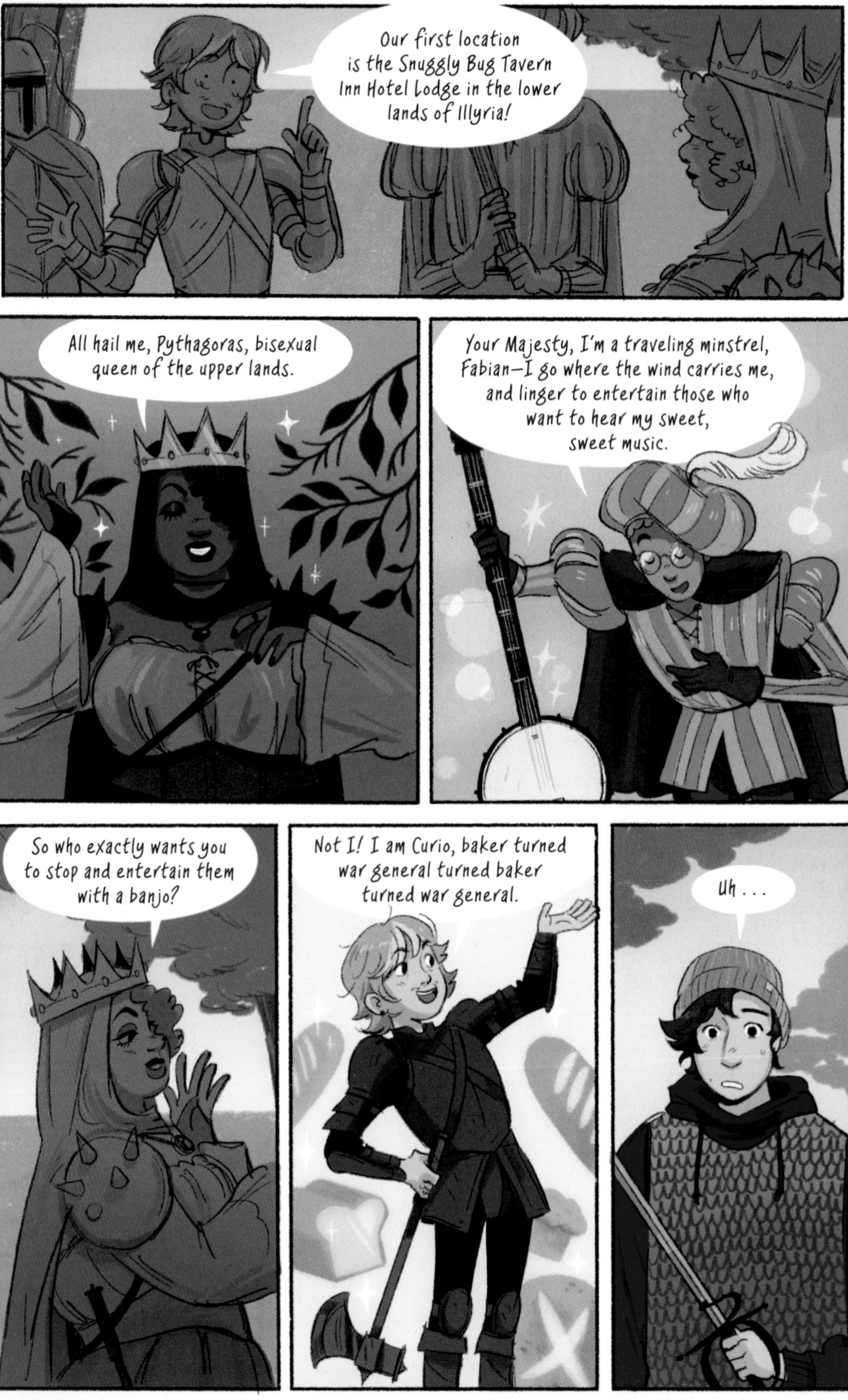
Our first location is the Snuggly Bug Tavern Inn Hotel Lodge in the lower lands of Illyria!
All hail me, Pythagoras, bisexual queen of the upper lands.
Your Majesty, I'm a traveling minstrel, Fabian—I go where the wind carries me, and linger to entertain those who want to hear my sweet, sweet music.
So who exactly wants you to stop and entertain them with a banjo?
Not I! I am Curio, baker turned war general turned baker turned war general.
Uh . . .

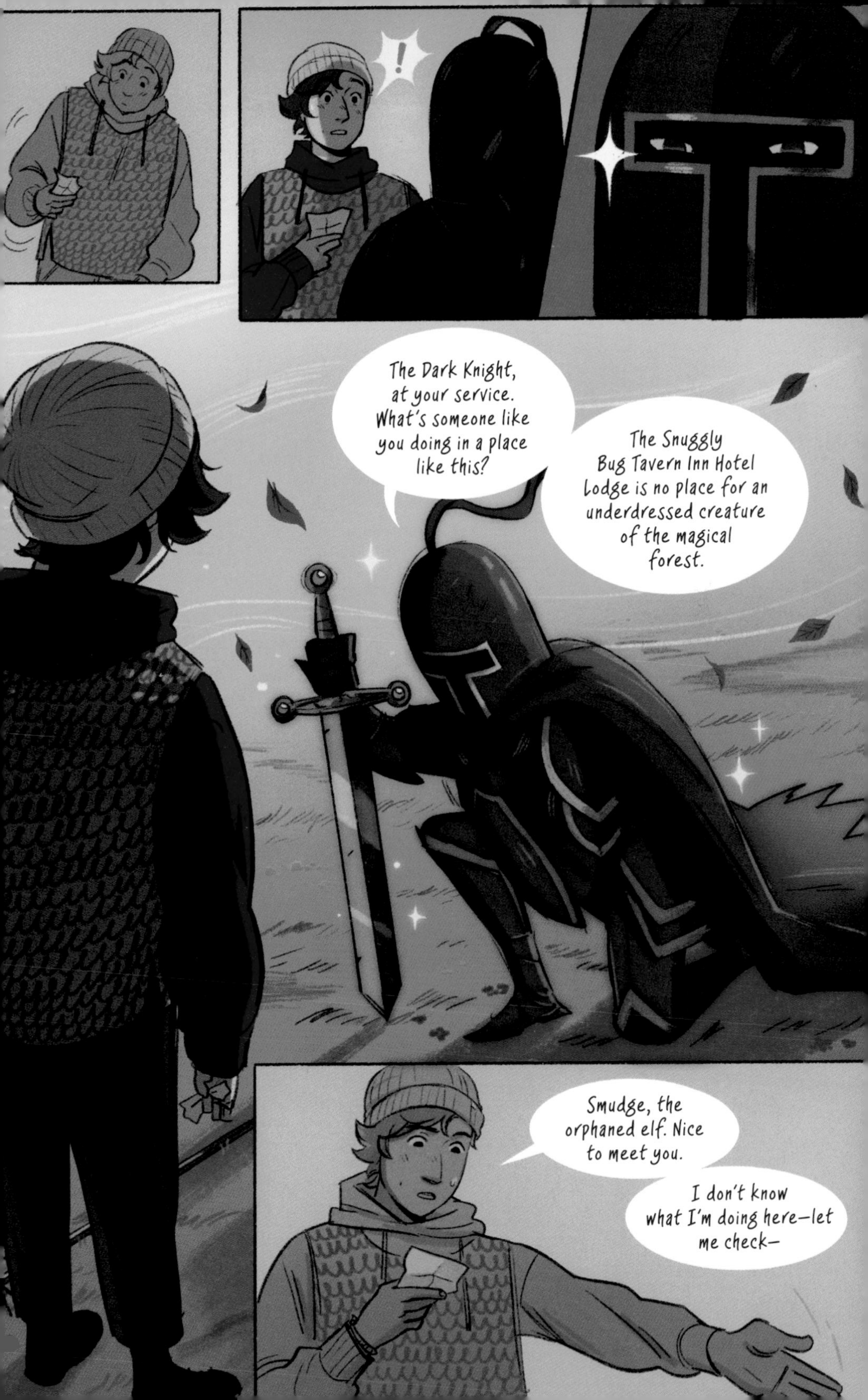
!
The Dark Knight, at your service. What's someone like you doing in a place like this?
The Snuggly Bug Tavern Inn Hotel Lodge is no place for an underdressed creature of the magical forest.
Smudge, the orphaned elf. Nice to meet you.
I don't know what I'm doing here—let me check—

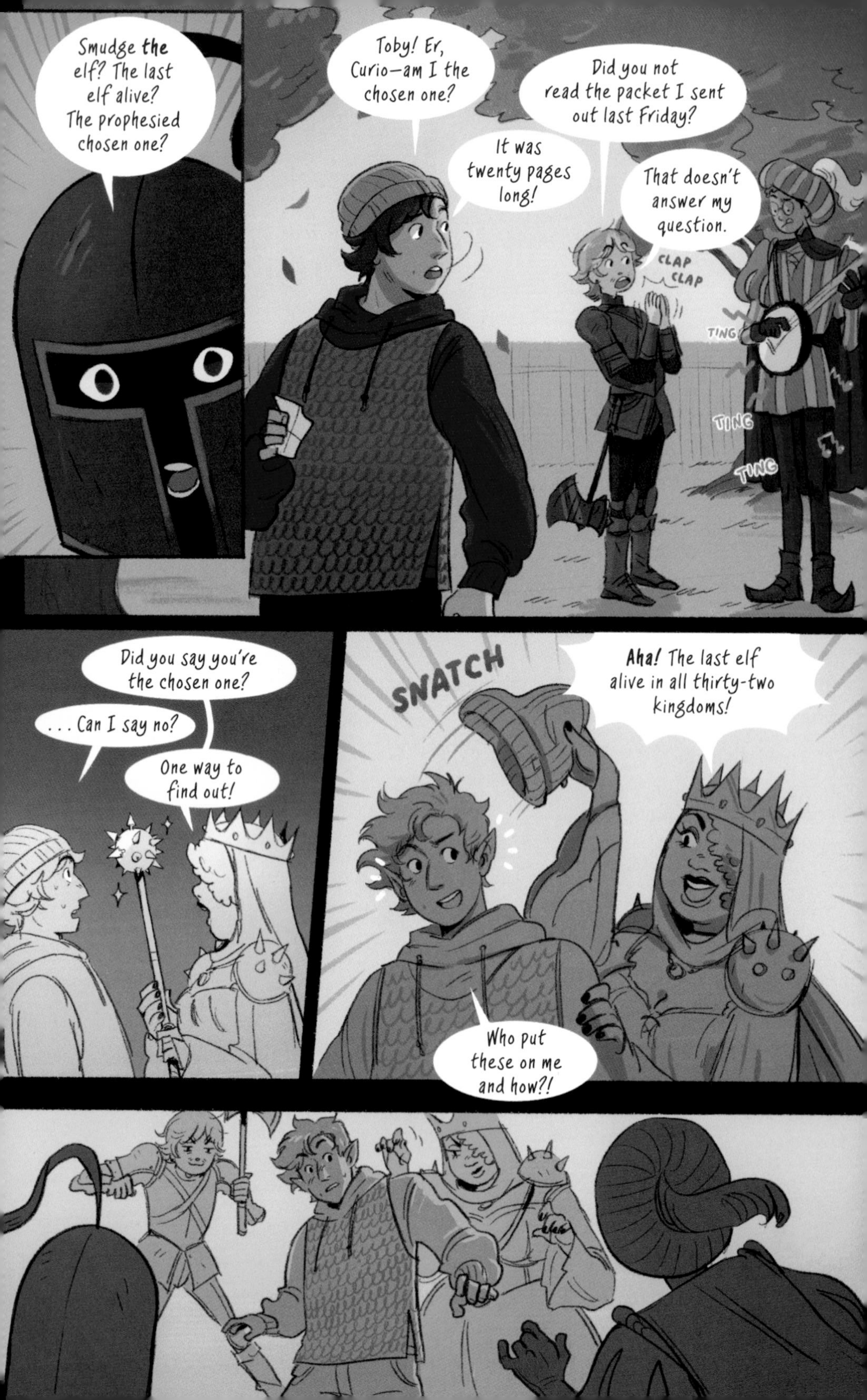

Smudge **the** elf? The last elf alive? The prophesied chosen one?
Toby! Er, Curio—am I the chosen one?
Did you not read the packet I sent out last Friday?
It was twenty pages long!
That doesn't answer my question.
CLAP CLAP
TING
TING
TING
Did you say you're the chosen one?
. . . Can I say no?
One way to find out!
SNATCH
Aha! The last elf alive in all thirty-two kingdoms!
Who put these on me and how?!

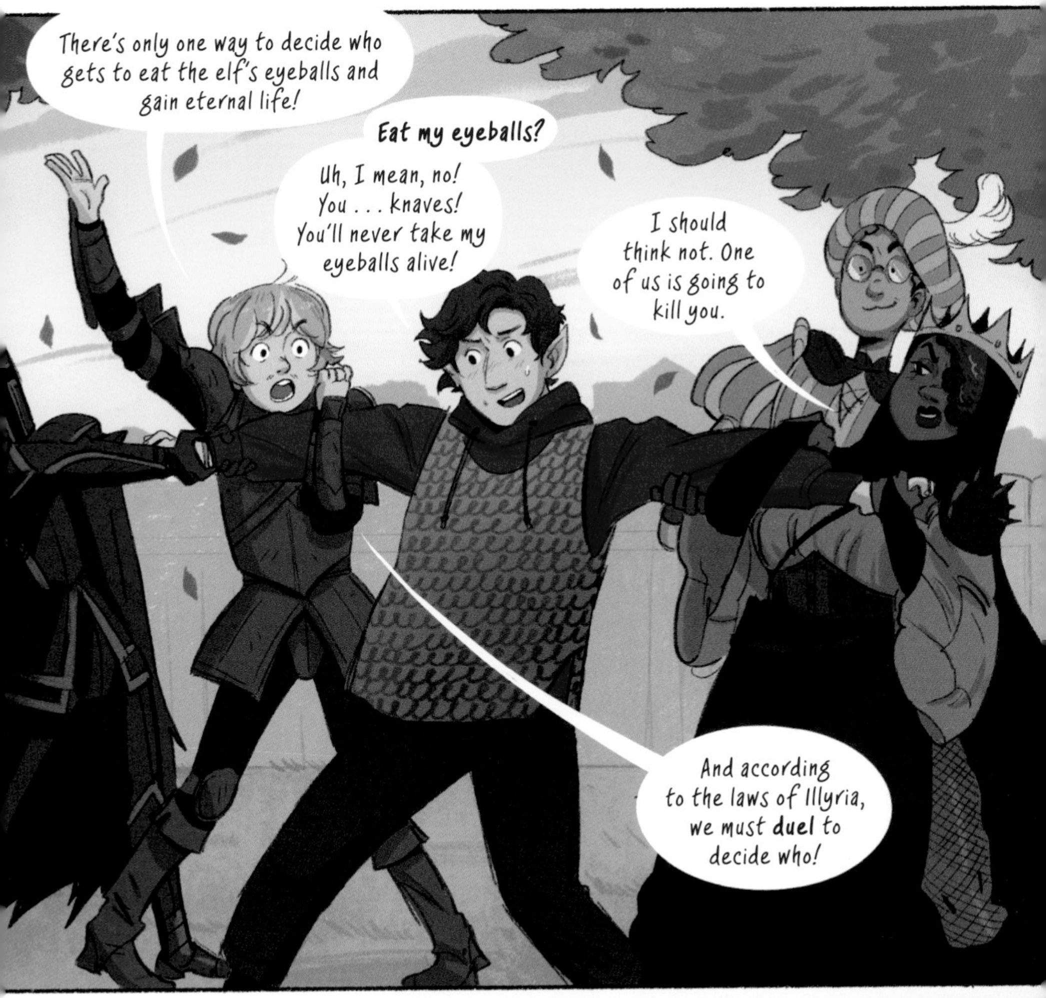
There's only one way to decide who gets to eat the elf's eyeballs and gain eternal life!
Eat my eyeballs?
Uh, I mean, no! You . . . knaves! You'll never take my eyeballs alive!
I should think not. One of us is going to kill you.
And according to the laws of Illyria, we must **duel** to decide who!

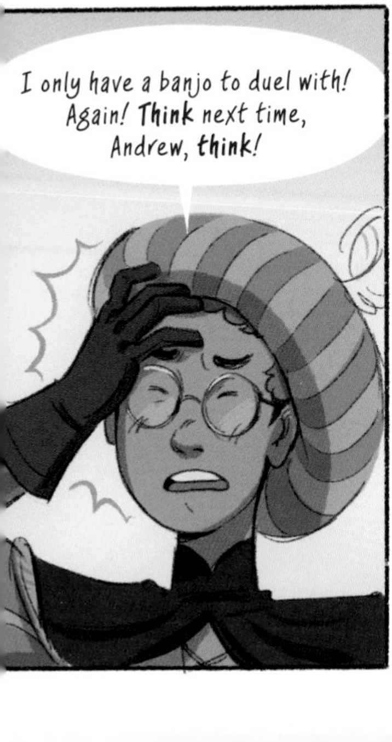
I only have a banjo to duel with! Again! **Think** next time, Andrew, **think**!

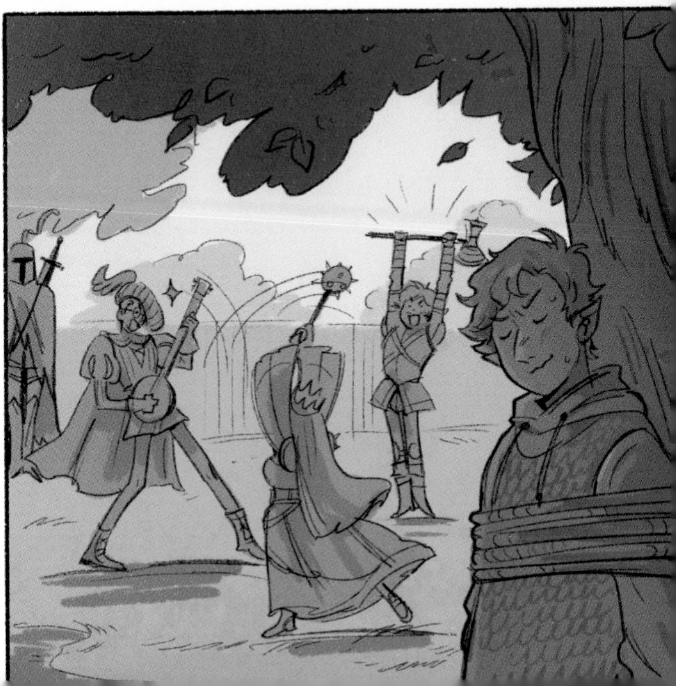

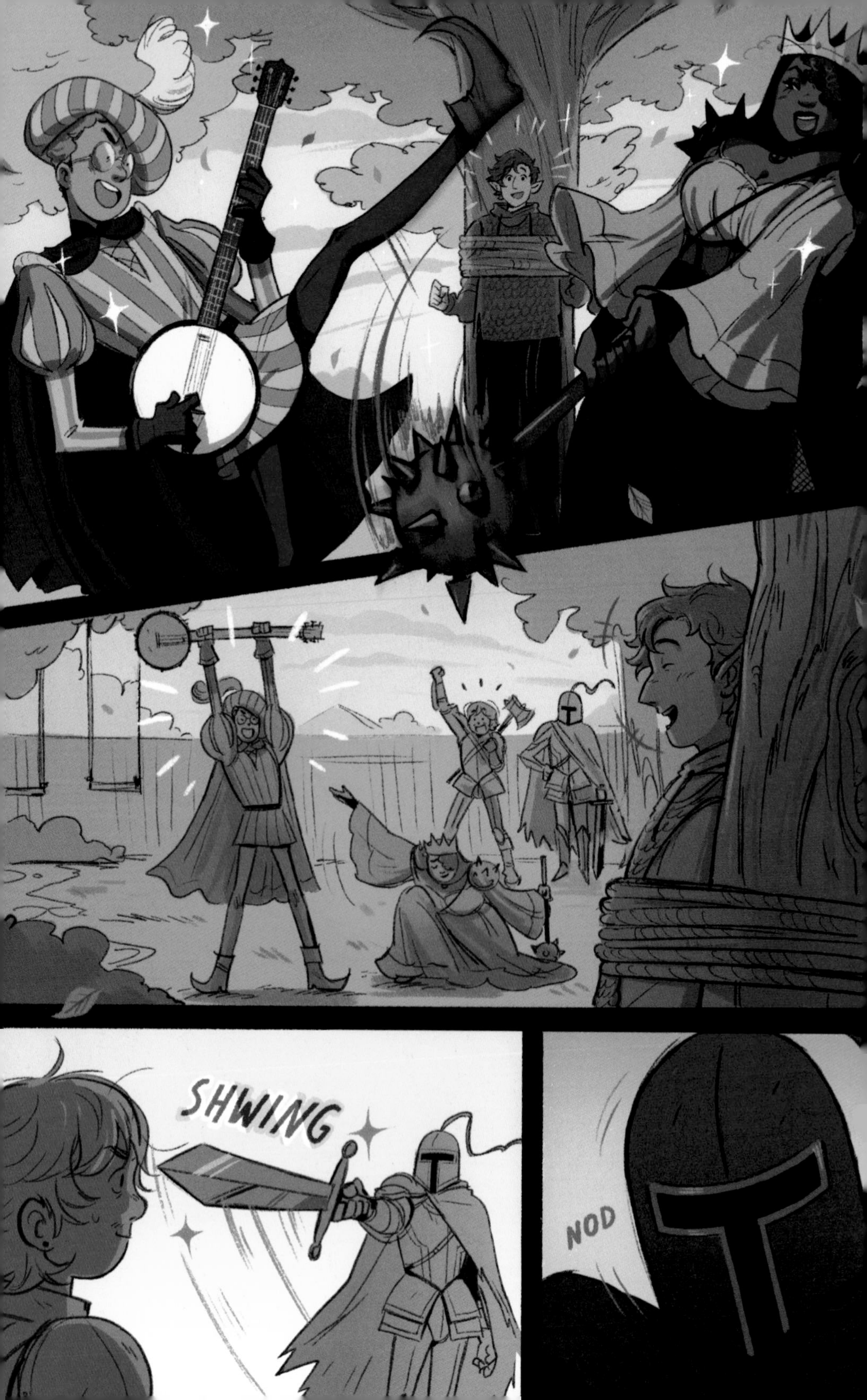
SHWING
NOD

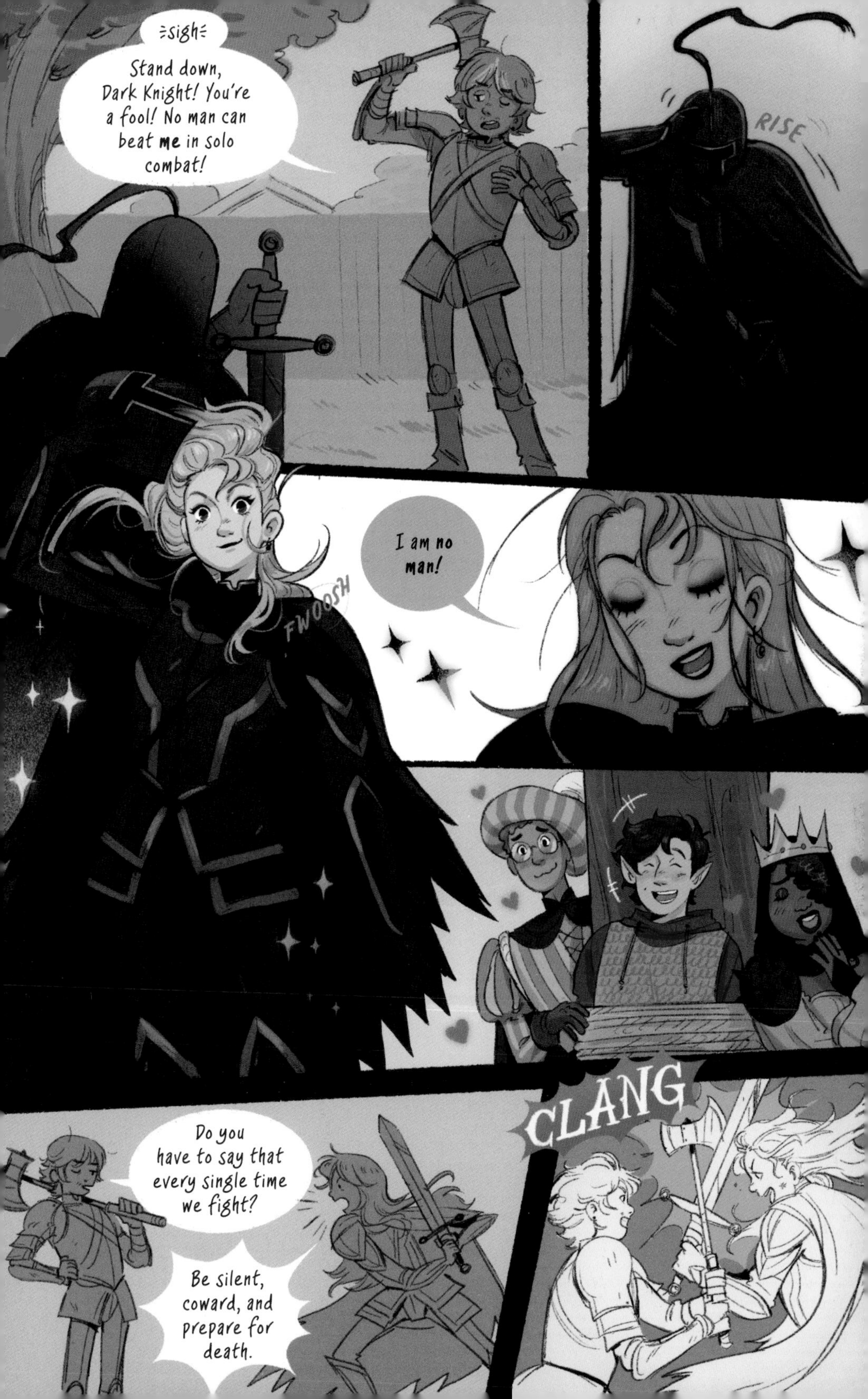

≈sigh≈
Stand down, Dark Knight! You're a fool! No man can beat **me** in solo combat!
RISE
FWOOSH
I am no man!
CLANG
Do you have to say that every single time we fight?
Be silent, coward, and prepare for death.

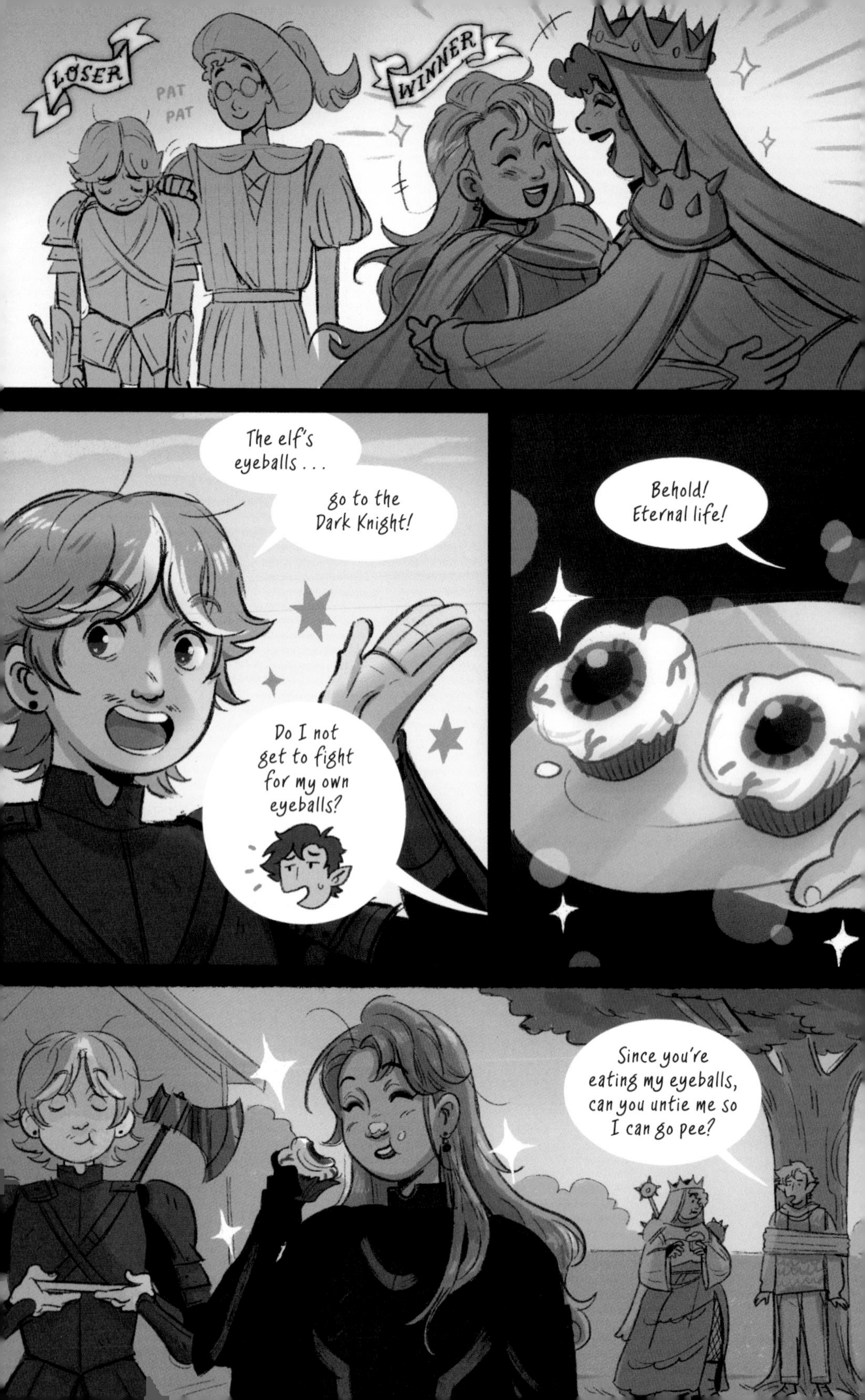
LOSER
PAT PAT
WINNER
The elf's eyeballs . . .
go to the Dark Knight!
Do I not get to fight for my own eyeballs?
Behold! Eternal life!
Since you're eating my eyeballs, can you untie me so I can go pee?

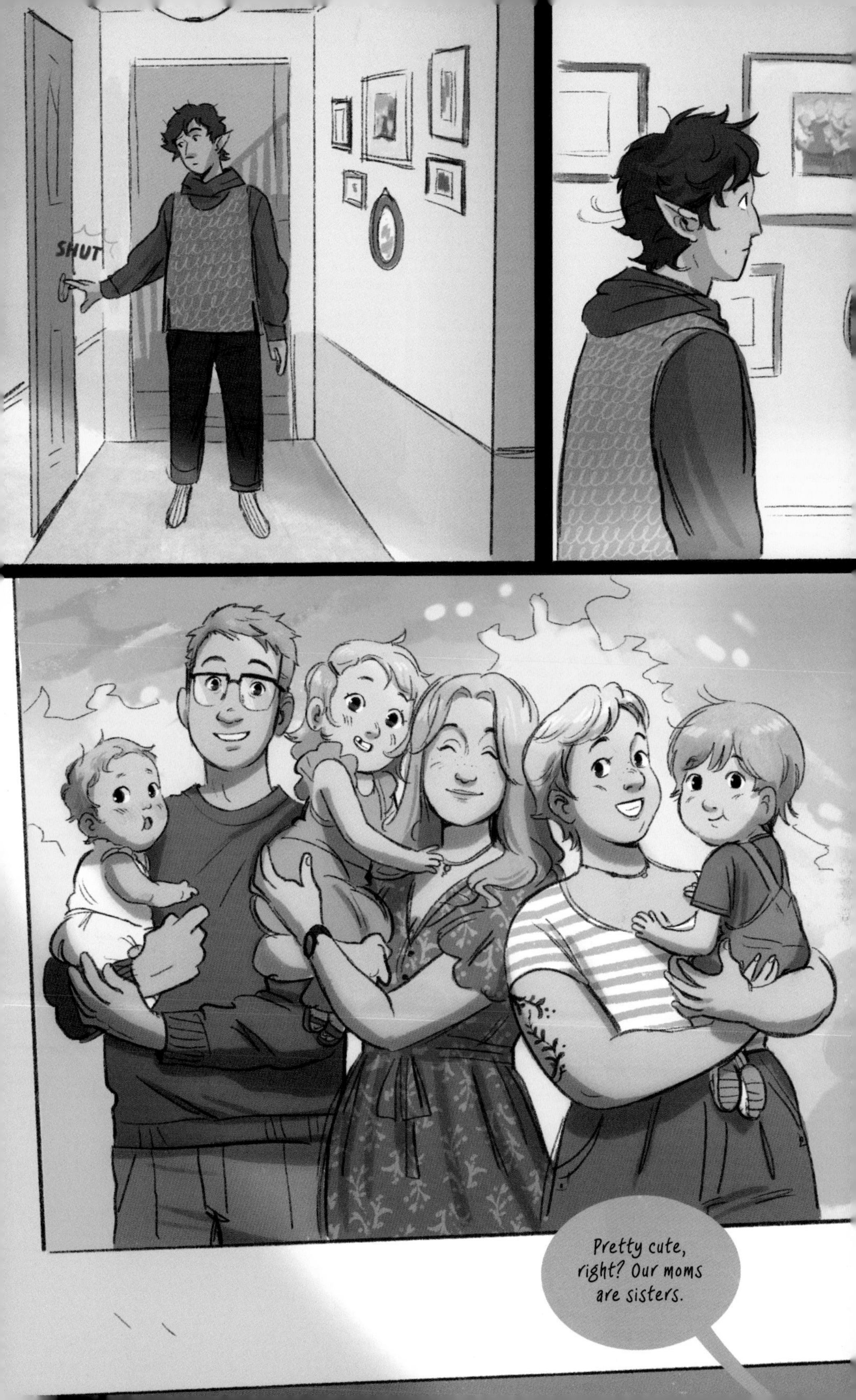
SHUT
Pretty cute, right? Our moms are sisters.

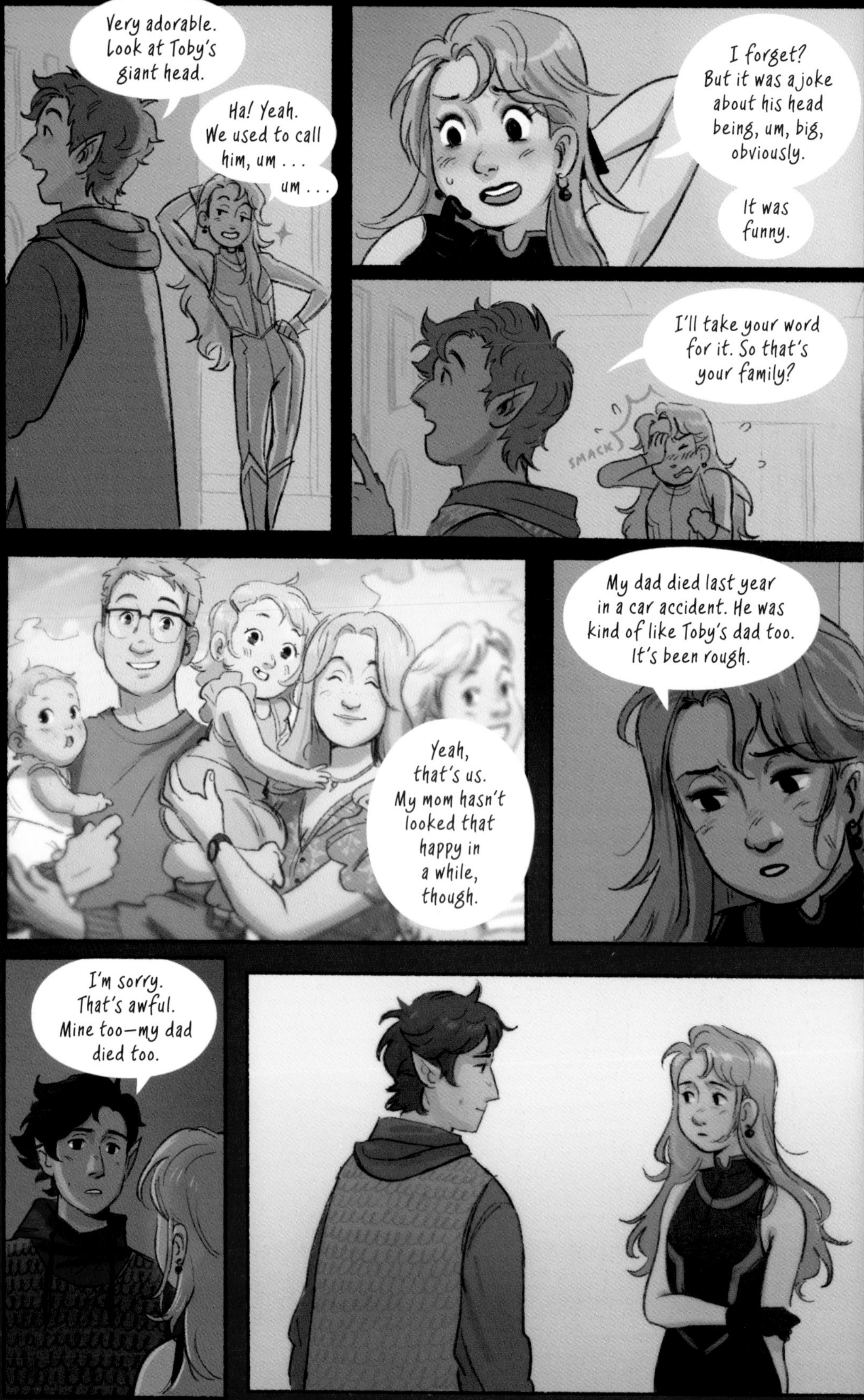
Very adorable. Look at Toby's giant head.
Ha! Yeah. We used to call him, um . . .
um . . .
I forget? But it was a joke about his head being, um, big, obviously.
It was funny.
I'll take your word for it. So that's your family?
SMACK
Yeah, that's us. My mom hasn't looked that happy in a while, though.
My dad died last year in a car accident. He was kind of like Toby's dad too. It's been rough.
I'm sorry. That's awful. Mine too—my dad died too.

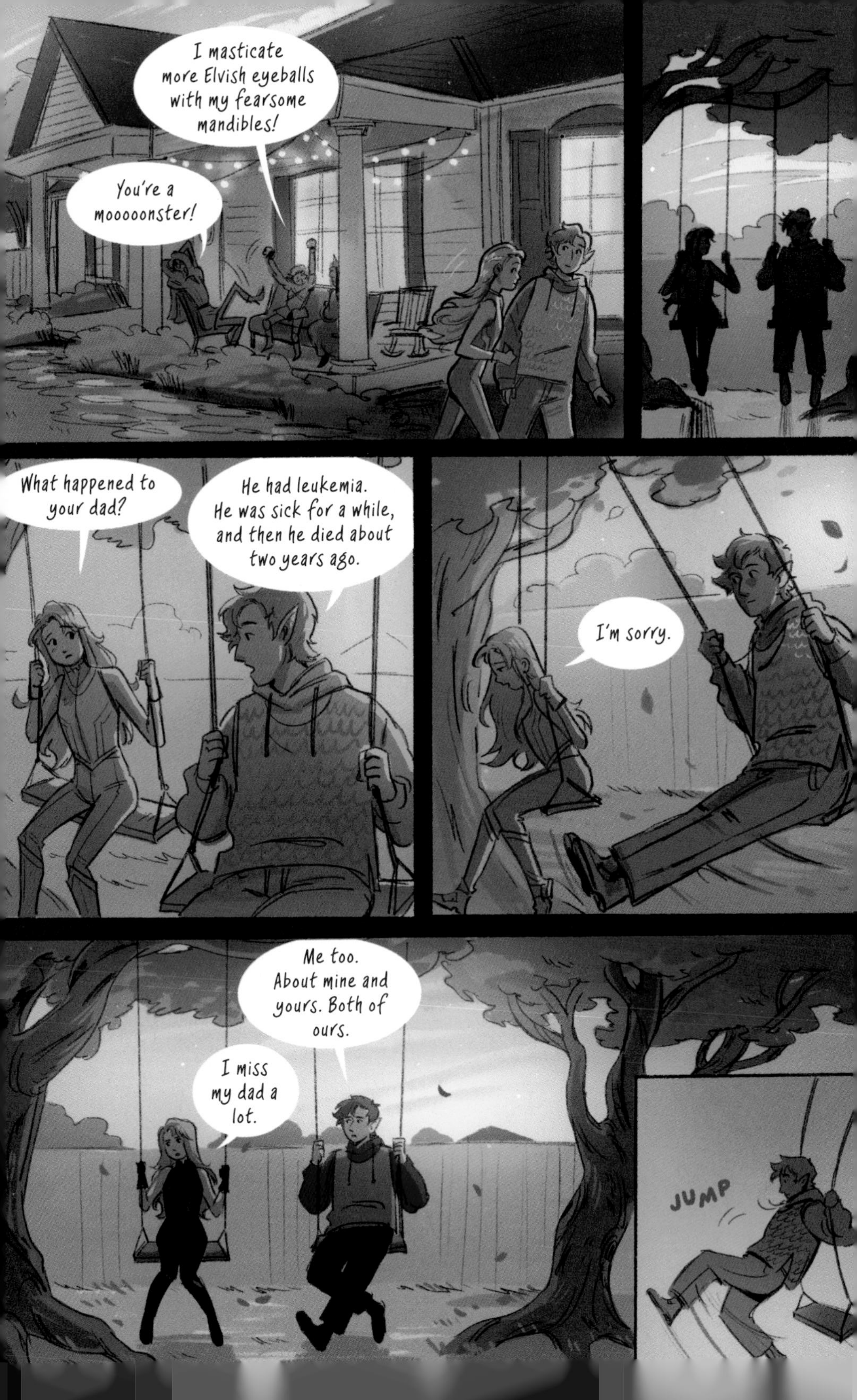
I masticate more Elvish eyeballs with my fearsome mandibles!
You're a mooooonster!
What happened to your dad?
He had leukemia. He was sick for a while, and then he died about two years ago.
I'm sorry.
I miss my dad a lot.
Me too. About mine and yours. Both of ours.
JUMP

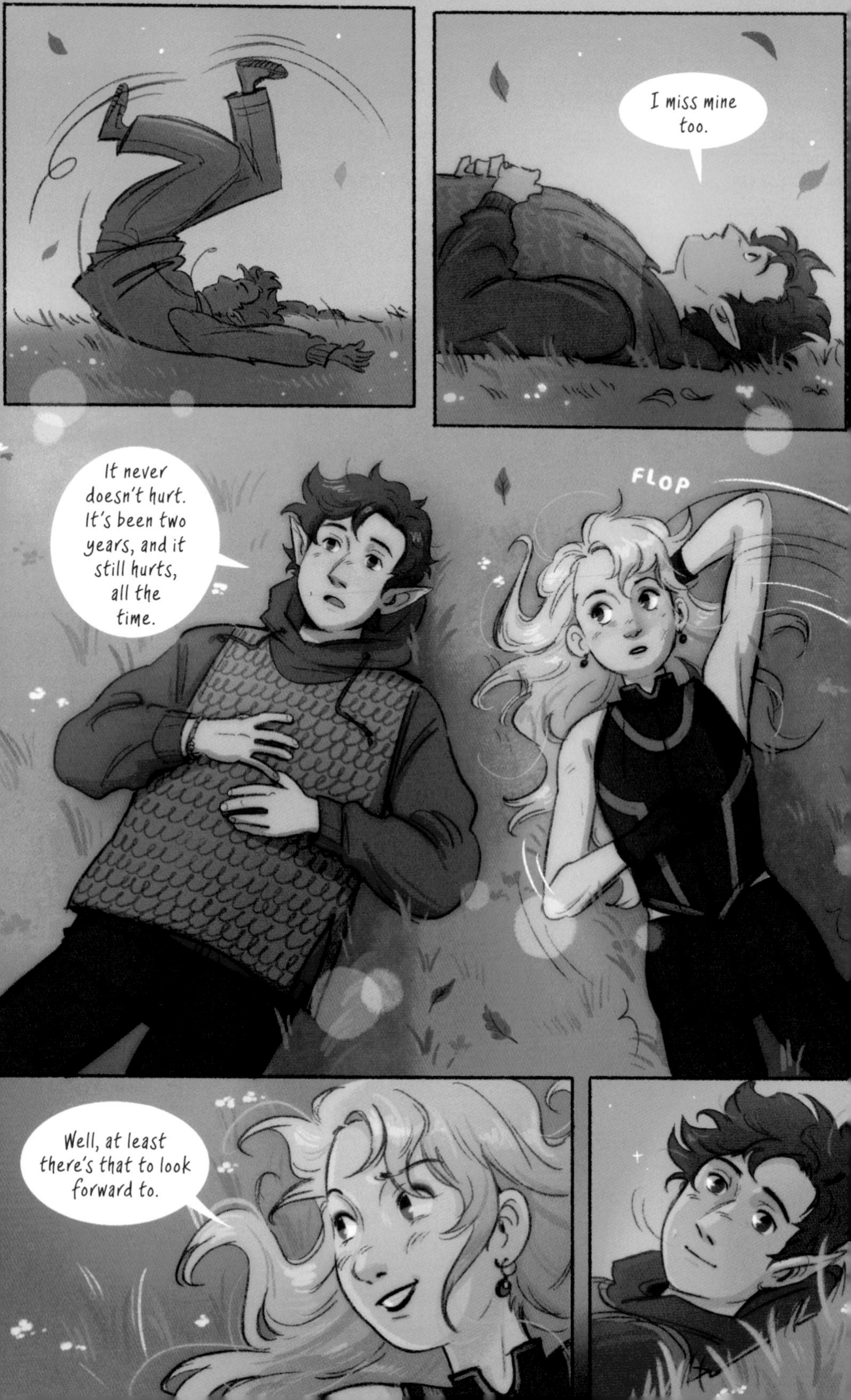
I miss mine too.
It never doesn't hurt. It's been two years, and it still hurts, all the time.
FLOP
Well, at least there's that to look forward to.

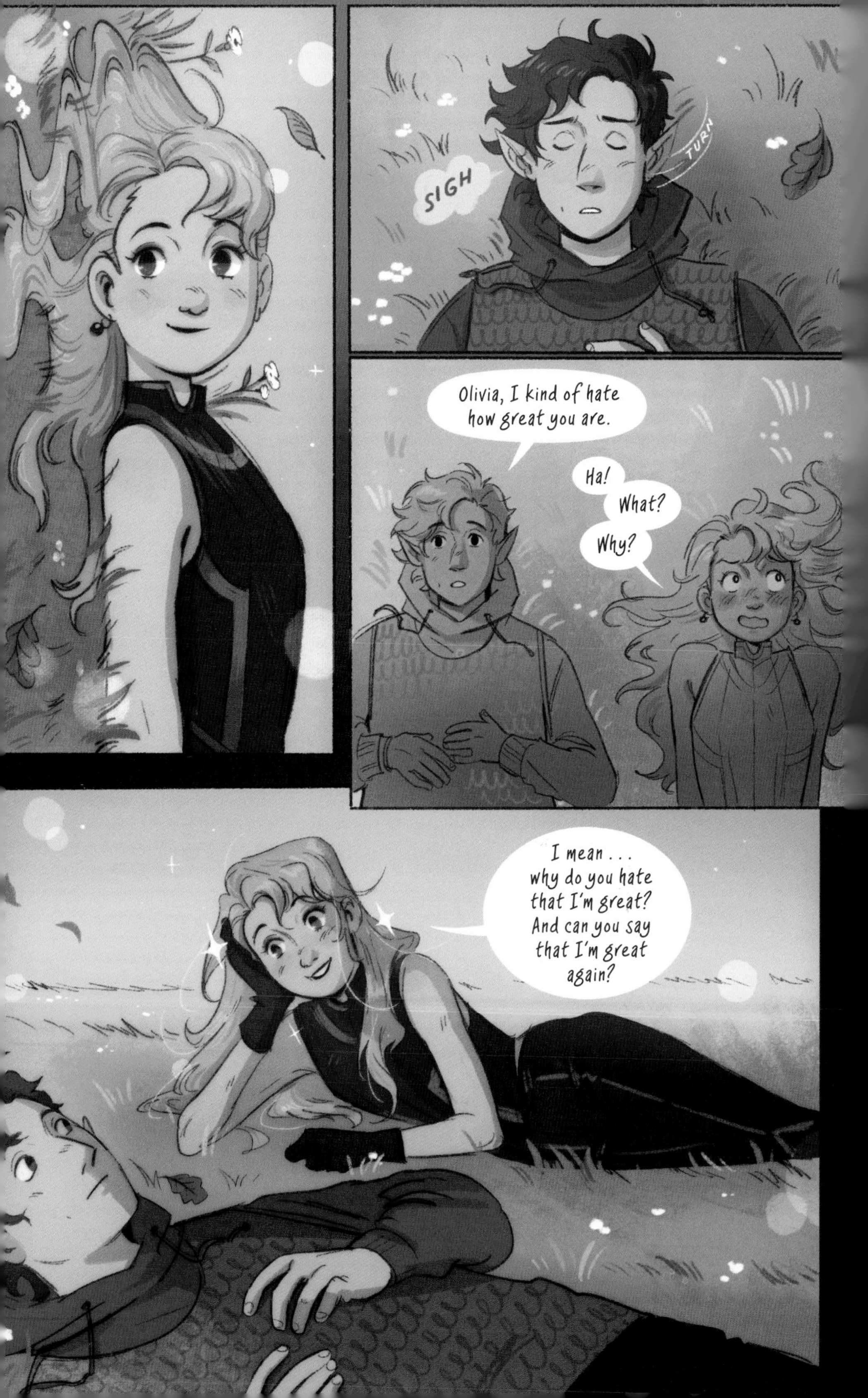
SIGH
TURN
Olivia, I kind of hate how great you are.
Ha!
What?
Why?
I mean . . . why do you hate that I'm great? And can you say that I'm great again?

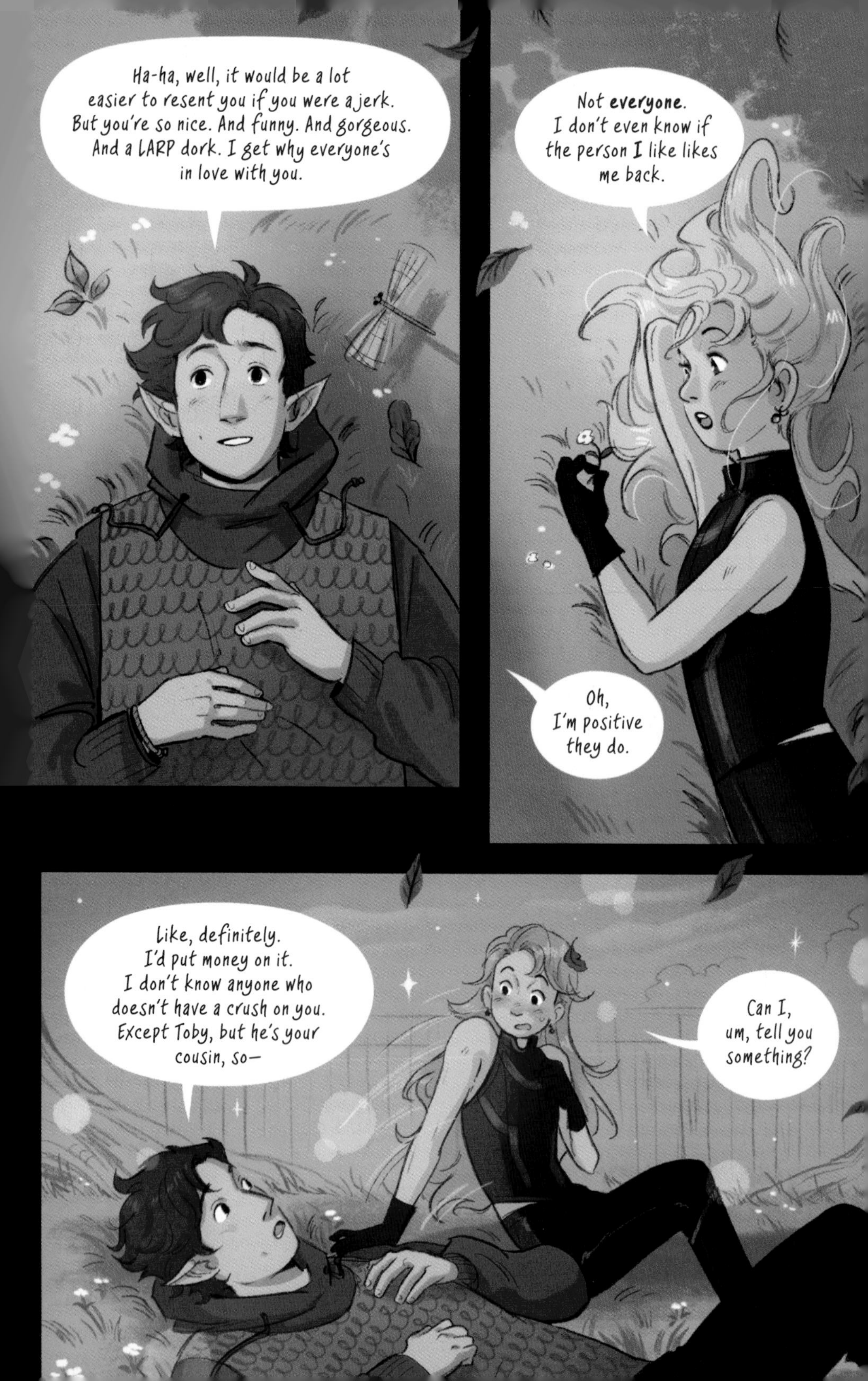
Ha-ha, well, it would be a lot easier to resent you if you were a jerk. But you're so nice. And funny. And gorgeous. And a LARP dork. I get why everyone's in love with you.
Not **everyone**. I don't even know if the person I like likes me back.
Oh, I'm positive they do.
Like, definitely. I'd put money on it. I don't know anyone who doesn't have a crush on you. Except Toby, but he's your cousin, so—
Can I, um, tell you something?

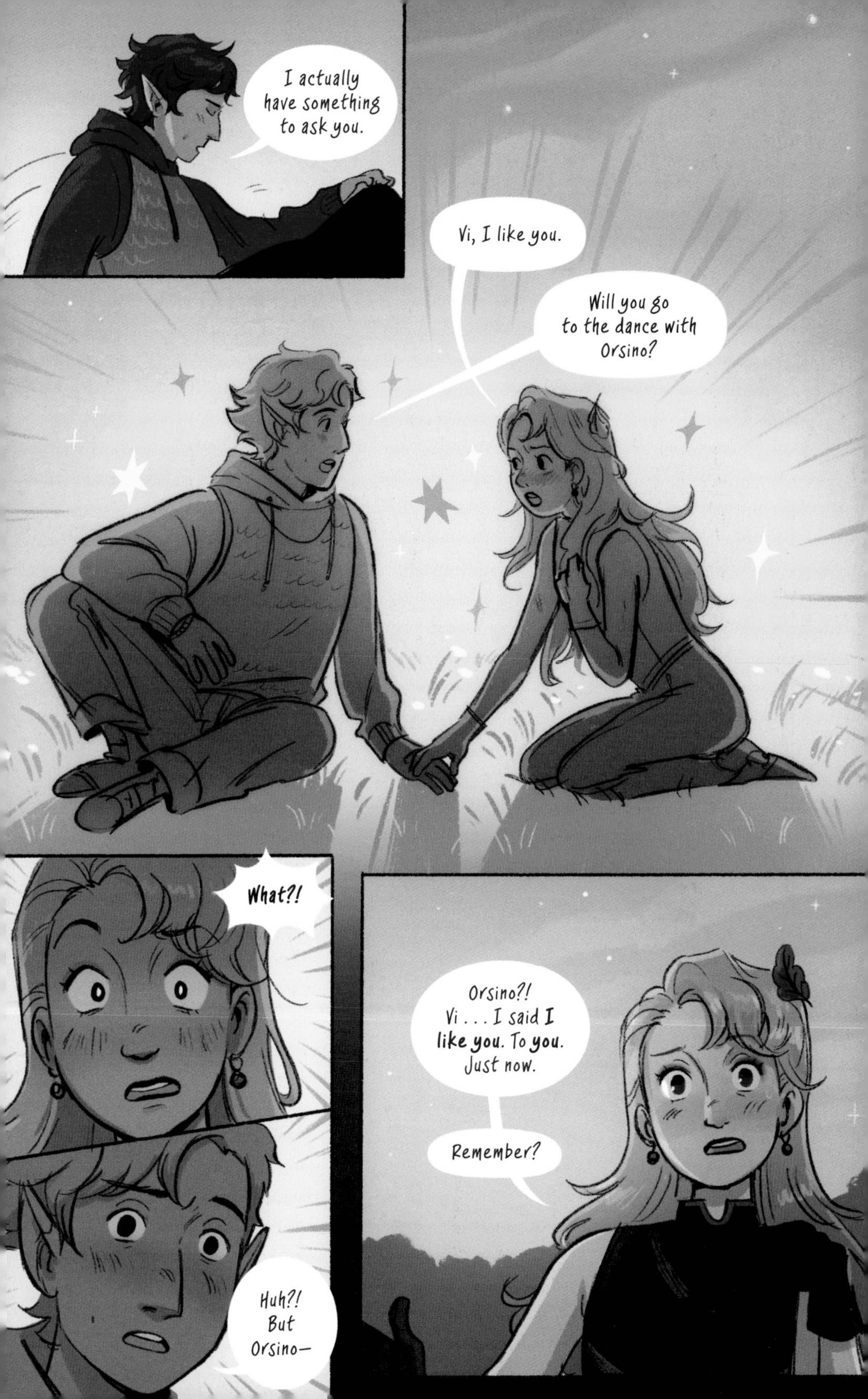
I actually have something to ask you.
Vi, I like you.
Will you go to the dance with Orsino?
What?!
Huh?! But Orsino—
Orsino?! Vi . . . I said **I like you**. To **you**. Just now.
Remember?

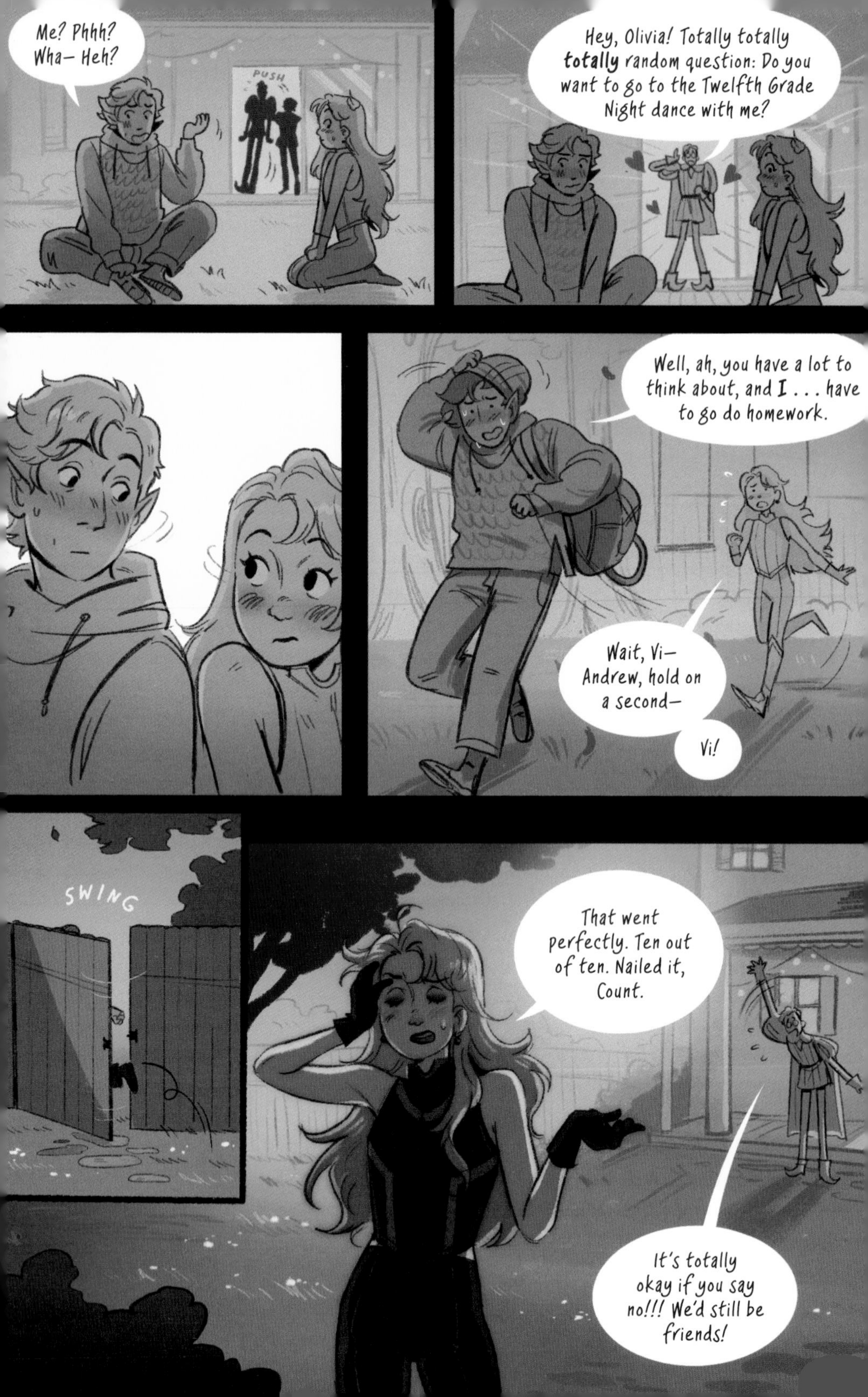
Me? Phhh?
Wha— Heh?
PUSH
Hey, Olivia! Totally totally **totally** random question: Do you want to go to the Twelfth Grade Night dance with me?
Well, ah, you have a lot to think about, and **I** . . . have to go do homework.
Wait, Vi— Andrew, hold on a second—
Vi!
SWING
That went perfectly. Ten out of ten. Nailed it, Count.
It's totally okay if you say no!!! We'd still be friends!

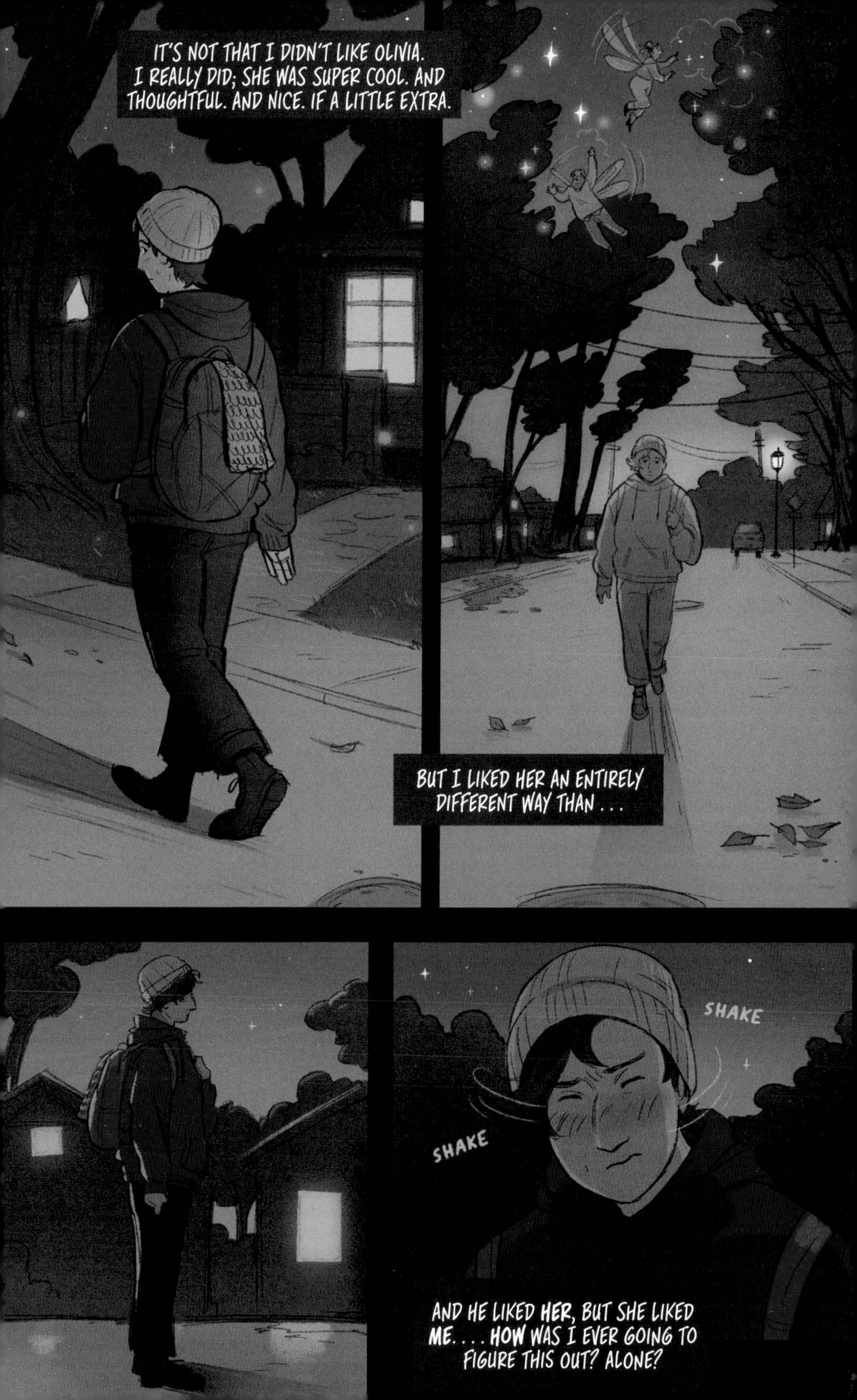
IT'S NOT THAT I DIDN'T LIKE OLIVIA. I REALLY DID; SHE WAS SUPER COOL. AND THOUGHTFUL. AND NICE. IF A LITTLE EXTRA.
BUT I LIKED HER AN ENTIRELY DIFFERENT WAY THAN . . .
SHAKE
SHAKE
AND HE LIKED HER, BUT SHE LIKED ME. . . . HOW WAS I EVER GOING TO FIGURE THIS OUT? ALONE?

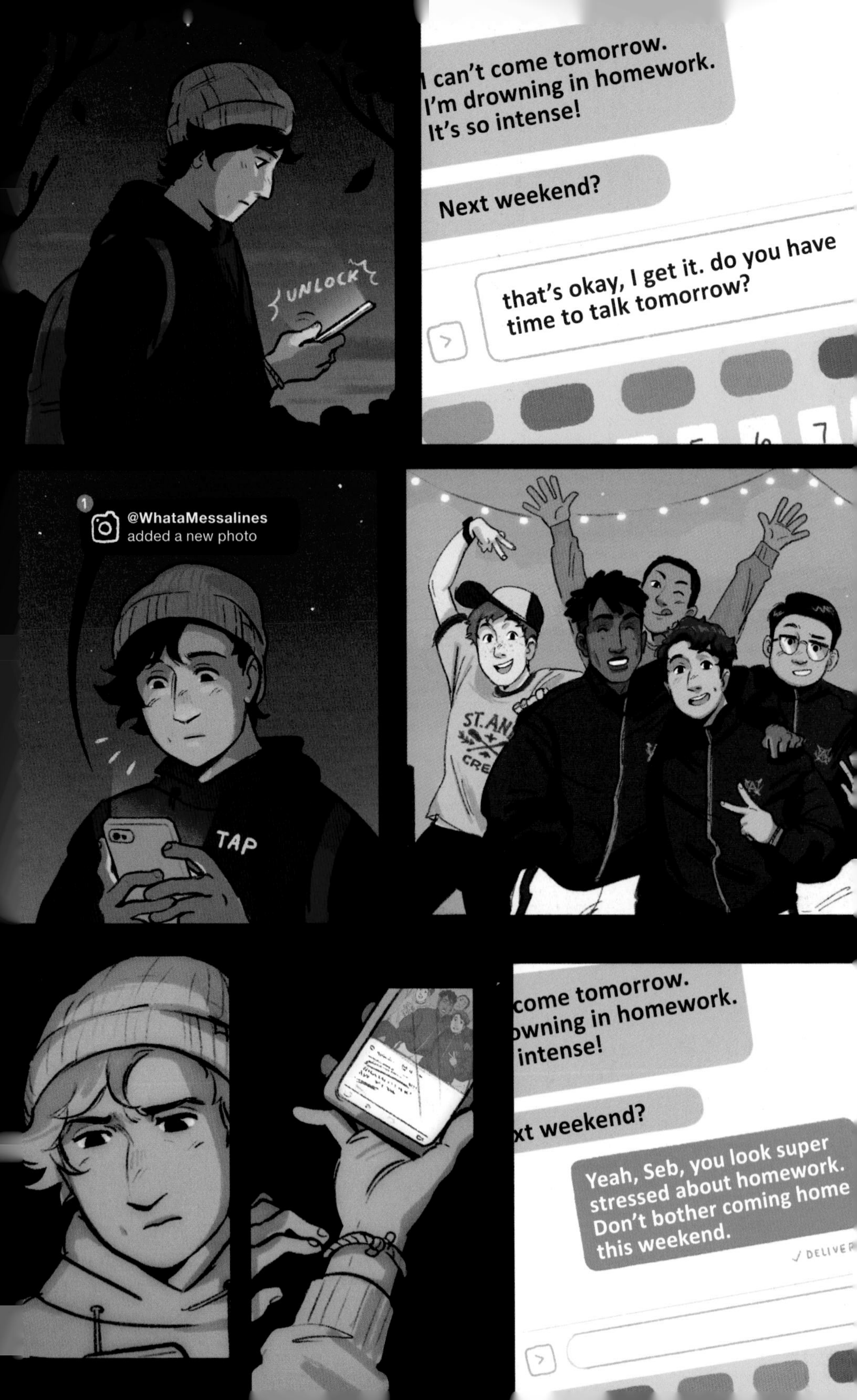
UNLOCK
I can't come tomorrow. I'm drowning in homework. It's so intense!
Next weekend?
that's okay, I get it. do you have time to talk tomorrow?
@WhataMessalines
added a new photo
TAP
ST. AN
come tomorrow.
owning in homework.
intense!
xt weekend?
Yeah, Seb, you look super stressed about homework. Don't bother coming home this weekend.
DELIVE

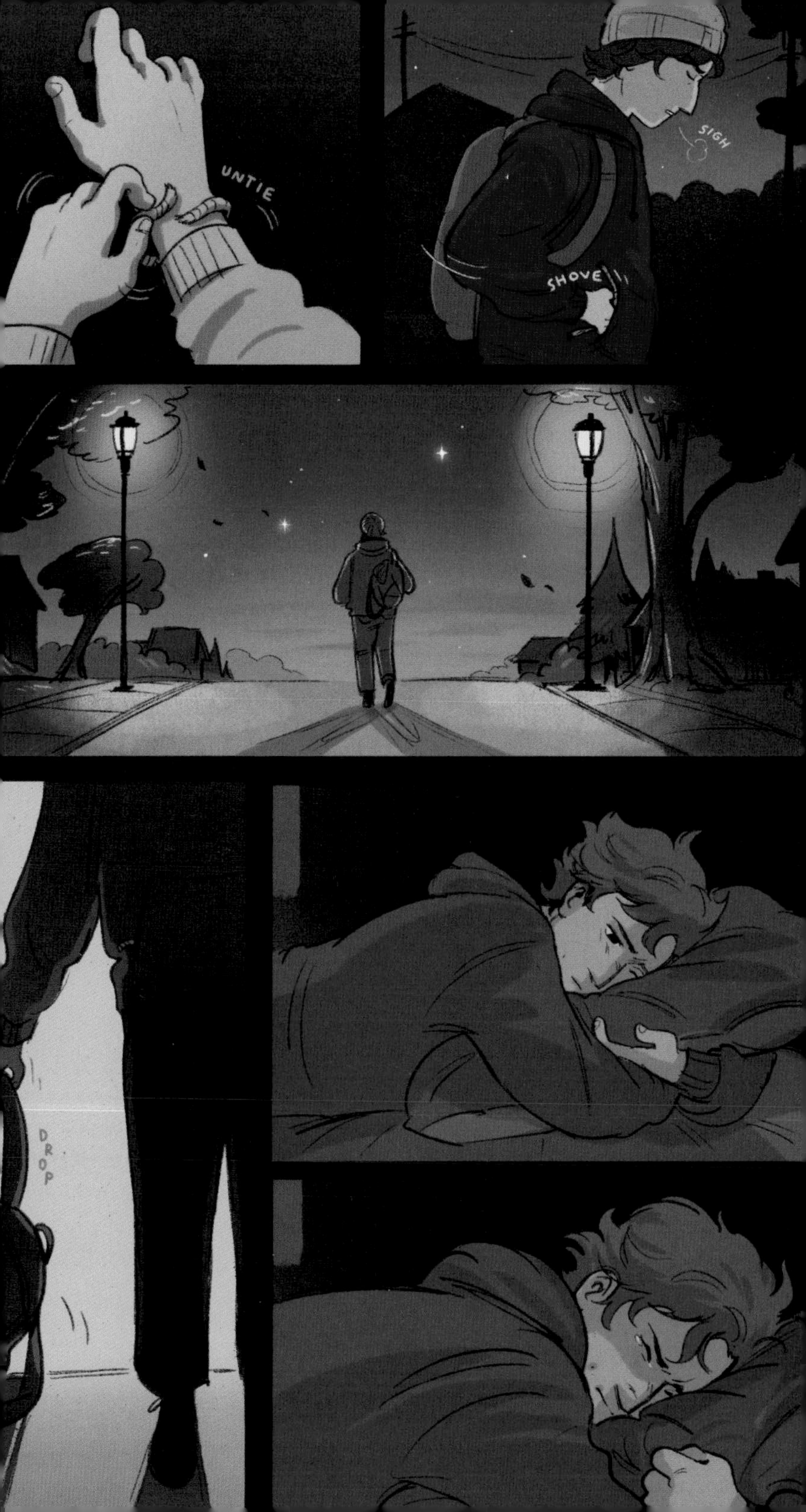
UNTIE
SIGH
SHOVE
DROP

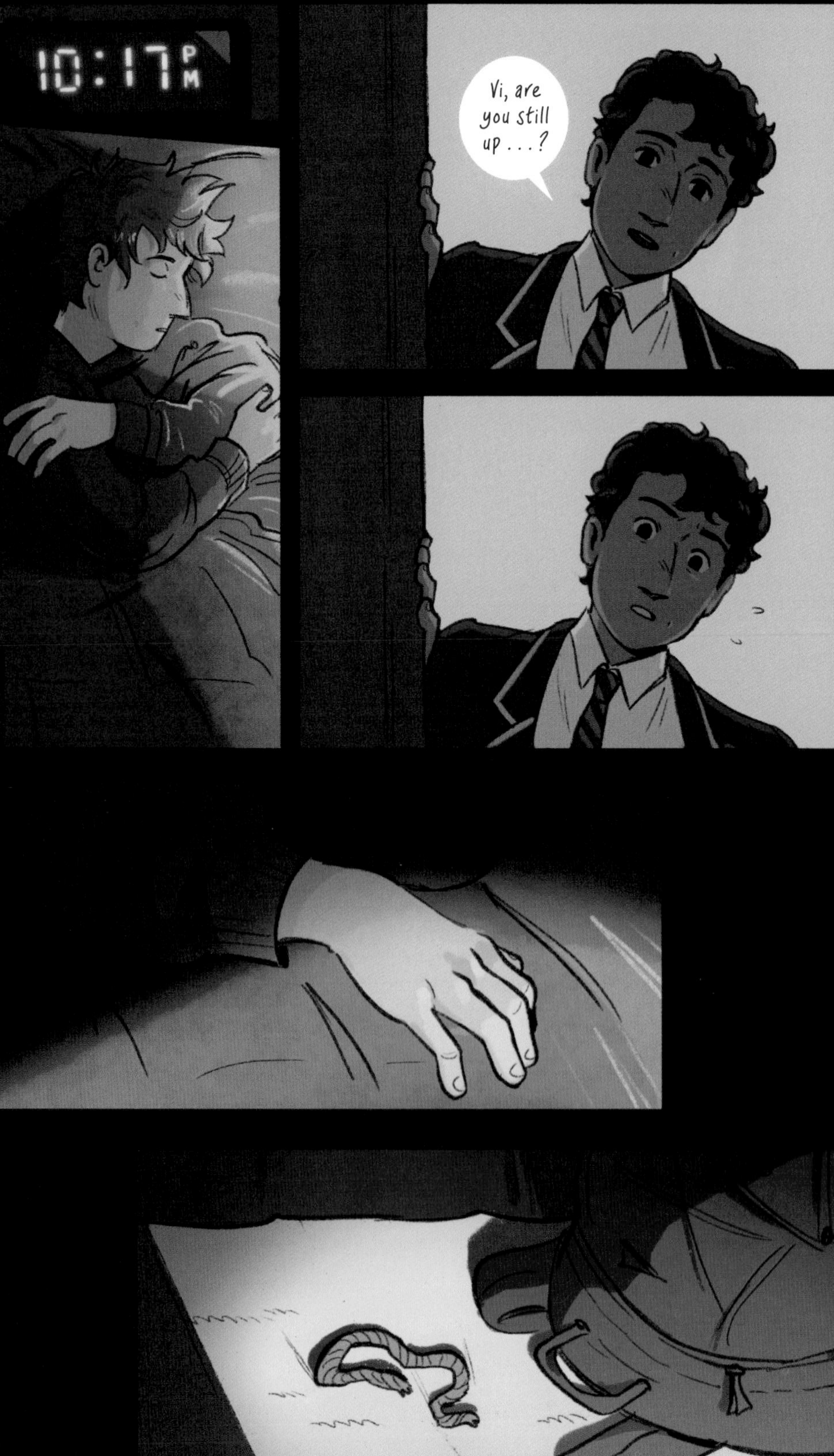
10:17 PM
Vi, are you still up . . . ?

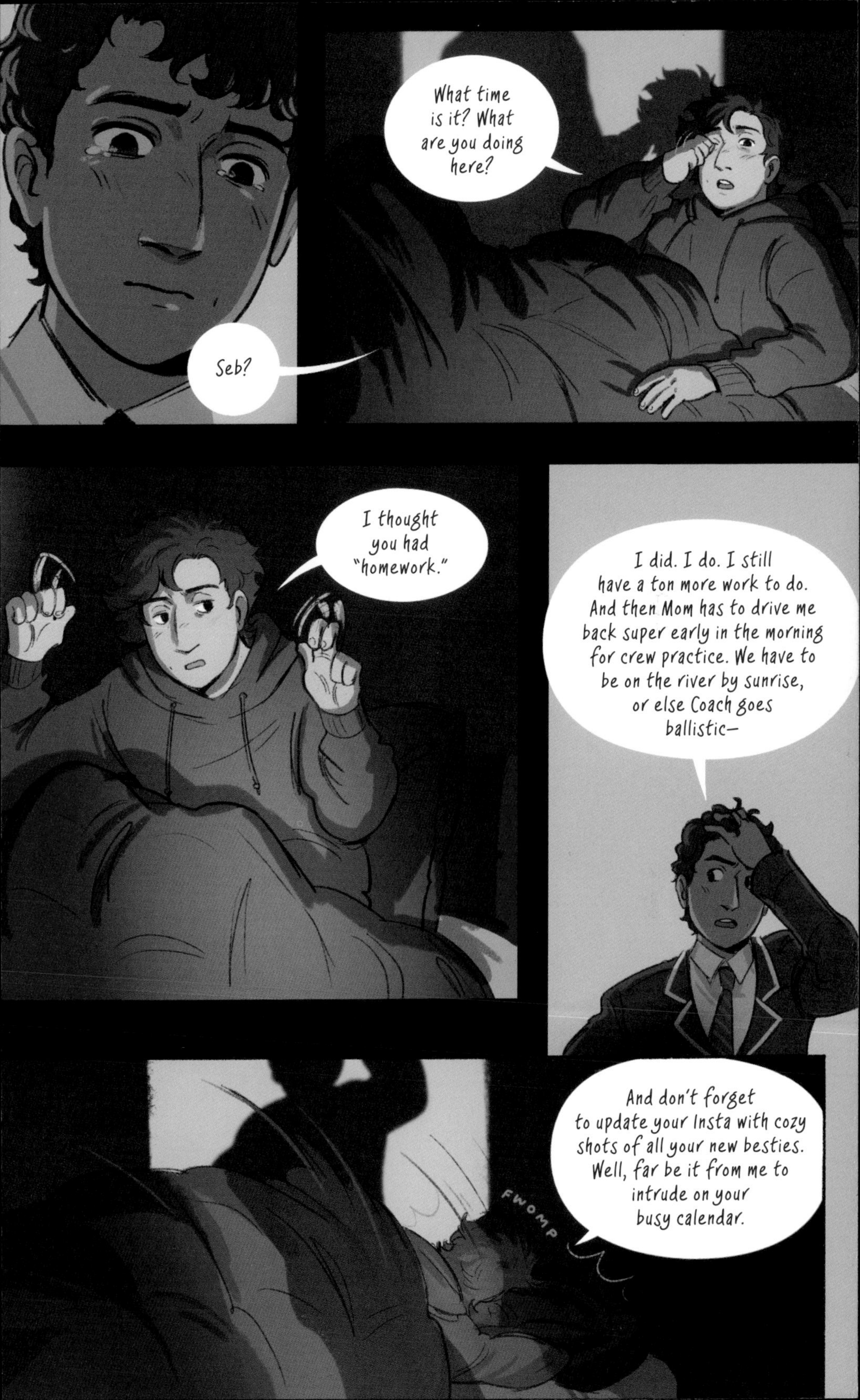
What time is it? What are you doing here?
Seb?
I thought you had "homework."
I did. I do. I still have a ton more work to do. And then Mom has to drive me back super early in the morning for crew practice. We have to be on the river by sunrise, or else Coach goes ballistic—
FWOMP
And don't forget to update your Insta with cozy shots of all your new besties. Well, far be it from me to intrude on your busy calendar.

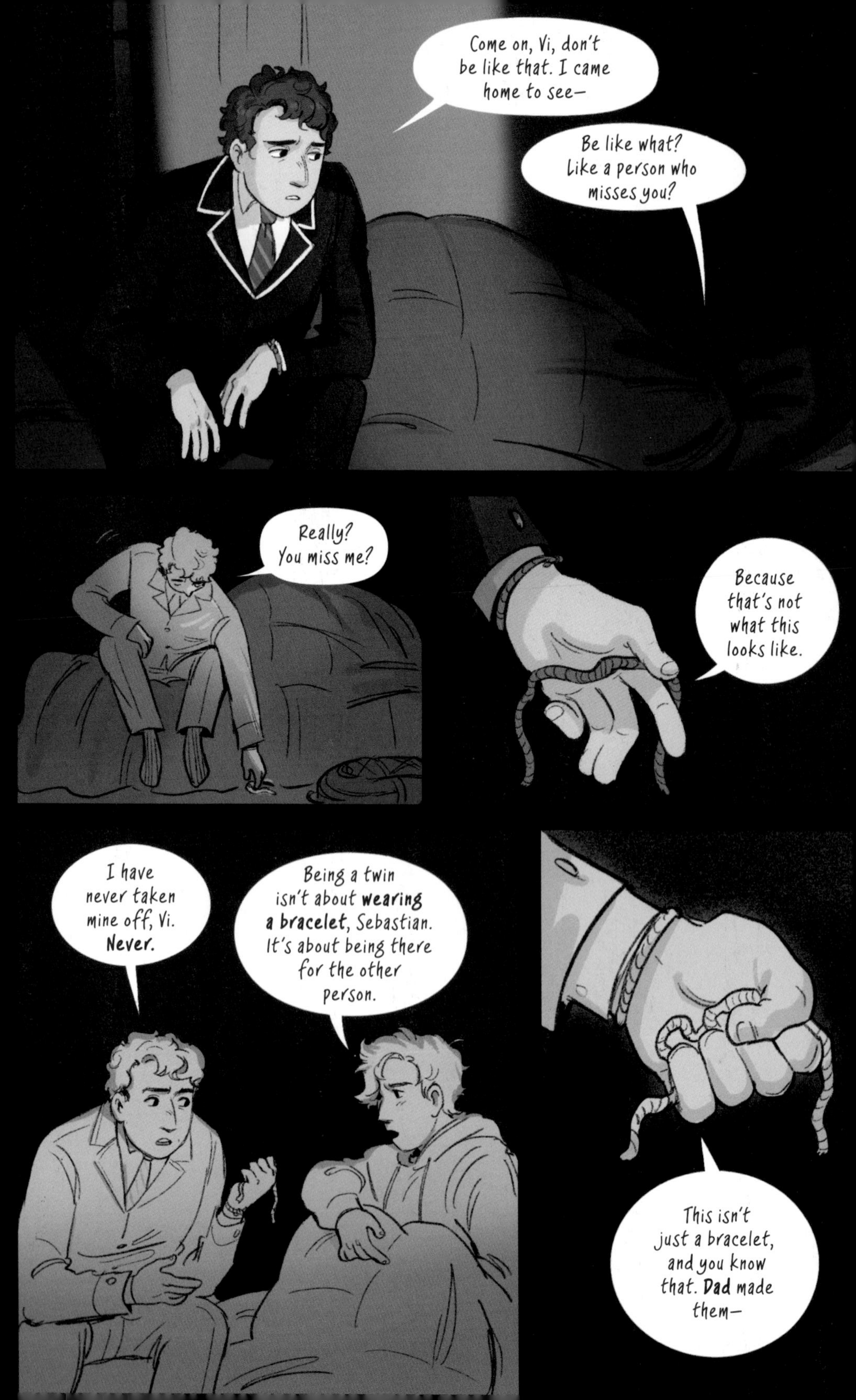
Come on, Vi, don't be like that. I came home to see—
Be like what? Like a person who misses you?
Really? You miss me?
Because that's not what this looks like.
I have never taken mine off, Vi. **Never.**
Being a twin isn't about **wearing a bracelet**, Sebastian. It's about being there for the other person.
This isn't just a bracelet, and you know that. **Dad** made them—

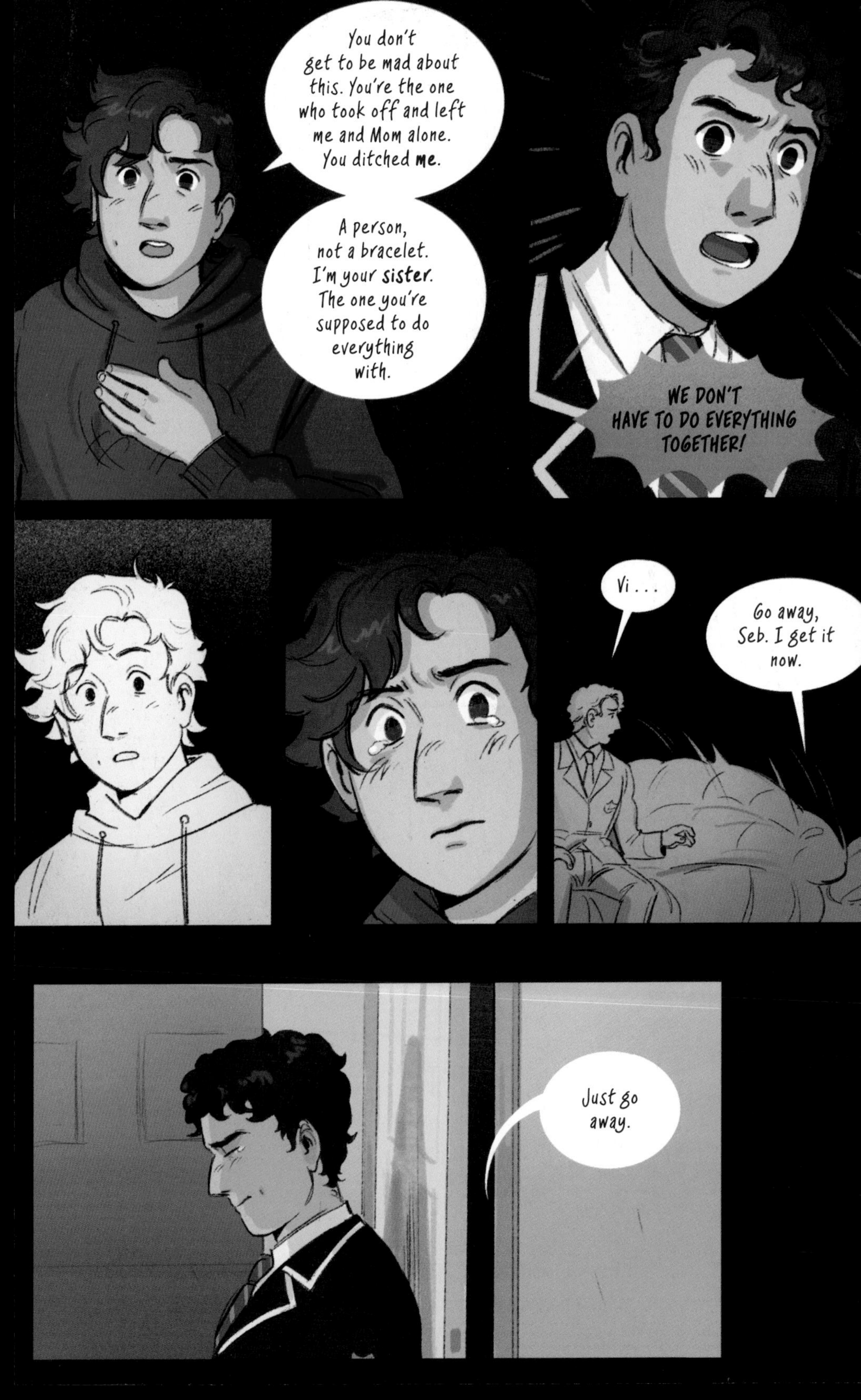
You don't get to be mad about this. You're the one who took off and left me and Mom alone. You ditched **me**.
A person, not a bracelet. I'm your **sister**. The one you're supposed to do everything with.
WE DON'T HAVE TO DO EVERYTHING TOGETHER!
Vi . . .
Go away, Seb. I get it now.
Just go away.

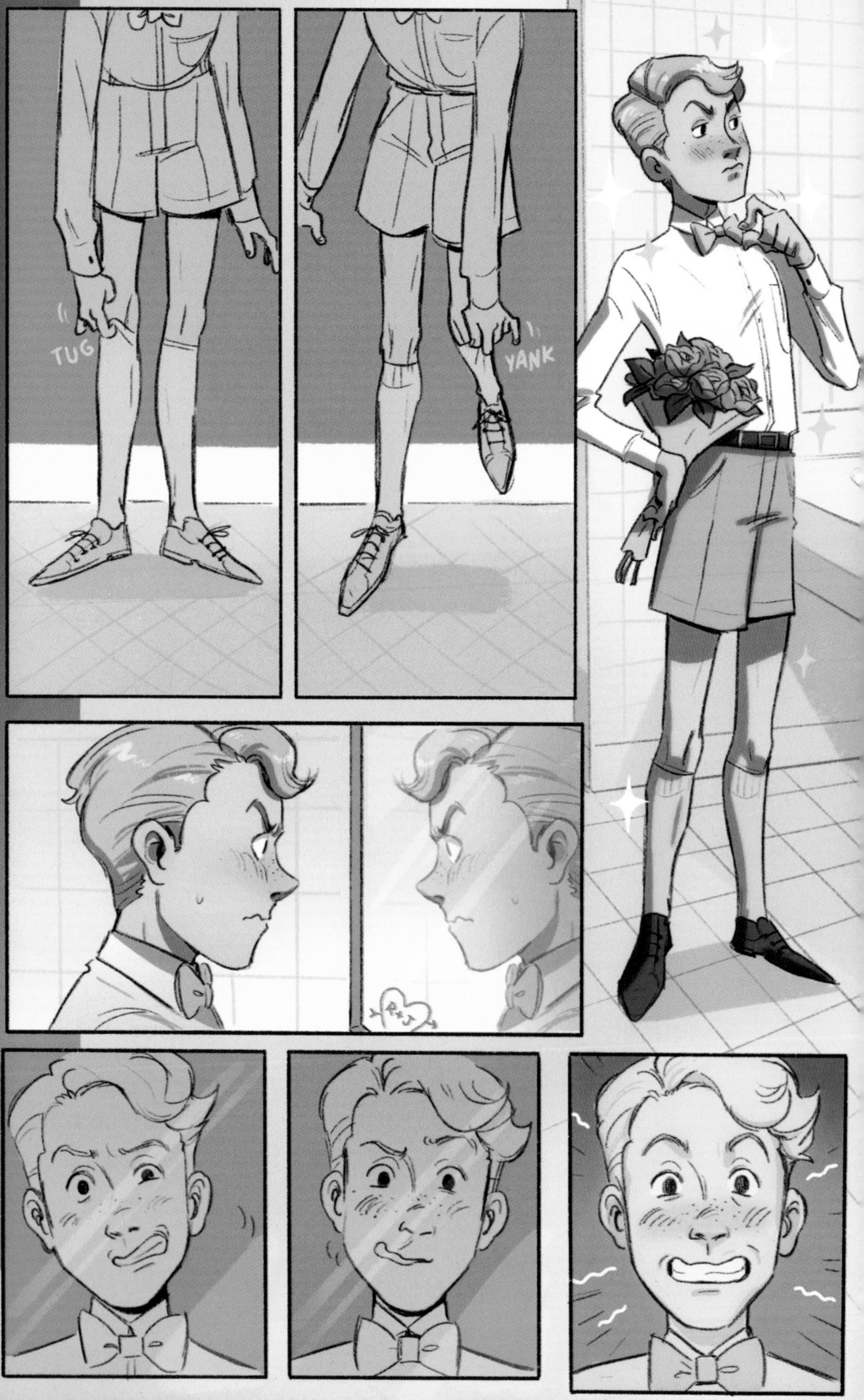
TUG
YANK

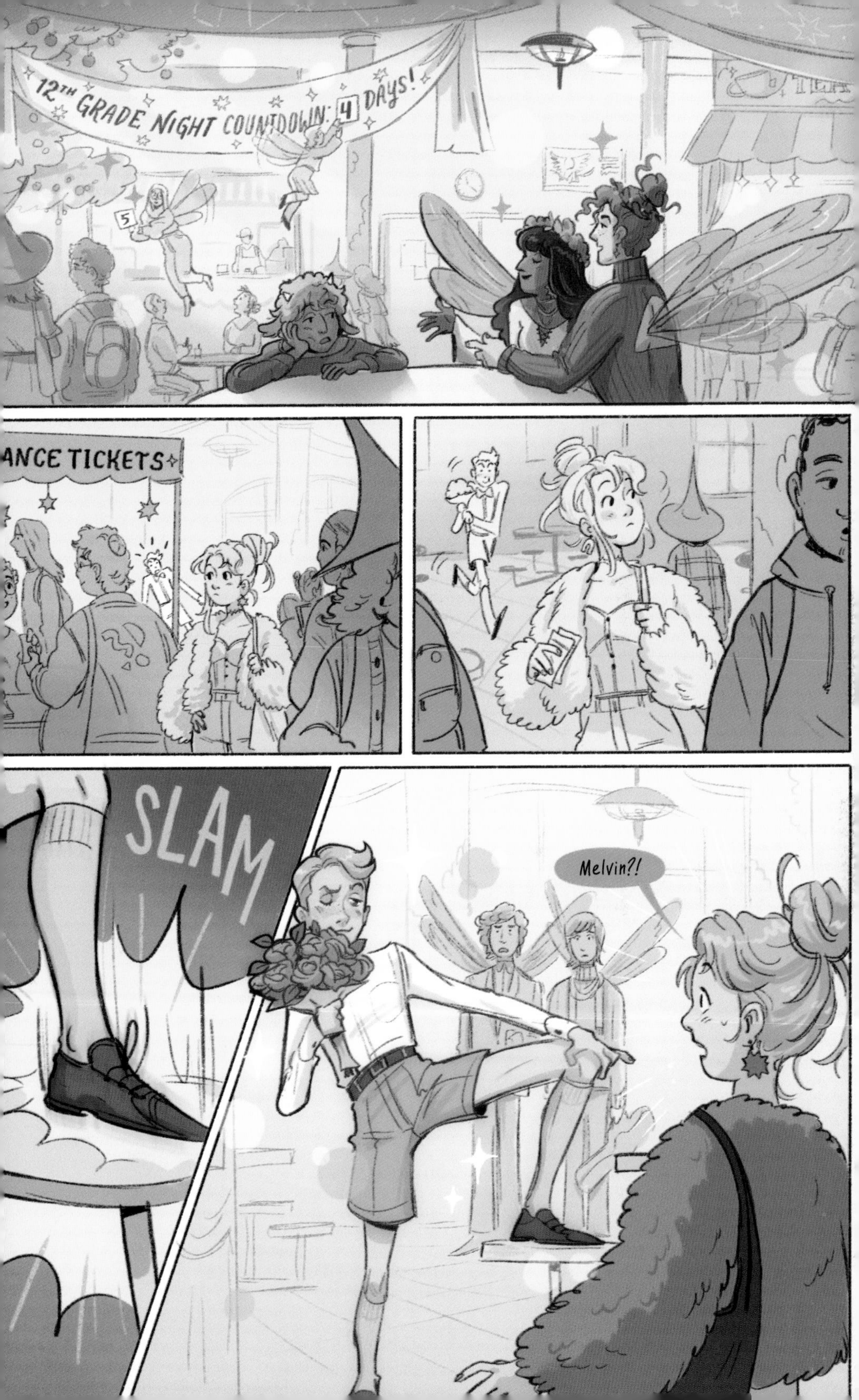
12TH GRADE NIGHT COUNTDOWN: 4 DAYS!
5
ANCE TICKETS
SLAM
Melvin?!

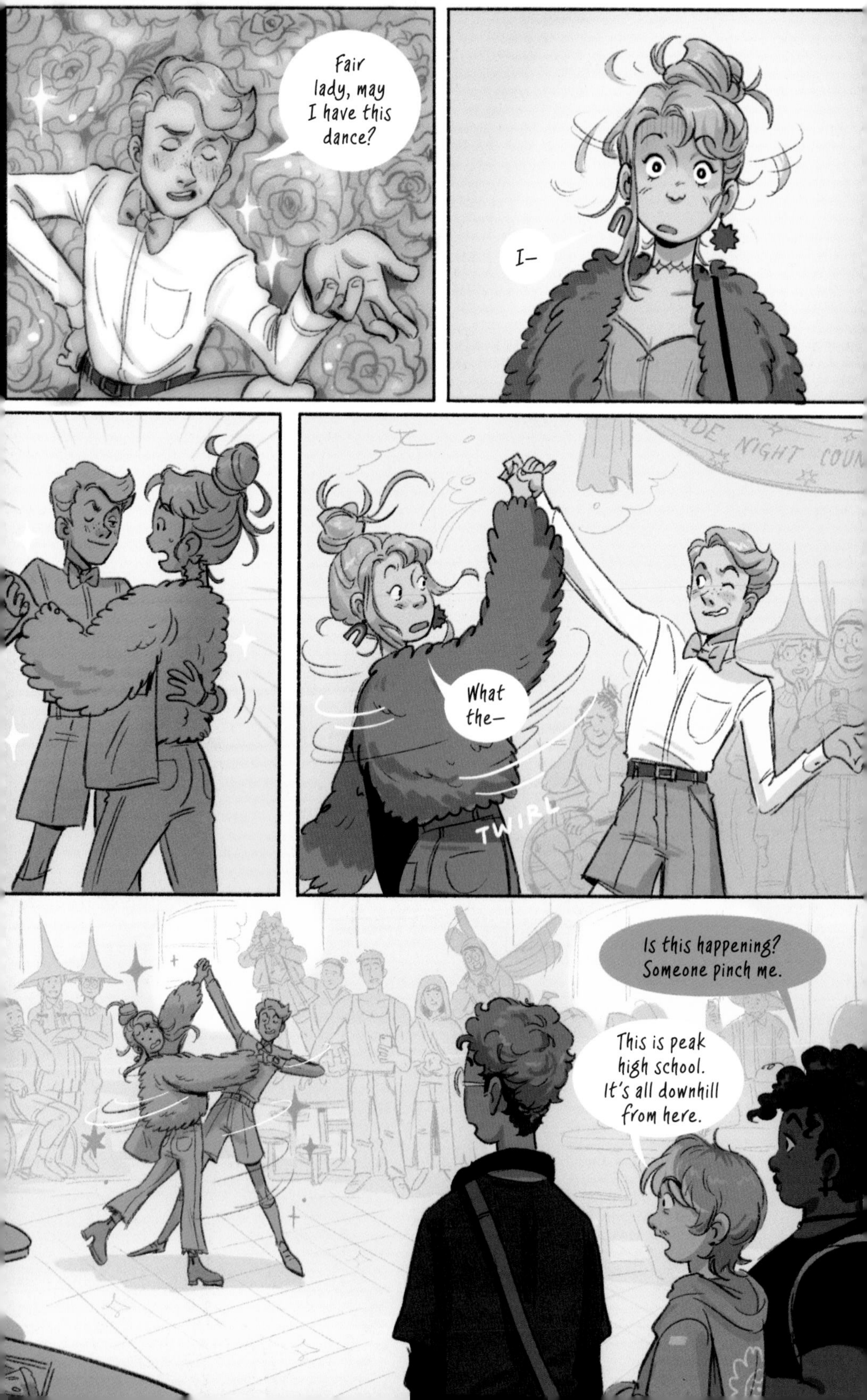

Fair lady, may I have this dance?
I—
ADE NIGHT COUN
What the—
TWIRL
Is this happening? Someone pinch me.
This is peak high school. It's all downhill from here.

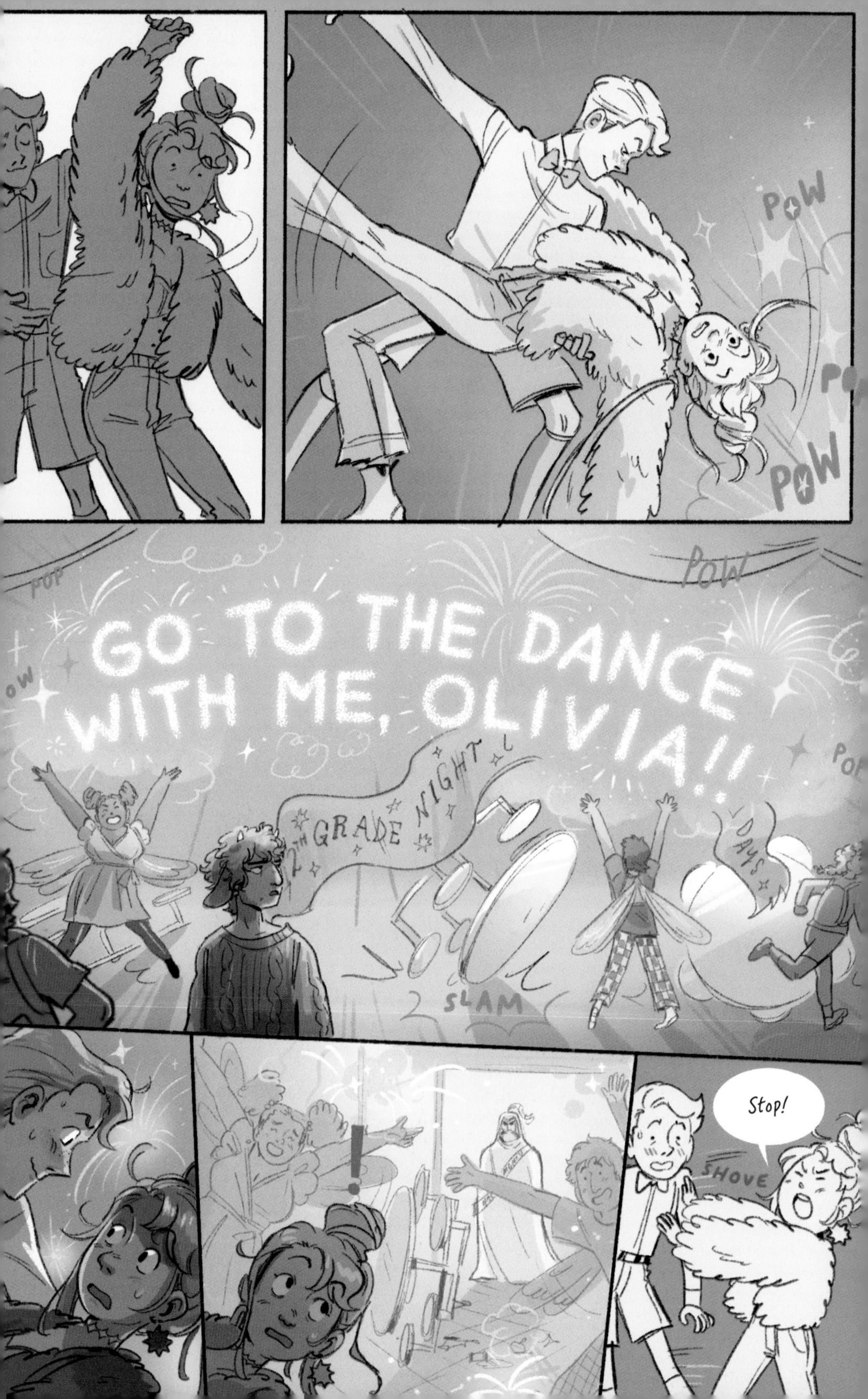
POW
POW
GO TO THE DANCE WITH ME, OLIVIA!!
POP
POW
GRADE NIGHT
SLAM
!
Stop!
SHOVE

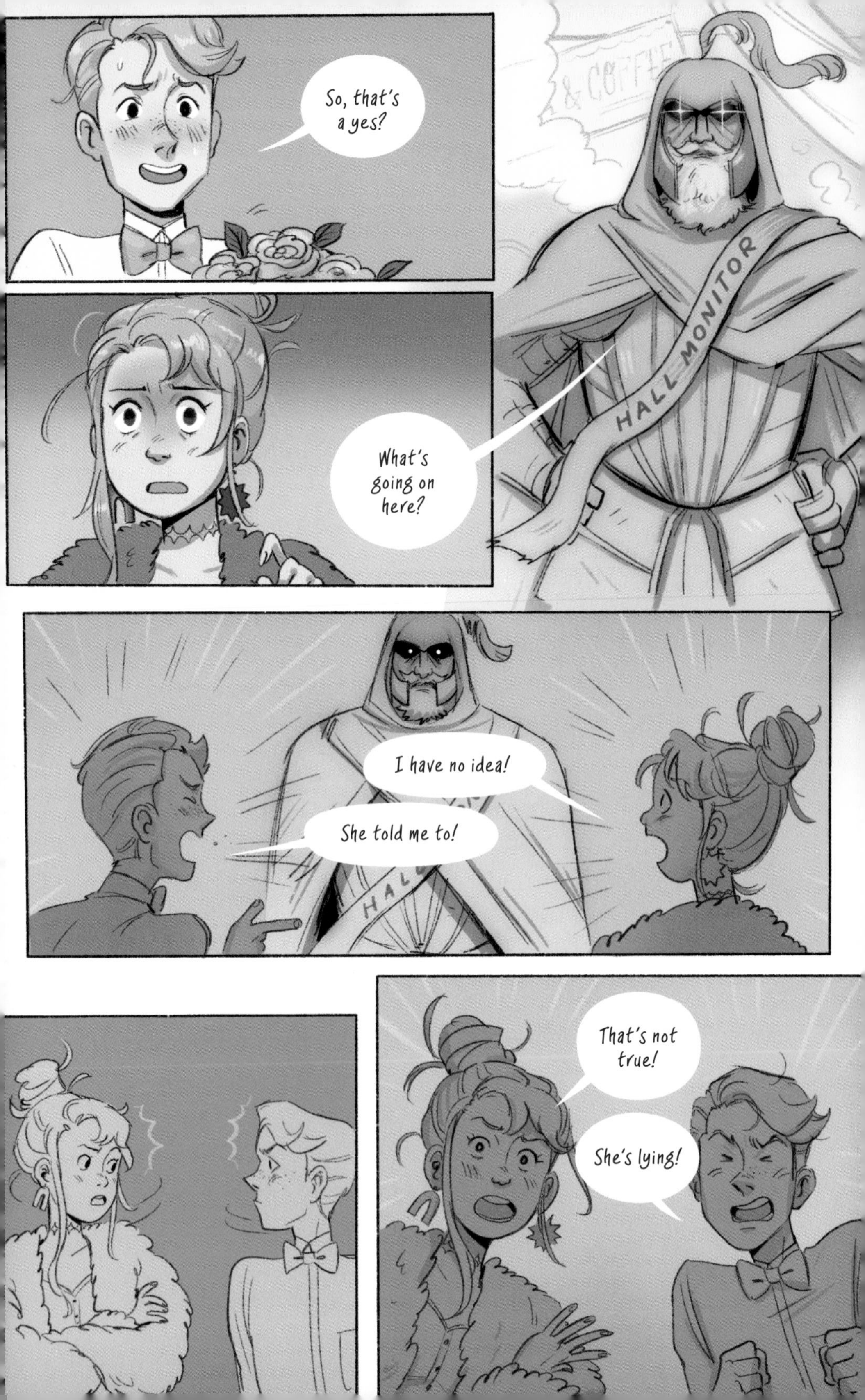
So, that's a yes?
&COFFEE
HALL MONITOR
What's going on here?
I have no idea!
She told me to!
That's not true!
She's lying!

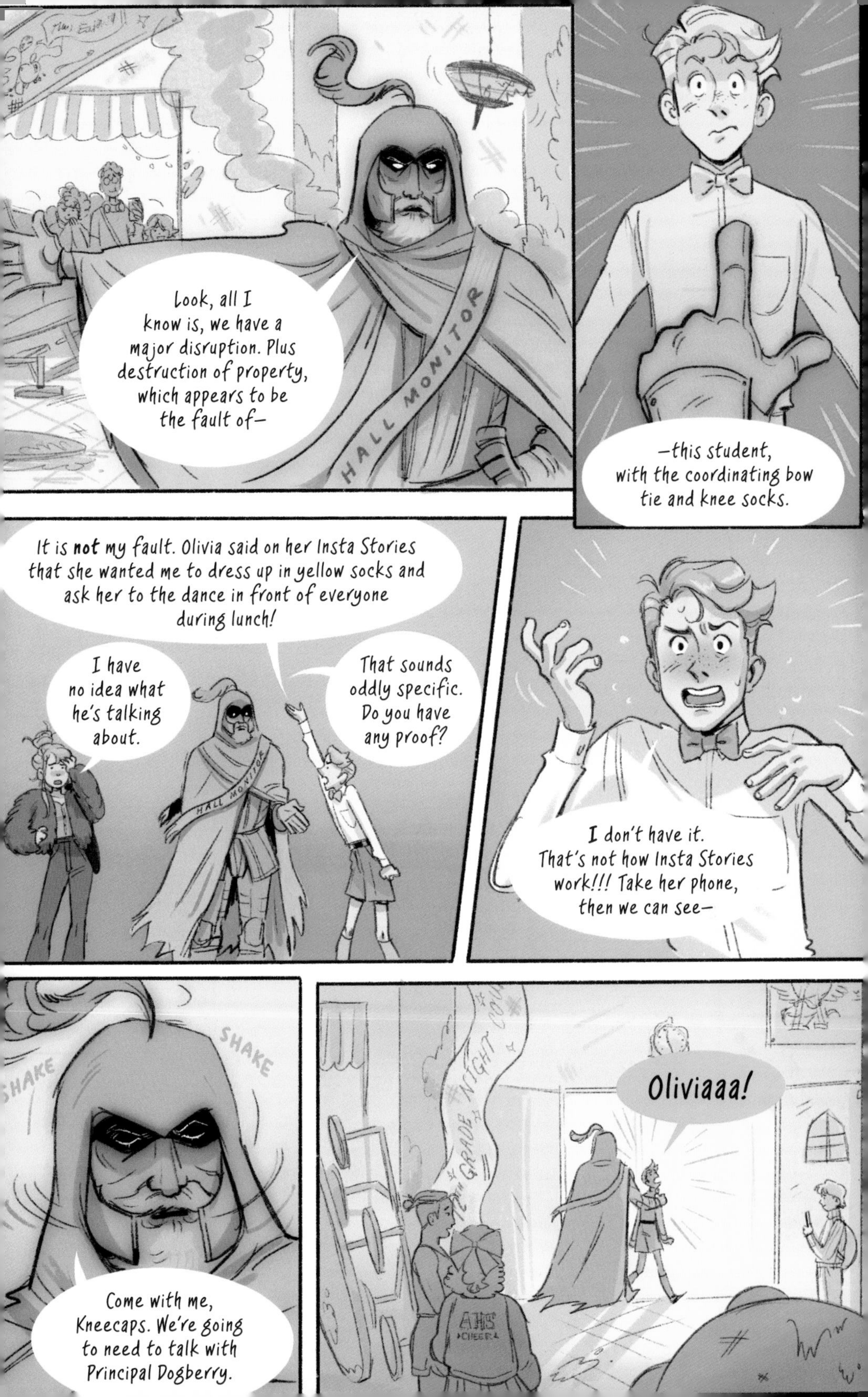
Look, all I know is, we have a major disruption. Plus destruction of property, which appears to be the fault of–
HALL MONITOR
–this student, with the coordinating bow tie and knee socks.
It is **not** my fault. Olivia said on her Insta Stories that she wanted me to dress up in yellow socks and ask her to the dance in front of everyone during lunch!
I have no idea what he's talking about.
That sounds oddly specific. Do you have any proof?
HALL MONITOR
I don't have it. That's not how Insta Stories work!!! Take her phone, then we can see–
SHAKE
SHAKE
Come with me, Kneecaps. We're going to need to talk with Principal Dogberry.
Oliviaaa!

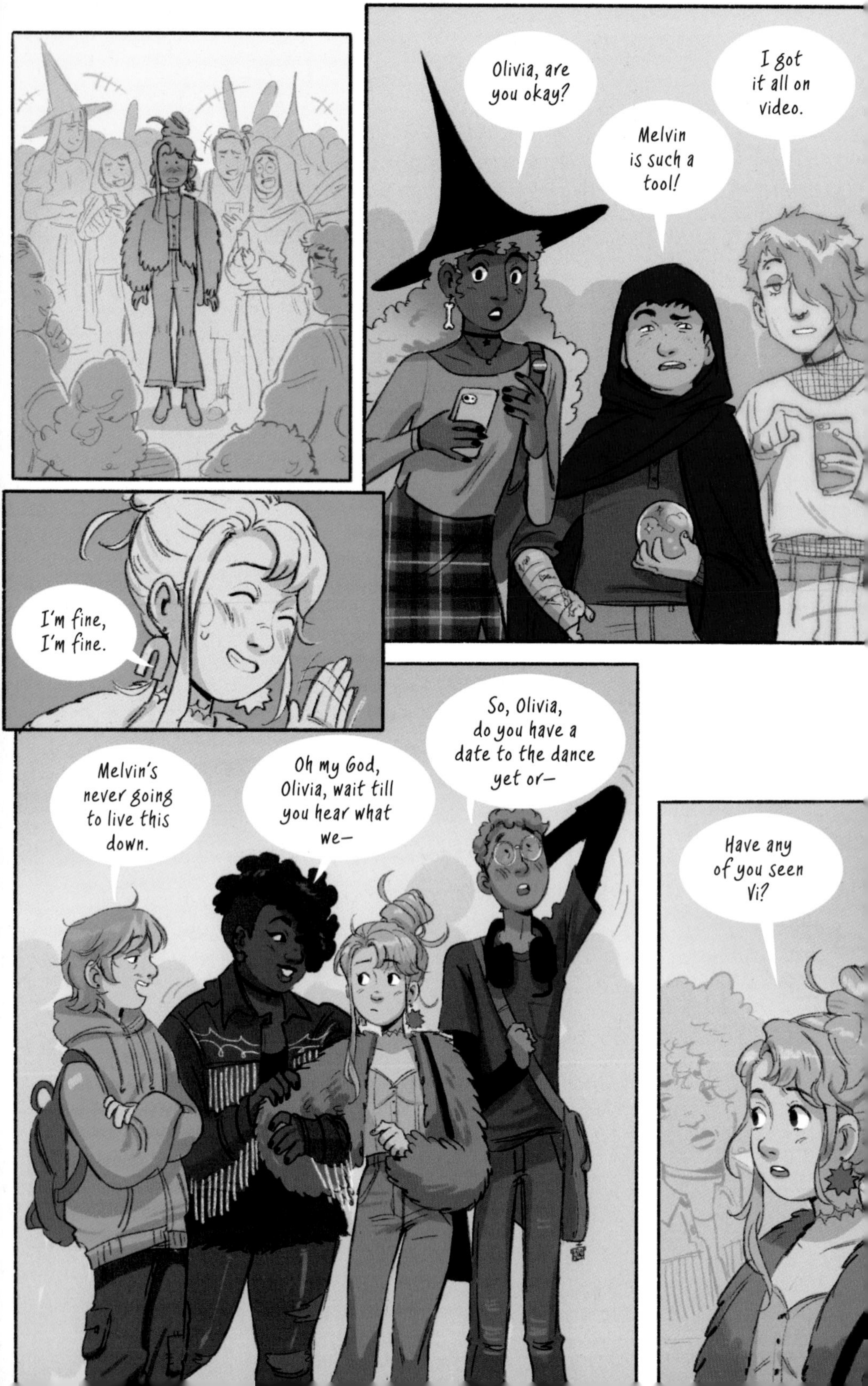
Olivia, are you okay?
Melvin is such a tool!
I got it all on video.
I'm fine, I'm fine.
Melvin's never going to live this down.
Oh my God, Olivia, wait till you hear what we—
So, Olivia, do you have a date to the dance yet or—
Have any of you seen Vi?

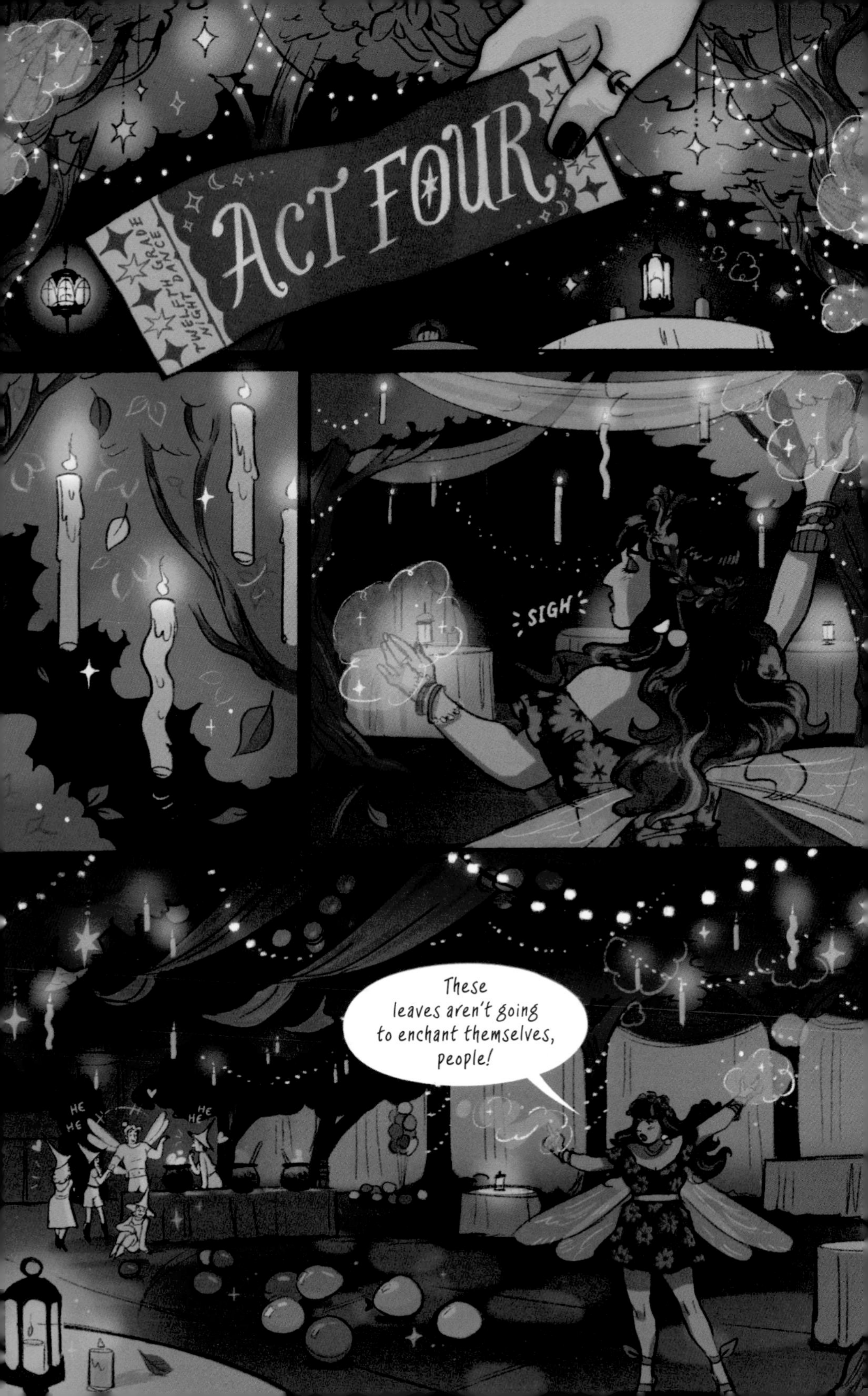
TWELFTH GRADE NIGHT DANCE
ACT FOUR
SIGH
HE HE
HE HE
These leaves aren't going to enchant themselves, people!

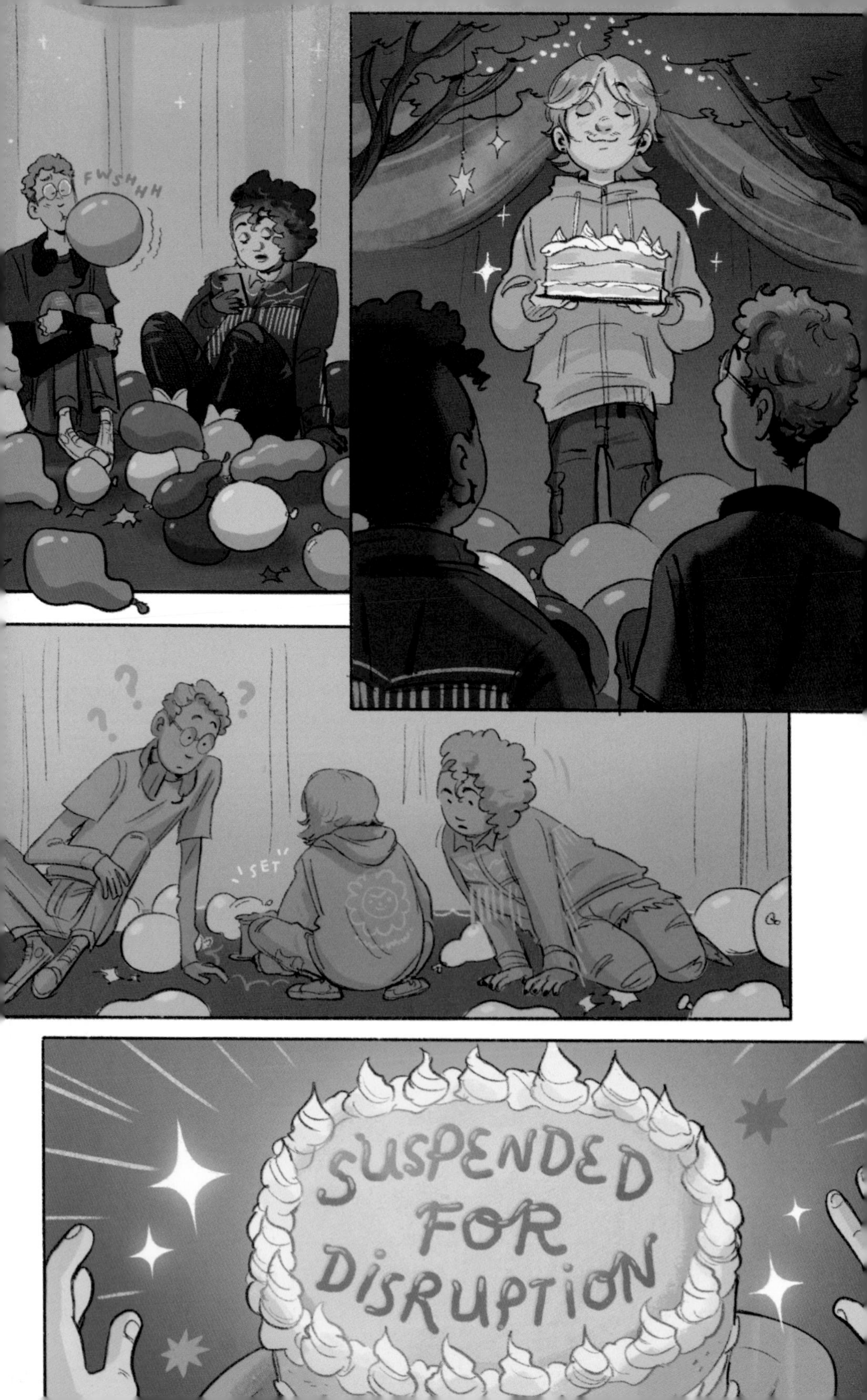
FWSHHH
SET
SUSPENDED FOR DISRUPTION

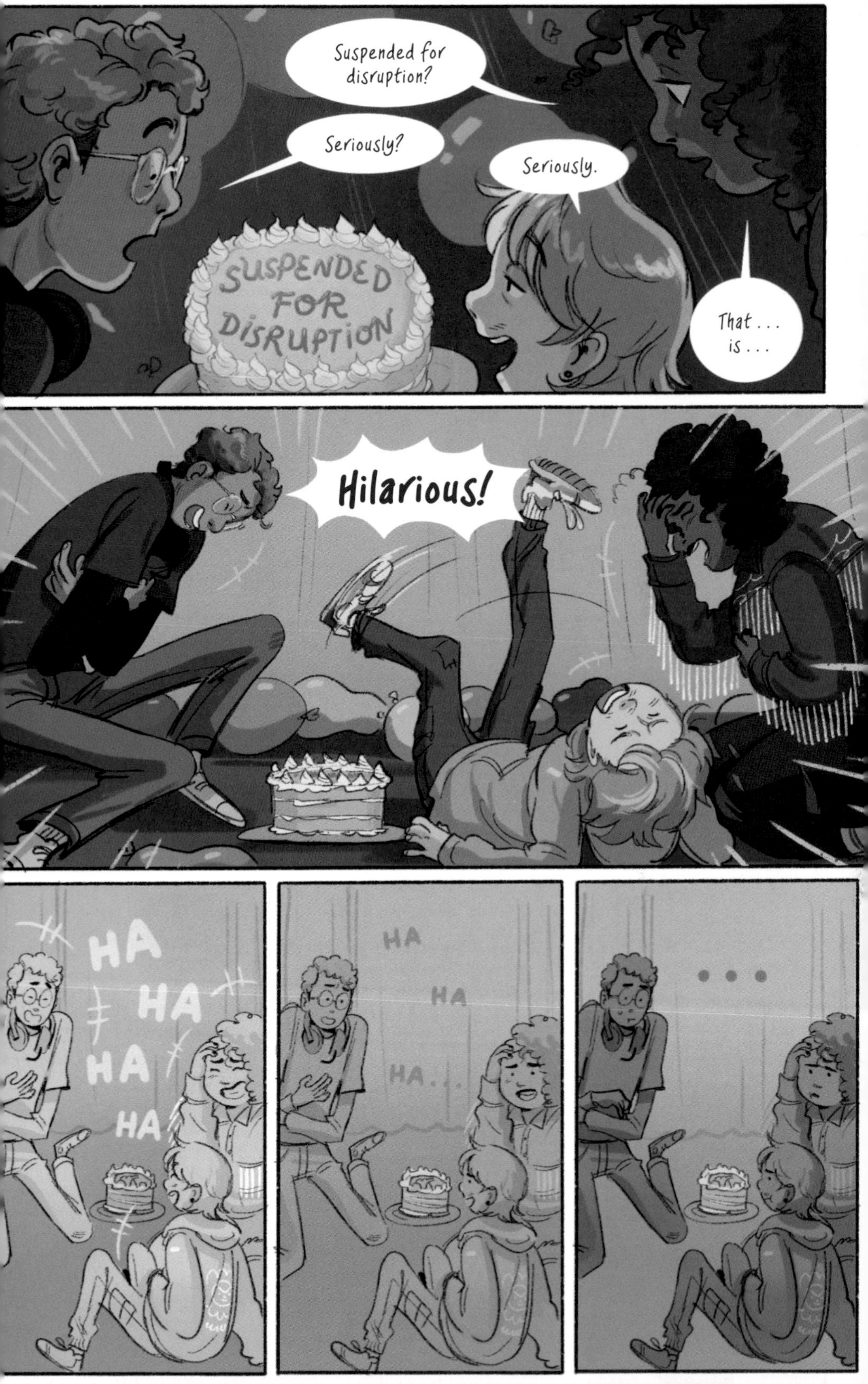
Suspended for disruption?
Seriously?
Seriously.
SUSPENDED FOR DISRUPTION
That . . . is . . .
Hilarious!
HA HA HA HA
HA HA HA. . .
. . .

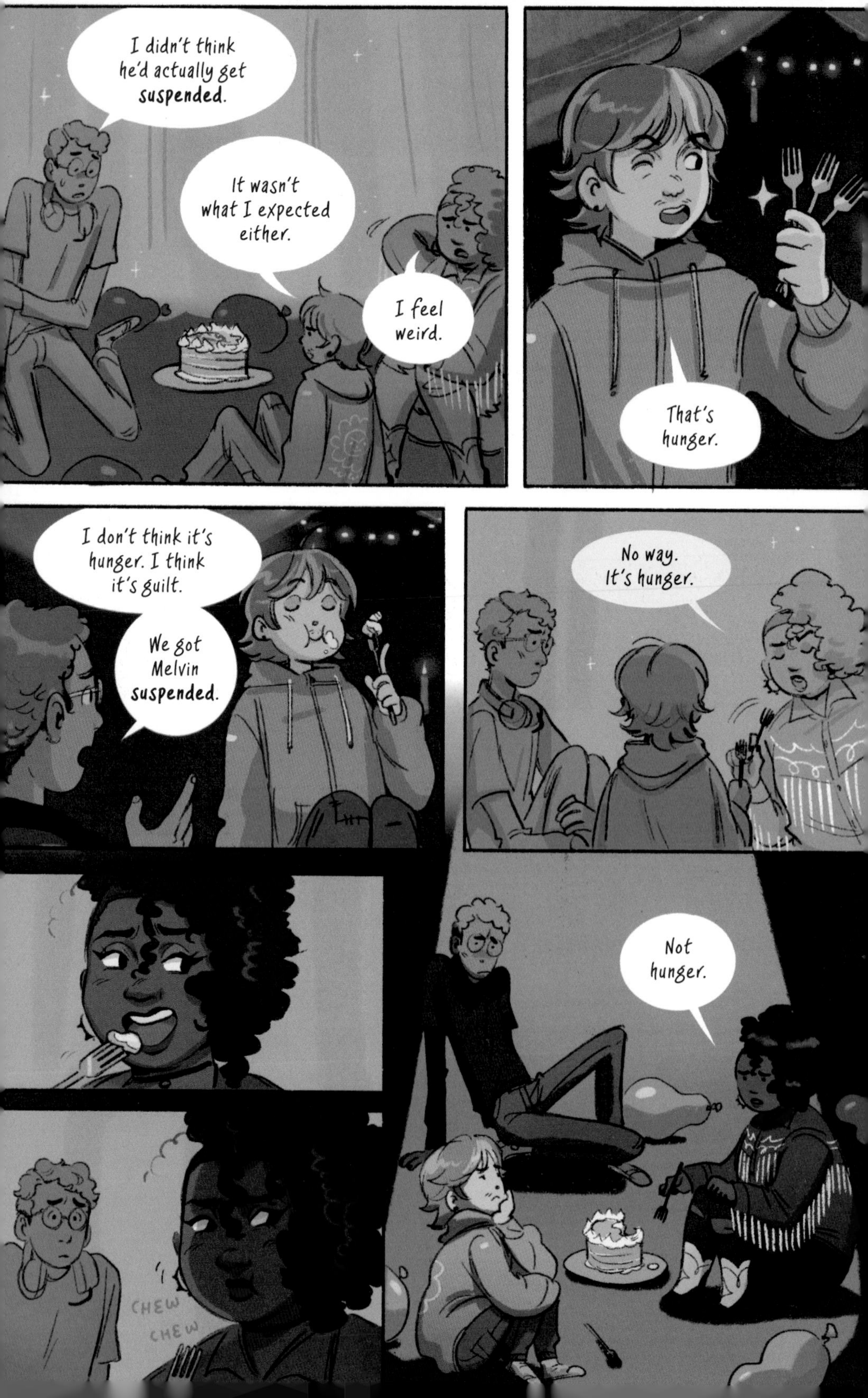
I didn't think he'd actually get suspended.
It wasn't what I expected either.
I feel weird.
That's hunger.
I don't think it's hunger. I think it's guilt.
We got Melvin suspended.
No way. It's hunger.
CHEW
CHEW
Not hunger.

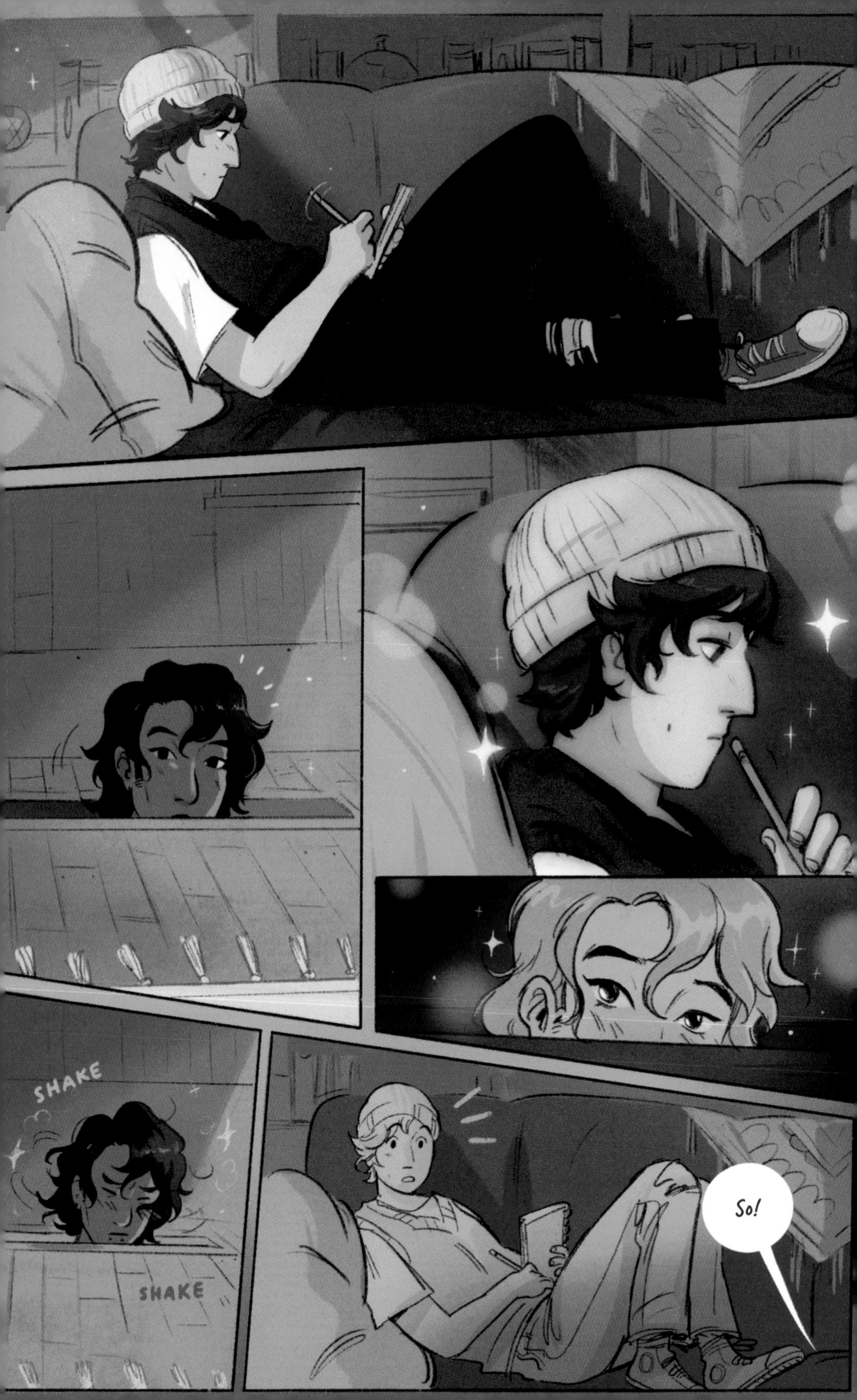
SHAKE
SHAKE
So!

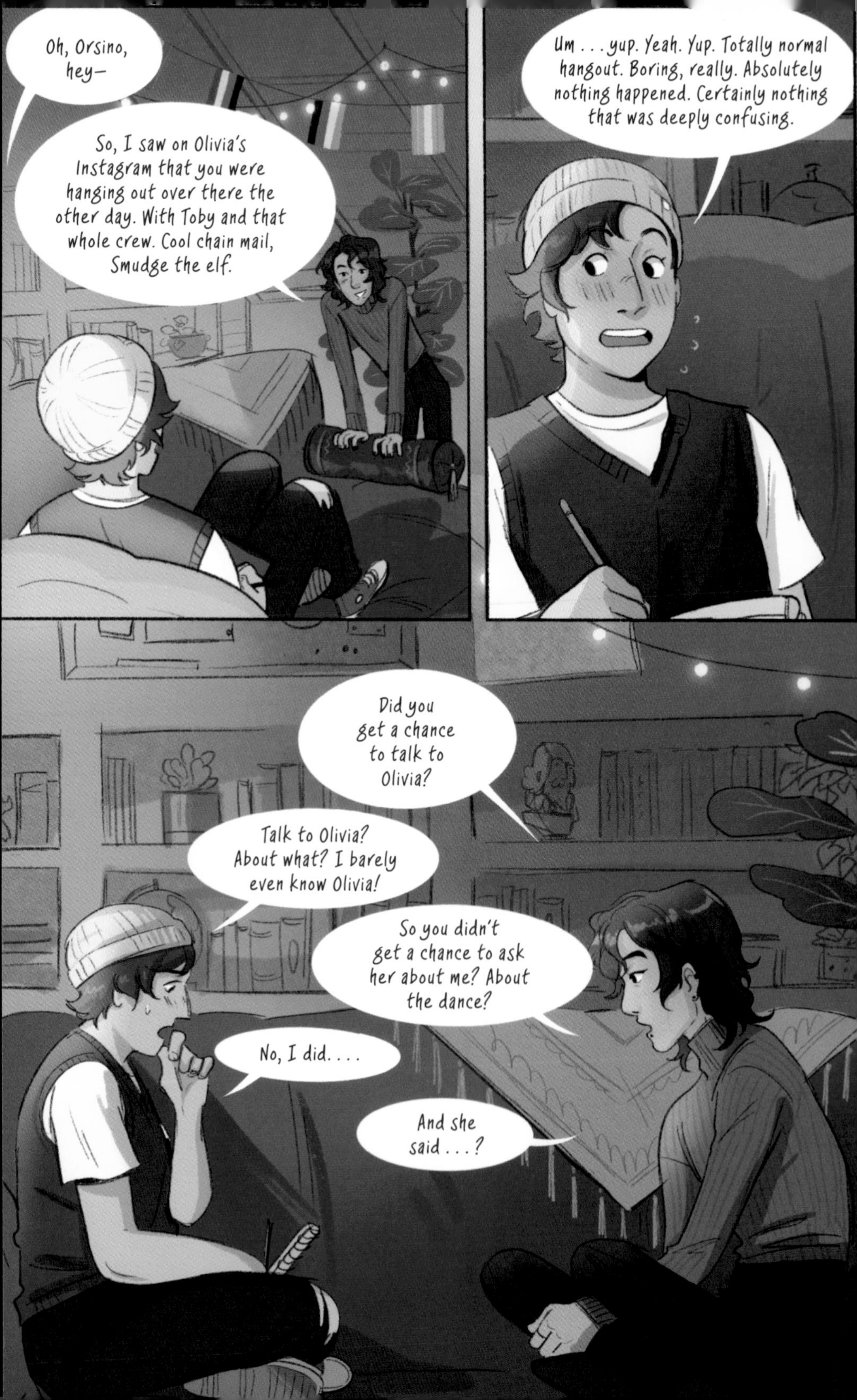
Oh, Orsino, hey—
So, I saw on Olivia's Instagram that you were hanging out over there the other day. With Toby and that whole crew. Cool chain mail, Smudge the elf.
Um . . . yup. Yeah. Yup. Totally normal hangout. Boring, really. Absolutely nothing happened. Certainly nothing that was deeply confusing.
Did you get a chance to talk to Olivia?
Talk to Olivia? About what? I barely even know Olivia!
So you didn't get a chance to ask her about me? About the dance?
No, I did. . . .
And she said . . . ?

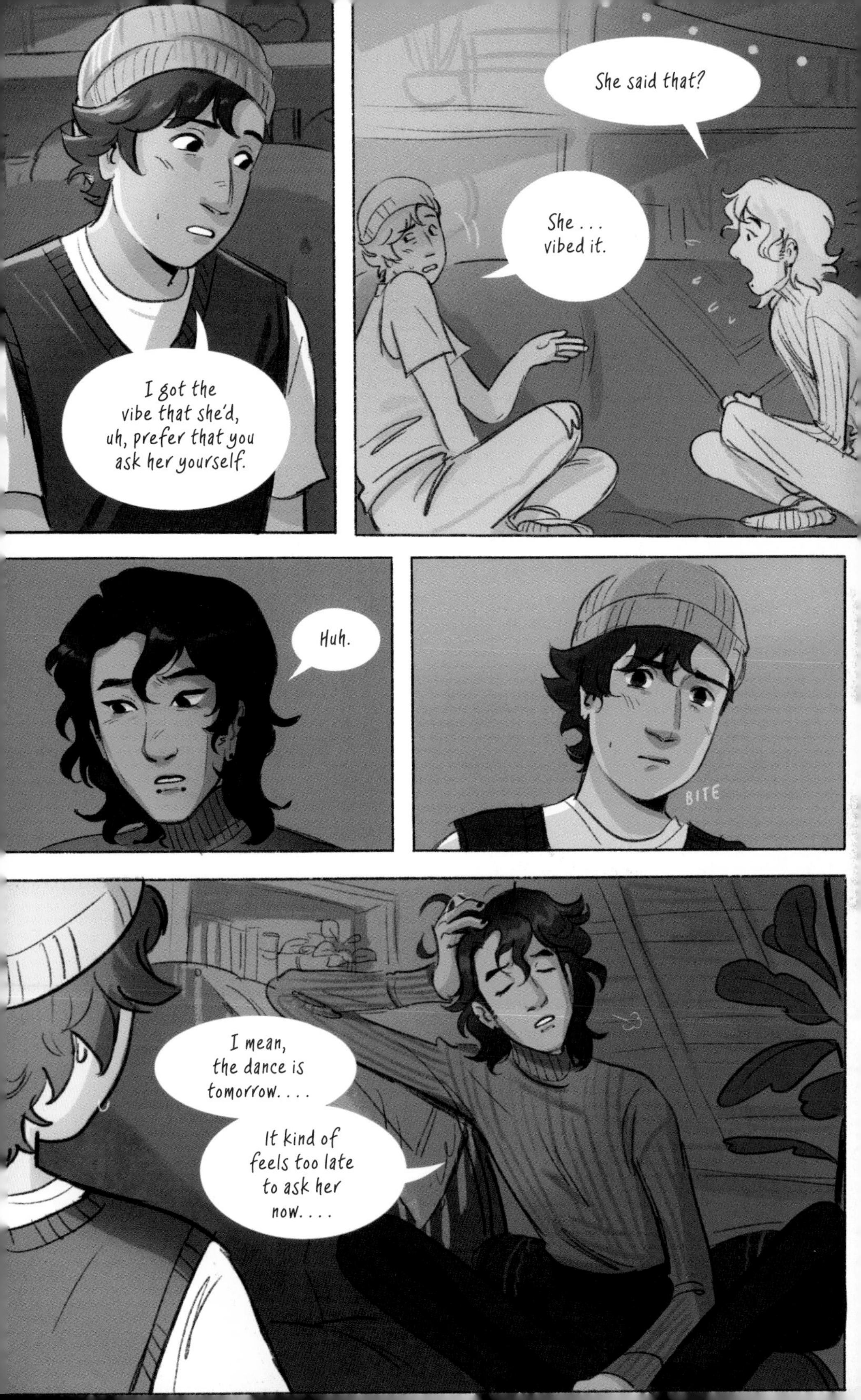
I got the vibe that she'd, uh, prefer that you ask her yourself.
She said that?
She . . . vibed it.
Huh.
BITE
I mean, the dance is tomorrow. . . .
It kind of feels too late to ask her now. . . .

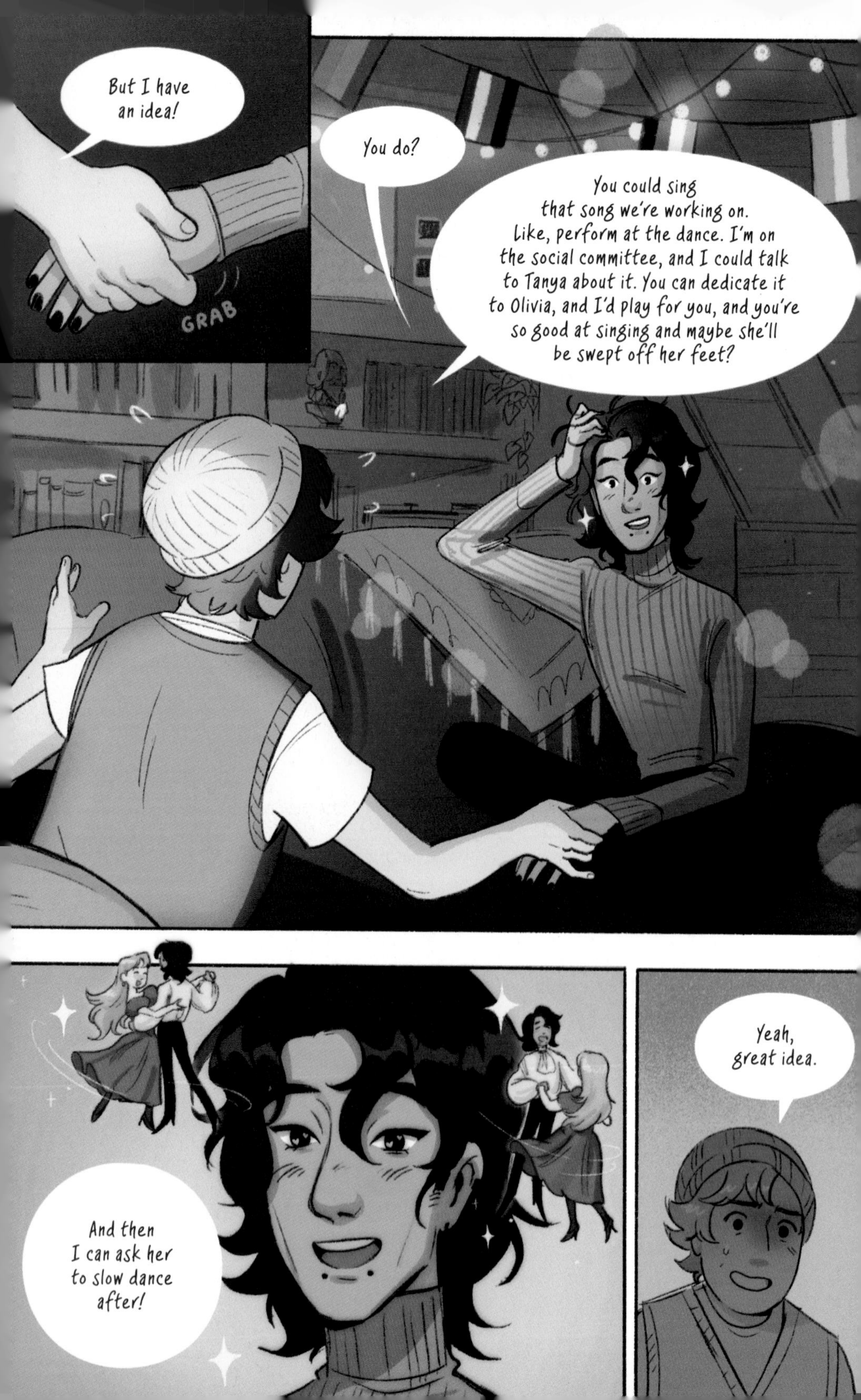
But I have an idea!
GRAB
You do?
You could sing that song we're working on. Like, perform at the dance. I'm on the social committee, and I could talk to Tanya about it. You can dedicate it to Olivia, and I'd play for you, and you're so good at singing and maybe she'll be swept off her feet?
And then I can ask her to slow dance after!
Yeah, great idea.

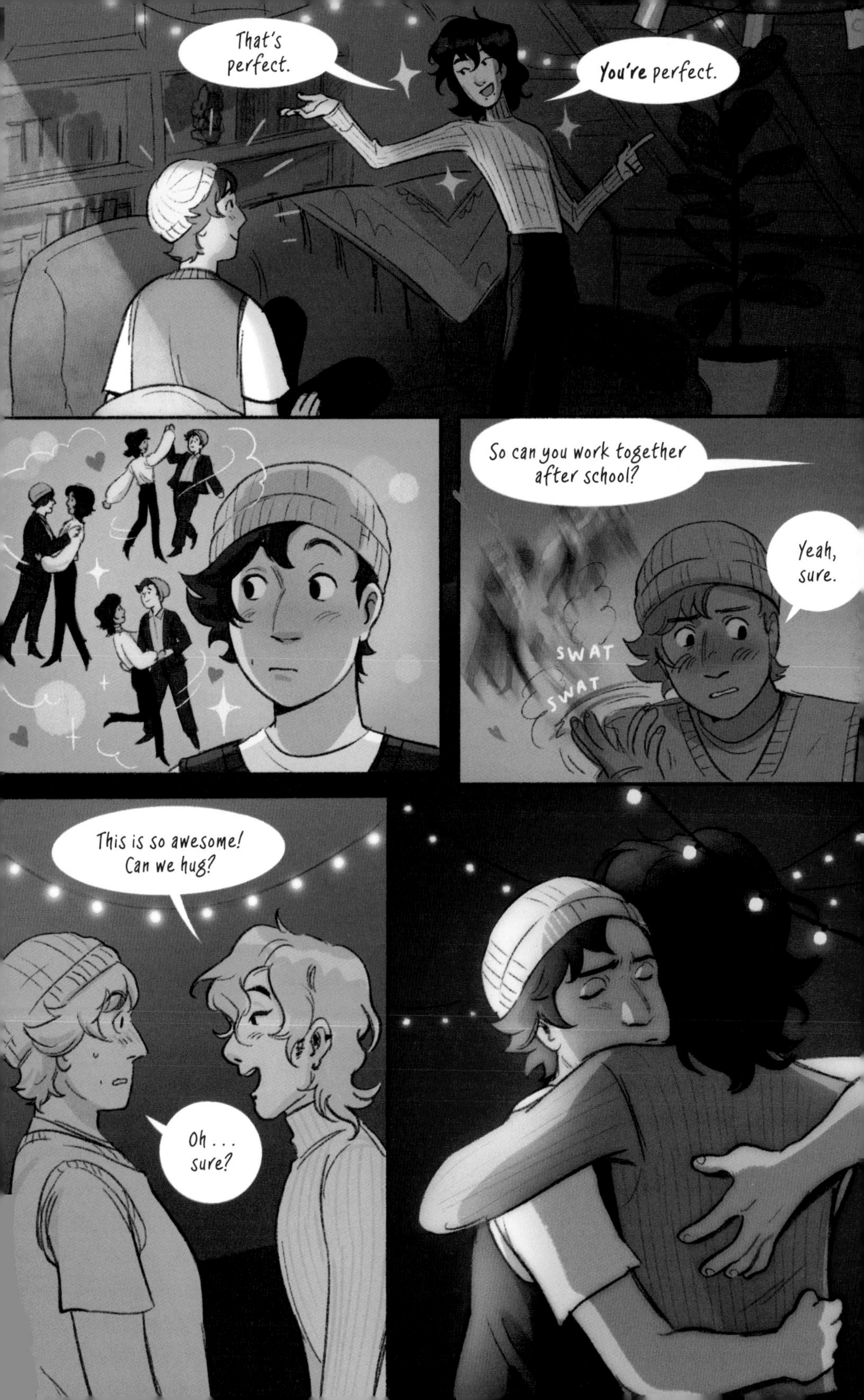
That's perfect.
You're perfect.
So can you work together after school?
Yeah, sure.
SWAT
SWAT
This is so awesome! Can we hug?
Oh . . . sure?

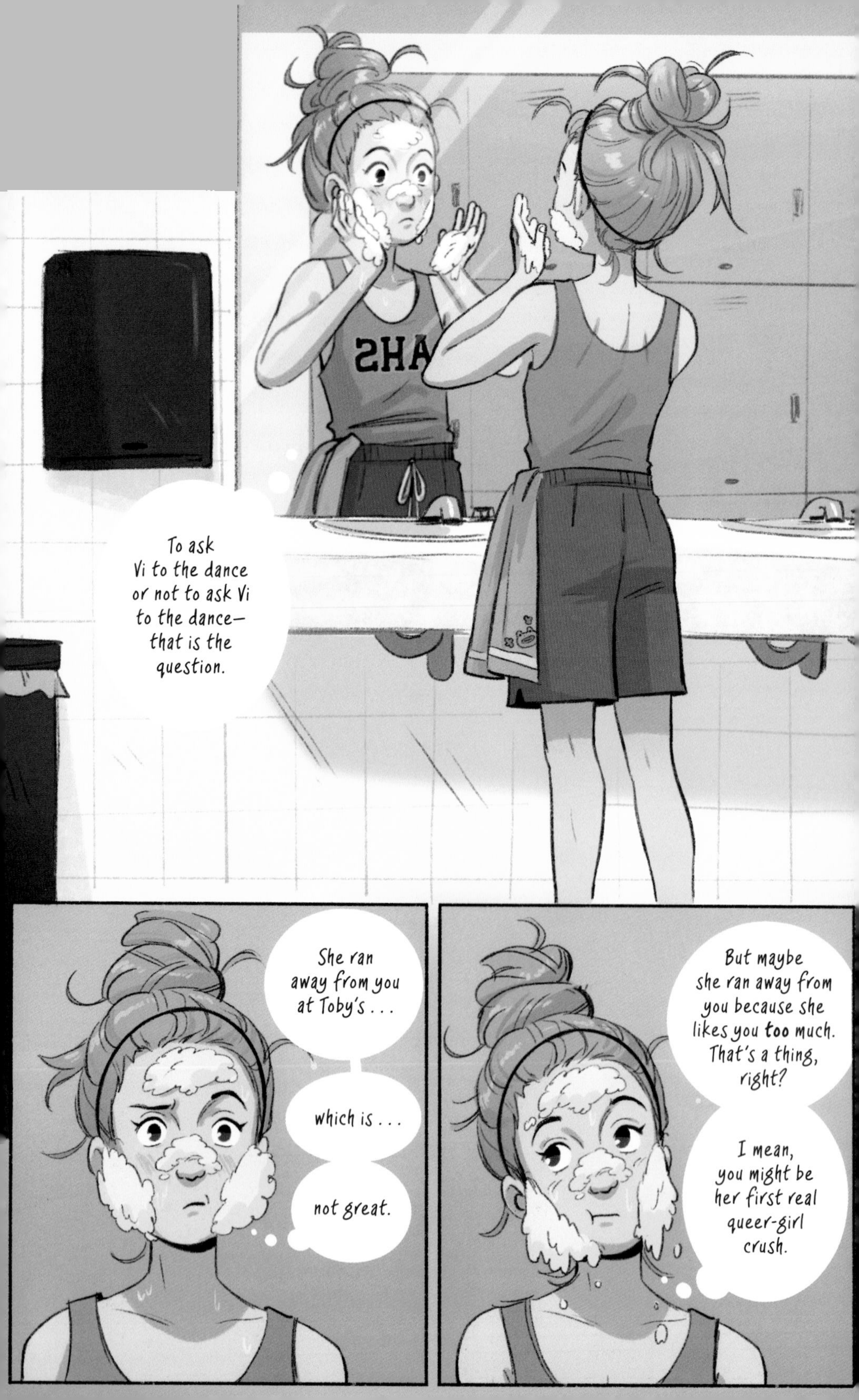
SHA
To ask Vi to the dance or not to ask Vi to the dance— that is the question.
She ran away from you at Toby's . . .
which is . . .
not great.
But maybe she ran away from you because she likes you **too** much. That's a thing, right?
I mean, you might be her first real queer-girl crush.

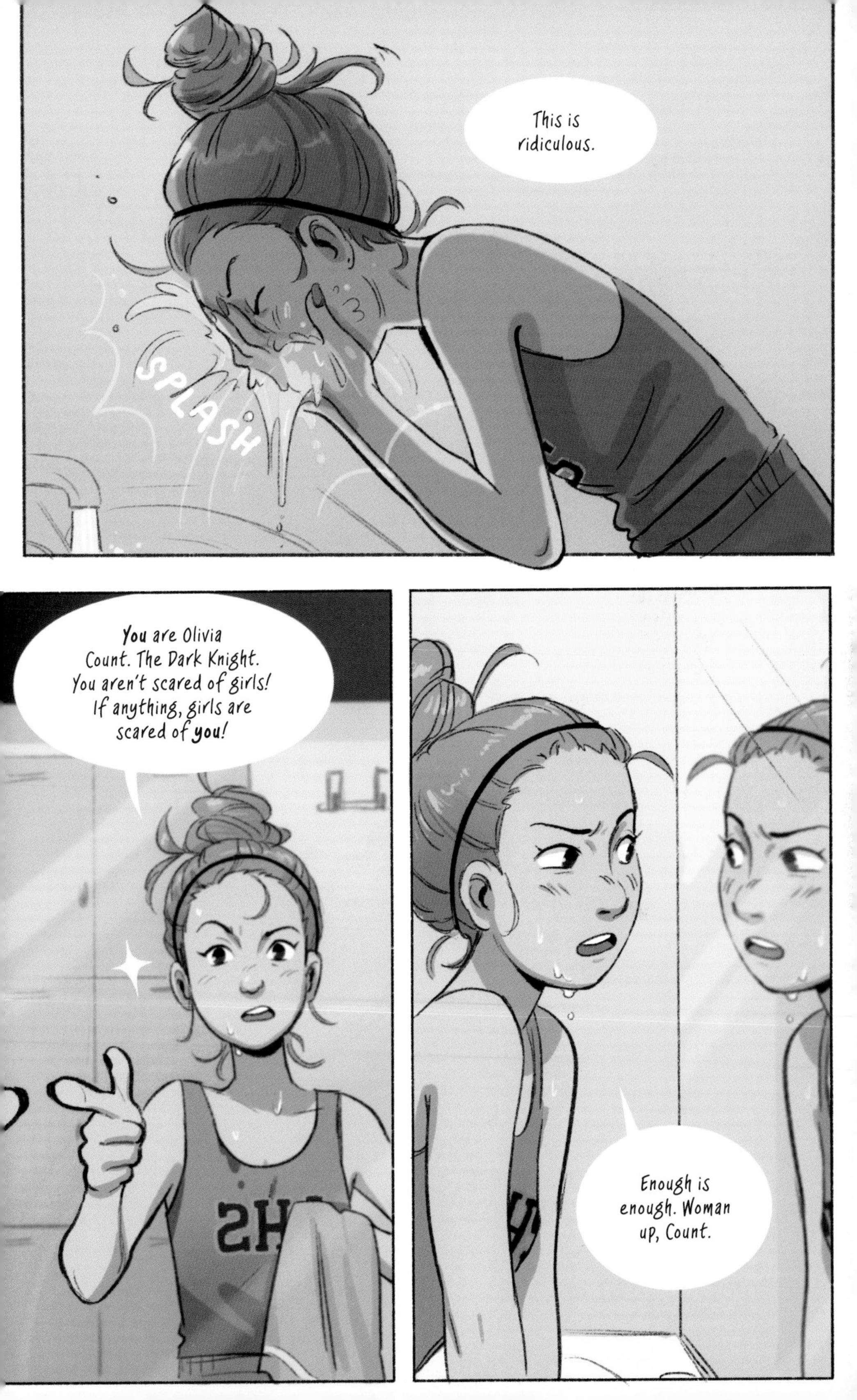
This is ridiculous.
SPLASH
You are Olivia Count. The Dark Knight. You aren't scared of girls! If anything, girls are scared of you!
Enough is enough. Woman up, Count.

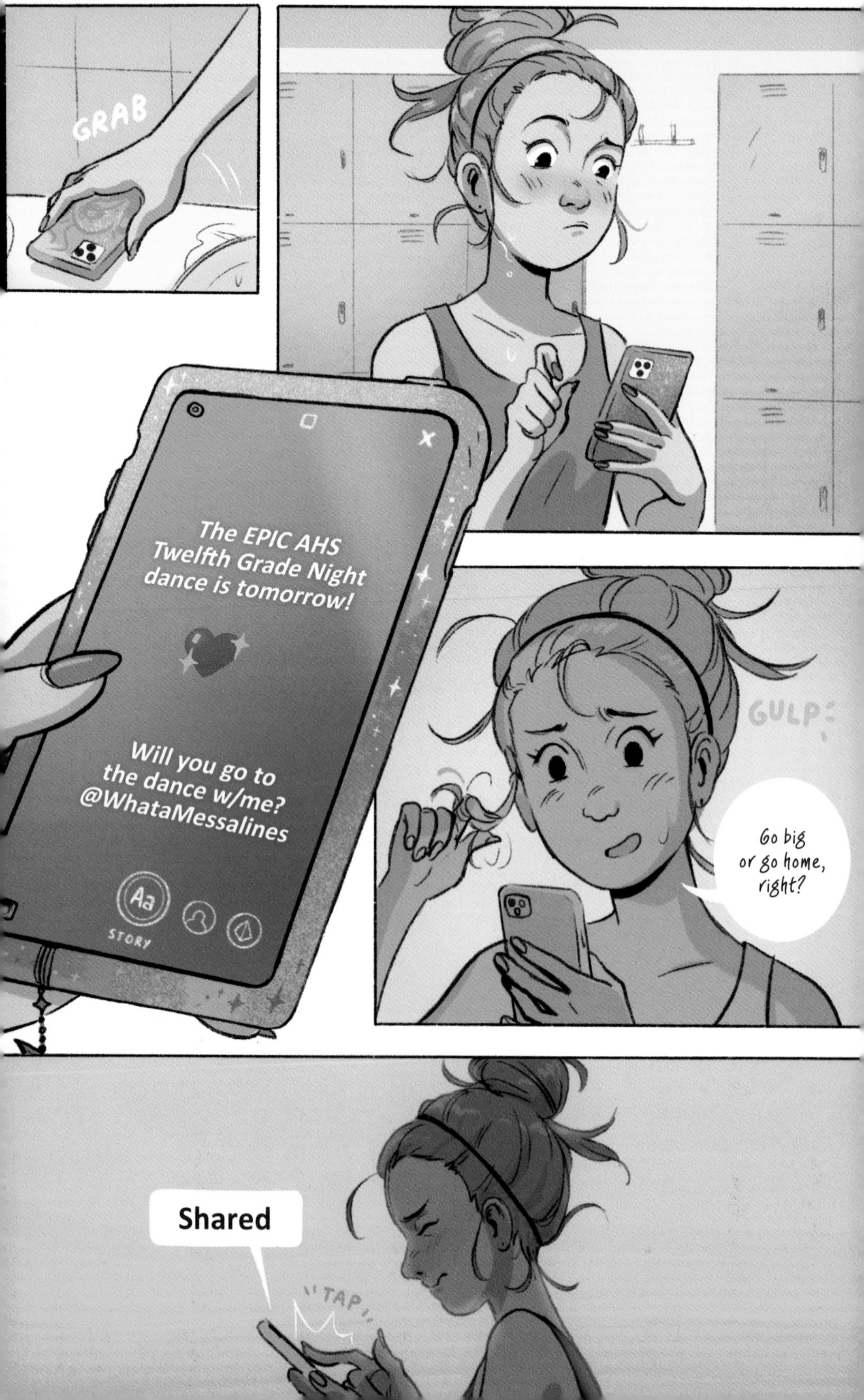
GRAB
The EPIC AHS Twelfth Grade Night dance is tomorrow!
Will you go to the dance w/me? @WhataMessalines
Aa
STORY
GULP
Go big or go home, right?
Shared
TAP

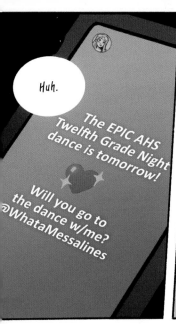

Huh.

The EPIC AHS Twelfth Grade Night dance is tomorrow!

Will you go to the dance w/me? @WhataMessalines

@CountTakesQueen

Olivia Count she/her

FOLLOW

MESSA

Wow.

Why yes, ridiculously hot stranger, I will go to the AHS Twelfth Grade Night dance with you.

Our first high school dance . . . There are some things we should do together.

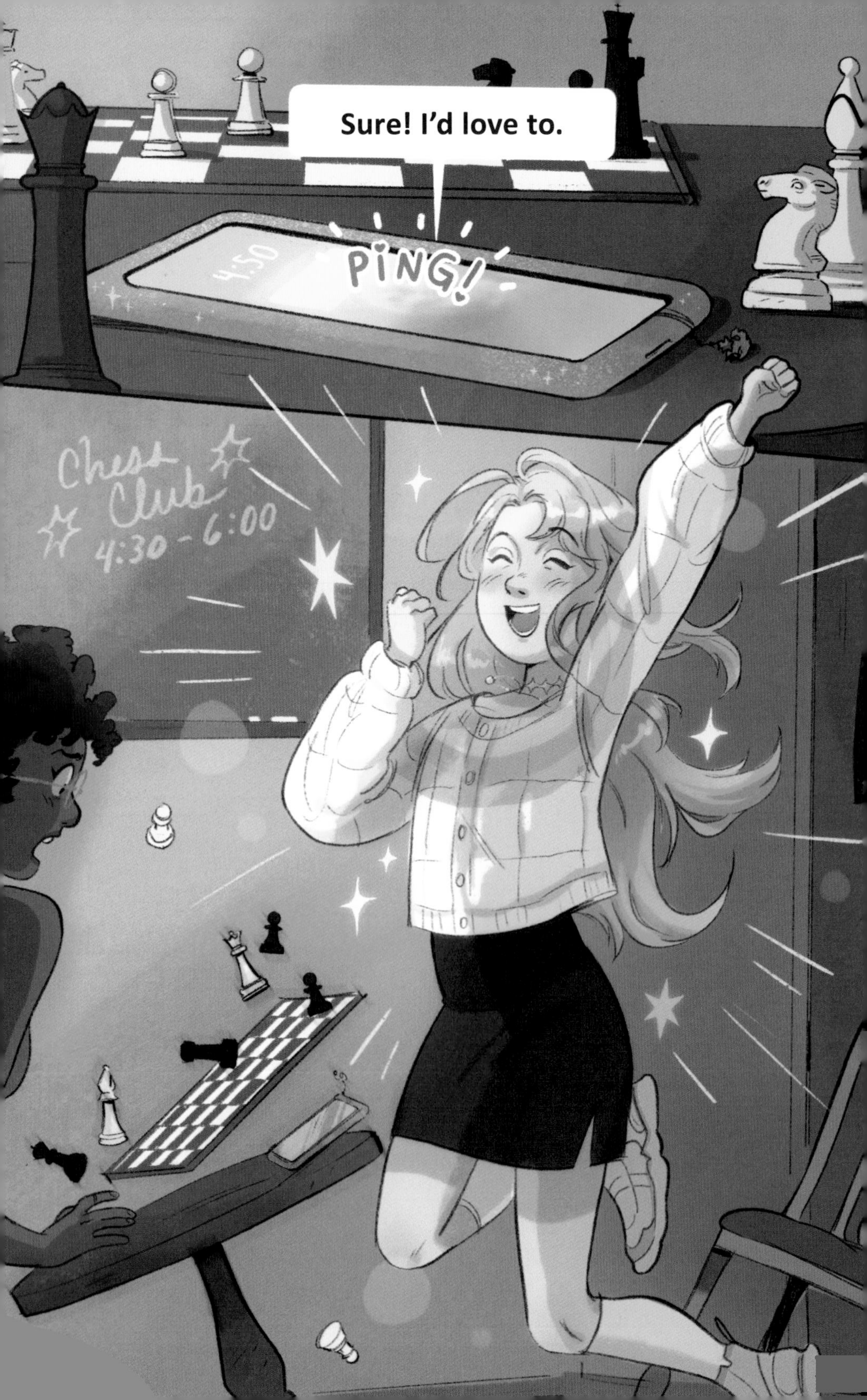
Sure! I'd love to.
PING!
4:50
Chess Club
4:30-6:00

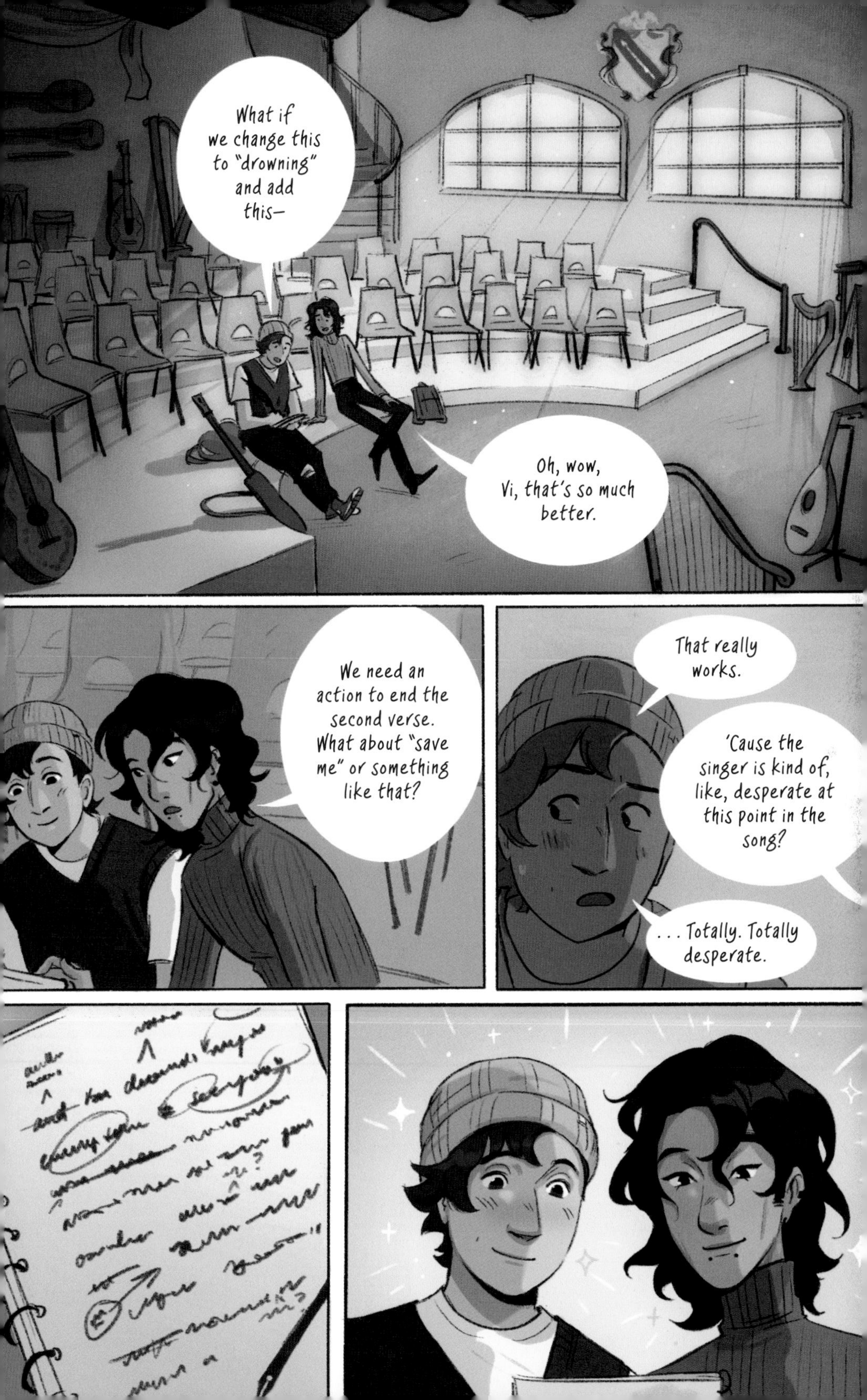
What if we change this to "drowning" and add this—
Oh, wow, Vi, that's so much better.
We need an action to end the second verse. What about "save me" or something like that?
That really works.
'Cause the singer is kind of, like, desperate at this point in the song?
. . . Totally. Totally desperate.

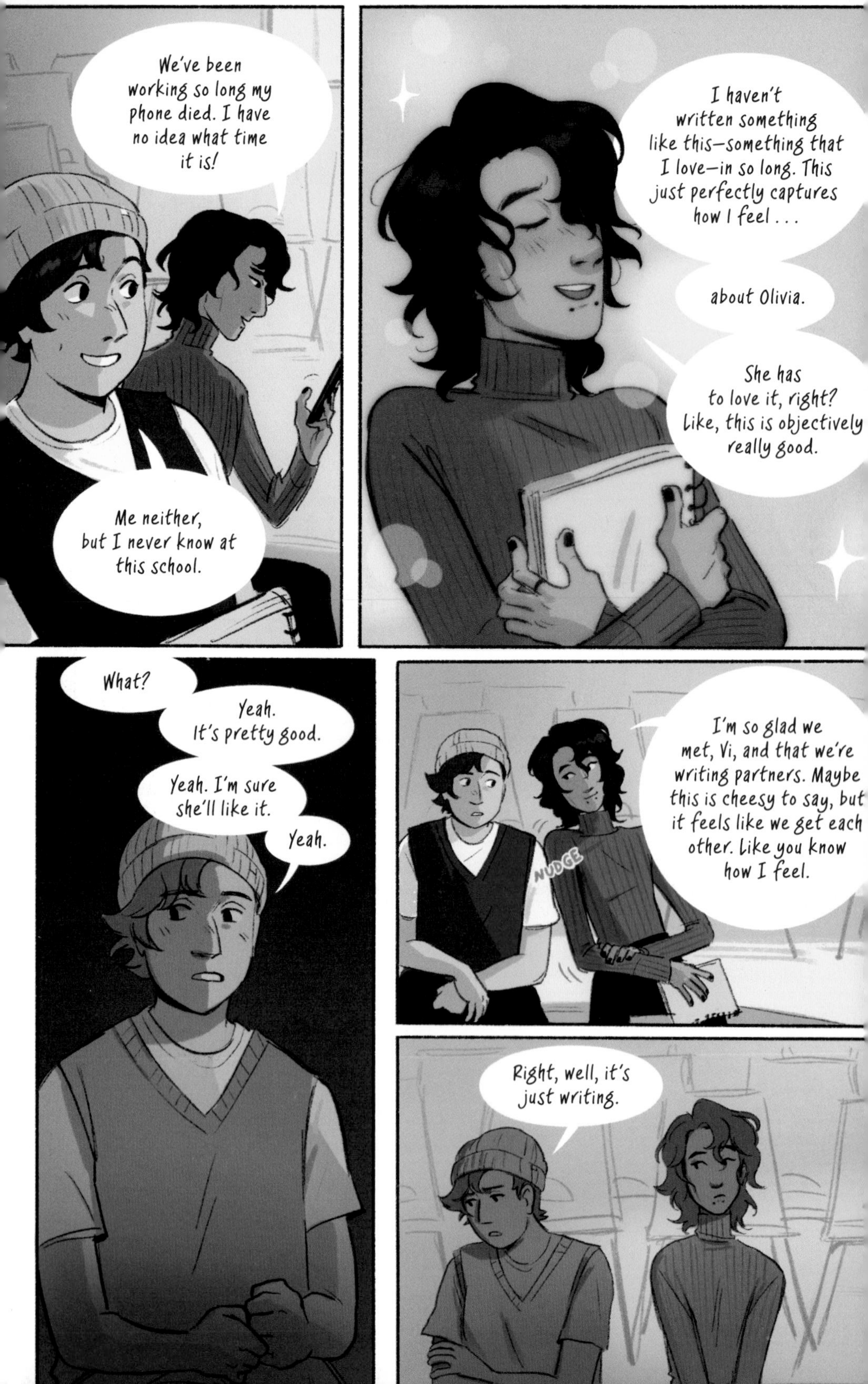

We've been working so long my phone died. I have no idea what time it is!
Me neither, but I never know at this school.
I haven't written something like this—something that I love—in so long. This just perfectly captures how I feel . . .
about Olivia.
She has to love it, right? Like, this is objectively really good.
What?
Yeah. It's pretty good.
Yeah. I'm sure she'll like it.
Yeah.
I'm so glad we met, Vi, and that we're writing partners. Maybe this is cheesy to say, but it feels like we get each other. Like you know how I feel.
NUDGE
Right, well, it's just writing.

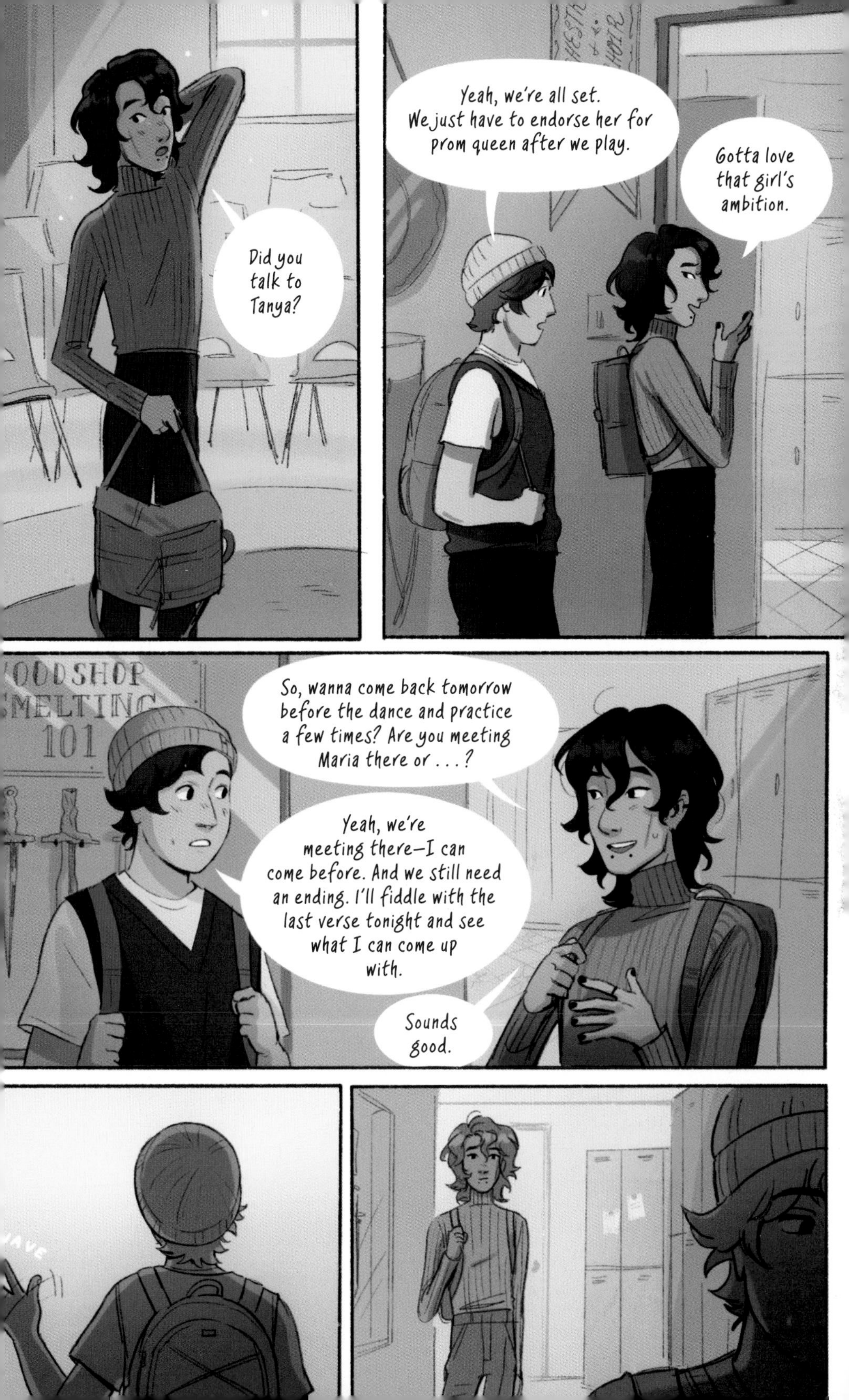
Did you talk to Tanya?
Yeah, we're all set. We just have to endorse her for prom queen after we play.
Gotta love that girl's ambition.
OODSHOP
MELTING
101
So, wanna come back tomorrow before the dance and practice a few times? Are you meeting Maria there or . . . ?
Yeah, we're meeting there—I can come before. And we still need an ending. I'll fiddle with the last verse tonight and see what I can come up with.
Sounds good.

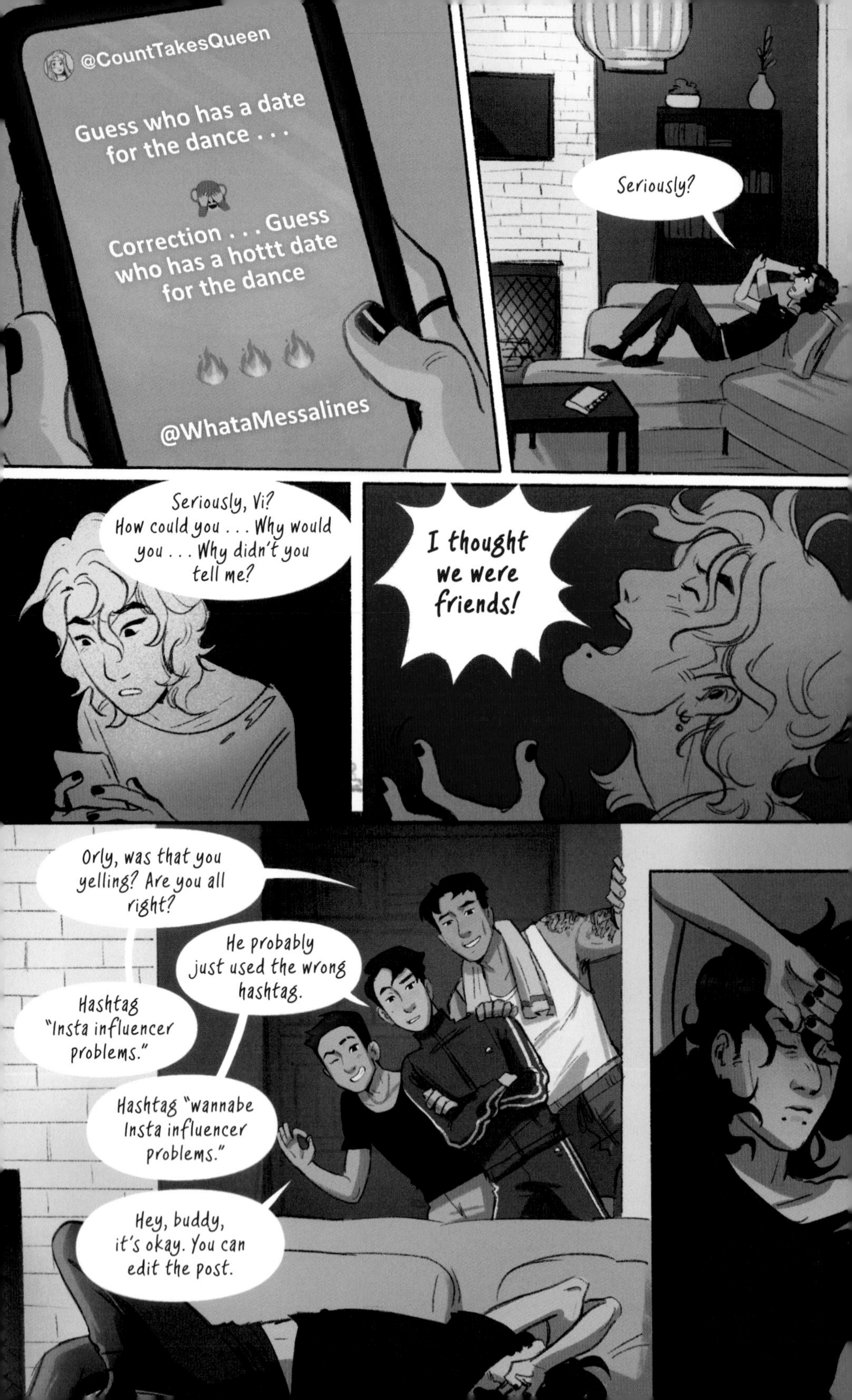
@CountTakesQueen
Guess who has a date for the dance . . .
Correction . . . Guess who has a hottt date for the dance
@WhataMessalines
Seriously?
Seriously, Vi? How could you . . . Why would you . . . Why didn't you tell me?
I thought we were friends!
Orly, was that you yelling? Are you all right?
He probably just used the wrong hashtag.
Hashtag "Insta influencer problems."
Hashtag "wannabe Insta influencer problems."
Hey, buddy, it's okay. You can edit the post.

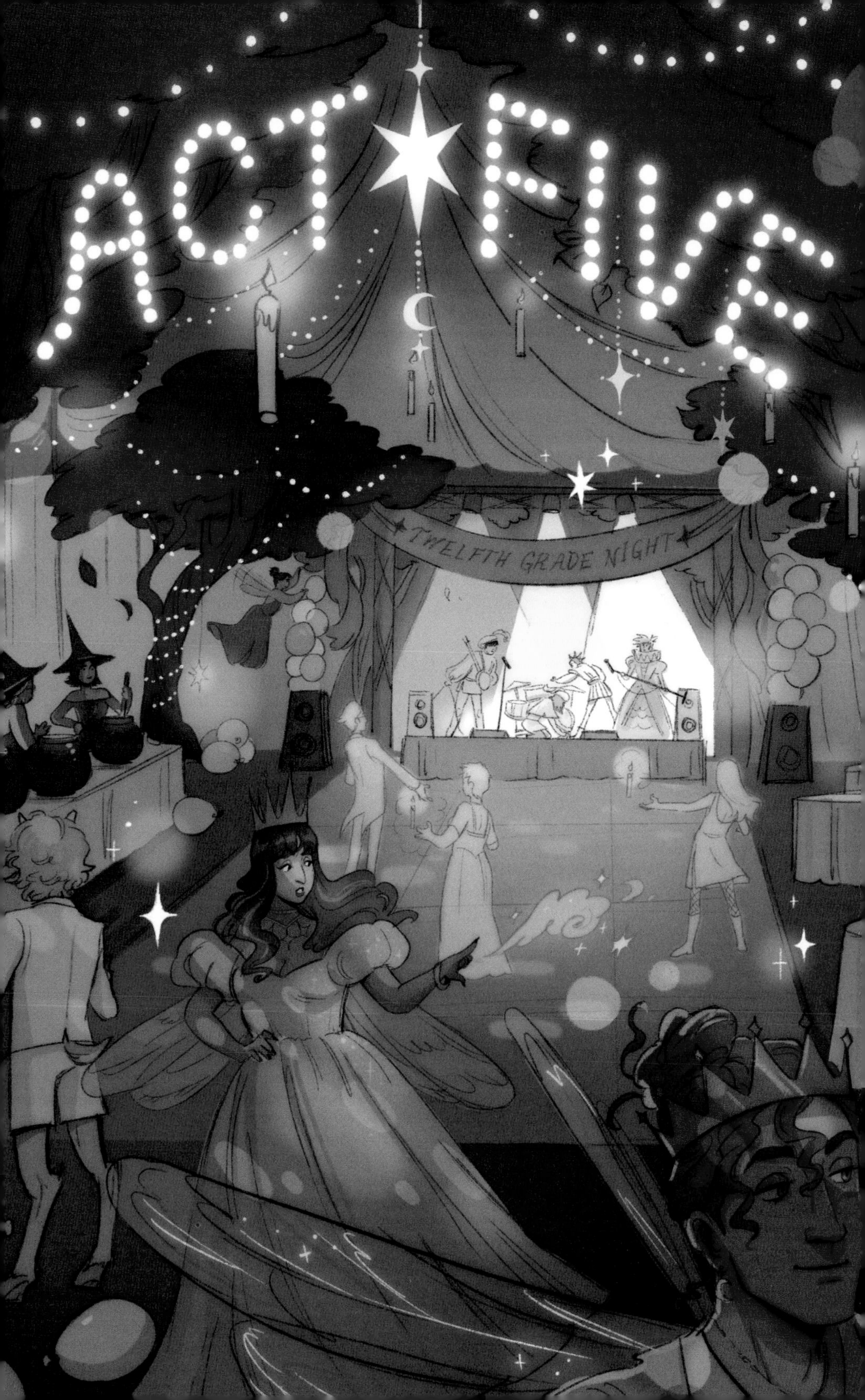
ACT FIVE
TWELFTH GRADE NIGHT

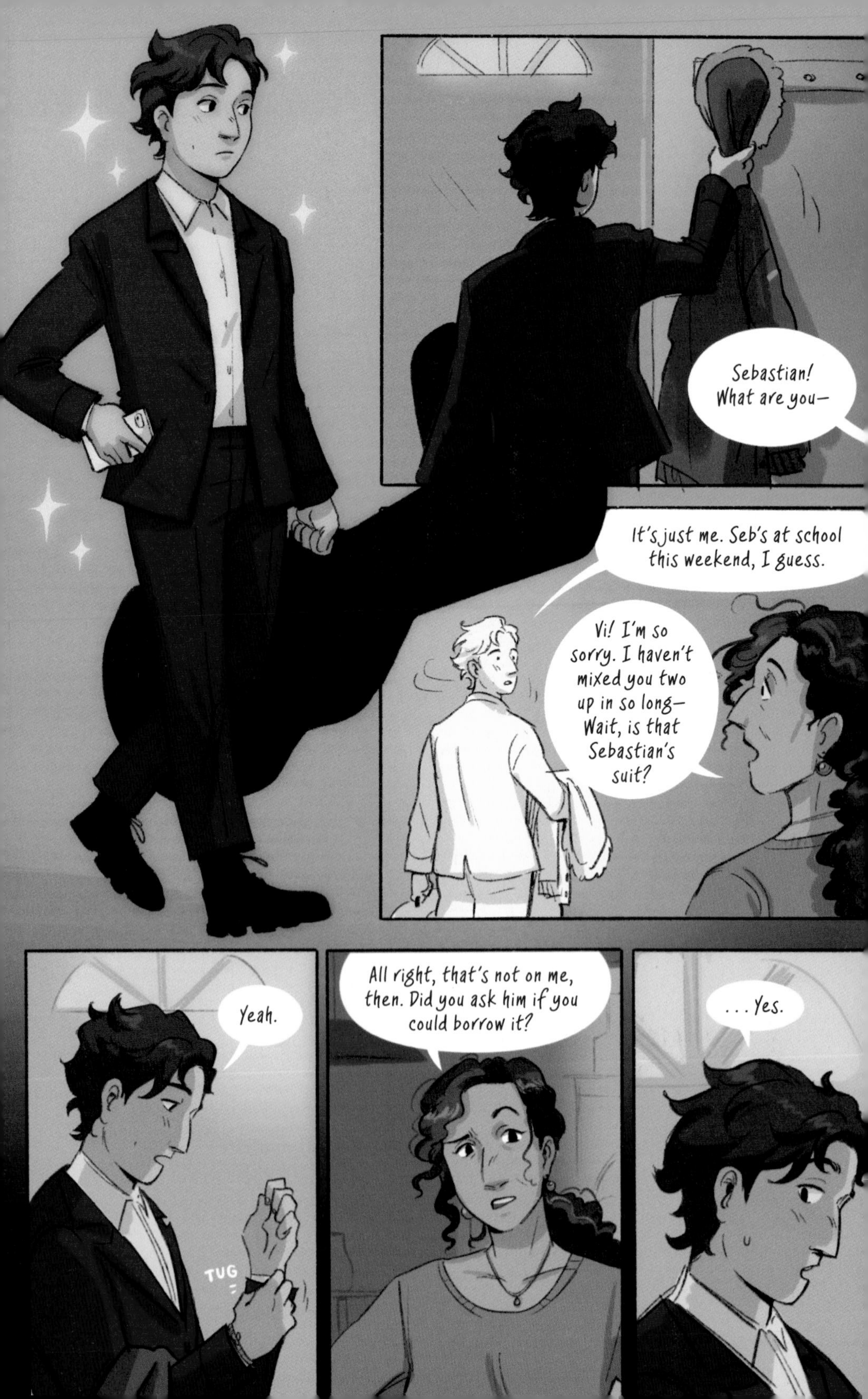
Sebastian! What are you—
It's just me. Seb's at school this weekend, I guess.
Vi! I'm so sorry. I haven't mixed you two up in so long— Wait, is that Sebastian's suit?
Yeah.
TUG
All right, that's not on me, then. Did you ask him if you could borrow it?
. . . Yes.

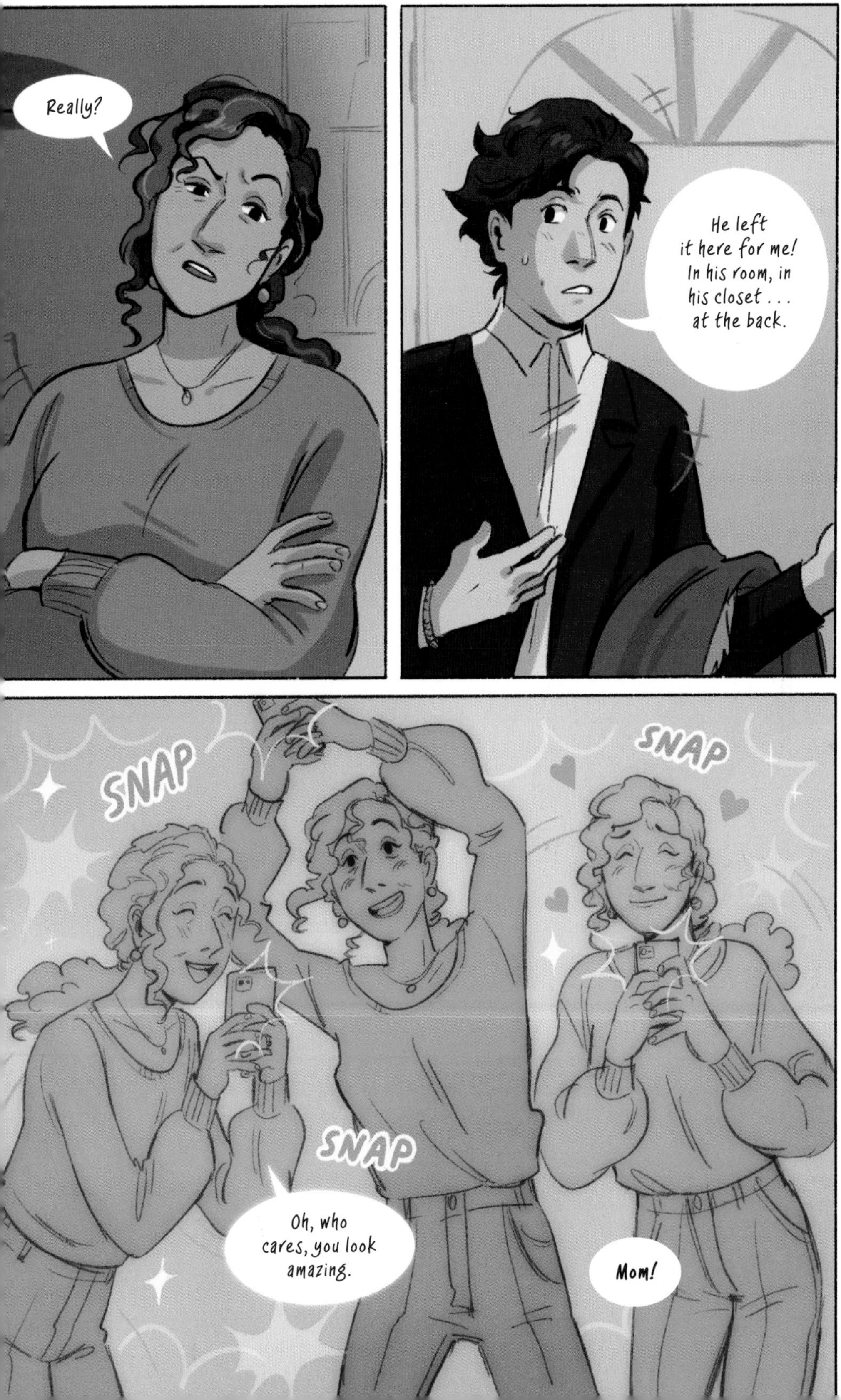
Really?
He left it here for me! In his room, in his closet . . . at the back.
SNAP
SNAP
SNAP
Oh, who cares, you look amazing.
Mom!

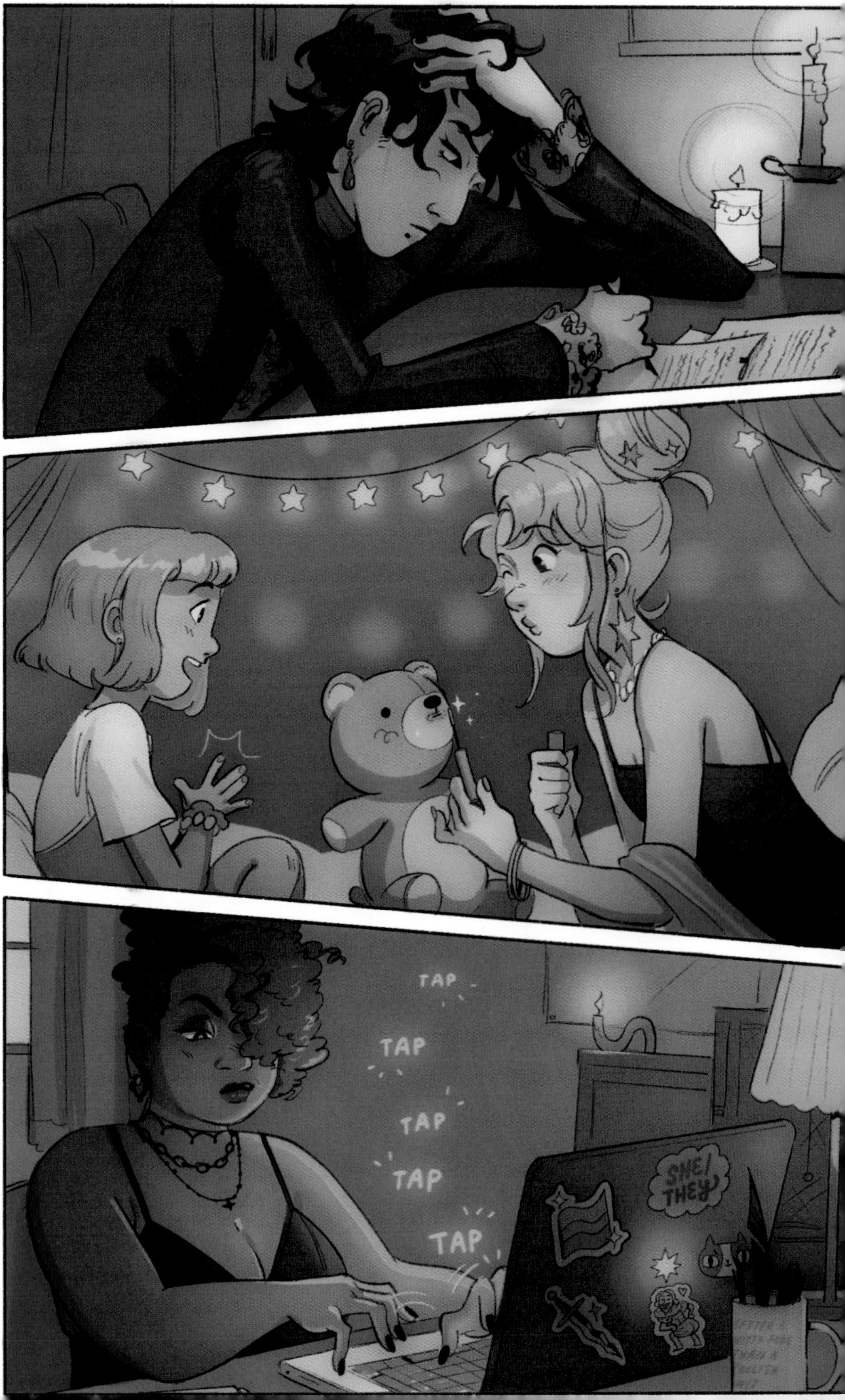
TAP
TAP
TAP
TAP
TAP
SHE/THEY

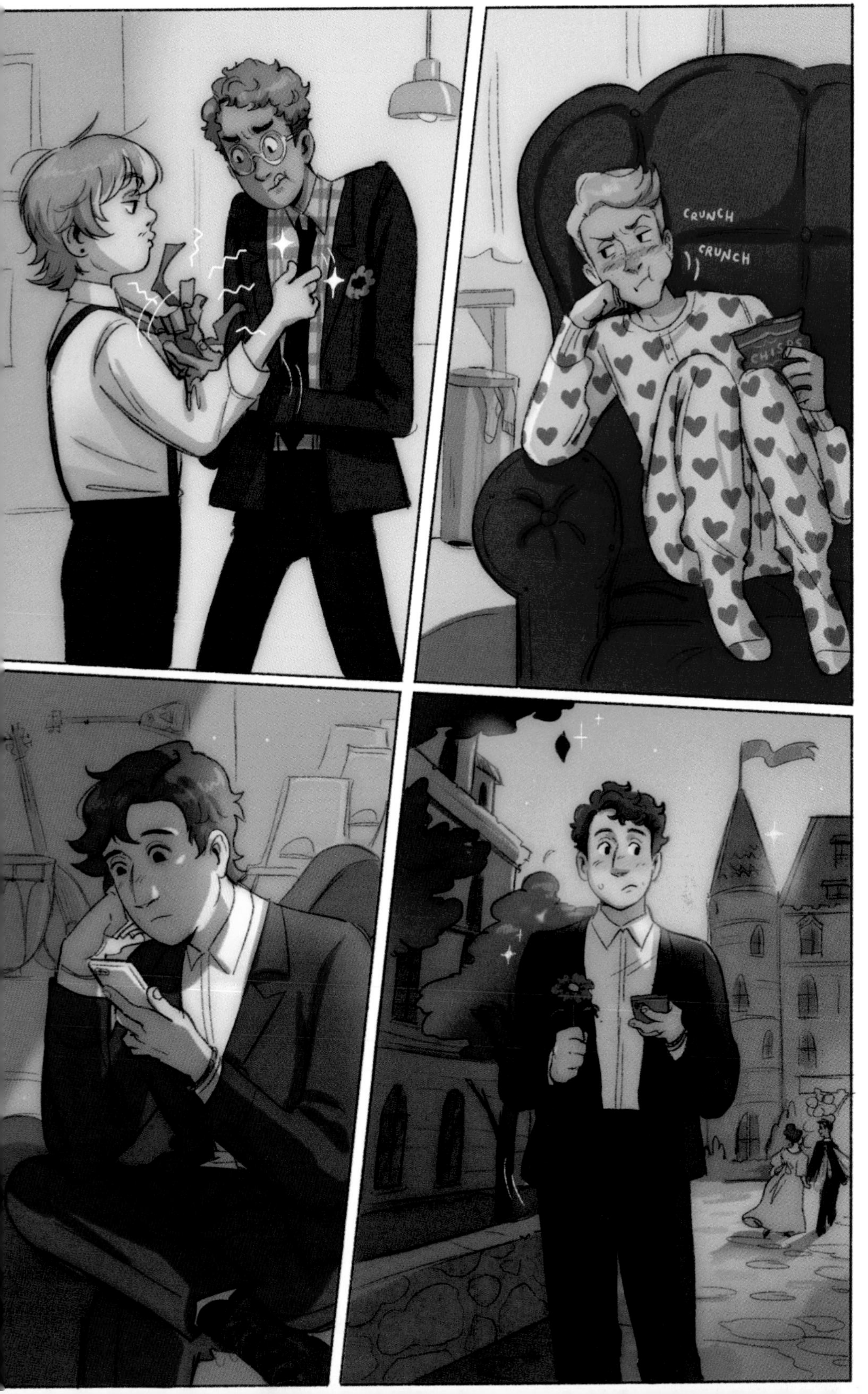
CRUNCH
CRUNCH
CHIPS

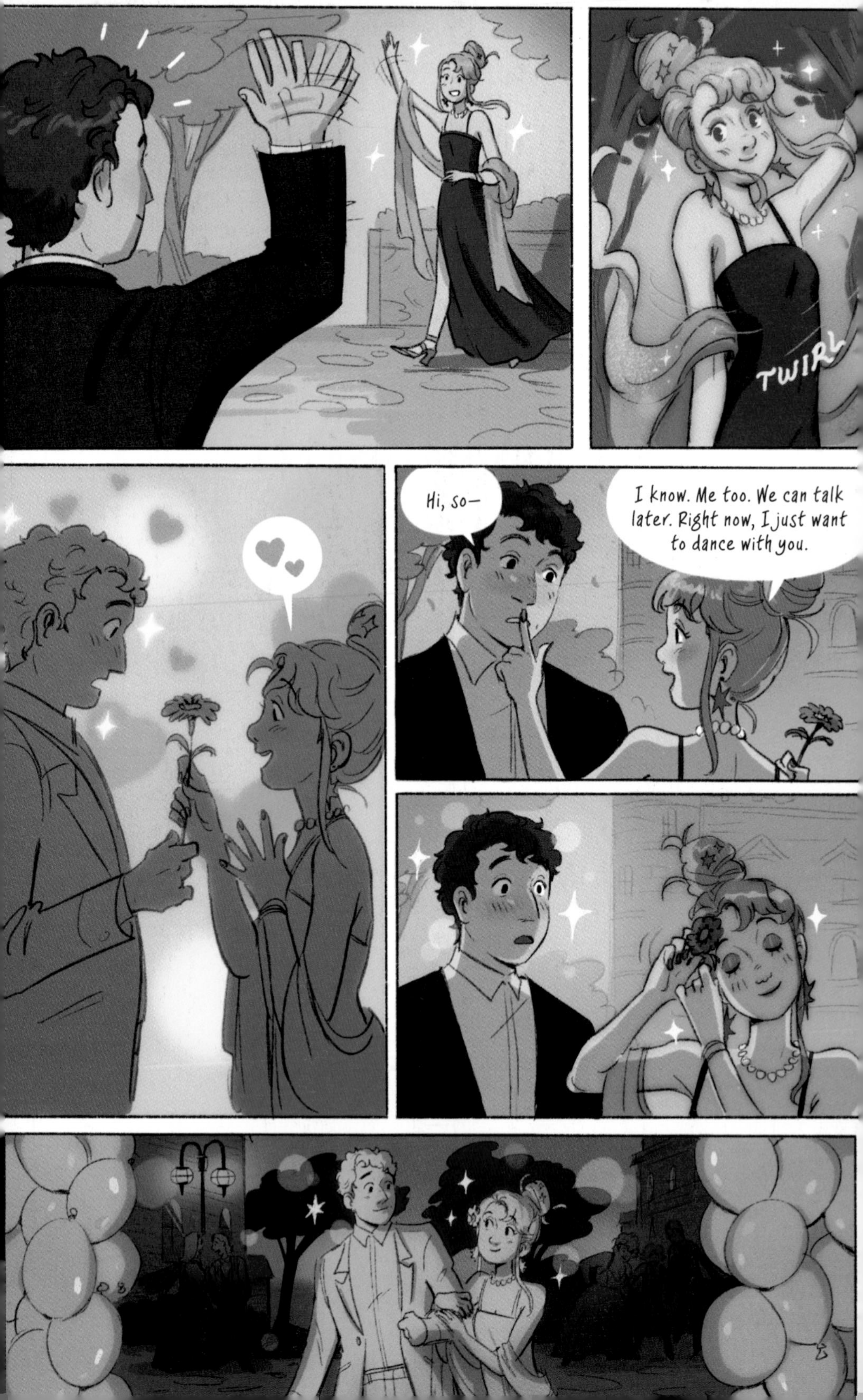
TWIRL
Hi, so—
I know. Me too. We can talk later. Right now, I just want to dance with you.

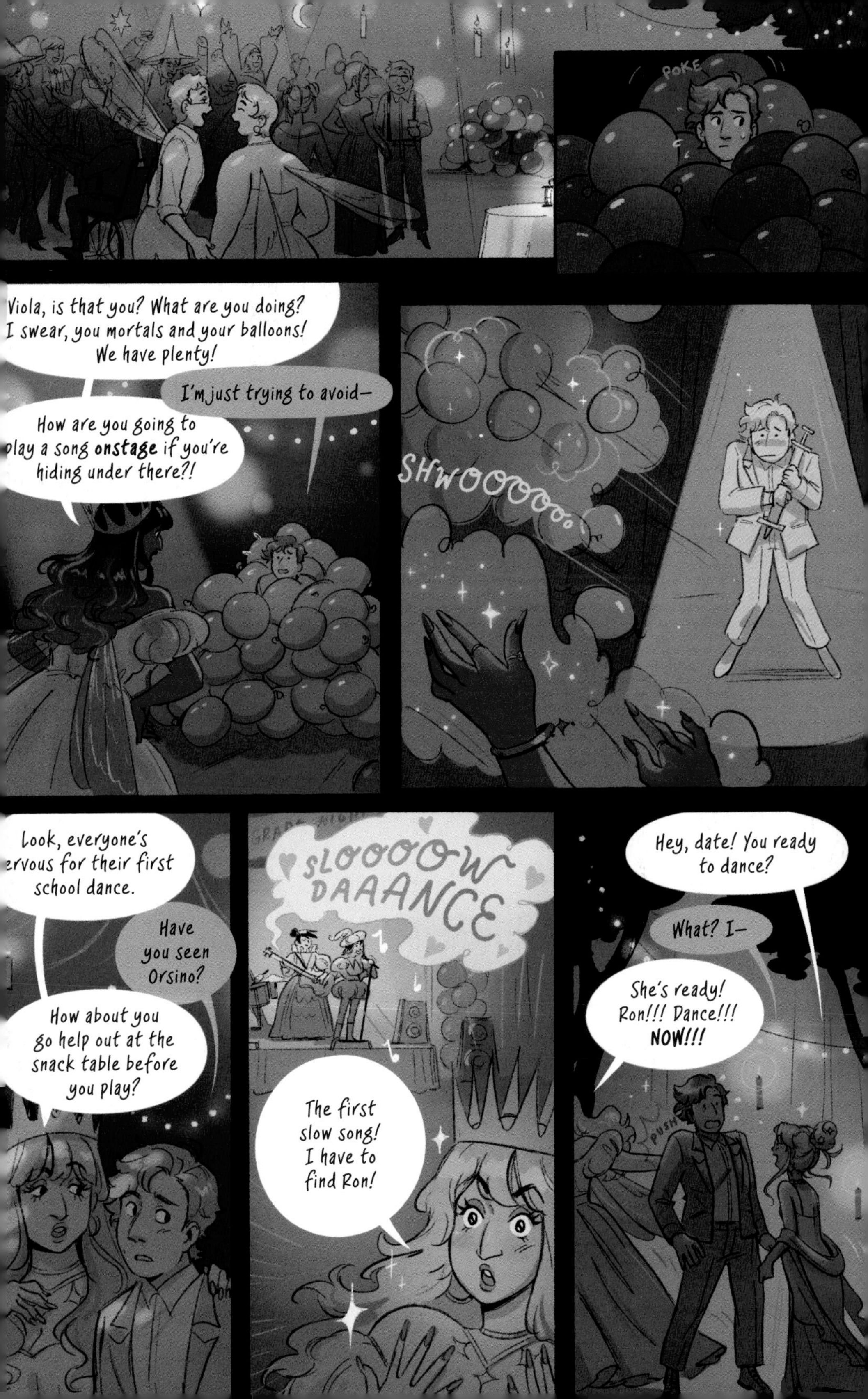
POKE
Viola, is that you? What are you doing? I swear, you mortals and your balloons! We have plenty!
I'm just trying to avoid—
How are you going to play a song onstage if you're hiding under there?!
SHWOOOOOOOO
Look, everyone's nervous for their first school dance.
Have you seen Orsino?
How about you go help out at the snack table before you play?
SLOOOOW DAAANCE
The first slow song! I have to find Ron!
Hey, date! You ready to dance?
What? I—
She's ready! Ron!!! Dance!!! NOW!!!
PUSH

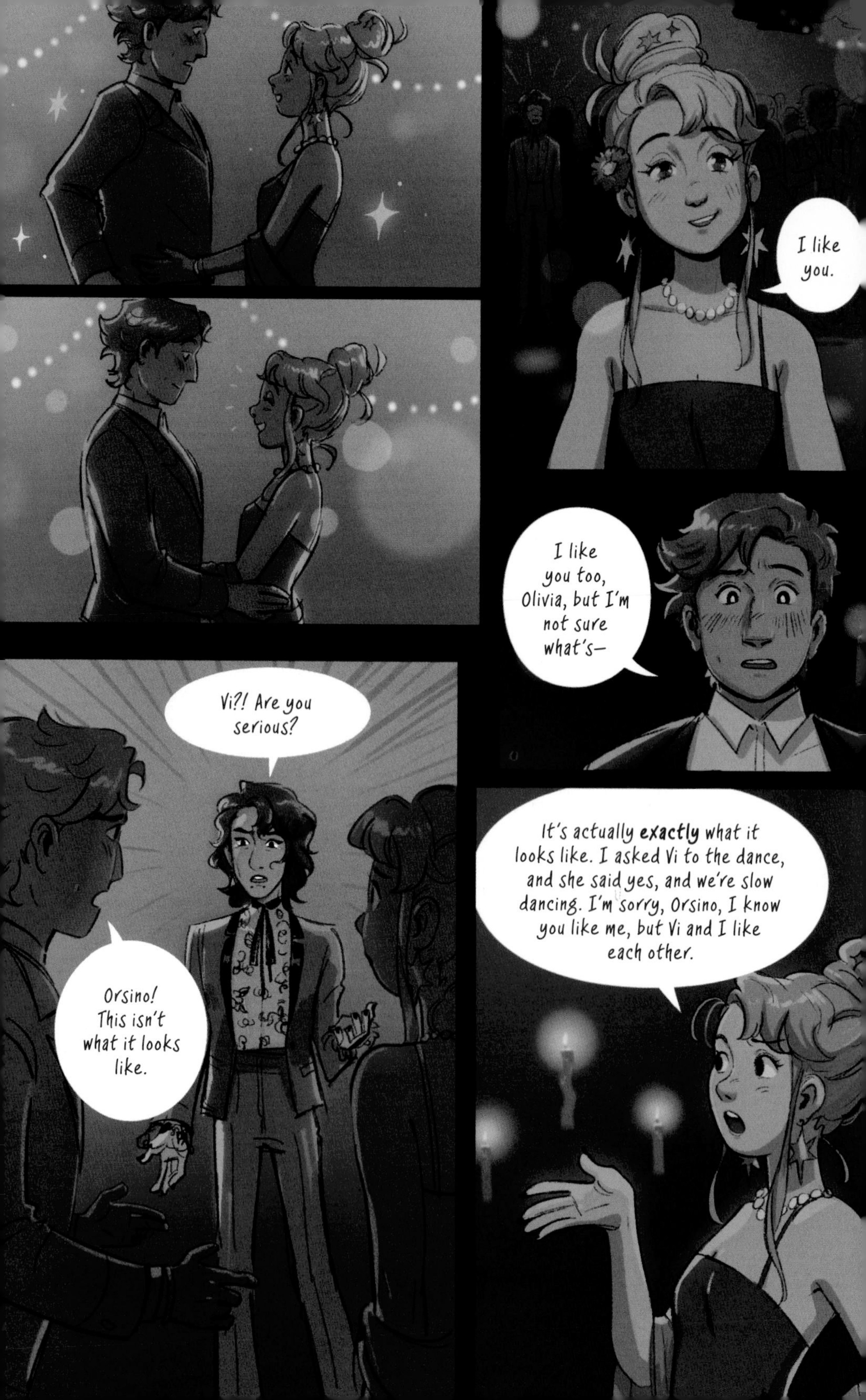
I like you.
I like you too, Olivia, but I'm not sure what's—
Vi?! Are you serious?
Orsino! This isn't what it looks like.
It's actually **exactly** what it looks like. I asked Vi to the dance, and she said yes, and we're slow dancing. I'm sorry, Orsino, I know you like me, but Vi and I like each other.

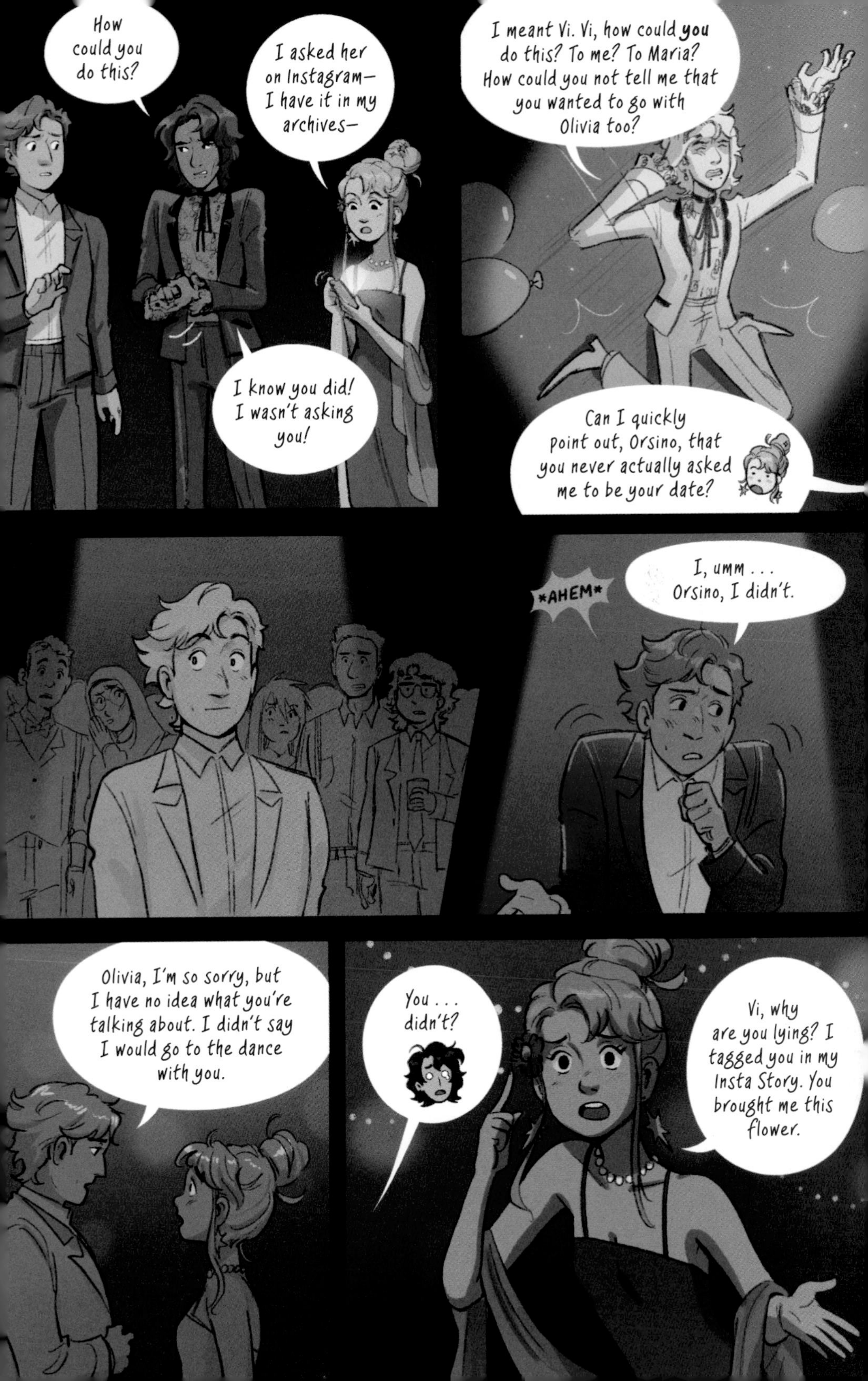
How could you do this?
I asked her on Instagram— I have it in my archives—
I know you did! I wasn't asking you!
I meant Vi. Vi, how could **you** do this? To me? To Maria? How could you not tell me that you wanted to go with Olivia too?
Can I quickly point out, Orsino, that you never actually asked me to be your date?
AHEM
I, umm . . . Orsino, I didn't.
Olivia, I'm so sorry, but I have no idea what you're talking about. I didn't say I would go to the dance with you.
You . . . didn't?
Vi, why are you lying? I tagged you in my Insta Story. You brought me this flower.

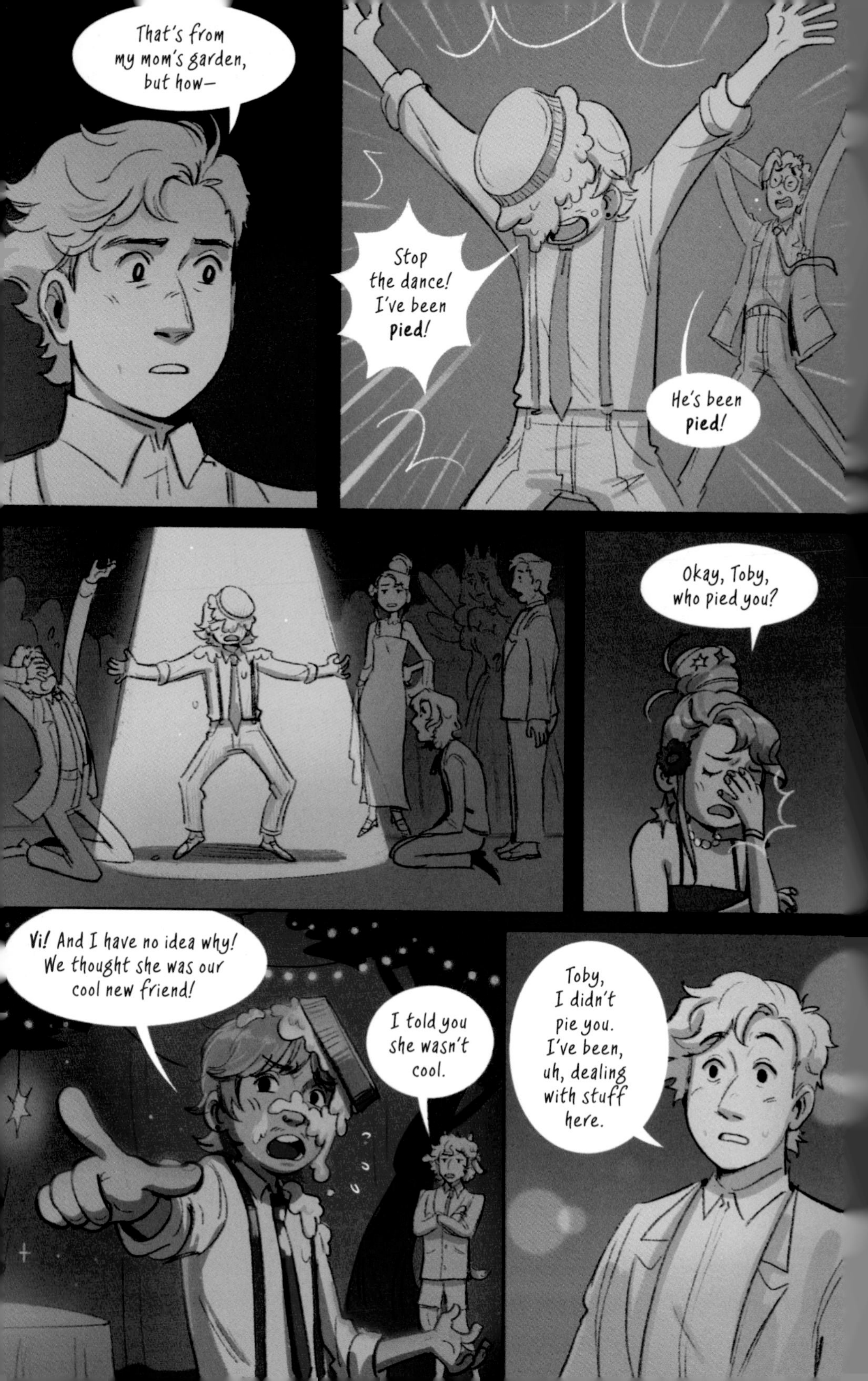

That's from my mom's garden, but how—
Stop the dance! I've been **pied**!
He's been **pied**!
Okay, Toby, who pied you?
Vi! And I have no idea why! We thought she was our cool new friend!
I told you she wasn't cool.
Toby, I didn't pie you. I've been, uh, dealing with stuff here.

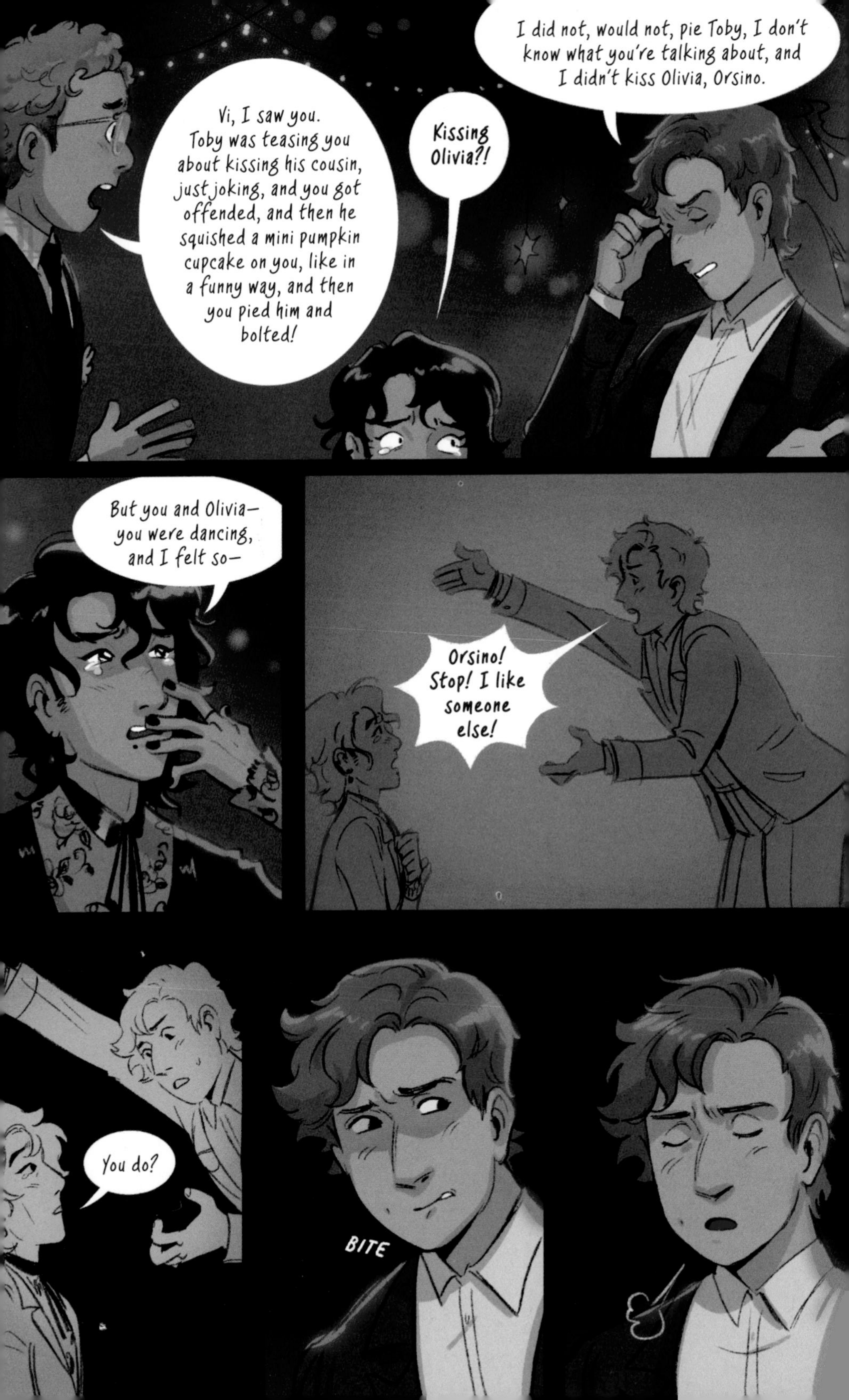
I did not, would not, pie Toby, I don't know what you're talking about, and I didn't kiss Olivia, Orsino.
Vi, I saw you. Toby was teasing you about kissing his cousin, just joking, and you got offended, and then he squished a mini pumpkin cupcake on you, like in a funny way, and then you pied him and bolted!
Kissing Olivia?!
But you and Olivia— you were dancing, and I felt so—
Orsino! Stop! I like someone else!
You do?
BITE

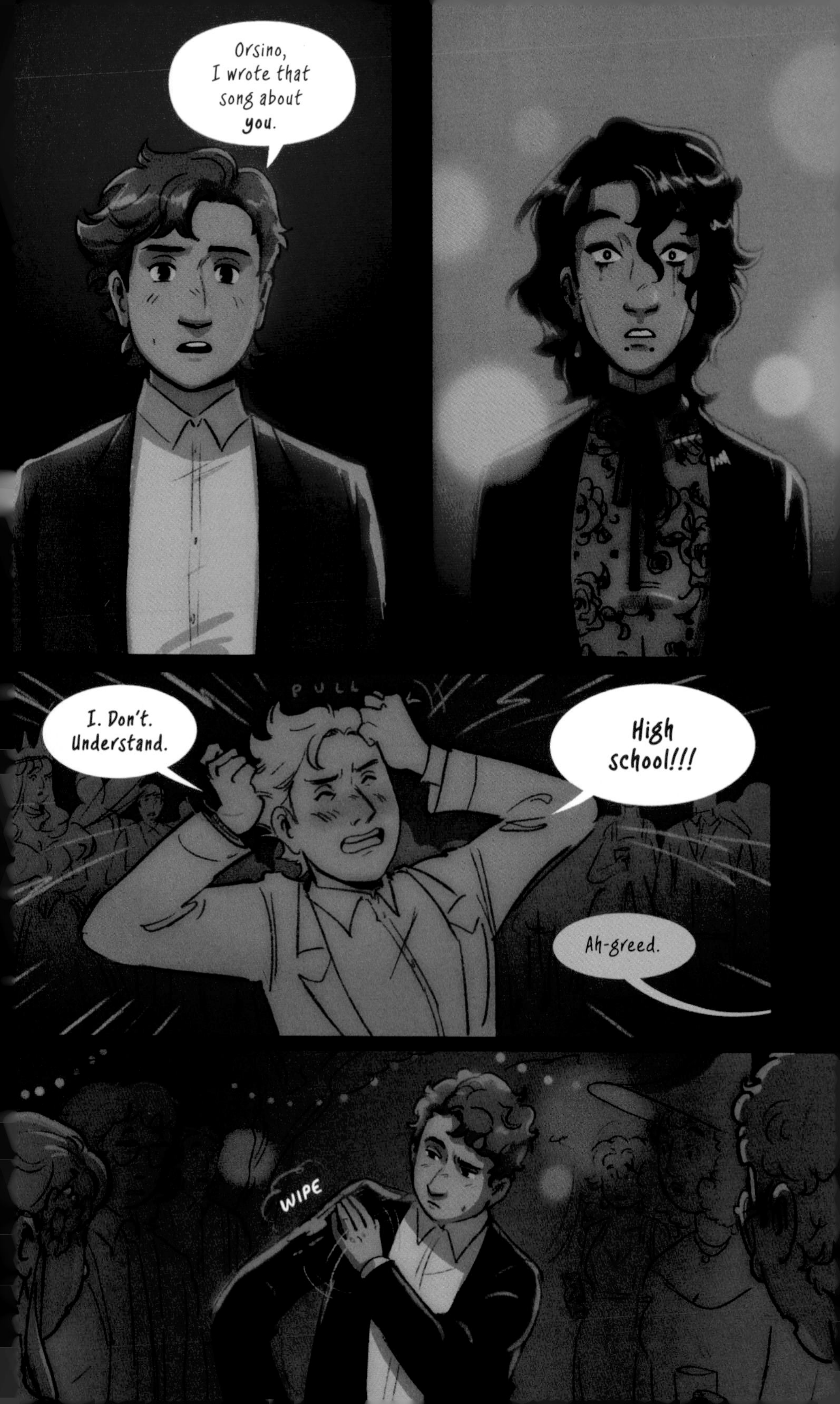
Orsino, I wrote that song about you.
PULL
I. Don't. Understand.
High school!!!
Ah-greed.
WIPE

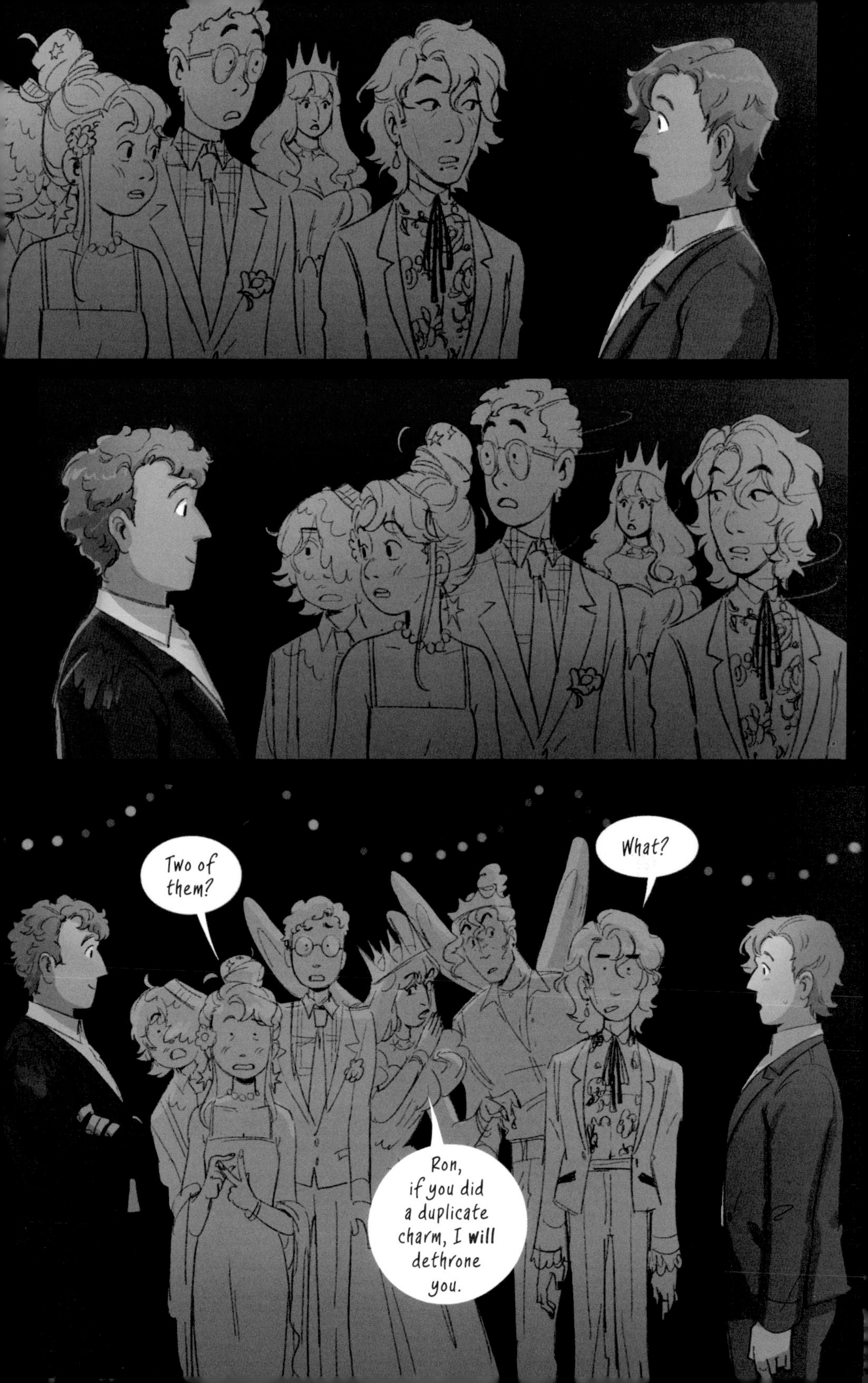
Two of them?
What?
Ron, if you did a duplicate charm, I will dethrone you.

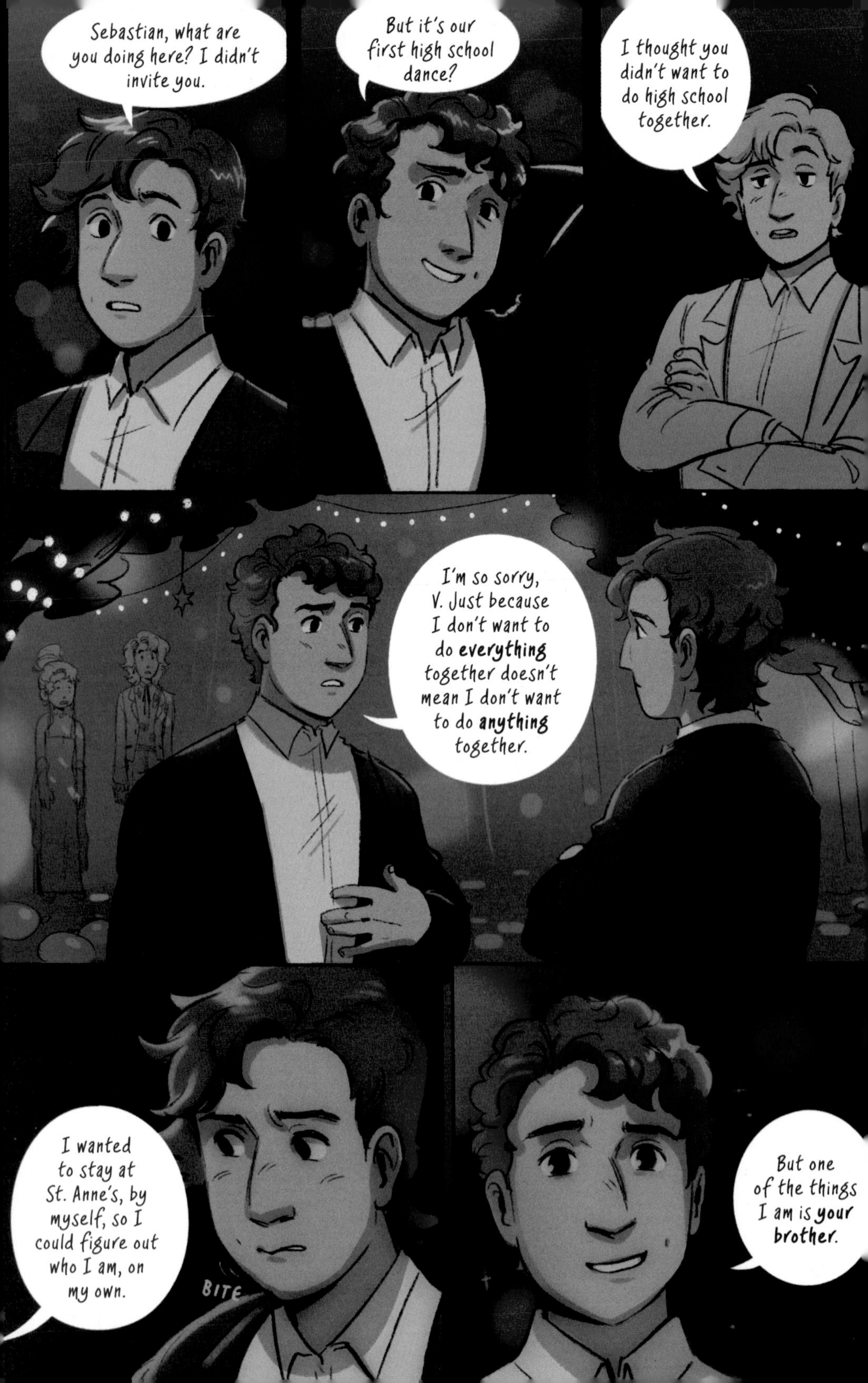
Sebastian, what are you doing here? I didn't invite you.
But it's our first high school dance?
I thought you didn't want to do high school together.
I'm so sorry, V. Just because I don't want to do **everything** together doesn't mean I don't want to do **anything** together.
I wanted to stay at St. Anne's, by myself, so I could figure out who I am, on my own.
BITE
But one of the things I am is **your brother**.

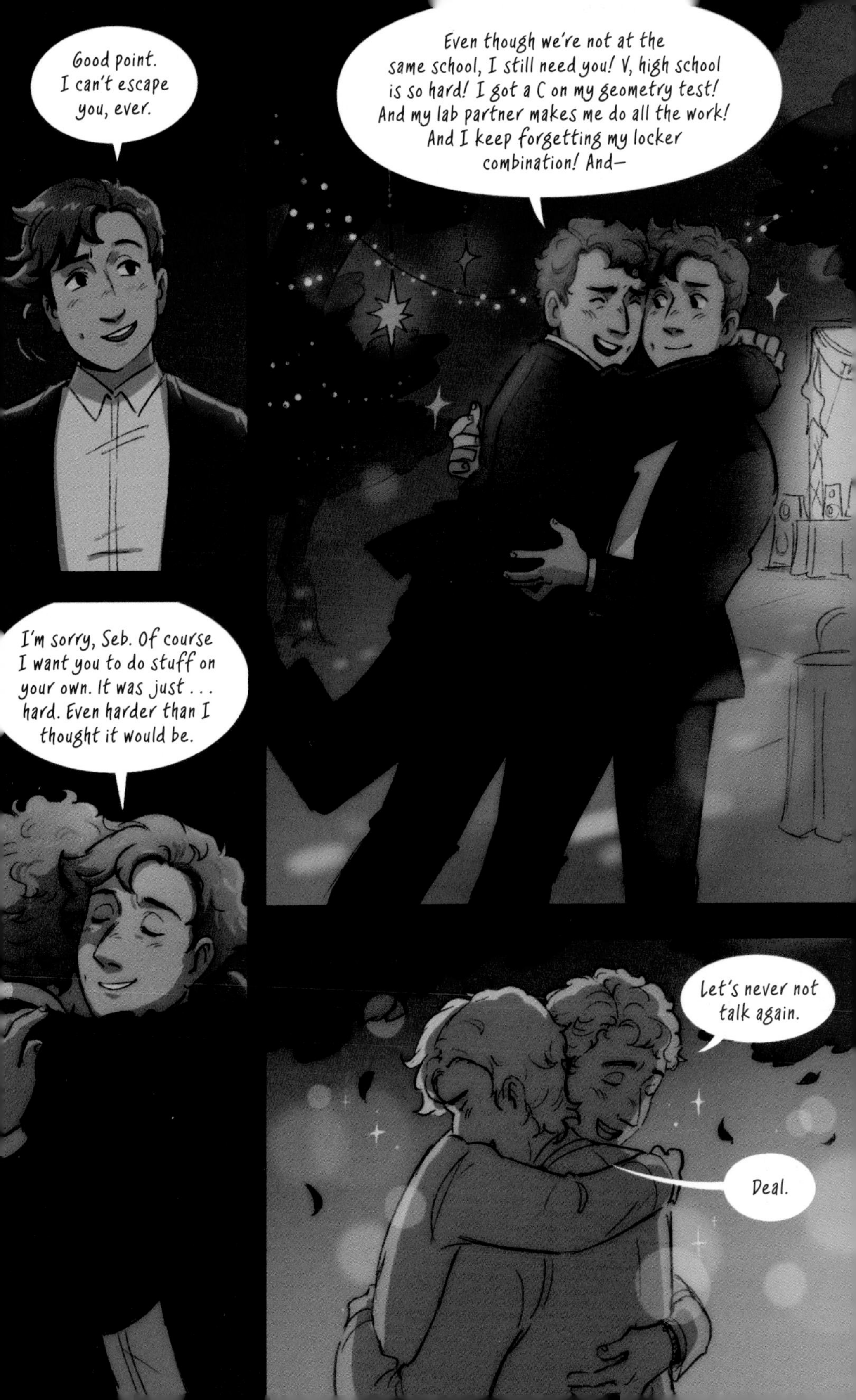
Good point. I can't escape you, ever.
Even though we're not at the same school, I still need you! V, high school is so hard! I got a C on my geometry test! And my lab partner makes me do all the work! And I keep forgetting my locker combination! And—
I'm sorry, Seb. Of course I want you to do stuff on your own. It was just . . . hard. Even harder than I thought it would be.
Let's never not talk again.
Deal.

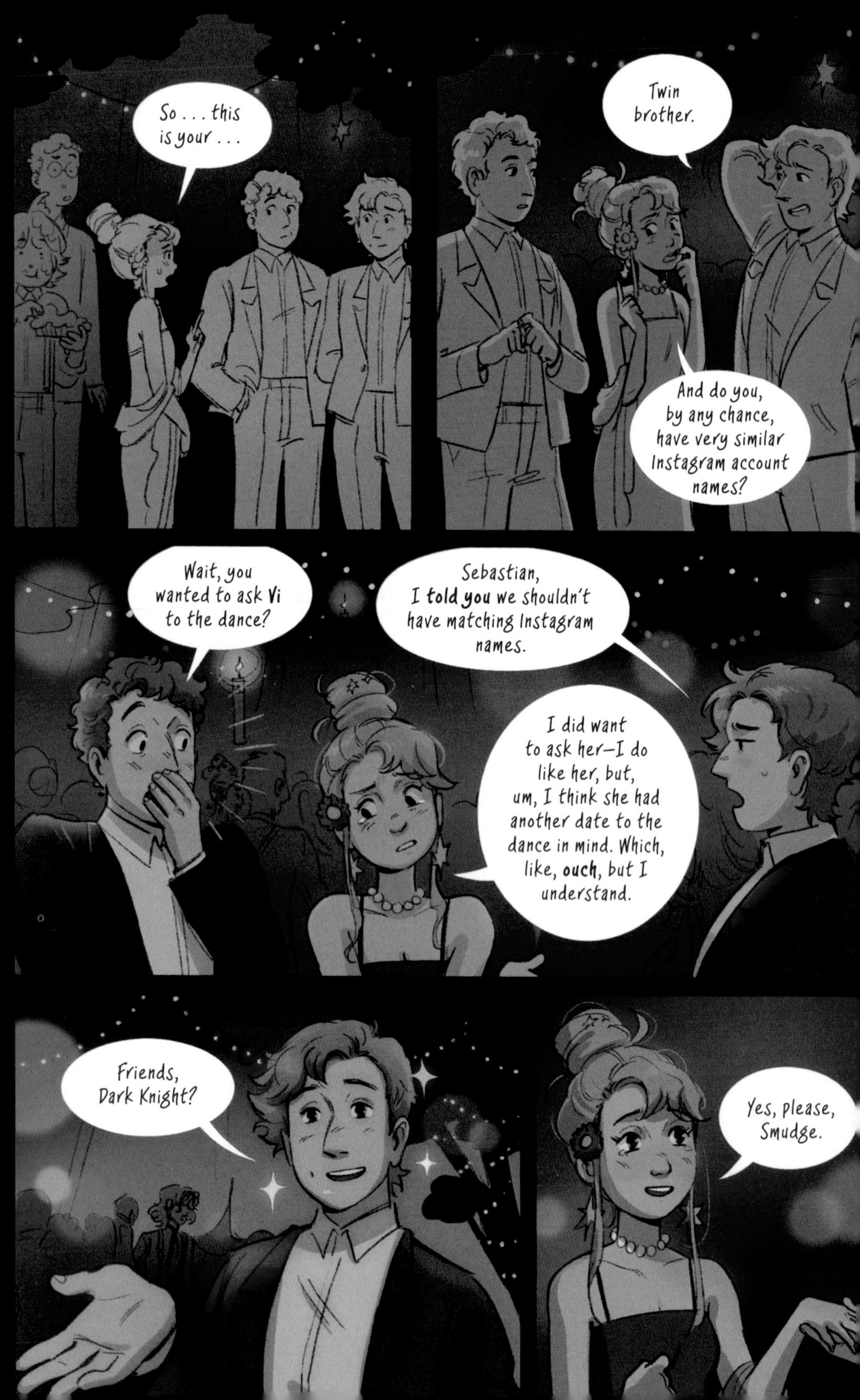

So . . . this is your . . .
Twin brother.
And do you, by any chance, have very similar Instagram account names?
Wait, you wanted to ask Vi to the dance?
Sebastian, I **told you** we shouldn't have matching Instagram names.
I did want to ask her—I do like her, but, um, I think she had another date to the dance in mind. Which, like, **ouch**, but I understand.
Friends, Dark Knight?
Yes, please, Smudge.

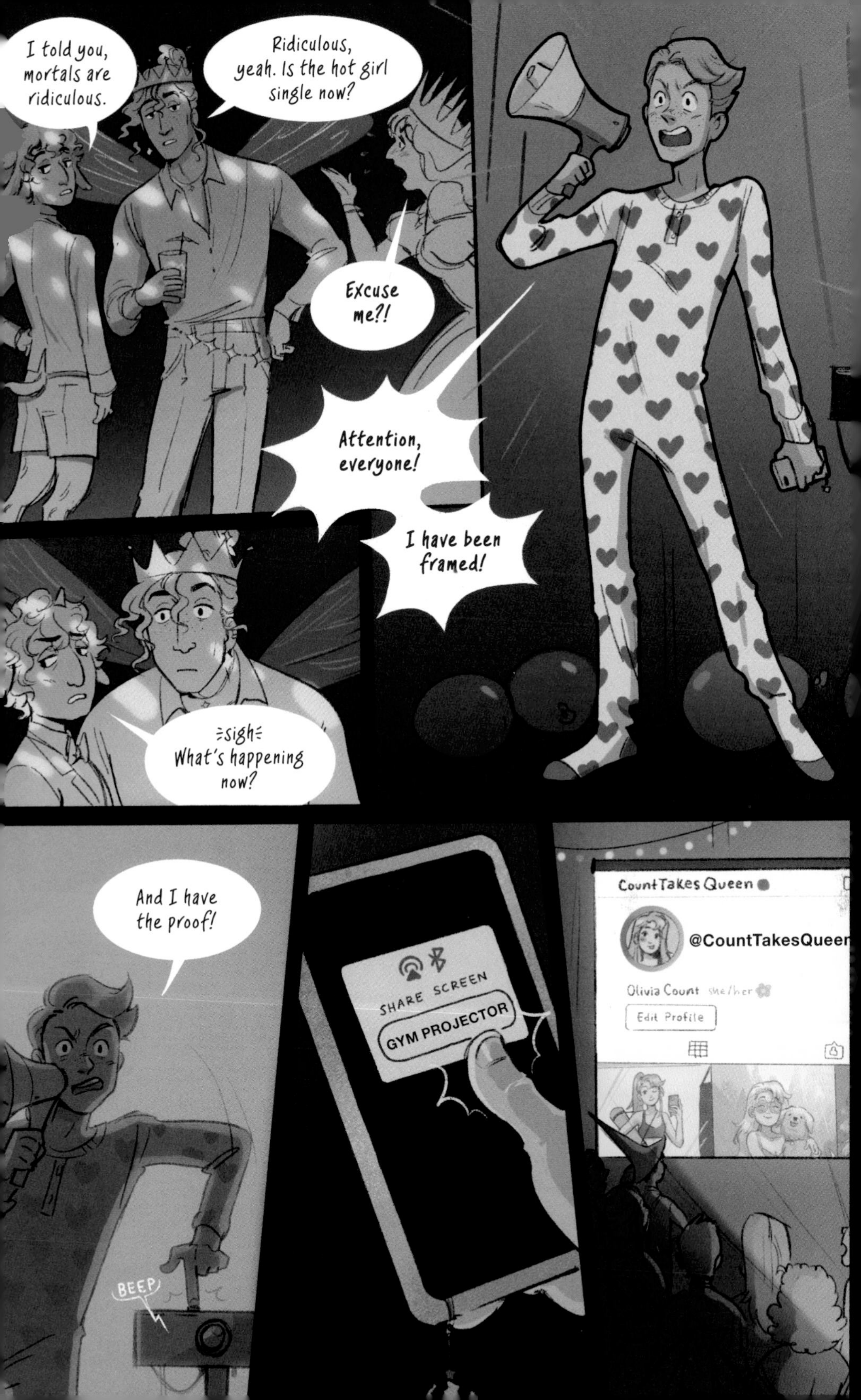
I told you, mortals are ridiculous.
Ridiculous, yeah. Is the hot girl single now?
Excuse me?!
Attention, everyone!
I have been framed!
≈sigh≈ What's happening now?
And I have the proof!
SHARE SCREEN
GYM PROJECTOR
BEEP
CountTakes Queen
@CountTakesQueen
Olivia Count she/her
Edit Profile

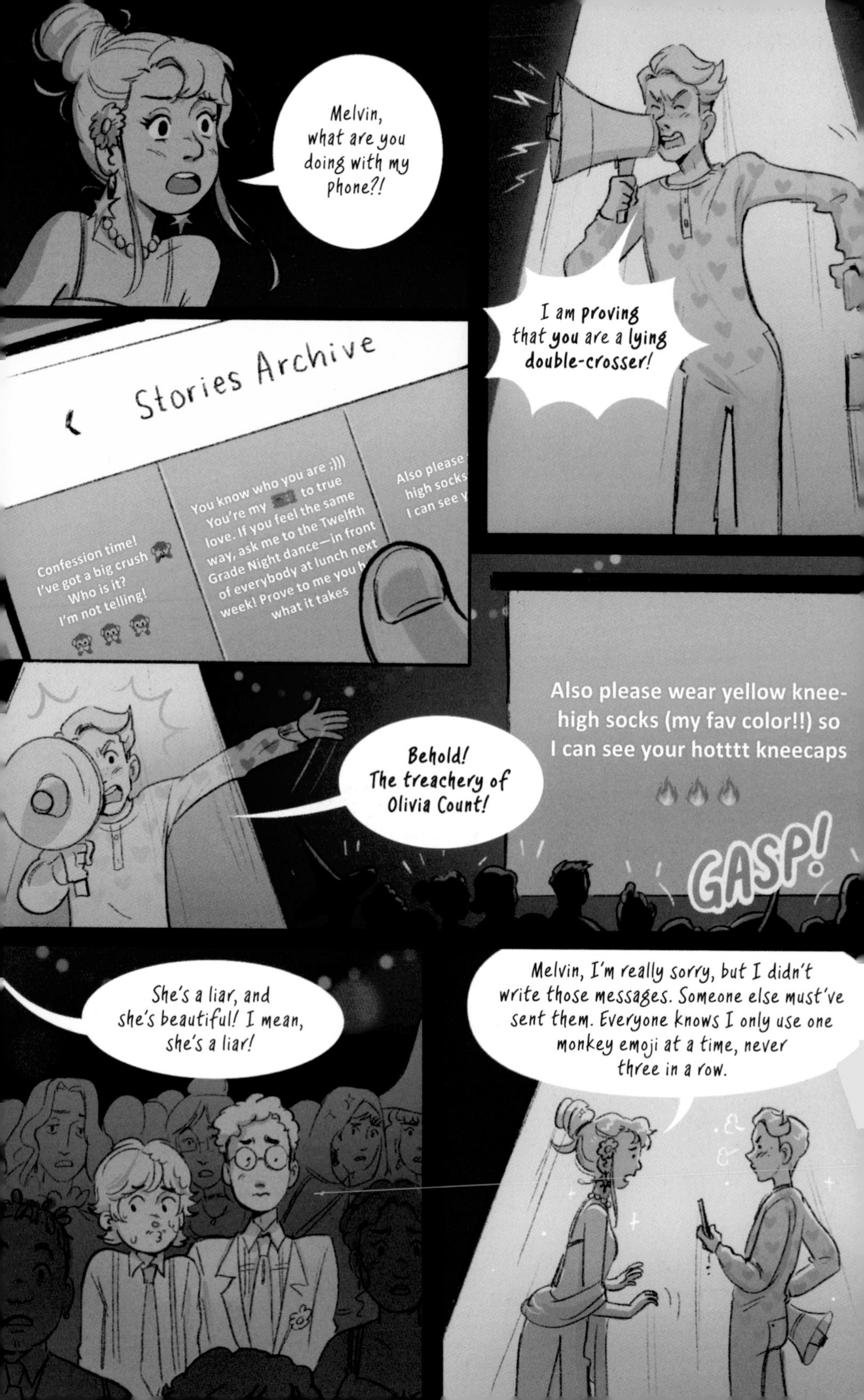
Melvin, what are you doing with my phone?!
I am proving that you are a lying double-crosser!
Stories Archive
Confession time! I've got a big crush Who is it? I'm not telling!
You know who you are ;))) You're my [redacted] to true love. If you feel the same way, ask me to the Twelfth Grade Night dance—in front of everybody at lunch next week! Prove to me you h what it takes
Also please high socks I can see y
Behold! The treachery of Olivia Count!
Also please wear yellow knee-high socks (my fav color!!) so I can see your hotttt kneecaps
GASP!
She's a liar, and she's beautiful! I mean, she's a liar!
Melvin, I'm really sorry, but I didn't write those messages. Someone else must've sent them. Everyone knows I only use one monkey emoji at a time, never three in a row.

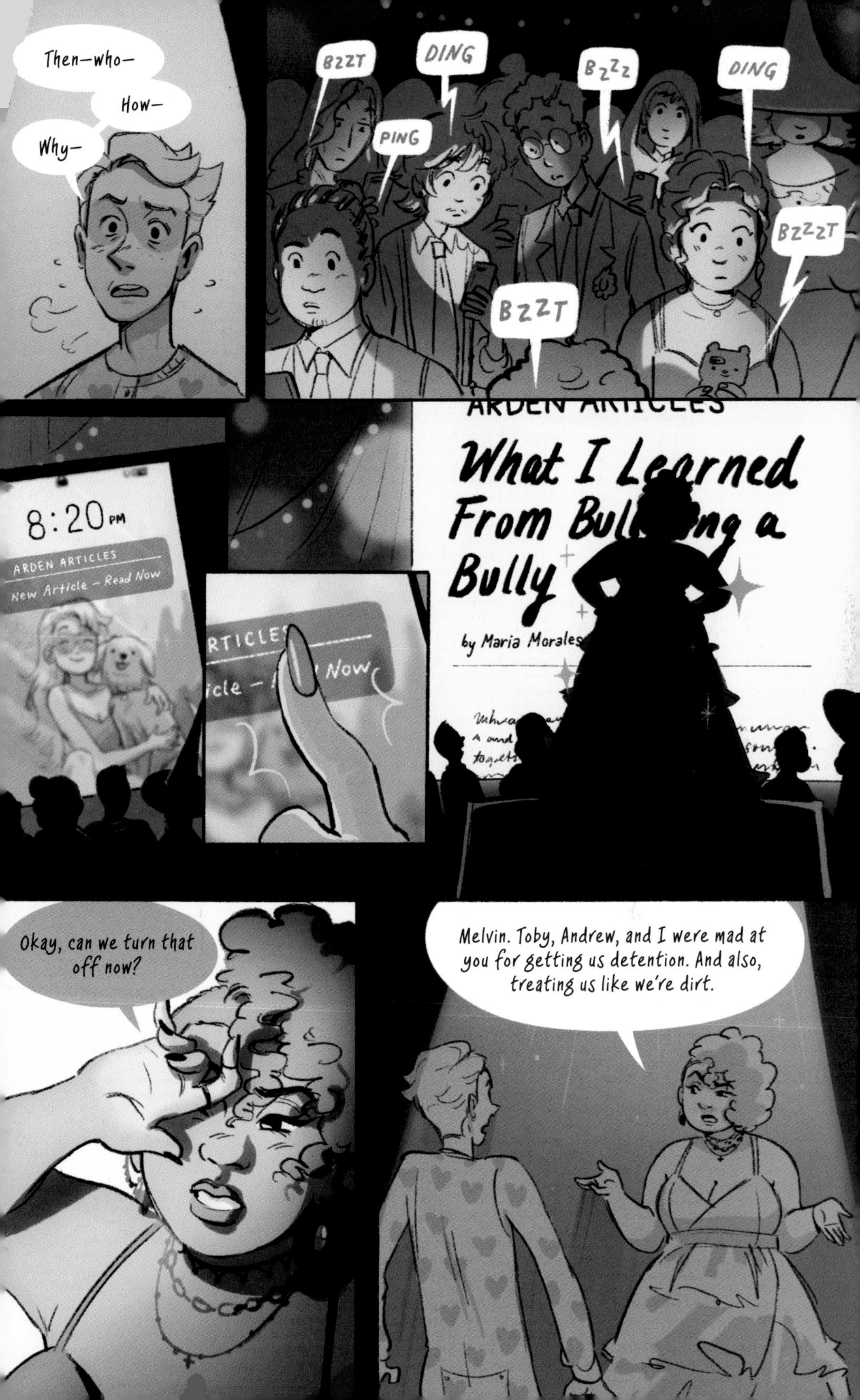
Then—who—
How—
Why—
BZZT
DING
BZZZ
DING
PING
BZZZT
BZZT
ARDEN ARTICLES
What I Learned From Bul[...]ng a Bully
by Maria Morales
8:20 PM
ARDEN ARTICLES
New Article – Read Now
Okay, can we turn that off now?
Melvin. Toby, Andrew, and I were mad at you for getting us detention. And also, treating us like we're dirt.

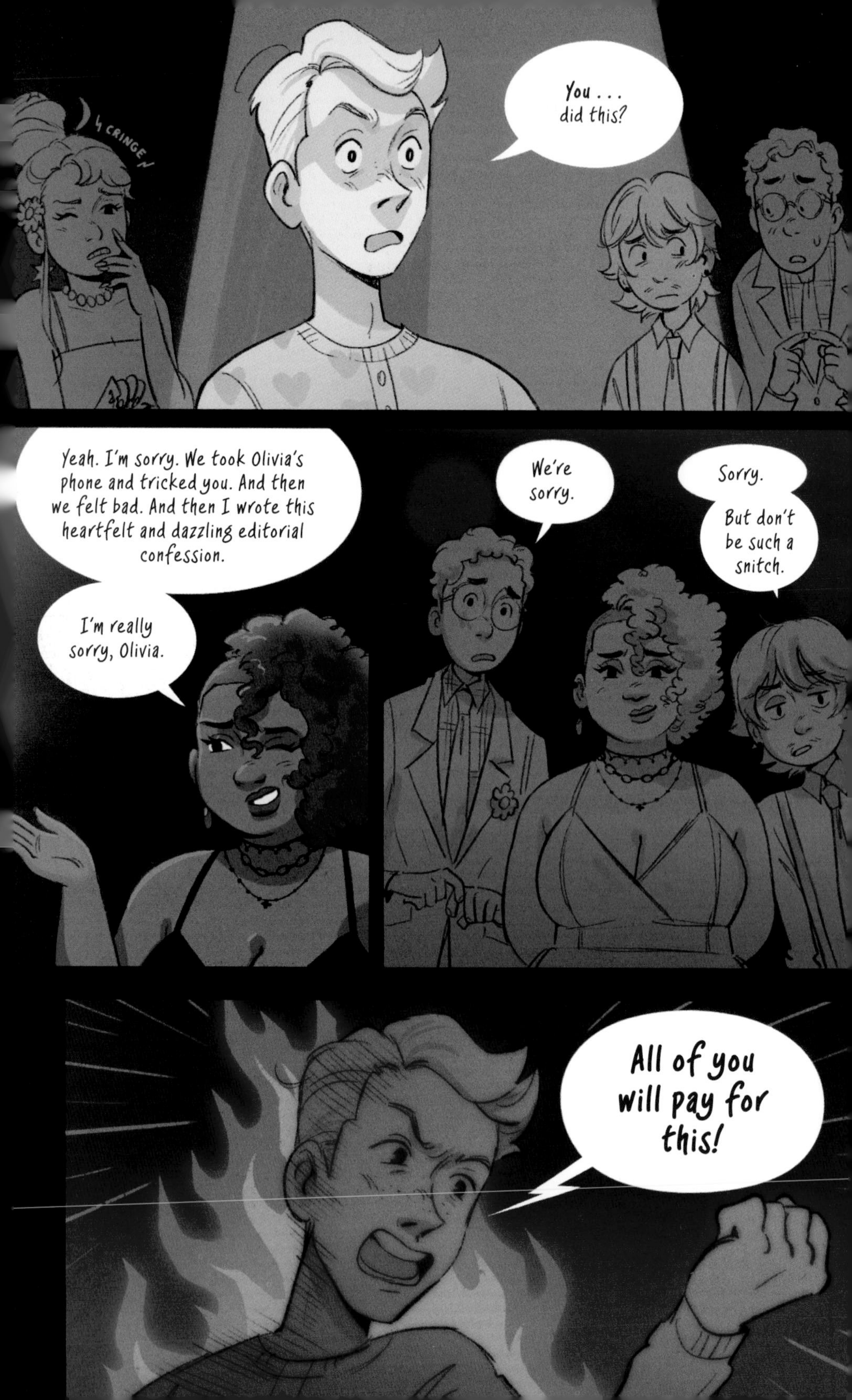
CRINGE
You . . . did this?
Yeah. I'm sorry. We took Olivia's phone and tricked you. And then we felt bad. And then I wrote this heartfelt and dazzling editorial confession.
I'm really sorry, Olivia.
We're sorry.
Sorry.
But don't be such a snitch.
All of you will pay for this!

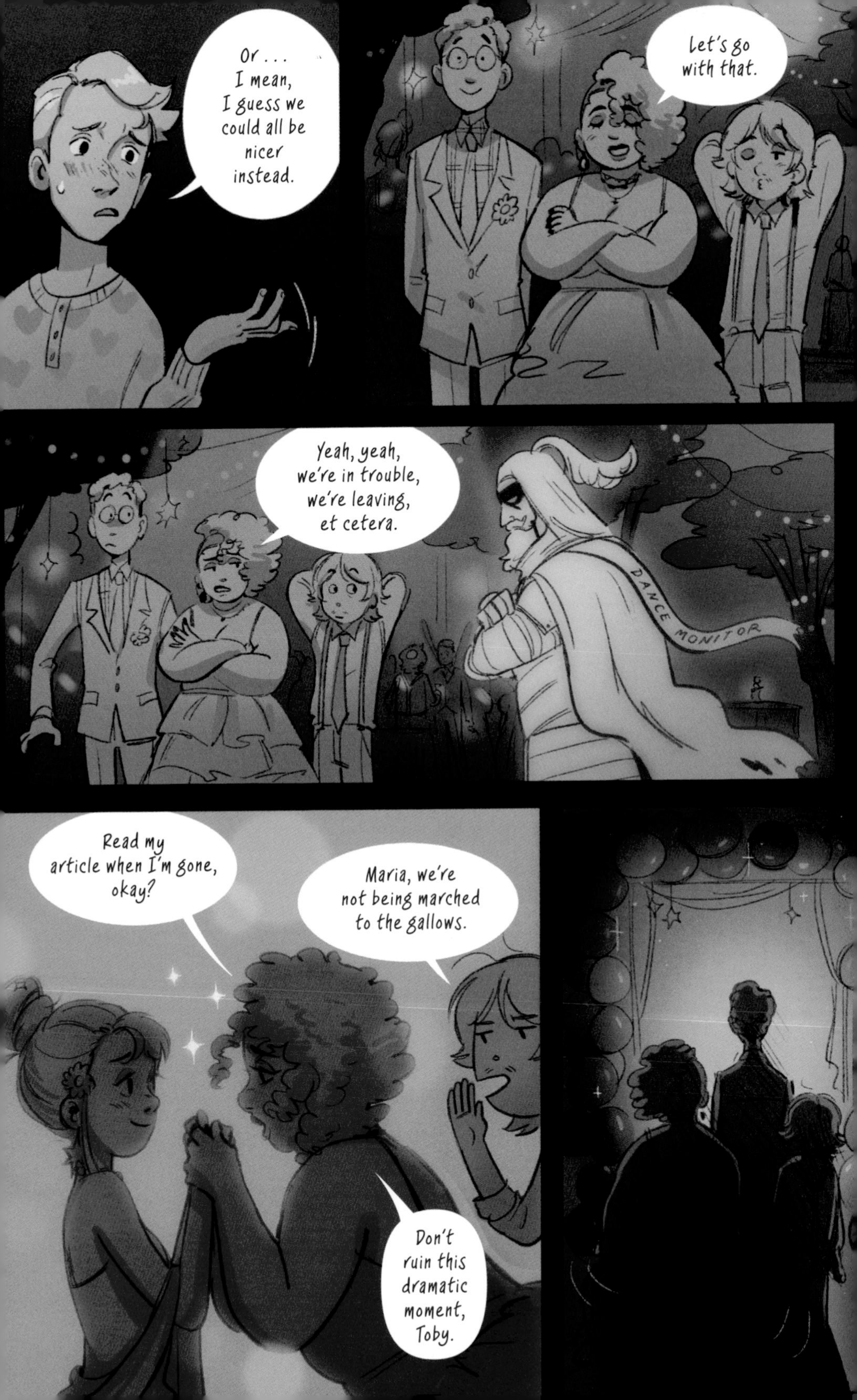

Or . . . I mean, I guess we could all be nicer instead.
Let's go with that.
Yeah, yeah, we're in trouble, we're leaving, et cetera.
DANCE MONITOR
Read my article when I'm gone, okay?
Maria, we're not being marched to the gallows.
Don't ruin this dramatic moment, Toby.

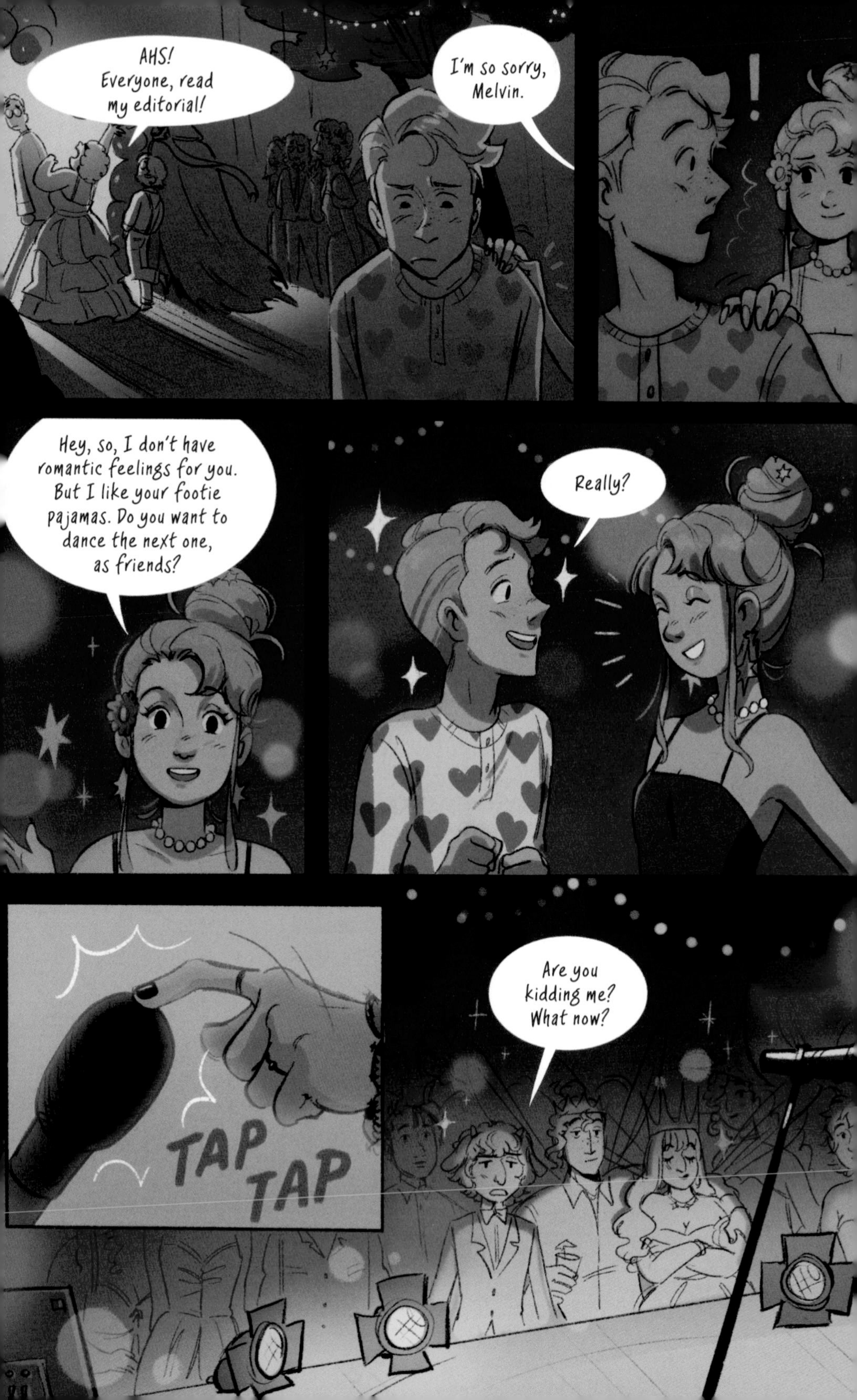
AHS! Everyone, read my editorial!
I'm so sorry, Melvin.
!
Hey, so, I don't have romantic feelings for you. But I like your footie pajamas. Do you want to dance the next one, as friends?
Really?
TAP TAP
Are you kidding me? What now?

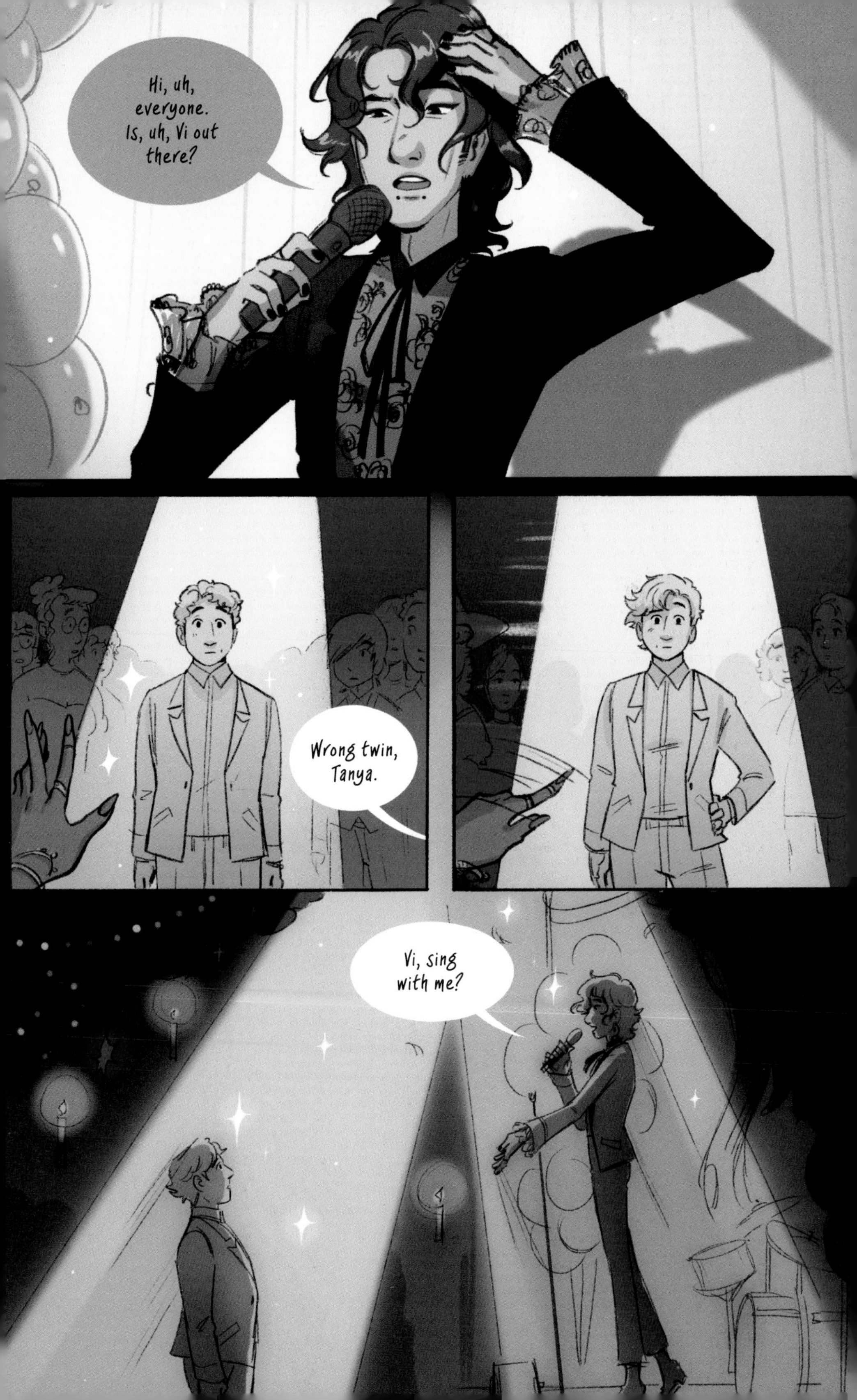
Hi, uh, everyone. Is, uh, Vi out there?
Wrong twin, Tanya.
Vi, sing with me?

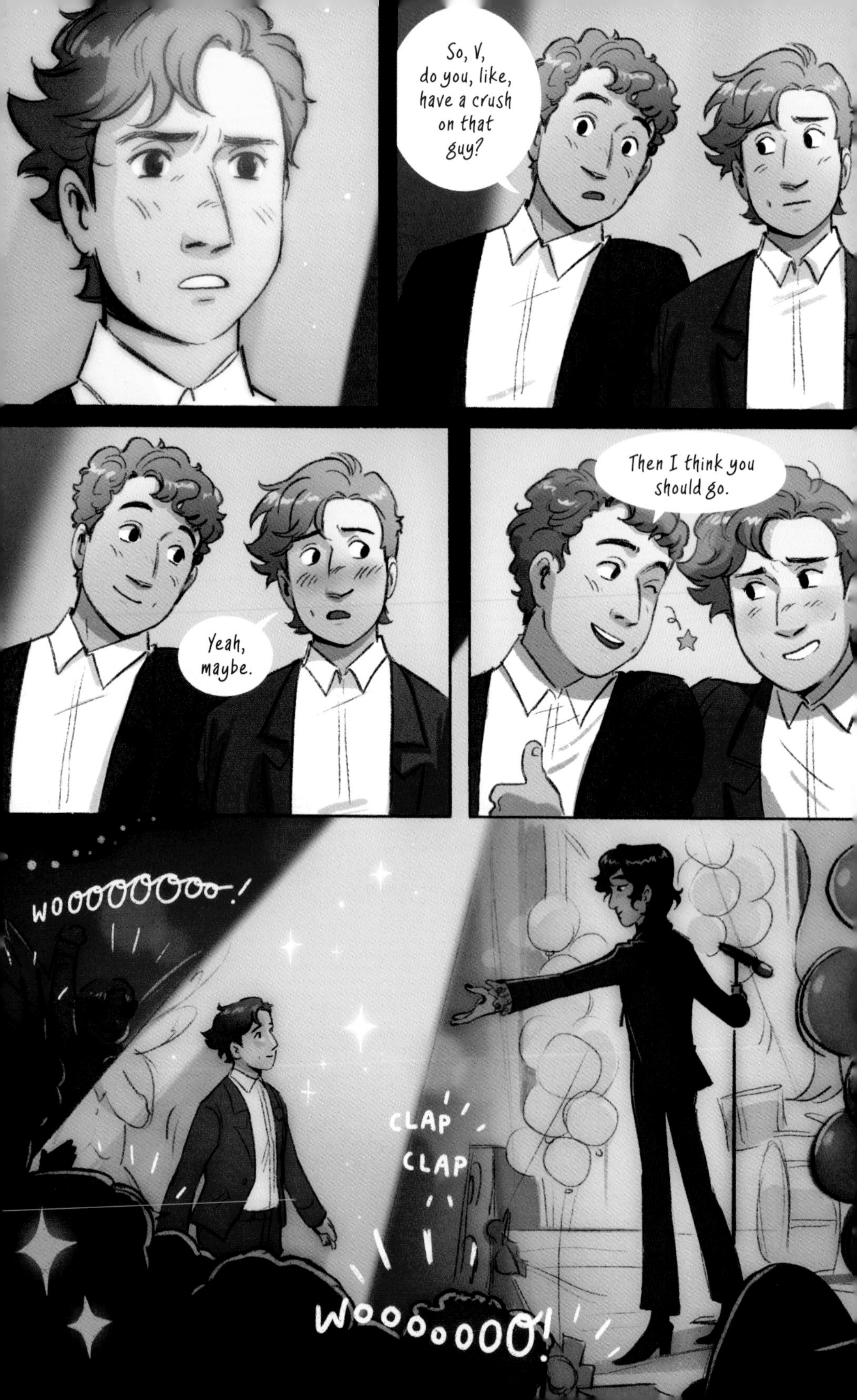
So, V, do you, like, have a crush on that guy?
Yeah, maybe.
Then I think you should go.
WOOOOOOOo!
CLAP
CLAP
WOOooOOO!

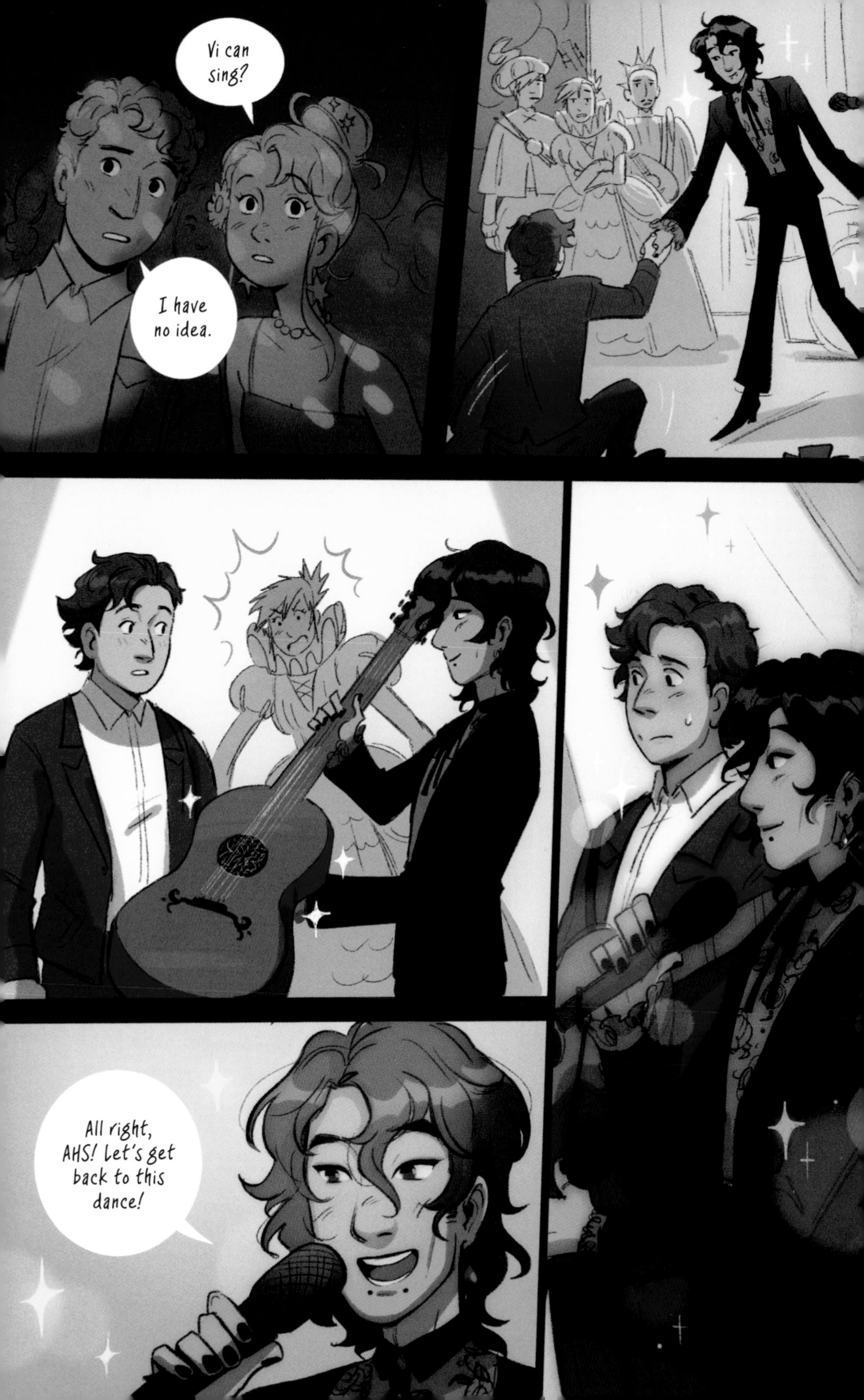
Vi can sing?
I have no idea.
All right, AHS! Let's get back to this dance!

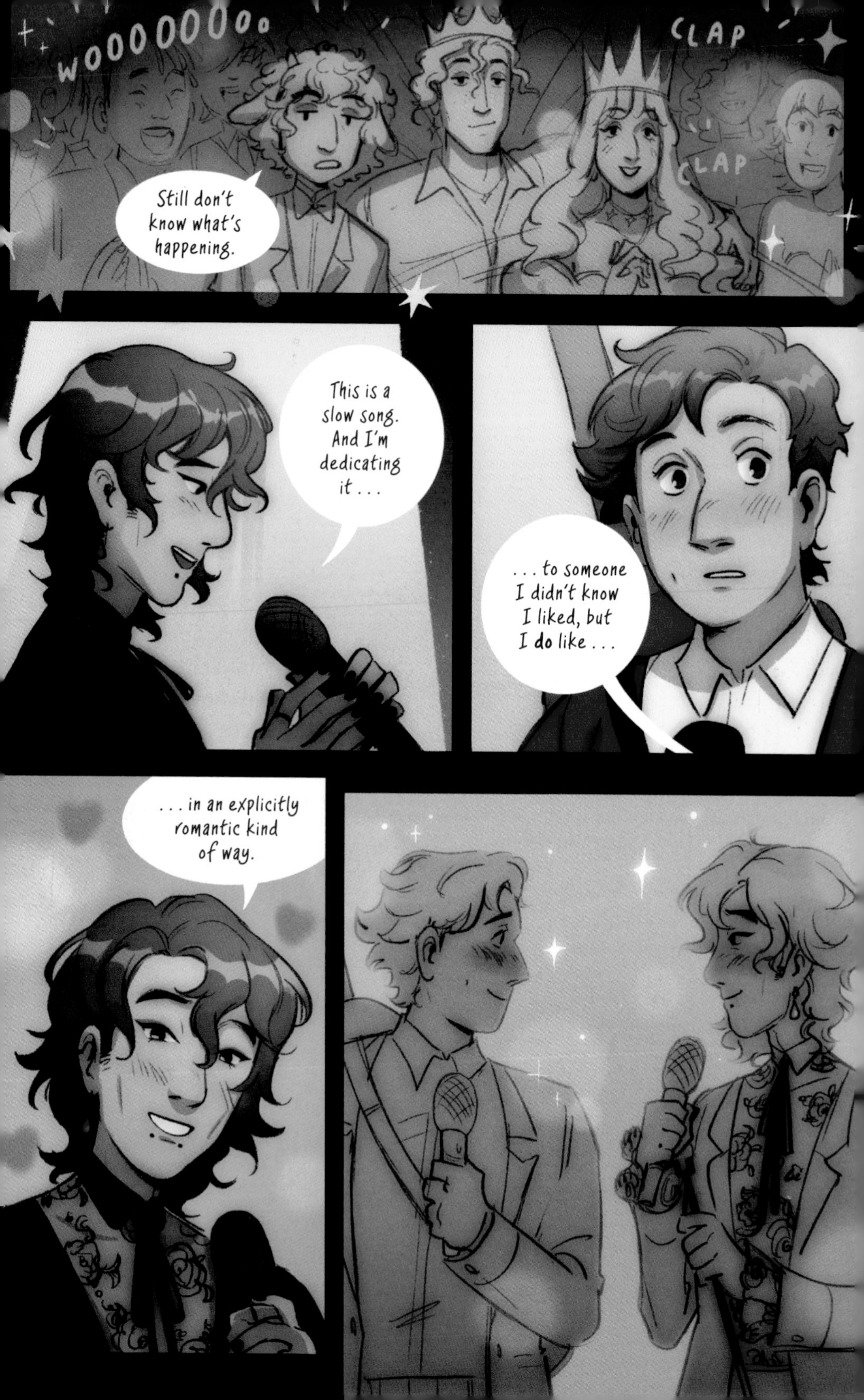
WOOOOOOOo
CLAP
CLAP
Still don't know what's happening.
This is a slow song. And I'm dedicating it . . .
. . . to someone I didn't know I liked, but I do like . . .
. . . in an explicitly romantic kind of way.

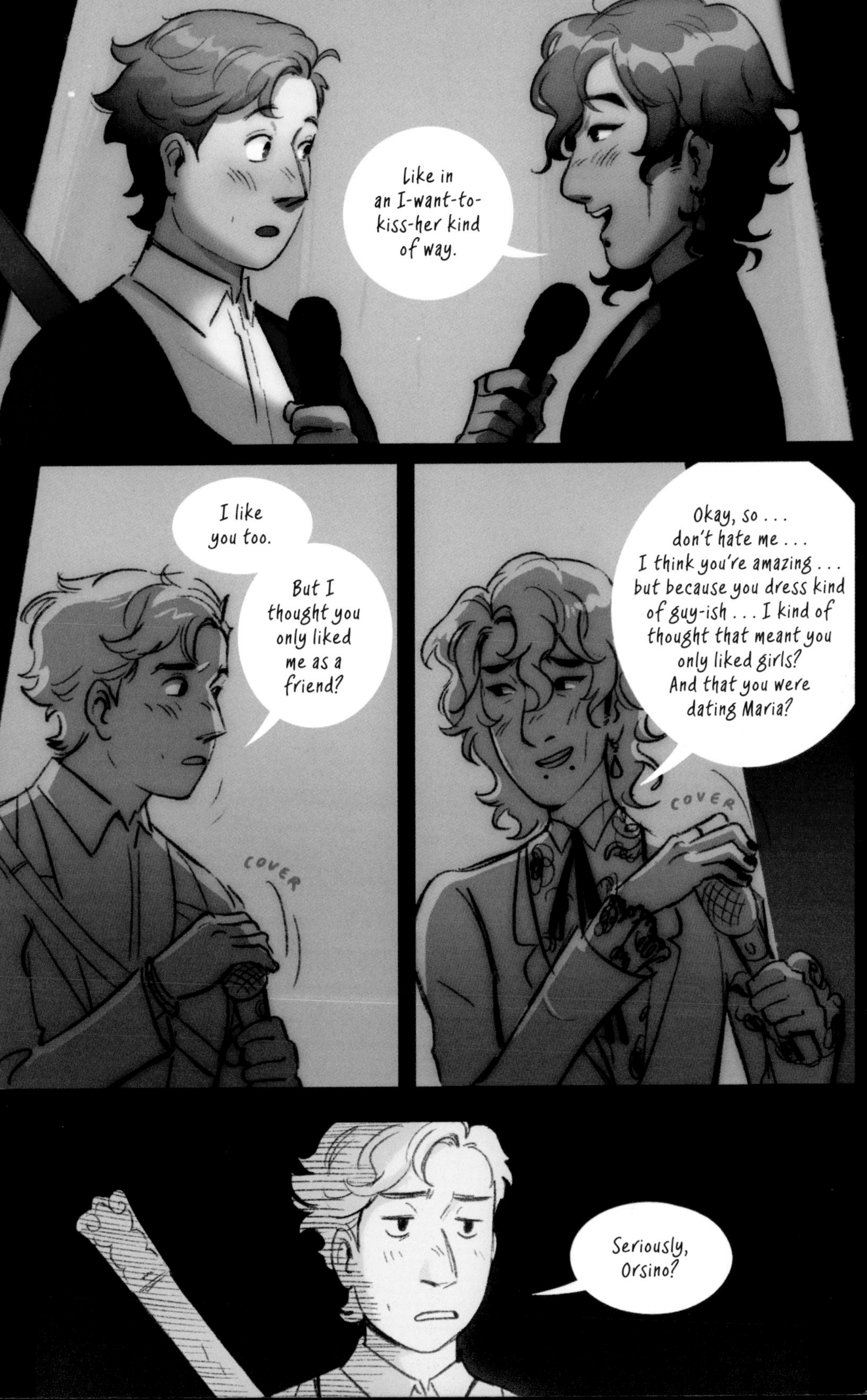
Like in an I-want-to-kiss-her kind of way.
I like you too.
But I thought you only liked me as a friend?
COVER
Okay, so . . . don't hate me . . . I think you're amazing . . . but because you dress kind of guy-ish . . . I kind of thought that meant you only liked girls? And that you were dating Maria?
COVER
Seriously, Orsino?

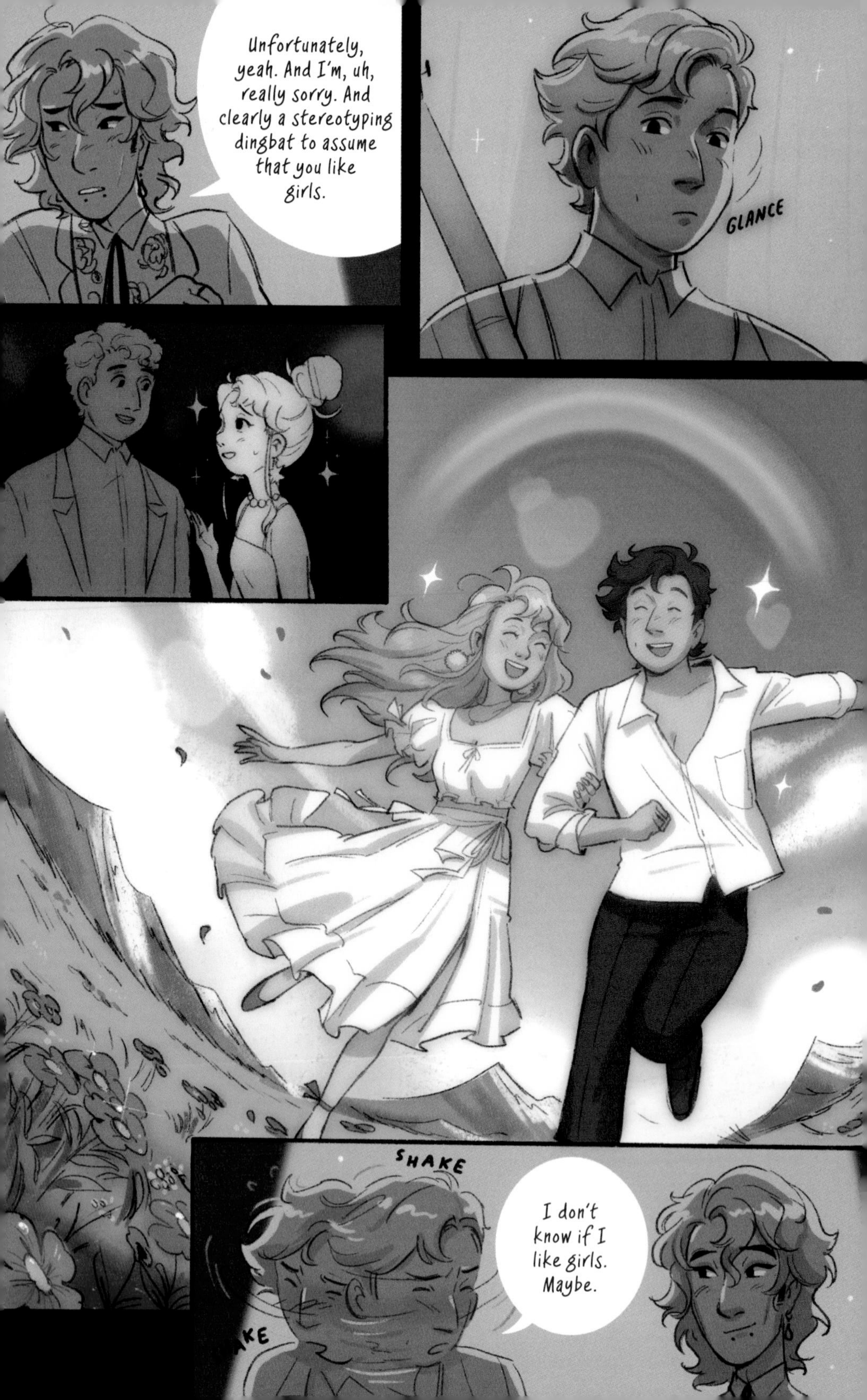
Unfortunately, yeah. And I'm, uh, really sorry. And clearly a stereotyping dingbat to assume that you like girls.
GLANCE
SHAKE
I don't know if I like girls. Maybe.

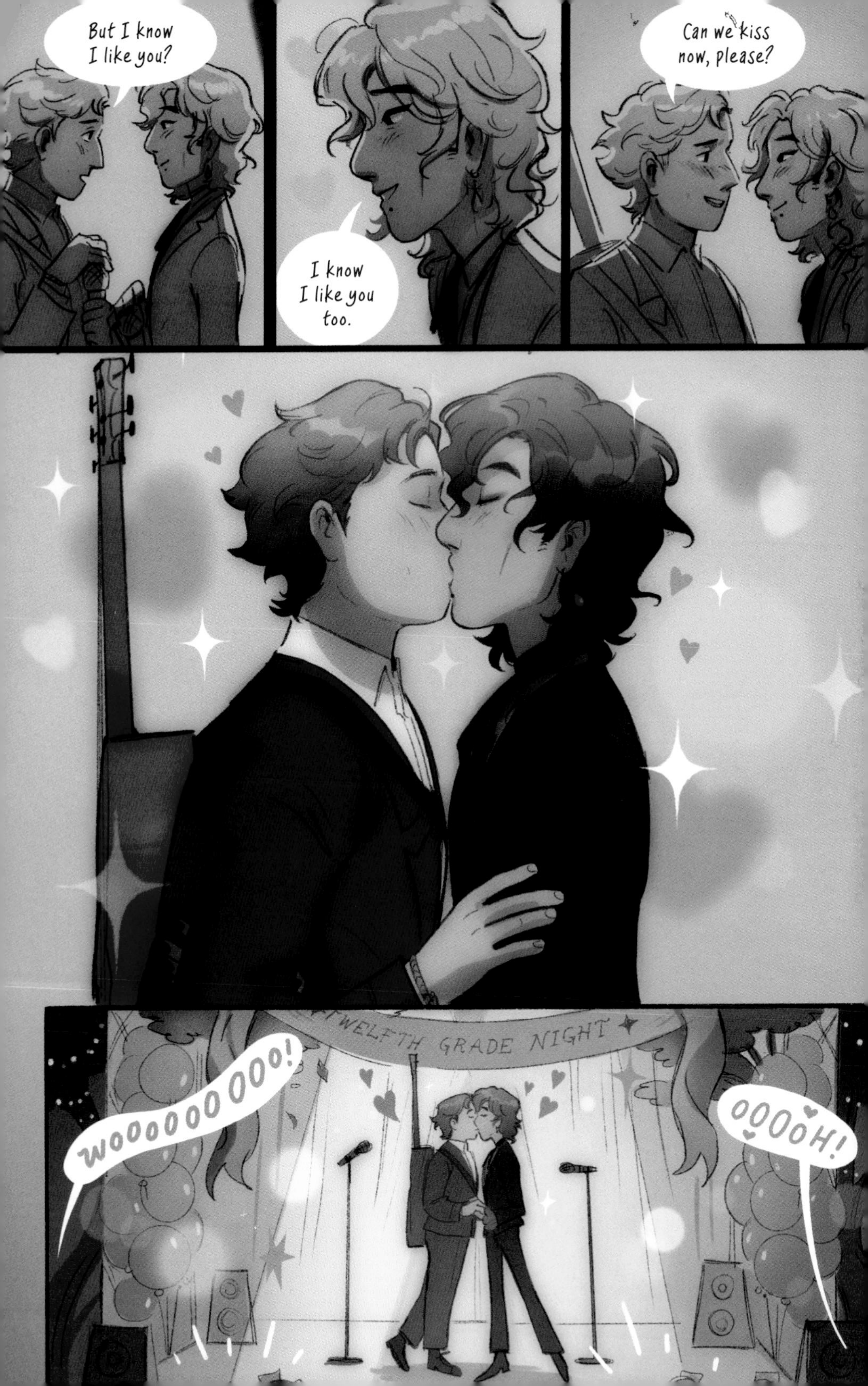
But I know I like you?
I know I like you too.
Can we kiss now, please?
TWELFTH GRADE NIGHT
WOOOOOOOOO!
OOOOH!

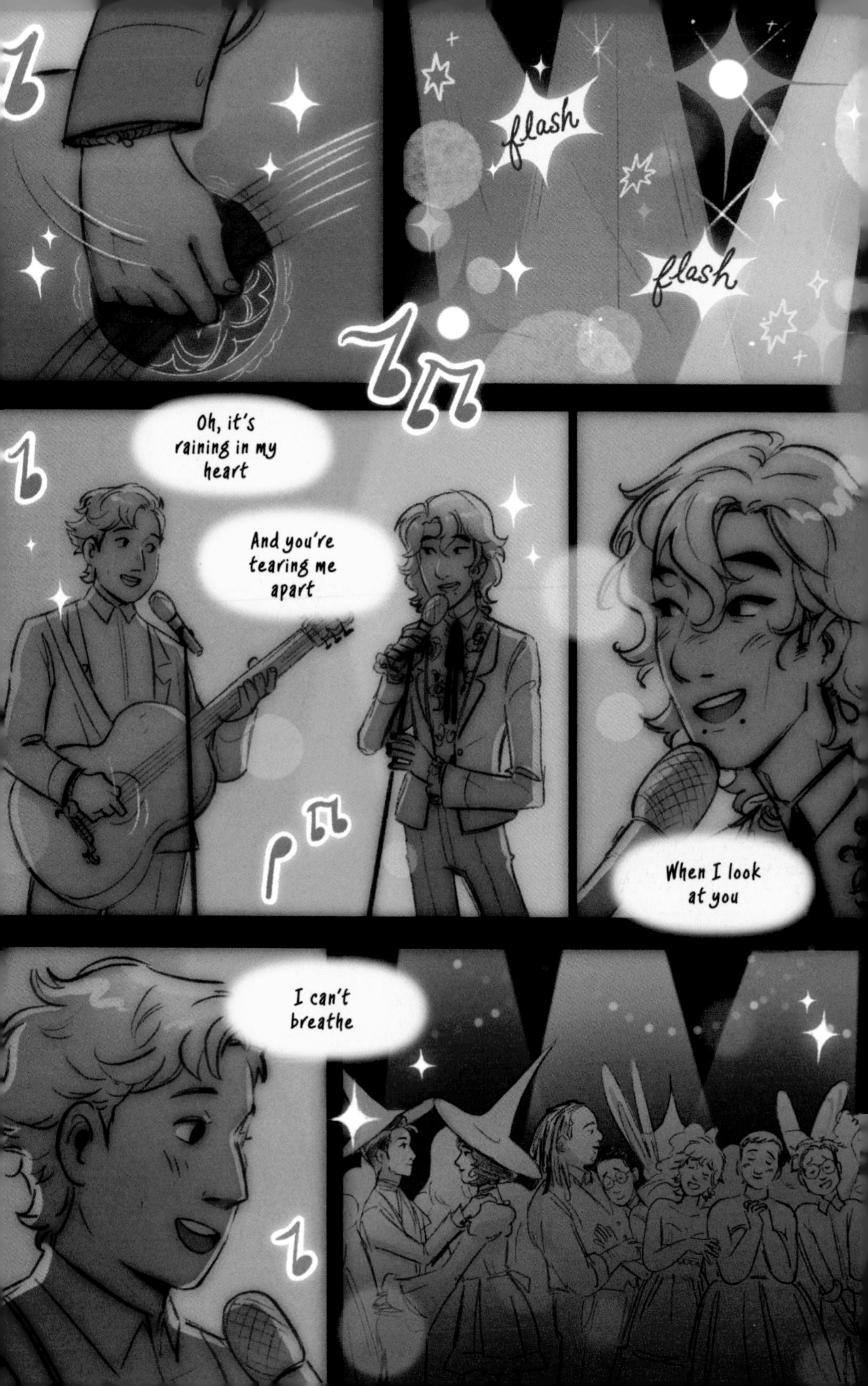
flash
flash
Oh, it's raining in my heart
And you're tearing me apart
When I look at you
I can't breathe

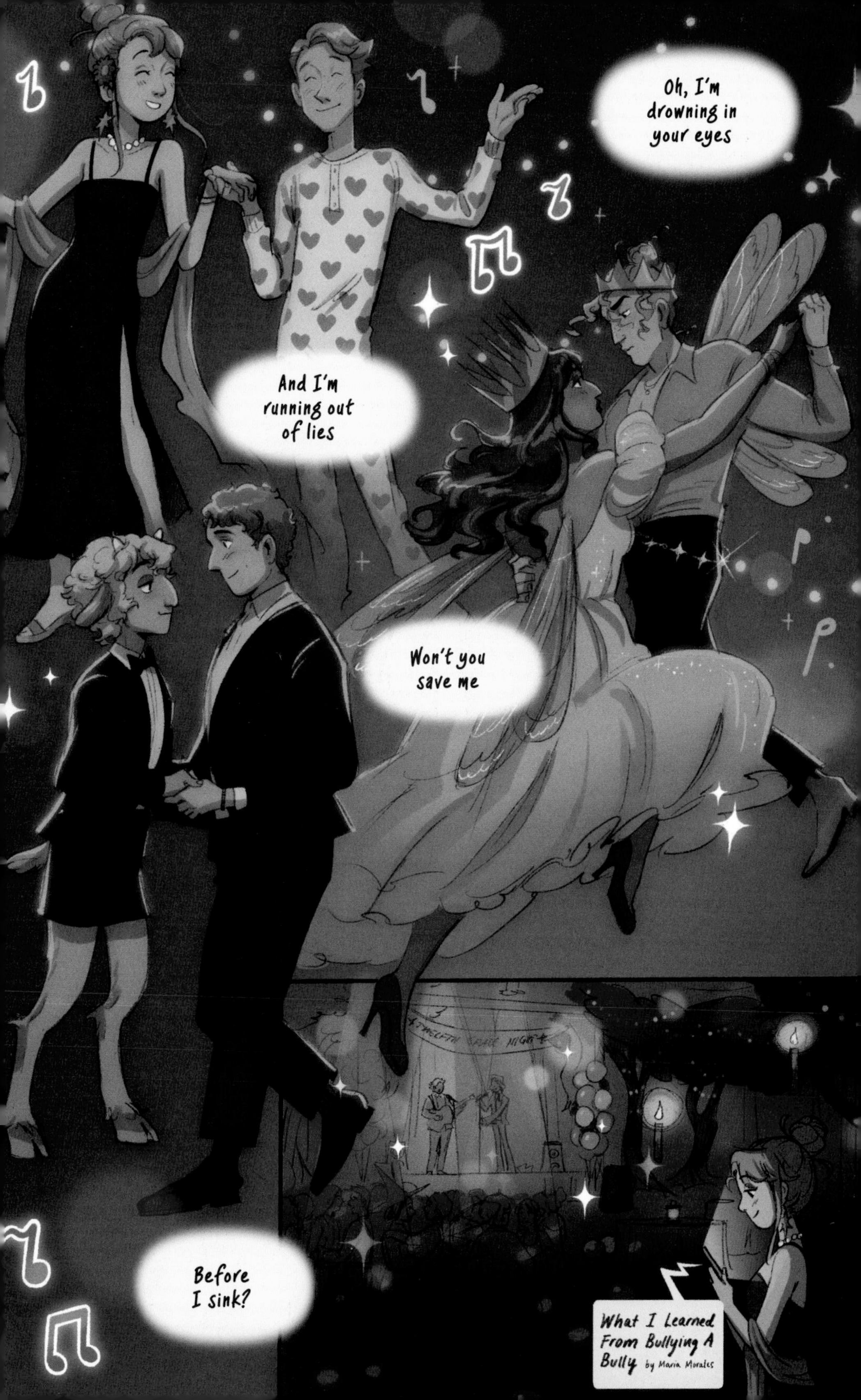
Oh, I'm drowning in your eyes
And I'm running out of lies
Won't you save me
Before I sink?
What I Learned From Bullying A Bully by Maria Morales

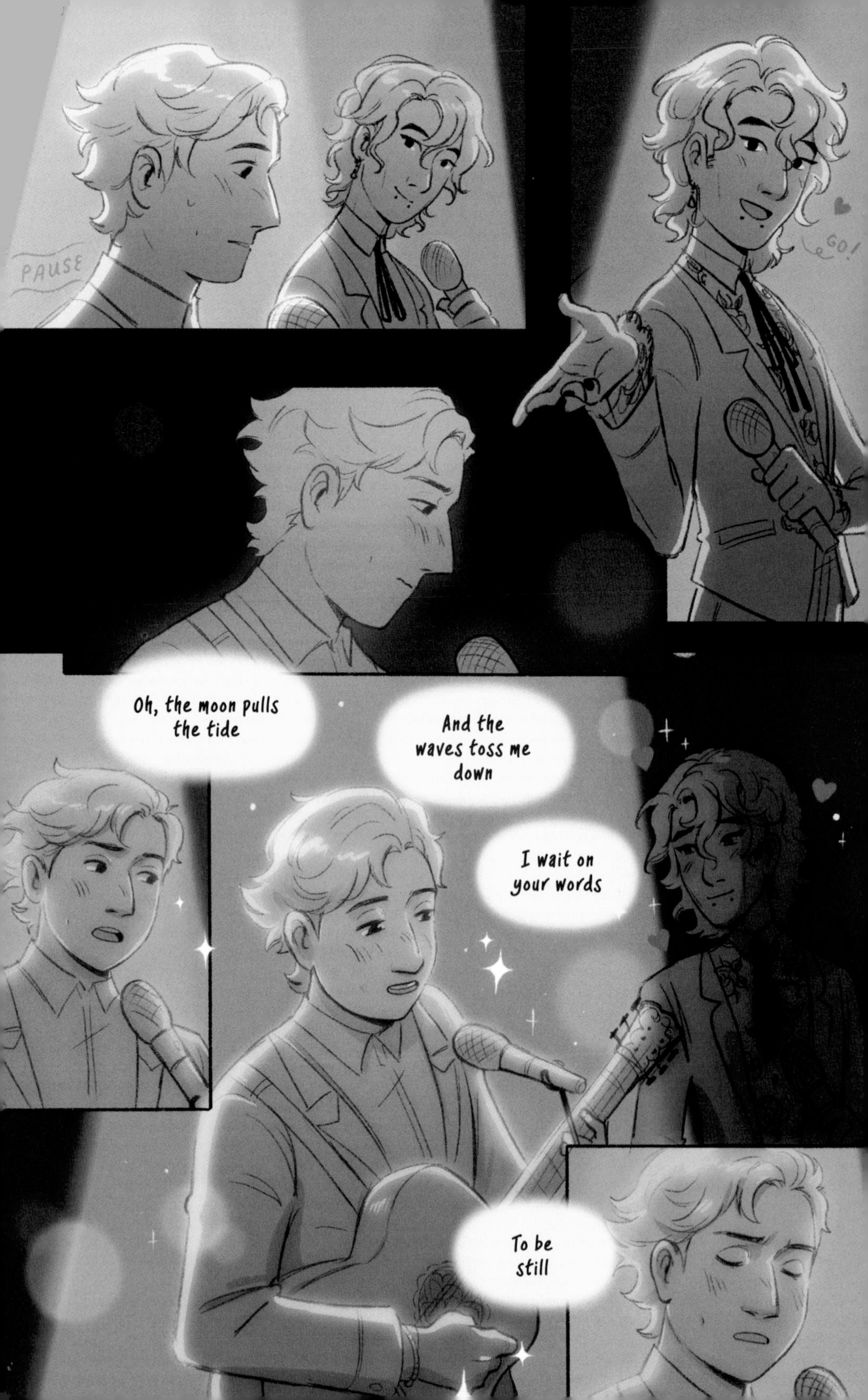
PAUSE
GO!
Oh, the moon pulls the tide
And the waves toss me down
I wait on your words
To be still

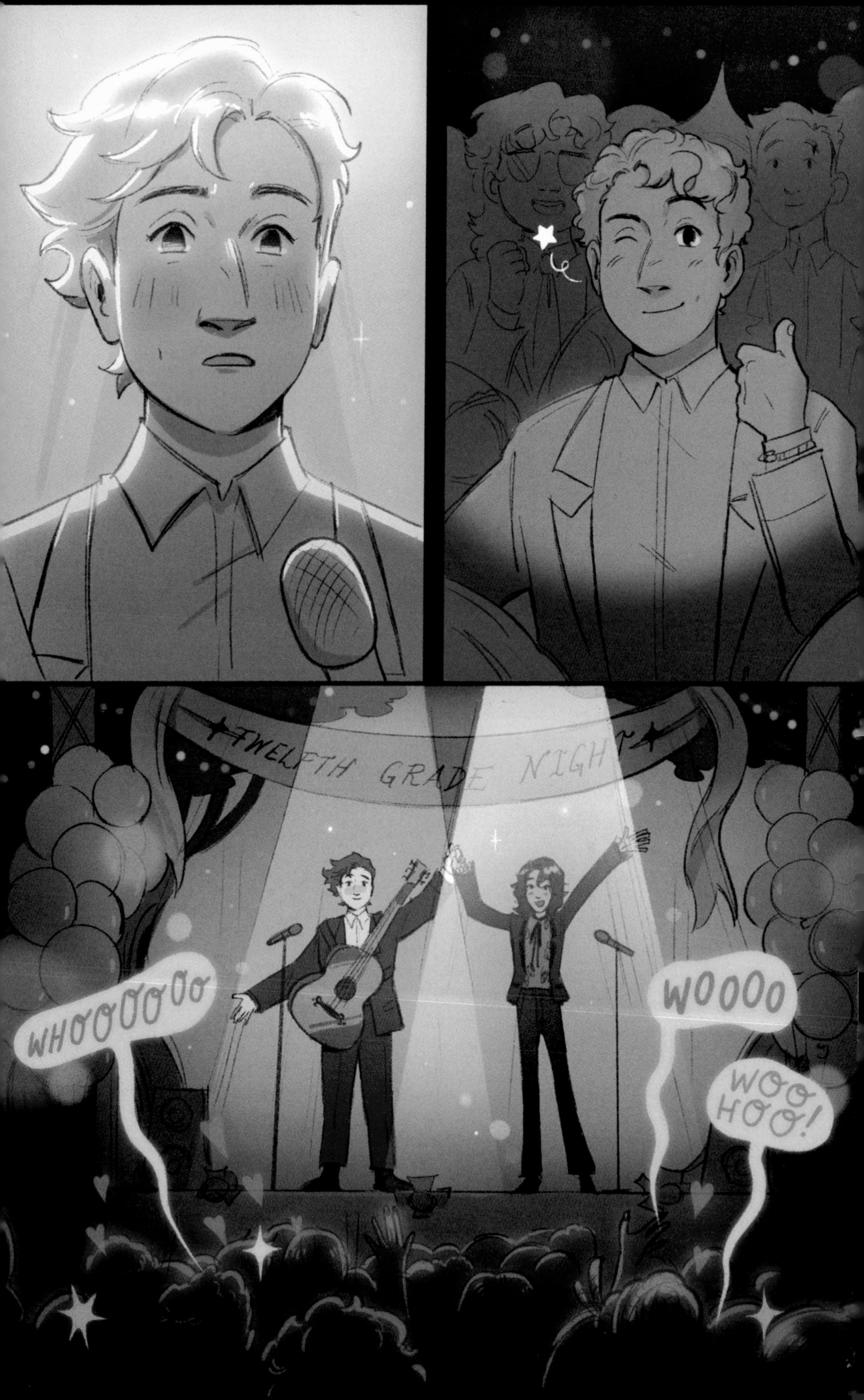
TWELFTH GRADE NIGHT
WHOOOOOO
WOOOO
WOO HOO!

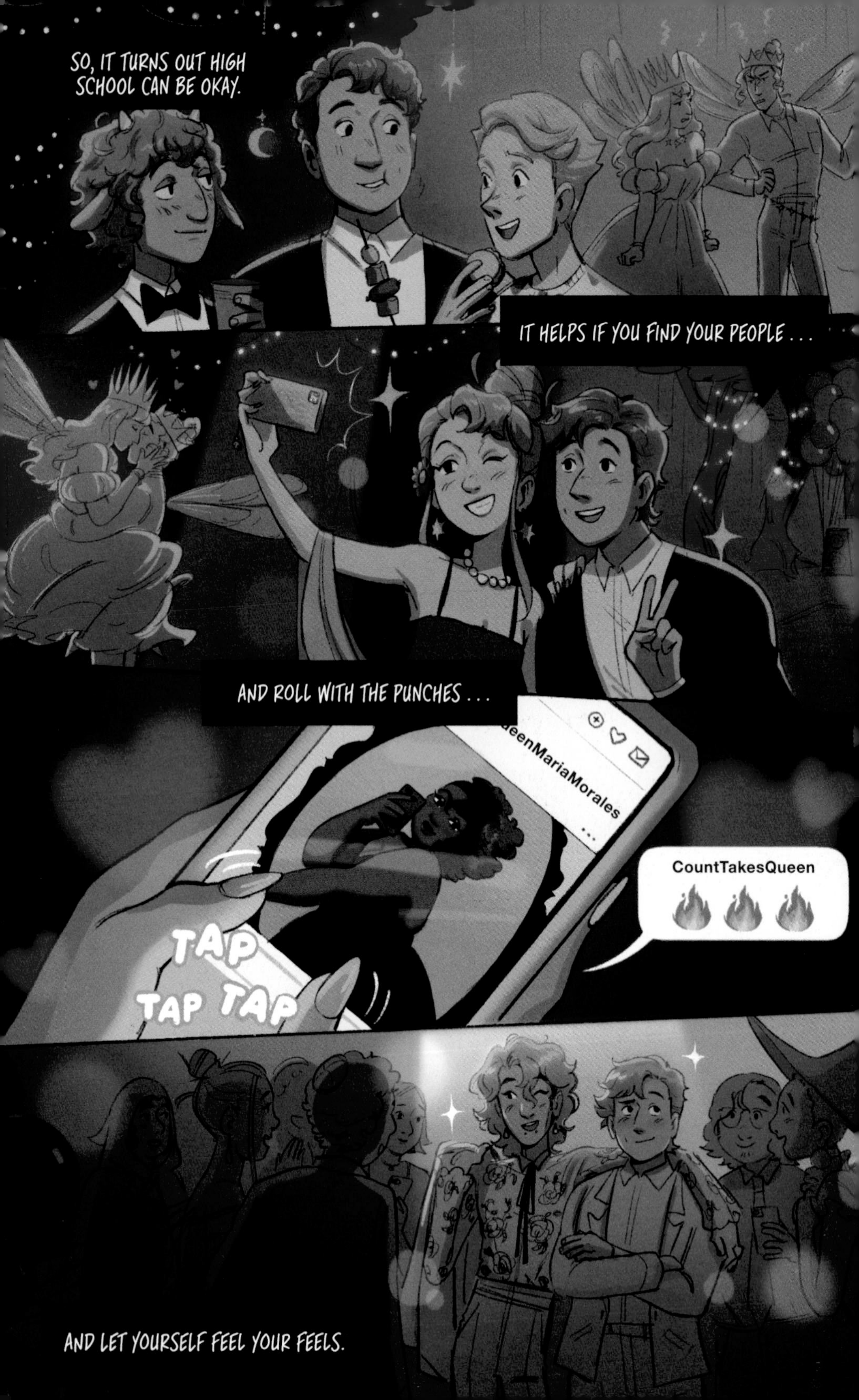
SO, IT TURNS OUT HIGH SCHOOL CAN BE OKAY.
IT HELPS IF YOU FIND YOUR PEOPLE . . .
AND ROLL WITH THE PUNCHES . . .
CountTakesQueen
🔥🔥🔥
TAP
TAP TAP
AND LET YOURSELF FEEL YOUR FEELS.

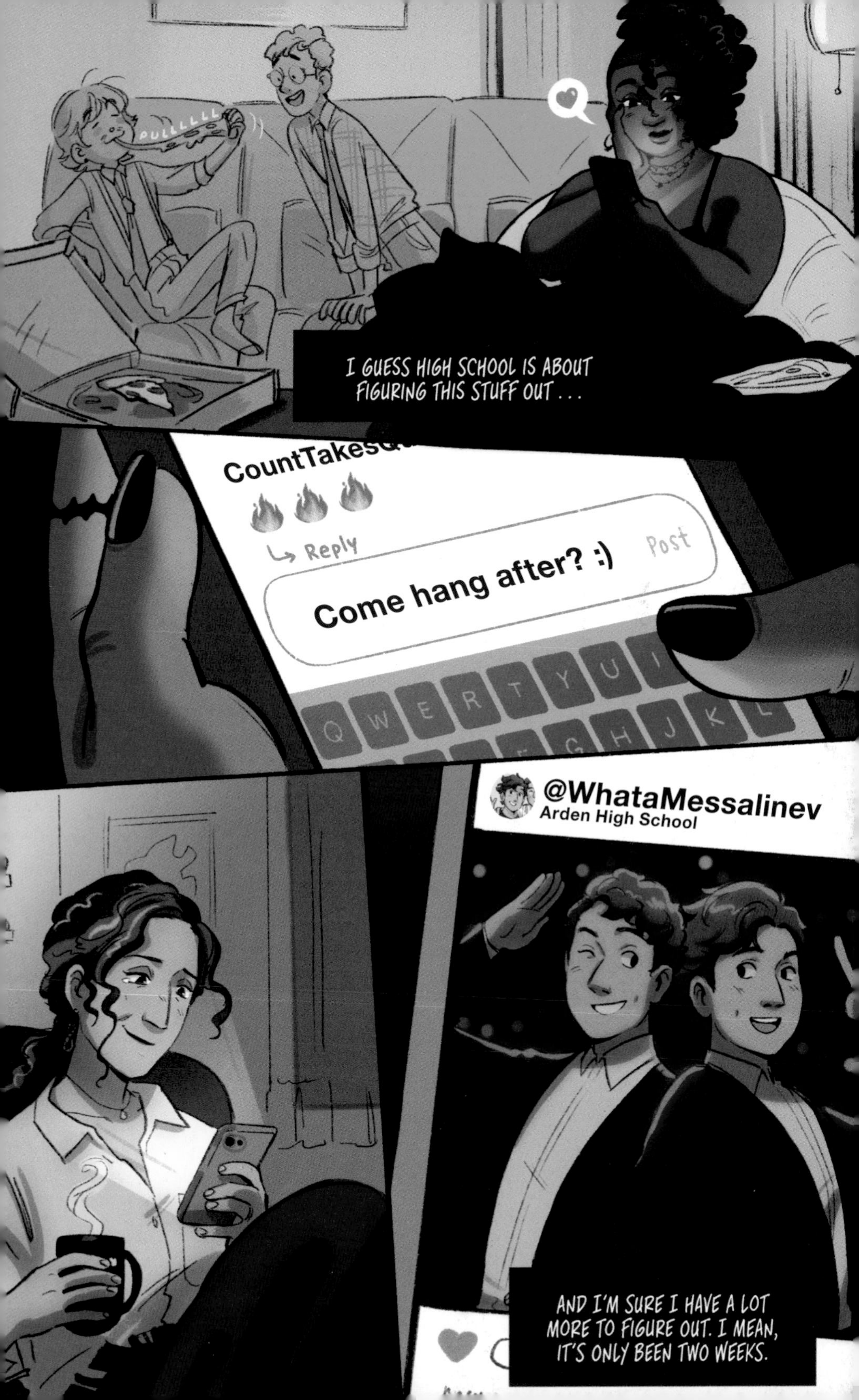
PULLLLLLL
I GUESS HIGH SCHOOL IS ABOUT FIGURING THIS STUFF OUT . . .
CountTakes
Reply
Post
Come hang after? :)
@WhataMessalinev
Arden High School
AND I'M SURE I HAVE A LOT MORE TO FIGURE OUT. I MEAN, IT'S ONLY BEEN TWO WEEKS.

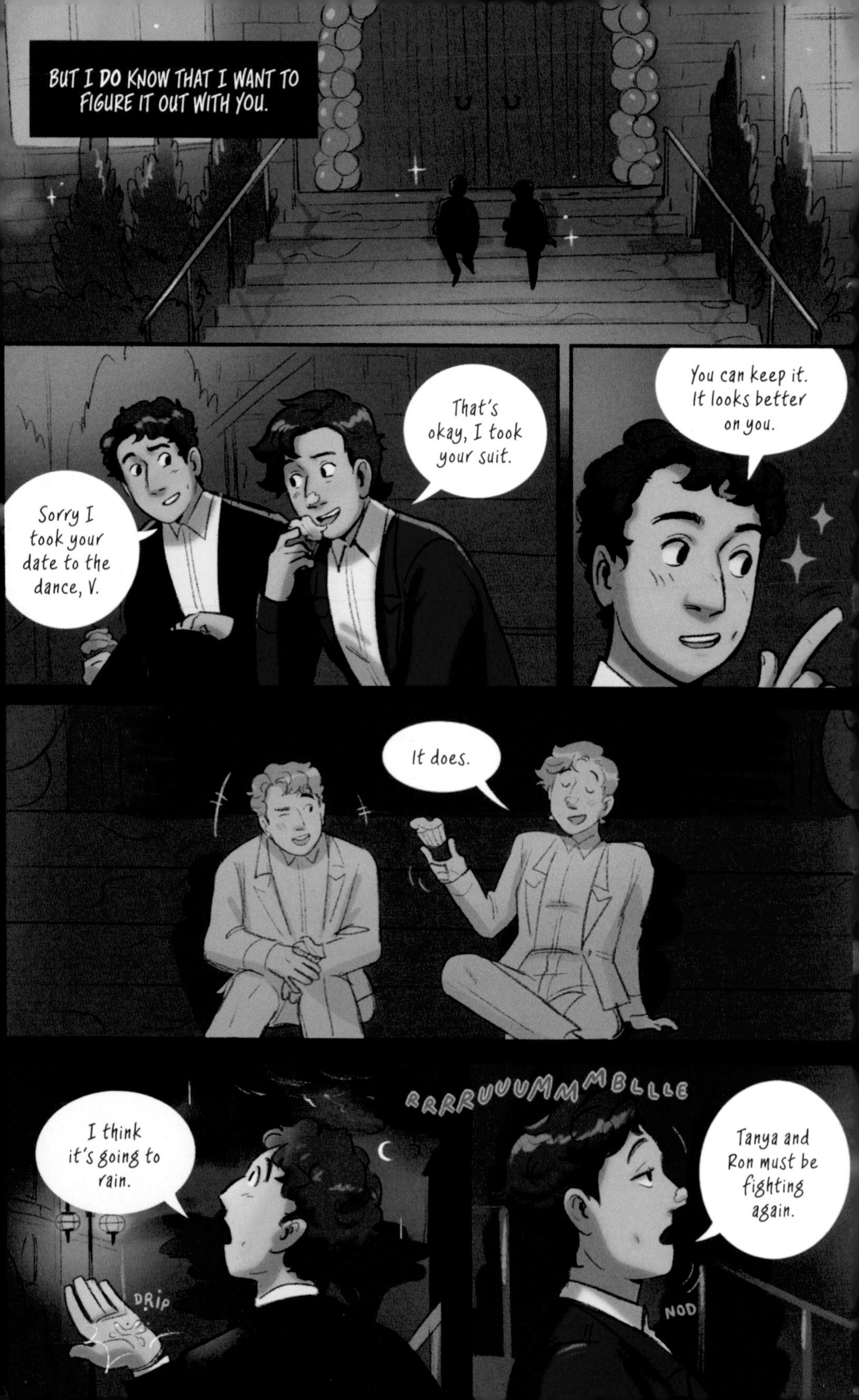
BUT I DO KNOW THAT I WANT TO FIGURE IT OUT WITH YOU.
Sorry I took your date to the dance, V.
That's okay, I took your suit.
You can keep it. It looks better on you.
It does.
I think it's going to rain.
DRIP
RRRRUUUMMMBLLLE
Tanya and Ron must be fighting again.
NOD

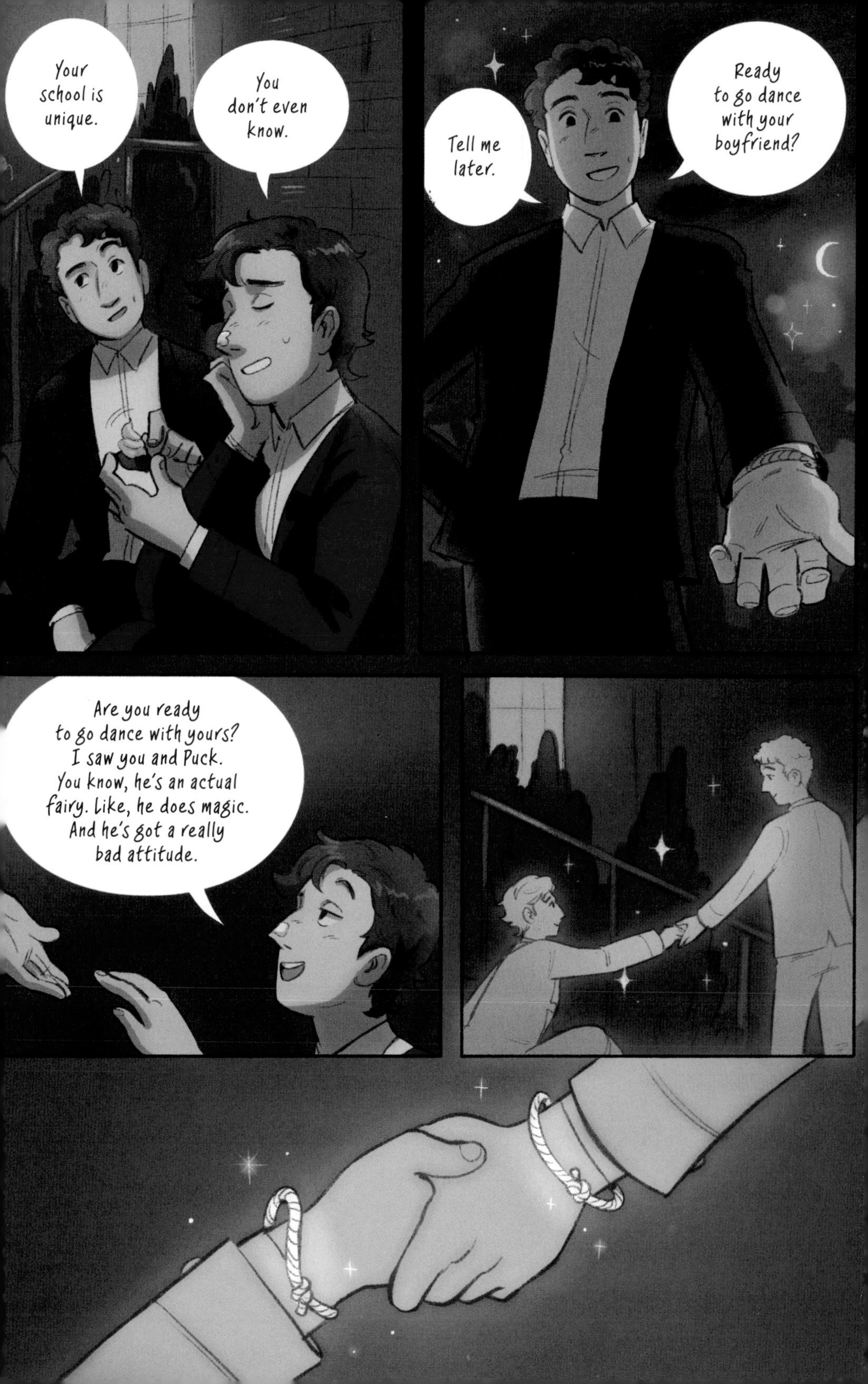
Your school is unique.
You don't even know.
Tell me later.
Ready to go dance with your boyfriend?
Are you ready to go dance with yours? I saw you and Puck. You know, he's an actual fairy. Like, he does magic. And he's got a really bad attitude.

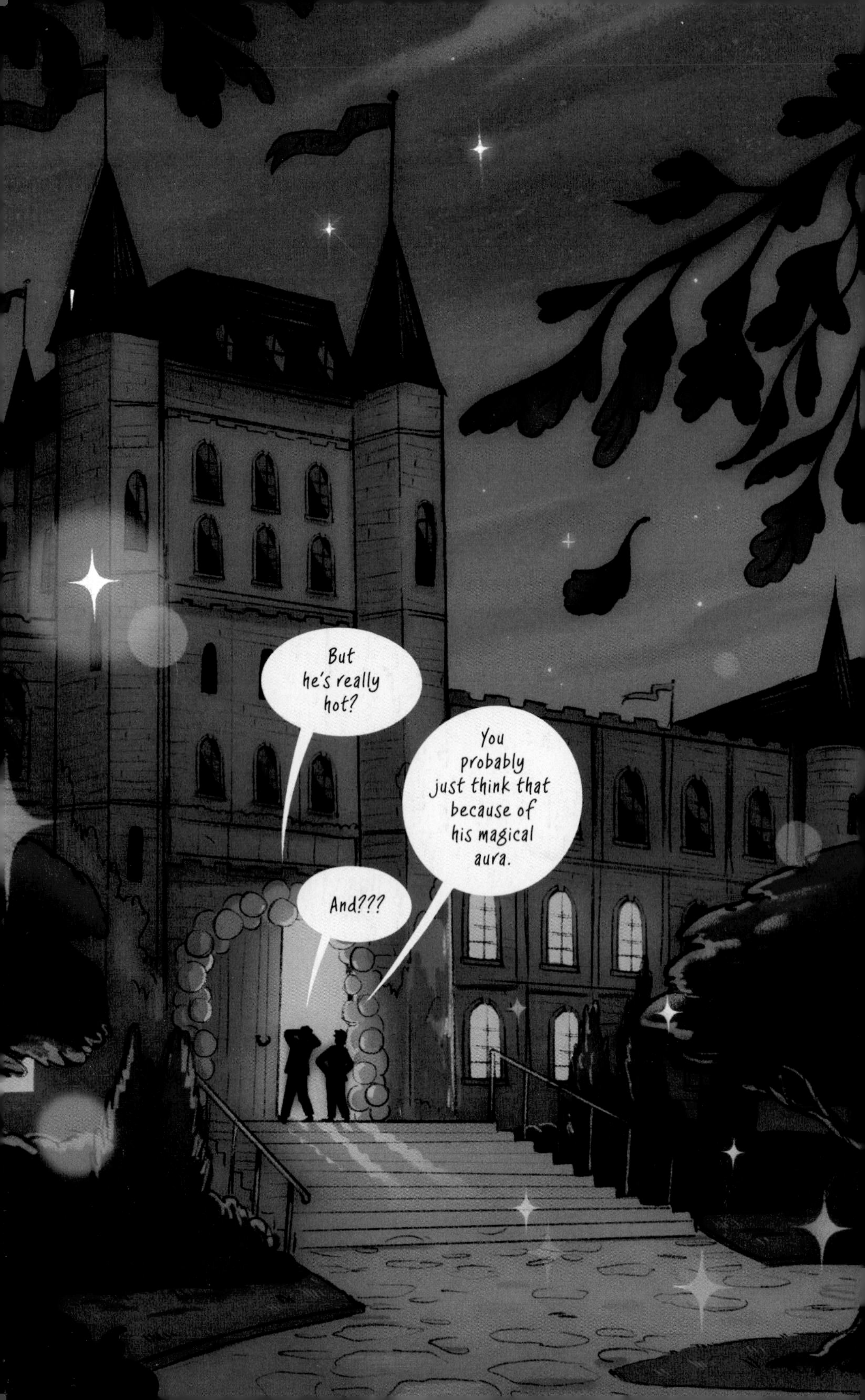
But he's really hot?
You probably just think that because of his magical aura.
And???